SILENT PARTNER

OTHER BOOKS BY JONATHAN KELLERMAN

SILENT PARTNER

JONATHAN KELLERMAN

 BANTAM BOOKS
NEW YORK · TORONTO · LONDON · SYDNEY · AUCKLAND

This novel is a work of fiction. Names, characters, places, and incidents are either the product of the author's imagination or are used fictitiously. Any resemblance to actual persons, living or dead, events, or locales is entirely coincidental.

SILENT PARTNER
A Bantam Book / October 1989

Grateful acknowledgment is made for permission to reprint the lyrics from "C.C. Rider" on page 264, copyright © 1965 Warner Bros. Inc. All rights reserved. Used by permission.

Library of Congress Cataloging-in-Publication Data

Kellerman, Jonathan.
 Silent partner / Jonathan Kellerman.
  p.   cm.
 ISBN 0-553-05370-1
 I. Title.
 PS3561.E3865S5   1989
 813'.54—dc19   89-6490
                                   CIP

Published simultaneously in the United States and Canada

Bantam Books are published by Bantam Books, a division of Bantam Doubleday Dell Publishing Group, Inc. Its trademark, consisting of the words "Bantam Books" and the portrayal of a rooster, is Registered in U.S. Patent and Trademark Office and in other countries. Marca Registrada. Bantam Books, 666 Fifth Avenue, New York, New York 10103.

PRINTED IN THE UNITED STATES OF AMERICA

B   0 9 8 7 6 5 4 3 2 1

This one's for Bob Elias.

If the rich could hire the poor to die for them,
the poor would make a very nice living.
—Yiddish saying

Special thanks to
Steve Rubin, Beverly Lewis,
Stuart Vener,
David Aftergood, and Al Katz

I've always hated parties and, under normal circumstances, never would have attended the one on Saturday.

But my life was a mess. I relaxed my standards. And stepped into a nightmare.

Thursday morning I was the good doctor, focusing on my patients, determined not to let my own garbage get in the way of work.

I kept my eye on the boy.

He hadn't yet gotten to the part where he tore the heads off the dolls. I watched him pick up the toy cars again and advance them toward each other in inevitable collision.

"Cah!"

The ringing concussion of metal against metal blocked out the whine of the video camera before dying. He tossed the cars aside as if they burned his fingers. One of them flipped over and rocked on its roof like a trapped turtle. He poked at it, then looked up at me, seeking permission.

I nodded and he snatched up the cars. Turning them over in his hands, he examined the shiny undercarriages, spun the wheels, simulated the sounds of revving engines.

"Voom voom. Cah."

A little over two, big and husky for his age, with the kind of fluid coordination that foretold athletic heroism. Blond hair, pug features, raisin-colored eyes that made me think of snowmen, an amber splash of freckles across nose and chubby cheeks.

A Norman Rockwell kid: the kind of son any red-blooded American father would be proud of.

His father's blood was a rusty stain on the central divider somewhere along the Ventura Freeway.

"Voom cah!"

In six sessions, it was as close as he'd come to speaking. I wondered about it, wondered about a certain dullness in the eyes.

The second collision was sudden, harder. His concentration was intense. The dolls would come soon.

His mother looked up from her seat in the corner. For the past ten minutes she'd read the same page of a paperback entitled *Will Yourself Successful!* Any pretense of casualness was betrayed by her body language. She sat high and stiff in the chair, scratched her head, stretched her long dark hair as if it were yarn, and kept coiling and uncoiling it around her fingers. One of her feet tapped out a nonstop four-four beat, sending ripples that coursed upward through the soft flesh of a pale, unstockinged calf and disappeared under the hem of her sun dress.

The third crash made her wince. She lowered the book and looked at me, blinking hard. Just short of pretty—the kind of looks that flower in high school and fade fast. I smiled. She snapped her head down and returned to her book.

"Cah!" The boy grunted, took a car in each hand, smashed them together like cymbals, and let go upon impact. They careened across the carpet in opposite directions. Breathing hard, he toddled after them.

"Cah!" He picked them up and threw them down hard. "Voom! Cah!"

He went through the routine several more times, then abruptly flung the cars aside and began scanning the room with hungry, darting glances. Searching for the dolls, though I always left them in the same place.

A memory problem or just denial? At that age, all you could do was infer.

Which was what I'd told Mal Worthy when he'd described the case and asked for the consult.

"You're not going to get hard proof."

"Not even trying for it, Alex. Just give me something I can work with."

"What about the mother?"

"As you'd expect, a mess."

"Who's working with her?"

"No one, for the moment, Alex. I tried to get her to see some-

*one but she refused. In the meantime, just do your thing for Darren
and if a little therapy for Mama takes place in the process, I won't raise
an objection. God knows she needs it—something like that happening
to someone her age."*

"How'd you get involved in an injury case, anyway?"

*"Second marriage. Father was my handyman. I handled the di-
vorce as a favor. She was the other woman and remembered me with
fondness. Actually, I used to do lots of P.I. in the beginning. Feels good
to get back into it. So tell me, how do you feel about working with one
this young?"*

"I've had younger. How verbal is he?"

*"If he talks I haven't heard it. She claims before the accident he
was putting a few words together, but I don't get the impression they
were saving up tuition for Cal Tech. If you could prove IQ loss, Alex, I
could translate it into dollars."*

"Mal—"

*He laughed over the phone. "I know, I know, Mr.—excuse me,
Dr. Conservative. Far be it from me to—"*

*"Good talking to you, Mal. Have the mother call me to set up
an appointment."*

*"—attempt to unduly influence an expert witness. However, while
you're analyzing the situation, you might consider imagining what it's
going to be like for her, raising a kid by herself, no training, no money.
Living with those memories. I just got pictures of the crash—they
almost made me lose my lunch. There are some deep pockets here,
Alex, and they deserve being dipped into."*

"Dah!" He'd found the dolls. Three men, a woman, a little boy.
Small, soft plastic and pink, with bland, guileless faces, anatomically
correct bodies, and detachable limbs. Next to them another pair of
cars, larger than the first two, one red, one blue. A miniature child's
car seat had been placed in the rear seat of the blue one.

I stood, adjusted the video camera so that it was trained on the
table, then sat on the floor next to him.

He picked up the blue car and positioned the dolls using a
familiar sequence: one man driving, another next to him, the woman
behind the driver, the child in the car seat. The red car was empty.
One male doll remained on the table.

He flapped his arms and tugged his nose. Holding the blue car
at arm's length, he looked away from it.

I patted his shoulder. "It's all right, Darren."

He inhaled, blew out air, picked up the red car and placed both vehicles on the floor, two feet apart, grille to grille. Taking another deep breath, he puffed up his cheeks and let out a scream, then smashed them together full force.

The male passenger and the woman flew out and landed on the carpet. The boy doll slumped in its harness, head down.

It was the driver doll that held his attention—lying across the front seat, its flight restrained by one foot caught in the steering wheel. Huffing, the boy struggled to pull it loose. Tugged and twisted, started to grunt with frustration, but finally managed to free it. He held it away from his body, examined its plastic face, and yanked its head off. Then he placed it next to the little boy.

I heard a gasp from across the room and turned. Denise Burkhalter ducked back behind her book.

Oblivious of her reaction, the boy dropped the headless body, picked up the female doll, hugged it, put it down. Then he returned to the male dolls—the decapitated driver and the front-seat passenger. Raising them over his head, he threw them against the wall, watched them hit, then fall.

He looked at the child slumped in the seat and picked up the head next to it. After rolling it under his palm, he tossed it aside.

He stepped toward the male doll that hadn't been moved—the driver of the other car—took another step, froze, then backed away.

The room was silent except for the hum of the camera. A page turned. He stood still for several moments, then was overtaken by a burst of hyperactivity so fierce it electrified the room.

Giggling, he rocked back and forth, wrung his hands and waved them in the air, sputtering and spitting. He ran from one side of the room to the other, kicking bookshelves, chairs, the desk, scuffing the baseboards, clawing the walls and leaving little greasy smudges on the plaster. His laughter rose in pitch before giving way to a croupy bark followed by a rush of tears. Throwing himself to the floor, he thrashed for a while, then curled fetally and lay there, sucking his thumb.

His mother remained behind her book.

I went to him and scooped him up in my arms.

His body was tense and he was chewing hard on his thumb. I held him in my lap, told him everything was okay, he was a good boy. His eyes opened for an instant, then closed. Milk-sweet breath mingled with the not unpleasant odor of child sweat.

"Do you want to go to Mommy?"

Drowsy nod.

She still hadn't moved. I said, "Denise." Nothing. I repeated her name.

She put the paperback in her purse, strung the purse over one shoulder, got up, and took him.

We left the library and walked toward the front of the house. By the time we reached the door he was sleeping. I held the door open. Cool air blew in. A gentle summer that kept threatening to heat up. From the distance came the sound of a motorized lawnmower.

"Any questions you want to ask me, Denise?"

"Nope."

"How'd he sleep this week?"

"The same."

"Six or seven nightmares?"

"About. I didn't count—do I still have to?"

"It would help to know what's going on."

No response.

"The legal part of the evaluation is over, Denise. I have enough information for Mr. Worthy. But Darren's still struggling—totally normal for what he's been through."

No response.

"He's come a long way," I said, "but he hasn't been able to act out the role of the . . . other driver yet. There's plenty of fear and anger still in him. It would help him to express it. I'd like to see him some more."

She looked at the ceiling.

"Those dolls," she said.

"I know. It's hard to watch."

She bit her lip.

"But it's helpful for Darren, Denise. We can try having you wait outside next time. He's ready for it."

She said, "It's far, coming up here."

"Bad traffic?"

"The pits."

"How long did it take you?"

"Hour and three quarters."

Tujunga to Beverly Glen. A forty-minute freeway ride. If you could handle freeways.

"Surface streets jammed?"

"Uh huh. And you've got some curvy roads up here."

"I know. Sometimes when—"

Suddenly she was backing away. "Why do you make yourself so hard to get to, living up here! If you want to help people, why do you make it so damned hard!"

I waited a moment before answering. "I know it's been rough, Denise. If you'd rather meet in Mr. Worthy's—"

"Oh, forget it!" And she was out the door.

I watched her carry her son across the deck and down the stairs. His weight caused her to waddle. Her ungainliness made me want to rush down and help her. Instead, I stood there and watched her struggle. She finally made it to the rental car, worked hard at opening the rear door with one hand. Bending low, she managed to get Darren's limp body into the car seat. Slamming the door shut, she walked around to the driver's side and threw open the front door.

Putting her key in the ignition, she lowered her head to the steering wheel and let it rest there. She sat that way for a while before turning on the engine.

Back in the library I turned off the video camera, removed the cassette, tagged it, and began my report, working slowly, with even greater precision than usual.

Trying to forestall the inevitable.

Several hours later the damned thing was finished; evicted from the helper role, I was, once again, someone who needed help. Numbness rolled over me, as inevitable as the tide.

I considered calling Robin, decided against it. Our last conversation had been anything but triumphant—tongue-biting civility finally sabotaged by depth charges of hurt and anger.

". . . freedom, space—I thought we were past that."

"Well, I never got past *freedom*, Alex."

"You know what I mean."

"No, I really don't."

"I'm just trying to figure out what you want, Robin."

"I've explained it over and over. What more can I say?"

"If it's space you want, you've got two hundred miles of it between us. Feeling any more fulfilled?"

"Fulfillment's not the issue."

"Then what is?"

"Stop it, Alex. Please."

"Stop what? Wanting to work this out?"

"Stop cross-examining me. You sound so hostile."

"How am I supposed to sound, a week stretched to a month? Where's the end point?"

"I . . . I wish I could answer that, Alex."

"Terrific—the endless dangle. And what was my big sin? Getting too involved? Okay, I can change that. Believe me, I can be cool as ice. In training I learned how to detach. But if I pull away, ten to one I'll be accused of male indifference."

"Stop it, Alex! I was up all night with Aaron. I can't handle this right now."

"Handle what?"

"All your words. They're coming at me like bullets."

"How're we supposed to work anything out without words?"

"We're not going to work anything out right now, so let's put it aside. Goodbye."

"Robin—"

"Say goodbye, Alex. Please. I don't want to hang up on you."

"Then don't."

Silence.

"Goodbye, Robin."

"Goodbye, Alex. I still love you."

The shoemaker's children go barefoot.

The shrink chokes on his words.

The low mood gathered strength and hit me full force.

Having someone to talk to would have helped. My list of confidants was damned short.

Robin at the top.

Then Milo.

He was off with Rick, on a fishing trip in the Sierras. But even if his shoulder had been available I wouldn't have cried on it.

Over the years, our friendship had taken on a certain rhythm: We talked about murder and madness over beer and pretzels, discussed the human condition with the aplomb of a pair of anthropologists observing a colony of savage baboons.

When the horrors piled up too high, Milo bitched and I listened. When he went off the wagon, I helped talk him back on it.

Sad-sack cop, supportive shrink. I wasn't ready to reverse the roles.

A week's worth of mail had piled up on the dining room table. I'd avoided opening it, dreading the superficial caresses of come-ons, coupons, and get-happy-quick schemes. But I needed, at that very moment, to keep my mind tethered to minutiae, free from the perils of introspection.

I carried the stack into the bedroom, pulled a wastebasket to the side of the bed, sat down, and began sorting. At the bottom of the pile was a buff-colored envelope. Heavy linen stock, a Holmby Hills return address, embossed silver script on the back flap.

Rich for my blood. An upscale sales pitch. I flipped the envelope over, expecting a computerized label, and saw my name and address printed in extravagant silver calligraphy. Someone had taken the time to do this one right.

I checked the postmark—ten days old. Opened the envelope and pulled out a buff-colored invitation card, silver-bordered, more calligraphy:

DEAR DOCTOR DELAWARE,

YOU ARE CORDIALLY INVITED TO JOIN
DISTINGUISHED ALUMNI AND MEMBERS OF THE
UNIVERSITY COMMUNITY AT A GARDEN PARTY AND
COCKTAIL RECEPTION HONORING

DOCTOR PAUL PETER KRUSE,
BLALOCK PROFESSOR OF PSYCHOLOGY AND HUMAN DEVELOPMENT,

UPON HIS APPOINTMENT AS

CHAIRMAN, THE DEPARTMENT OF PSYCHOLOGY

SATURDAY, JUNE 13, 1987, FOUR IN THE AFTERNOON
SKYLARK
LA MAR ROAD
LOS ANGELES, CALIFORNIA 90077

RSVP, THE PSYCHOLOGY DEPARTMENT

Kruse as chairman. An *endowed* chair, the ultimate reward for exceptional scholarship.

It made no sense; the man was anything but a scholar. And though it had been years since I'd had anything to do with him, there was no reason to believe he'd changed and become a decent human being.

Back in those days, he'd been an advice columnist and a darling of the talk-show circuit, armed with the requisite Beverly Hills practice and a repertoire of truisms couched in pseudoscientific jargon.

His column had appeared monthly in a supermarket-rack "women's" magazine—the kind of throwaway that prints articles on the latest miracle crash diet, closely followed by recipes for chocolate fudge cake, and combines exhortations to "be yourself" with sexual IQ tests designed to make anyone taking them feel inadequate.

Endowed professor. He'd made only the slimmest pretense of conducting research—something to do with human sexuality that never produced a shred of data.

But he hadn't been expected to be academically productive, because he hadn't been a member of the tenured faculty, just a clinical associate. One of scores of practitioners seeking academic cachet through association with the University.

Associates gave occasional lectures on their specialties—in Kruse's case that had been hypnosis and a manipulative form of psychotherapy he called Communication Dynamics—and served as therapists and supervisors of the clinical-psych graduate students. A nifty symbiosis, it freed up the "real" professors for their grant applications and committee meetings while earning the associates parking permits, priority tickets to football games, and admission to the Faculty Club.

From that to Blalock Professor. Incredible.

I thought of the last time I'd seen Kruse—about two years ago. Chance passers-by on campus, we'd pretended not to notice each other.

He'd been walking toward the psych building, all custom tweeds, elbow patches, and fuming briar, a female student at each elbow. Letting loose with some profundity while copping fast feels.

I looked down at all that silver writing. Cocktails at four. Hail to the chief.

Probably something to do with a Holmby Hills connection, but still the appointment defied comprehension.

I checked the date of the party—two days from now—then reread the address at the bottom of the invitation.

Skylark. The very rich christened their houses as if they were offspring.

La Mar Road, no numbers. Translation: *We own all of it, peasants.*

I pictured the scene two days hence: fat cars, weak drinks, and numbing banter wafting across money-green lawns.

Not my idea of fun. I tossed the invitation in the trash and forgot about Kruse. Forgot about the old days.

But not for long.

2

I slept poorly and woke with the sun on Friday. With no patients scheduled, I dived into busywork: messengering the video of Darren to Mal, finishing other reports, paying and mailing bills, feeding the koi and netting debris out of their pond, cleaning the house until it sparkled. That took until noon and left the rest of the day open for wallowing in misery.

I had no appetite, tried running, couldn't get the tightness out of my chest and gave up after a mile. Back home, I gulped a beer so quickly it made my diaphragm ache, followed it with another and took the six-pack into the bedroom. I sat in my underwear and watched images float across the TV screen. Soap operas: perfect-looking people suffering. Game shows: real-looking people regressing.

My mind wandered. I stared at the phone, reached out for the receiver. Pulled back.

The shoemaker's children . . .

At first I'd thought the problem had something to do with business—with forsaking the world of high tech for the hand-cramping, poorly compensated life of an artisan.

A Tokyo music conglomerate had approached Robin about adapting several of her guitars into prototypes for mass production. She was to draw up the specifications; an army of computerized robots would do the rest.

They flew her first-class to Tokyo, put her up in a suite at the Okura Hotel, sushied and sake'd her, sent her home laden with exquisite gifts, sheaves of contracts printed on rice paper, and promises of a lucrative consultantship.

All that hard sell notwithstanding, she turned them down, never explaining why, though I suspected it had something to do with her roots. She'd grown up the only child of a mercilessly perfectionistic cabinetmaker who worshipped handwork, and an ex-showgirl who grew bitter playing Betty Crocker and worshipped nothing. A daddy's girl, she used her hands to make sense of the world. Endured college until her father died, then eulogized him by dropping out and handcrafting furniture. Finally she found her perfect pitch as a luthier, shaping, carving, and inlaying custom guitars and mandolins.

We were lovers for two years before she agreed to live with me. Even then she held on to her Venice studio. After returning from Japan, she began escaping there more and more. When I asked her about it she said she had to catch up.

I accepted it. We'd never spent that much time together. Two headstrong people, we'd fought hard for independence, moving in different worlds, merging occasionally—sometimes it seemed randomly—in passionate collision.

But the collisions grew less and less frequent. She started spending nights at the studio, claiming fatigue, turning down my offers to pick her up and drive her home. I was keeping busy enough to avoid thinking about it.

I'd retired from child psychology at the age of thirty-three after overdosing on human misery, had lived comfortably off investments made in Southern California real estate. Eventually I began to miss clinical work, but continued to resist the entanglement of long-term psychotherapy. I dealt with it by limiting myself to forensic consultations referred by lawyers and judges—custody evaluations, trauma cases involving children, one recent criminal case that had taught me something about the genesis of madness.

Short-term work, with little or no follow-up. The surgical side of psych. But enough to make me feel like a healer.

A post-Easter lull left me with time on my hands—time spent alone. I began to realize how far Robin and I had drifted from each other, wondered if I'd missed something. Hoping for spontaneous cure, I waited for her to come around. When she didn't, I cornered her.

She shrugged off my concerns, suddenly remembered something she'd forgotten at the studio and was gone. After that, I saw her even less. Phone calls to Venice triggered her answering machine. Drop-ins were maddeningly unsatisfying: Usually she was surrounded by sad-eyed musicians cradling mangled instruments and singing one form of blues or the other. When I caught her alone she used the roar of saws and lathes, the hiss of the spray gun, to blot out discourse.

I gritted my teeth, backed off, told myself to be patient. Adapted by creating a heavy workload of my own. All during the spring, I evaluated, wrote reports, and testified like a demon. Lunched with lawyers, got stuck in traffic jams. Made lots of money and had no one to spend it on.

As summer neared, Robin and I had become polite strangers. Something had to give. Early in May, it did.

A Sunday morning, rich with hope. She'd come home late Saturday afternoon to retrieve some old sketches, had ended up spending the night, making love to me with a workmanlike determination that scared me but was better than nothing.

When I woke, I reached across the bed to touch her, felt only percale. Sounds filtered from the living room. I jumped out of bed, found her dressed, handbag over one shoulder, heading for the door.

"Morning, babe."

"Morning, Alex."

"Leaving?"

She nodded.

"What's the rush?"

"Lots of things to do."

"On Sunday?"

"Sunday, Monday, it doesn't matter." She put her hand on the doorknob. "I made juice—there's a pitcher in the fridge."

I walked over to her, put my hand on her wrist.

"Stay just a little longer."

She eased away. "I really have to go."

"Come on, take a breather."

"I don't need a breather, Alex."

"At least stay for a while and let's talk."

"About what?"

"Us."

"There's nothing to talk about."

Her apathy was forced, but it pushed my button anyway. Months of frustration were compressed into a few moments of blazing soliloquy:

She was selfish. Self-obsessed. How did she think it felt to live with a hermit? What had I done to deserve this kind of treatment?

Then a laundry list of my virtues, of every lofty service I'd performed for her since the day we'd met.

When I was through she put down her bag and took a seat on the couch. "You're right. We do need to talk."

She stared out the window.

I said, "I'm listening."

"I'm trying to collect my thoughts. Words are your business, Alex. I can't compete with you on that level."

"No one needs to compete with anyone. Just talk to me. Tell me what's on your mind."

She shook her head. "I don't know how to put this without being hurtful."

"Don't worry about that. Just let it out."

"Whatever you say, doctor." Then: "Sorry, this is just very hard."

I waited.

She clenched her hands, unflexed them and spread them out. "Look around this room—the furniture, the artwork—everything exactly the way it was the first time I saw it. Picture-perfect—*your* perfect taste. For five years, I've been a boarder."

"How can you say that? This is your home."

She started to reply, shook her head and turned away.

I stepped into her line of vision, pointed to the ash-burl trestle table in the dining room. "The only furniture that means anything to me is *that*. Because *you* built it."

Silence.

"Say the word and I'll chop everything to matchsticks, Robin. We'll start from scratch. Together."

She put her face in her hands, sat that way for a while, and finally looked up, wet-eyed. "This isn't about interior decorating, Alex."

"What *is* it about?"

"*You*. The kind of person you are. Overwhelming. Overpowering. It's about the fact that you've never thought to ask if I wanted anything different—if I had ideas of my own."

"I never thought that kind of thing mattered to you."

"I never hinted that it did—it's me, too, Alex. Accepting, going along, fitting into your preconceived notions. Meanwhile, I've been living a lie—viewing myself as strong, self-sufficient."

"You *are* strong."

She laughed without joy. "That was Daddy's line: You are *strong* girl, beautiful *strong* girl. He used to get mad at me when my confidence lagged, yelled at me and told me over and over that I was different from the other girls. *Stronger* than them. To him, strong meant using your hands, creating. When the other girls were playing with Barbies, I was learning how to load a band saw. Sanding my knuckles to the bone. Constructing a perfect miter joint. Being *strong.* For years I bought into it. Now here I am, finally taking a good look in the mirror, and all I see is another weak woman living off a man."

"Did the Tokyo deal have anything to do with this?"

"The Tokyo deal made me stop and think about what I wanted out of life, made me realize how far I was from it—how beholden I've always been to someone."

"Babe, I never meant to hem you in—"

"That's the *problem!* I'm a *babe*—a damn *baby!* Helpless and ready to be fixed by Doctor Alex!"

"I don't view you as a patient," I said, "I love you, for God's sake."

"Love," she said. "Whatever the hell that means."

"I know what it means to me."

"Then you're just a better person than I am, okay? Which is the crux of the problem, isn't it! Doctor Perfect. Ph.D. problem-solver. Looks, brains, charm, money, all those patients who think you're God."

She got up, walked the floor. "Dammit, Alex, when I first met you, you had problems—the burnout, all those self-doubts. You were a *mortal* and *I* could care for *you.* I helped you through that, Alex. I was one of the main reasons you pulled out of it, I know I was."

"You were, and I *still* need you."

She smiled. "No. Now you're fixed, my darling. Perfectly tuned. And there's nothing left for me to do."

"That's crazy. I've been miserable not seeing you."

"Temporary reaction," she said. "You'll cope."

"You must think I'm pretty shallow."

She walked some more, shook her head. "God, I'm listening to myself and realizing it all comes down to jealousy, doesn't it? Stupid, childish jealousy. The same way I used to feel about the popular girls. But I can't help it—you've got it all together. Everything organized into a neat little routine: run your three miles, take a shower, work a little, cash your checks, play your guitar, read your journals. Fuck me until we both come, then fall asleep, grinning. You buy tickets to Hawaii, we take a vacation. Show up with a picnic basket, we take lunch. It's an assembly line, Alex, with you pushing the buttons, and one thing Tokyo taught me was that I don't want an assembly line. The crazy thing is, it's a great life. If I let you, you'd take care of me forever, make my life one perfect, sugar-coated dream. I know lots of women would kill for something like that, but it's not what *I* need."

Our eyes met. I felt stung, turned away.

"Oh, God," she said, "I'm hurting you. I just hate this."

"I'm fine. Just go on."

"That's all of it, Alex. You're a wonderful man, but living with you has started to *scare* me. I'm in danger of disappearing. You've been hinting about marriage. If we married, I'd lose even more of my self. Our children would come to see me as someone dull and unstimulating and bitter. Meanwhile, Daddy would be out in the wide world performing heroics. I need time, Alex—breathing space. To sort things out."

She moved toward the door. "I have to go now. Please."

"Take all the time you need," I said. "All the space. Just don't cut me off."

She stood trembling in the doorway. Ran to me, kissed my forehead, and was gone.

Two days later I came home and found a note on the ash-burl table:

Dear Alex,

Gone up to San Luis. Cousin Terry had a baby. Going to help her, be back in about a week. Don't hate me.

Love,
R

3

One of the cases I'd just finished working on involved a five-year-old girl as the hostage in a vicious custody battle between a Hollywood producer and his fourth wife.

For two years the parents, encouraged to wage war by lawyers on retainer, had been unable to reach a settlement. Finally the judge got disgusted and asked me to come up with recommendations. I evaluated the girl and asked that another psychologist be appointed to examine the parents.

The consultant I recommended was a former classmate named Larry Daschoff, a sharp diagnostician whose ethics I respected. Larry and I had remained amicable over the years, trading referrals, getting together occasionally for lunch or handball. But as a friend he fell in the casual category and I was surprised when he called me at 10:00 P.M. on Friday.

"Dr. D.? It's Dr. D.," he shouted, cheerful as usual. A hurricane of noise roared in the background—squealing tires and gunshots from a blaring TV competing with what sounded like a schoolyard during recess.

"Hi, Larry. What's up?"

"What's up is Brenda is at the law library cramming for her torts course and I've got all five monsters to myself."

"The joys of parenthood."

"Oh, yeah." The noise level rose. A small voice whined, "Daddy! Daddy! Daddy!"

"One second, Alex." He put his hand over the phone and I heard him say, "Wait till I'm off the phone. *No,* not now. *Wait.* If he bothers you, just stay *away* from him. Not *now,* Jeremy, I don't want to hear it. I'm *talking on the phone, Jeremy.* If you don't cool it, it's *no Cocoa Puffs and twenty minutes off your bedtime!*"

He came back on the line. "I've become an instant fan of aversion therapy, D. Fuck Anna Freud and Bruno Bettelheim. Both of them probably locked themselves in their studies to write their books while someone else raised their kids. Did old Anna even have kids? I think she stayed married to Daddy. Anyway, first thing Monday I'm sending away for half a dozen cattle prods. One for each of them and one to shove up my own ass for encouraging Brenda to go back to school. If Robin ever comes up with a creative idea like that, change the subject fast."

"I'll be sure to do that, Larry."

"You okay, D.?"

"Just a little tired."

He was too good a therapist not to know I was holding back. Too good, also, to pursue the issue.

"Anyway, D., I read your report on the Featherbaugh mess and concur in every respect. With parents like these, what would really benefit the kid would be orphanhood. Barring that, I agree that some half-assed joint custody arrangement's probably the least terrible way to go. Want to take bets on the chances of its working out?"

"Only if I can wager on the down side."

"No way." He excused himself again, yelled for someone to turn down the TV. No compliance followed. "People are really fucked up, aren't they, D.? How's that for a major insight after thirteen years as a mind prober? Nobody wants to work at anything anymore—God knows I'm no day at the beach and neither is Brenda. If we can stick it out all these years, anyone should be able to."

"I always thought of you two as the perfect couple."

"One born every moment." He chuckled. "We're talking Italian marriage—mucho passione, mucho screamo. Bottom line, she puts up with me because of my erotic prowess."

"That so?"

"*That so?*" he mimicked. "D., that was pretty damn shrinky sounding, not up to your usual level of sparkling repartee. Sure you're okay?"

"I'm fine. Really."

"If you say so. Anyway, on to my main reason for calling. Get the invite to Kruse's big bash?"

"It's gracing the bottom of my wastebasket—that sparkling enough?"

"Not by a long shot. Not planning on going?"

"You've got to be kidding, Larry."

"I don't know. It could be fun in a *mondo bizarro* kind of way—see how the other half lives, stand on the sidelines making nasty analytic comments while suppressing our bourgeois envy."

I remembered something. "Larry, weren't you Kruse's research assistant for a while?"

"Not *for a while,* D. Just one semester—and yes, I'm being defensive. The guy was a sleaze. My excuse is that I was broke—just married, slaving over the dissertation, and my NIMH stipend ran out mid-semester."

"C'mon, 'fess up, Larry. It was a plum job. You guys sat around all day watching dirty movies."

"Not fair, Delaware. We were exploring the frontiers of human sexuality." He laughed. "Actually, we sat around all day and watched *undergraduates* watch dirty movies. Oh, for those licentious seventies—could you see getting away with that today?"

"A tragic loss to science."

"Catastrophic. Truth be told, D., it *was* total bullshit. Kruse got away with it because he'd brought in money—a private grant—to study the effects of pornography on sexual arousal."

"Did he come up with anything?"

"Major data: fuck films make college sophomores horny."

"I knew that when *I* was a sophomore."

"You were a late bloomer, D."

"Did he publish?"

"Where? *Penthouse?* Nah, he used the results to go on talk shows and cheerlead for porn as a healthy sexual outlet, et cetera, et cetera. Then, in the 'uptight eighties,' he made a complete about-face—supposedly, he'd 'reanalyzed' his data. Started giving speeches about porn promoting violence against women."

"Lots of integrity, our new department head."

"Oh, yeah."

"How'd he climb this high, Larry? He used to be part-time help."

"Part-time help with full-time connections."

"The name on the endowment—Blalock?"

"You got it. Old moolah—steel, railroads—one of those families that gets a penny every time someone west of the Mississippi breathes."

"What's Kruse's connection?"

"Way I hear it, Mrs. Blalock had a kid with problems, Kruse was the kid's therapist. Must have made it all better because Mommy's been pouring money into the department for years—on condition that Kruse administer it. He's been promoted, given everything he wants. His latest want is to be department head, so, *voila,* party time."

"Tenure for sale," I said. "I didn't know things had gotten that bad."

"That bad and worse, Alex. I still give those lectures in family therapy, so I'm involved enough in the department to know that the financial situation sucks. Remember how they used to push pure research at us, look down their noses at anything even remotely applied? How Ratman Frazier used to keep telling us *relevant* was a dirty word? It finally caught up with them. Nobody wants to fund grants to study the eyeblink reflex in decorticate lobsters. On top of that, undergraduate enrollment's way down—psych's not a hip major anymore. Nowadays everyone, including my oldest, wants to be a business major, inside-trade their way to health and happiness. Which means budget cuts, layoffs, empty classrooms. They've had a hiring freeze for nineteen months—even the full profs have got their noses to the floor. Kruse brings in Blalock money, he can eat tenure for breakfast. In the words of my oldest: Money talks, Dad. Bullshit walks. Hell, even Frazier's jumped on the bandwagon. Last I heard he was into mail-order, marketing stop-smoking tapes."

"You're kidding."

"I kid you not."

"What does Frazier know about how to quit smoking? About anything *human?*"

"Since when is that important? Anyway, that's the situation. Now, about Saturday. I managed to farm out all five cupcakes for three hours tomorrow. I *could* use the time to pump iron, watch the game, or do something else comparably thrilling, but the idea of getting all spiffed up and saturating myself with free drinks and *haute-cuisine* munchies at some Holmby Hills pleasure dome didn't sound half bad."

"The drinks are bound to be lousy, Larry."

"Better than what I'm drinking now. Diluted apple juice. Looks like piss. It's all that's left in the house—I forgot to go shopping. I've been shoveling sugared cereal into the kids for two days." He sighed. "I'm a trapped man, D. We're talking terminal cabin fever. Come to the damned party and trade cynical barbs with me for a couple of hours. I'll R-S-Veep for both of us. Bring Robin, parade her around, and let the rich farts know money can't buy everything."

"Robin can't make it. Out of town."

"Business?"

"Yup."

Pause.

"Listen, D., if you're tied up, I understand."

I thought about it for a moment, considered another lonely day and said, "No, I'm free, Larry."

And set the gears in motion.

4

Holmby Hills is the highest-priced spread in L.A., a tiny pocket of mega-affluence sandwiched between Beverly Hills and Bel Air. Financially, light-years from my neighborhood, but only about a mile or so due south.

My map put La Mar Road in the heart of the district, a winding bit of dead-end filament terminating in the rolling hills that overlook the L.A. Country Club. Not far from the Playboy Mansion, but I didn't imagine Hef had been invited to this bash.

At four-fifteen I put on a lightweight suit and set out on foot. Traffic was heavy on Sunset—surfers and sun-worshippers returning from the beach, gawkers headed east clutching maps to the stars' homes. Fifty yards into Holmby Hills everything went hushed and pastoral.

The properties were immense, the houses concealed behind high walls and security gates and backed by small forests. Only the merest outline of slate gable or Spanish tile tower floating above the greenery suggested habitation. That, and the phlegmy rumble of unseen attack dogs.

La Mar appeared around a bend, an uphill strip of single-lane asphalt nicked into a wall of fifty-foot eucalyptus. In lieu of a city street sign, a varnished slab of pine had been nailed to one of the trees above the emblems of three security companies and the red-and-white badge of the Bel Air Patrol. Rustic lettering burned into the slab spelled out LA MAR. PRIVATE. NO OUTLET. Easy to miss at forty miles per, though a blue Rolls-Royce Corniche sped past me and hooked onto it without hesitation.

I followed the Rolls's exhaust trail. Twenty feet in, twin field-stone gateposts tacked with another PRIVATE ROAD warning fed into eight-foot stone walls topped with three feet of gold-finialed wrought iron. The iron was laced with alternating twenty-foot sections of vines—English ivy, passion fruit, honeysuckle, wisteria. Controlled profusion masquerading as something natural.

Beyond the walls was a gray-green canvas—more five-story eucalyptus. A quarter-mile later the foliage got even thicker, the road darker and cooler. Mounds of moss and lichen patched the field-stone. The air smelled wet and menthol-clean. A bird chirped timidly, then abandoned its song.

The road curved, straightened, and revealed its end point: a towering stone arch sealed by wrought-iron gates. Scores of cars were lined up, a double file of chrome and lacquer.

As I got closer I could see that the division was purposeful: sparkling luxury cars in one queue; compacts, station wagons, and similar plebeian transport in the other. Heading the dream-mobiles was a spotless white Mercedes coupe, one of those custom jobs with a souped-up engine, bumper guards and spoilers, gold-plating—and a vanity plate that said PPK PHD.

Red-jacketed valets hopped around newly arrived vehicles like fleas on a summer pelt, throwing open car doors and pocketing keys. I made my way to the gate and found it locked. Off to one side was a speaker box on a post. Next to the speaker were a punch-pad, keyslot, and phone.

One of the red-jackets saw me, held out his palm, and said, "Keys."

"No keys. I walked."

His eyes narrowed. In his hand was an oversized iron key chained to a rectangle of varnished wood. On the wood was burnt lettering: FR. GATE.

"*We* park," he insisted. He was dark, thick, round-faced, fuzzy-bearded, and spoke in a Mediterranean accent. His palm wavered.

"No car," I said. "I walked." When his face stayed blank, I pantomimed walking with my fingers.

He turned to another valet, a short, skinny black kid, and whispered something. Both of them stared at me.

I looked up at the top of the gate, saw gold letters: SKYLARK.

"This is Mrs. Blalock's home, right?"

No response.

"The University party? Dr. Kruse?"

The bearded one shrugged and trotted over to a pearl-gray Cadillac. The black kid stepped forward. "Got an invitation, sir?"

"No. Is one necessary?"

"We-ell." He smiled, seemed to be thinking hard. "You'all got no car, you'all got no invitation."

"I didn't know it was necessary to bring either."

He clucked his tongue.

"Is a car necessary for collateral?" I asked.

The smile disappeared. "You'all walked?"

"That's right."

"Where d'you'all live?"

"Not far from here."

"Neighbor?"

"Invited guest. My name is Alex Delaware. Dr. Delaware."

"One minute." He walked to the box, picked up the telephone, and spoke. Replacing the receiver, he said "One minute" again, and ran to open the doors of a white stretch Lincoln.

I waited, looked around. Something brown and familiar caught my eye: a truly pathetic vehicle pushed to the side of the road, away from the others. Quarantined.

Easy to see why: a scabrous Chevy station wagon of senile vintage, rust-pocked and clotted with lumpy patches of primer. Its tires needed air; its rear compartment was crammed with rolled clothing, shoes, cardboard cartons, fast-food containers, and crumpled paper cups. On the tailgate window was a yellow, diamond-shaped sticker: MUTANTS ON BOARD.

I smiled, then noticed that the clunker had been positioned in a way that prevented exit. A score of cars would have to be moved in order to free it.

A fashionably thin middle-aged couple climbed out of the white Lincoln and were escorted to the gate by the bearded valet. He put the oversized key in the slot, punched a code, and one iron door swung open. Slipping through, I followed the couple onto a sloping drive paved with black bricks shaped like fish scales. As I walked past him, the valet said, "Hey," but without enthusiasm, and made no effort to stop me.

When the gate had closed after him, I pointed to the Chevy and said, "That brown station wagon—let me tell you something about it."

He came up next to the wrought iron. "Yes? What?"

"That car is owned by the richest guy at this party. Treat it well—he's been known to give huge tips."

He swiveled his head and stared at the station wagon. I began walking. When I looked back he was playing musical cars, creating a clearing around the Chevy.

A hundred yards past the gate the eucalyptus gave way to open skies above a golf course-quality lawn trimmed to stubble. The grass was flanked by ramrod columns of barbered Italian cypress and beds of perennials. The outer reaches of the grounds had been bulldozed into hillocks and valleys. The highest of the mounds were at the farthest reaches of the property, capped by solitary black pines and California junipers pruned to look windswept.

The fish-scale drive humped. From over the crest came the sound of music—a string section playing something baroque. As I neared the top I saw a tall old man dressed in butler's livery walking toward me.

"Dr. Delaware, sir?" His accent fell somewhere between London and Boston; his features were soft, generous, and pouchy. His loose skin was the color of canned salmon. Tufts of cornsilk circled a sun-browned dome. A white carnation graced his buttonhole.

Jeeves, out of central casting.

"Yes?"

"I'm Ramey, Dr. Delaware, just coming to get you, sir. Please forgive the inconvenience, sir."

"No problem. I guess the valets aren't equipped to deal with pedestrians."

We stepped over the crest. My eye was drawn toward the horizon. Toward a dozen peaks of green copper tile roof, three stories of white stucco and green shutters, columned porticoes, balustered balconies and verandas, arched doors and fanlight windows. A monumental wedding cake surrounded by acres of green icing.

Formal gardens fronted the mansion: gravel paths, more cypress, a maze of boxwood hedges, limestone fountains, reflecting pools, hundreds of beds of roses so bright they seemed fluorescent. Partygoers clutching long-stemmed glasses strolled the paths and admired the plantings. Admired themselves in the mirrored water of the pools.

The butler and I walked in silence, kicking up gravel. The sun beat down, thick and warm as melting butter. In the shadow of the tallest fountain sat a Philharmonic-sized group of grim, formally dressed musicians. Their conductor, a young, long-haired Asian, lifted his baton, and the players broke into dutiful Bach.

The strings were augmented by tinkling glass and a ground bass of conversation. To the left of the gardens a huge flagstone patio was filled with round white tables shaded by yellow canvas umbrellas. On each table was a centerpiece of tiger lilies, purple irises, and white carnations. A yellow-and-white-striped tent, large enough to house a circus, sheltered a long white-lacquered bar manned by a dozen elbow-greased bartenders. Three hundred or so people sat at the tables and drank. Half that amount crowded the bar. Waiters circulated with trays of drinks and canapés.

"Yes, sir. Can I get you a drink, sir?"

"Soda water would be fine."

"Excuse me, sir." Ramey widened his stride, walked ahead of me, disappeared into the bar throng, and emerged moments later with a frosty glass and a yellow linen napkin. He handed them to me just as I reached the patio.

"Here you are, sir. Sorry again for the inconvenience."

"No problem. Thanks."

"Would you care for anything to eat, sir?"

"Nothing right now."

He gave a small bow and walked off. I stood alone, sipping my soda, scanning the crowd for a friendly face.

The crowd, it soon became obvious, was divided into two discrete groups, a sociologic split that echoed the double-filed cars.

Center stage was dominated by the big rich, an assemblage of swans. Deeply tan and loose-limbed in conservative *haute couture,* they greeted each other with cheek-pecks, laughed softly and discreetly, drank steadily and not so discreetly, and made no notice of the ethnically diverse bunch sitting off to the side.

The University people were the magpies, intense, watchful, brimming with nervous chatter. They'd congregated, reflexively, into tight little cliques, talking behind their hands while darting their eyes. Some were conspicuously sleek in off-the-rack suits and special-occasion party dresses; others had made a point of dressing down. A few still gaped at their surroundings, but most were content to observe the rituals of the swans with a mixture of raw hunger and analytic contempt.

I'd finished half my soda when a ripple spread through the patio—through both camps. Paul Kruse appeared in its wake, weaving his way adroitly through Town and Gown. A small, lovely-looking silver-blond woman in a strapless black dress and three-inch heels hung on his arm. She was in her early thirties but wore her hair like a prom queen—ruler-straight down to her waist, the ends puffed and curled extravagantly. The dress clung to her like a coat of pitch.

Around her neck was a diamond choker. She kept her eyes fastened on Kruse as he grinned and worked his audience.

I took a good look at the new department chairman. By now he had to be close to sixty, fighting entropy with chemistry and good posture. His hair was still long, a dubious shade of corn-yellow and cut new-wave surfer-style, with a flap over one eye. Once, he'd resembled a male model, with the kind of coarse handsomeness that photographs well but loses something in the translation to reality. And his good looks were still in evidence. But his features had fallen; the jawline seemed weaker, the ruggedness dissolved into something mushy and vaguely dissolute. His tan was so deep he looked overbaked. It put him in sync with the moneyed crowd, as did his custom-tailored suit. The suit was featherweight but conspicuously tweedy and arm-patched—an almost snotty concession to academia. I watched him flash a mouthful of white caps, shake the hands of the men, kiss the ladies, and move on to the next set of well-wishers.

"Smooth, huh?" said a voice at my back.

I turned around, looked down on two hundred pounds of broken-nosed, bushy-mustached square meal packed into five feet five inches of round can, wrapped in a brown plaid suit, pink shirt, black knit tie, and scuffed brown penny loafers.

"Hello, Larry." I started to extend my hand, then saw that both of his were occupied: a glass of beer in the left, a plate of chicken wings, egg rolls, and partially gnawed rib bones in the right.

"I was over by the roses," said Daschoff, "trying to figure out how they get them to flower like that. Probably fertilize them with old dollar bills." He raised his eyebrows and tilted his head toward the mansion. "Nice little cottage."

"Cozy."

He eyed the conductor. "That's Narahara, the *wunderkind*. God knows what he cost."

He lifted the mug to his mouth and drank. A fringe of foam coated the bottom half of his mustache.

"Budweiser," he said. "I expected something more exotic. But at least it's full strength."

We sat down at an empty table. Larry crossed his legs with effort and took another, deeper swallow of beer. The movement inflated his chest and strained the buttons of his jacket. He unbuttoned it and sat back. A beeper was clipped to his belt.

Larry is almost as wide as he is tall and he waddles; the reason-able assumption is obesity. But in swim trunks he's as firm as a frozen side of beef—a curious mixture of hypertrophied muscle marbled with suet, the only guy under six feet to have played defensive tackle for the University of Arizona. One time, back in grad school, I watched him bench-press twice his weight at the university gym without breathing hard, then top it off with one-handed push-ups.

He ran blunt fingers through steel-wool hair, wiped his mustache, and watched as Kruse charmed his way through the crowd. The new department head's route took him closer to our table—near enough to observe the mechanics of small talk but too far to hear what was being said. It was like watching a mime show. Something entitled *Party Games.*

"Your mentor's in fine form," I said.

Larry swallowed more beer and held out his hands. "I told you I was dead *busted,* D. Would have worked for the devil himself—a bargain-basement Faust."

"No need to explain, doctor."

"Why not? It still bugs me, being a party to bullshit." More beer. "Entire semester a waste. Kruse and I had virtually nothing to do with each other—I doubt if we spoke ten sentences the entire time. I didn't like him because I thought he was shallow and a phony. And he resented me 'cause I was male—all his other assistants were women."

"Then why'd he hire you?"

"Because his research subjects were males and they were unlikely to relax watching dirty movies with a bunch of women around taking notes. Not likely to answer the kinds of questions he was asking, either—how often they jerked off, their most frequent masturbation fantasies. Did they do it in public toilets? How often and who they fucked, how long it took them to come. What was their deep-seated primal attitude toward liver in a can."

"Frontiers of human sexuality," I said.

He shook his head. "Sad thing is, it *could* have been valuable. Look at all the clinical data Masters and Johnson came up with. But Kruse wasn't serious about collecting data. It was as if he was going through the motions."

"Didn't the granting agency care?"

"No agency. These were private suckers—rich porn freaks. He promised to make them respectable, put the academic imprimatur on their hobby."

I turned and looked at Kruse. The blonde in the black dress was teetering on spiked heels.

"Who's the woman with him?"

"*Mrs.* K. You don't remember? Suzanne?"

I shook my head.

"Suzy Straddle? The talk of the department?"

"I must have slept through it."

"You must have been *comatose,* D. She was a campus celebrity. Former porn actress, got her nickname for being . . . limber. Kruse met her at some Hollywood party while doing 'research.' She couldn't have been more than eighteen or nineteen. He left his second wife for her . . . or maybe it was the third—who keeps track? Got her enrolled in the university as an English major. I think she lasted three weeks. Ring a bell yet?"

I shook my head. "When was this?"

" '74."

"In '74 I was up in San Francisco—at Langley Porter."

"Oh, yeah, you double-shifted—internship and dissertation same year. Well, D., your precociousness may have dumped you in the job market one year sooner than the rest of us, but you missed out on Suzy. She was really supposed to be something. I actually worked with her—for a week. Kruse assigned her to the study, doing secretarial work. She couldn't type, screwed up the files. Sweet kid, actually. But somewhat basic."

The honoree and spouse had come closer. Suzanne Kruse tagged along after her husband as if bolted to a track. She looked fragile, with bony shoulders, a tight-corded neck bisected by a diamond choker, nearly flat chest, hollow cheeks, and sharply pointed chin. Her arms were shapely but sinewy, bony hands ending in long, spindly fingers. Her nails were long and red-lacquered. They clutched her husband's sleeve, digging into the tweed.

"Must be true love," I said. "He stuck with her all these years."

"Don't bet that it's wholesome monogamy. Kruse's got a rep as a major-league pussy hound and Suzy's known to be tolerant." He cleared his throat. *"Submissive."*

"Literally?"

He nodded. "Remember those parties Kruse used to throw at his place in Mandeville Canyon the first year he joined the faculty? Oh, yeah, you were in Frisco." He stopped, ate an egg roll and ruminated. "Wait, I think they were still going on in '75. You were back by '75, right?"

"Graduated," I said. "Working at the hospital. I met him once. We didn't like each other. He wouldn't have invited me."

"No one was *invited,* Alex. These were open houses. In every sense of the word."

He chucked me under the chin. "You probably wouldn't have

gone, anyway, because you were a *good boy*, so serious. Actually, I never got further than the door, myself. Brenda took one look at them coating the floor with Wesson oil and hauled my ass out of there. But people who went said they were plus-four orgies, if you could stand fucking other shrinks. *Oh! Calcutta!* meets B. F. Skinner—what a scary idea, huh? And Suzy Straddle was one of the main attractions—tied up, harnessed, muzzled, and flogged."

"How do you know all this?"

"Campus gossip. Everyone knew—it was no secret. Back then, no one thought it was all that weird. Pre-microbe days—sexual freedom, liberating the id, expanding the boundaries of consciousness, et cetera. Even the radical libbers in our class thought Kruse was on the cutting edge of something *meaningful*. Or maybe it just got their rocks off being dominant. Either way, it was *philosophically* acceptable to flog Suzy because she was fulfilling some need of her own."

"Kruse do the flogging?"

"Everyone did. It was a real gang scene—she was an equal-opportunity floggee. There, look at her, how she's holding on to him for dear life. Doesn't she seem submissive? Probably a passive-dependent personality, perfect symbiotic fit for a power junkie like Kruse."

To me she looked scared. Adhering to her husband, but staying in the background. I watched her step forward and smile when spoken to, then retreat. Tossing her long hair, checking her nails. Her smile was as flat as a decal, her dark eyes unnaturally bright.

She moved so that the sun hit the diamond choker and threw off sparks. I thought of a dog collar.

Kruse turned abruptly to take someone's hand and his wife was caught off balance. Throwing her arm out for support, she took hold of his sleeve and held on tighter, wrapping herself around him. He continued to knead her bare shoulder, but for all the attention he paid to her, she might have been a sweater.

Love. Whatever the hell that means.

"Low self-esteem," said Larry. "You'd have to be down on yourself to fuck on film."

"Guess so."

He drained his mug. "Going for a refill. Can I get you something?"

I held up my half-full soda glass. "Still working on this."

He shrugged and went to the bar.

The Kruses had circled away from our table toward one filled with magpies. A fizz of small talk; then he laughed, a deep, self-satisfied sound. He said something to a male graduate student, pumped the student's hand while running his eyes over the young man's pretty wife. Suzanne Kruse kept smiling.

Larry returned. "So," he said, settling, "how's it going with you?"

"Great."

"Yeah, me too. That's why we're here without our women, right?"

I sipped soda and gazed at him. He maintained eye contact but busied himself with a chicken wing.

The therapist's look. Gravid with concern.

Genuine concern, but I wanted no part of it. Suddenly I felt like bolting. A quick jog back to the big stone arch, farewell to Gatsbyland.

Instead, I dipped into my own bag of shrink-moves. Parried a question with a question.

"How's Brenda doing in law school?"

He knew full well what was going on, answered anyway. "Top ten percent of the class for the second year in a row."

"You must be proud of her."

"Sure. Except there's another entire year to go. Check me same time next year and see if I'm still functioning."

I nodded. "I've heard it's a rotten process."

His grin lost its warmth. "Anything that produces lawyers would have to be, wouldn't it? Like turning sirloin into shit. My favorite part is when she comes home and cross-examines me about the house and the kids."

He wiped his mouth and leaned in close. "One part of me understands it—she's bright, brighter than I am, I always expected her to go for something other than housework. She was the one who said no, her own mother had worked full time, farmed her out to babysitters, she resented it. She got pregnant on our honeymoon, nine months later we had Steven, then the rest of them, like after-shocks. Now, all of a sudden, she needs to find herself. Clara Darrow."

He shook his head. "The problem is the timing. Here I am, finally getting to a point where I don't have to hustle referrals. The associates are reliable, the practice is basically running itself. The baby starts first grade next year, we could take some time off, travel. Instead, she's gone twenty hours a day while I play Mr. Mom."

He scowled. "Be careful, my friend—though with Robin it'll probably be different, she's already had her career, might be ready to settle down."

I said, "Robin and I are separated."

He stared at me, shook his head, again. Rubbed his chin and sighed. "Shit, I'm sorry. How long's it been?"

"Five weeks. Temporary vacation that just seemed to stretch."

He drained his beer. "I'm really sorry. I always thought you guys were the perfect couple."

"I thought so, too, Larry." My throat got tight and my chest burned. I was certain that everyone was looking at me, though when I looked around, no one was. Just Larry, eyes as soft as a spaniel's.

"Hope it works out," he said.

I stared into my glass. The ice had melted to slush. "Think I will have something stronger."

I elbowed my way through the crush at the bar and ordered a double gin and tonic that fell just short of single strength. On the way back to the table I came face to face with Kruse. He looked at me. His eyes were light-brown flecked with green, the irises unusually large. They widened—with recognition I was certain—then flicked away and focused somewhere over my shoulder. Simultaneously, he shot out his hand, grasped mine firmly, covered it with his other, and moved our arms up and down while exclaiming, "So nice you could come!" Before I had a chance to reply, he'd used the handshake as leverage to propel himself past me, spinning me halfway around before relinquishing his grip and moving on.

Politician's hustle. I'd been expertly manipulated.

Again.

I turned, saw his tailored back retreating, followed by the shimmering silver sheet of his wife's hair swaying in counterpoint to her narrow, tight derrière.

The two of them walked several steps before being taken in hand by a tall, handsome middle-aged woman.

Slim and impeccably assembled in a custard-yellow silk cocktail dress, white rose corsage, and strategically placed diamonds, she could have been any President's First Lady. Her hair was chestnut accented with pewter, combed back and tied in a chignon that crowned a long, full-jawed face. Her lips were thin, molded in a half-smile.

Finishing-school smile. Genetic poise.

I heard Kruse say, "Hello, Hope. Everything's just beautiful."

"Thank you, Paul. If you've a moment, there are some people I'd like you to meet."

"Of course, dear."

The exchange sounded rehearsed, lacking in warmth, and had excluded Suzanne Kruse. The three of them left the patio, Kruse and the First Lady side by side, the former Suzy Straddle following like a servant. They headed for a group of swans basking in the reflected light of one of the pools. Their arrival was heralded by the cessation of chatter and the lowering of glasses. A lot of flesh was pressed. Within seconds the swans were all listening raptly to Kruse. But the woman in yellow seemed bored. Even resentful.

I returned to the table, took a deep drink of gin. Larry raised his glass and touched it to mine.

"Here's to old-fashioned girls, D. Long may they fucking live."

I tossed back what was left of my gin and sucked on the ice. I hadn't eaten all day, felt a light buzz coming on and shook my head to clear it. The movement brought a swatch of custard-yellow into view.

The First Lady had left Kruse's side. She scanned the grounds, took a few steps, stopped and flicked her head toward a yellow spot on the lawn. Discarded napkin. A waiter rushed to pick it up. Like a captain on the bow of a frigate, the chestnut-haired woman shaded her eyes with her hand and continued to scan the grounds. She glided to one of the rosebeds, lifted a blossom and inspected it. Another waiter bearing shears was at her side immediately. A moment later the flower was in her hair and she was moving on.

"That's our hostess?" I said. "In the pale-yellow dress?"

"No idea, D. Not exactly my social circle."

"Kruse called her Hope."

"Then that's her. Hope Blalock. Springs eternal."

A moment later, he said, "Some hostess. Notice how we're all kept outside, no one gets into the house?"

"Like dogs that haven't been housebroken."

He laughed, lifted one leg off the chair and made a rude sound with his lips. Then he cocked his head at a nearby table. "Speaking of animal training, observe the maze-and-electrode crowd."

Eight or nine grad students sat surrounding a man in his late fifties. The students favored corduroy, jeans, and plain cotton shifts, lank hair and wire-rims. Their mentor was stoop-shouldered, bald, and wore a clipped white beard. His suit was mud-colored hopsacking, a couple of sizes too large. It shrouded him like a monk's habit. He talked nonstop and jabbed his finger a lot. The students looked glassy-eyed.

"The Ratman himself," said Larry. "And his merry band of Ratkateers. Probably going on about something sexy like the correlation between electroshock-induced defecation and stimulation voltage following experimentally induced frustration of a partially reinforced escape response acquired under widely spaced trials. In fucking squirrels."

I laughed. "Looks like he lost weight. Maybe he's doing weight-loss tapes, too."

"Nope. Heart attack last year—it's why he gave up being department head and passed it along to Kruse. The tapes started right after that. Fucking hypocrite. Remember how he used to put down the clinical students, say we shouldn't consider our doctorates a *union card for private practice*? What an asshole. You should see the ads he's been running for his little no-smoking racket."

"Where've they run?"

"Trashy magazines. One square inch of black-and-white in the back along with pitches for military schools, stuff-envelopes-and-make-a-fortune schemes, and Oriental pen pals. Only reason I found out is, one of my patients sent away for it and brought the cassette in to show me. 'Use the Behavioral Approach to Quit Smoking,' the Ratman's name right there on the plastic, along with this tacky mimeographed brochure listing his academic credentials. He actually narrates the damned thing, D., in that pompous monotone. Trying to sound compassionate, as if he'd been working with people instead of rodents all these years." He gave a disgusted look. "Union cards."

"Is he making any money?"

"If he is, he sure ain't spending it on clothes."

Larry's beeper went off. He pulled it off his belt, held it to his ear for a moment. "The service. 'Scuse me, D."

He stopped a waiter, asked for the nearest phone, and was directed to the big white house. I watched him duck-walk through the formal gardens, then got up, ordered another gin and tonic, and stood there at the bar drinking it, enjoying the anonymity. I was starting to feel comfortably fuzzy when I heard something that set off an internal alarm.

Familiar tones, inflections.

A voice from the past.

I told myself it was imagination. Then I heard the voice again and searched the crowd.

I saw her, over several sets of shoulders.

A time-machine jolt. I tried to look away, couldn't.

Sharon, exquisite as ever.

I knew her age without calculating. Thirty-four. A birthday in May. May 15—how strange to still remember . . .

I stepped closer, got a better look: maturity but no diminution of beauty.

A face out of a cameo.

Oval, fine-boned, clean-jawed. The hair thick, wavy, black and glossy as caviar, brushed back from a high, flawless forehead, spilling over square shoulders. Milk-white complexion, unfashionably sun-shy. High cheekbones gently defined, rouged naturally with coins of dusty rose. Small, close-set ears, a single pearl in each. Black eyebrows arching above wide-set deep-blue eyes. A thin, straight nose, gently flaring nostrils.

I remembered the feel of her skin . . . pale as porcelain but warm, always warm. I craned to get a better view.

She had on a knee-length navy-blue linen dress, short-sleeved and loose-fitting. Unsuccessful camouflage: the contours of her body fought the confines of the dress and won. Full, soft breasts, wasp waist, rich flare of hip tapering to long legs and sculpted ankles. Her arms were smooth white stalks. She wore no rings or bracelets, only the pearl studs and a matching string of opera-length pearls that rode the swell of her bosom. Blue pumps with medium heels added an inch to her five and a half feet. In one hand was a matching blue purse. The other hand caressed it.

No wedding ring.

So what?

With Robin at my side, I would have taken brief notice.

Or so I tried to convince myself.

I couldn't keep my eyes off her.

She had *her* eyes on a man—one of the swans, old enough to be her father. Big square bronze face corrugated with deep seams. Narrow, pale eyes, brush-cut hair the color of iron filings. Well-built, despite his age, and perfectly turned out in double-breasted blue blazer and gray flannel slacks.

Oddly boyish—one of those youthful older men who populate the better clubs and resorts and are able to bed younger women without incurring snickers.

Her lover?

What business was that of mine?

I kept staring. Romance didn't seem to be what was fueling her attention. The two of them were off in one corner and she was arguing with him, trying to convince him of something. Barely moving her lips and straining to look casual. He just stood there, listening.

Sharon at a party; it didn't fit. She'd hated them as much as I had.

But that had been a long time ago. People change. Lord knew that applied to her.

I raised my glass to my lips, watched her tug on one earlobe—some things stayed the same.

I edged closer, bumped into a matron's padded haunch and received a glare. Mumbling apologies, I pressed forward. The crush of drinkers was unyielding. I wedged my way through, seeking a voyeur's vantage—deliciously close but safely out of view. Telling myself it was just curiosity.

Suddenly she turned her head and saw me. She pinkened with recognition and her lips parted. We locked in on each other. As if dancing.

Dancing on a terrace. A nest of lights in the distance. Weightless, formless . . .

I felt dizzy, bumped into someone else. More apologies.

Sharon kept looking straight at me. The brush-cut man was facing the other way, looking contemplative.

I retreated further, was swallowed by the crowd, and returned to the table short of breath, clutching my glass so tightly my fingers hurt. I counted blades of grass until Larry returned.

"The call was about the baby," he said. "She and her little playmate got into a fight. She's tantrumming and insisting on being taken home. The other girl's mother says they're both hysterical—overtired. I've got to go pick her up, D. Sorry."

"No problem. I'm ready to leave myself."

"Yeah, turned out to be pretty turgid, didn't it? But at least I got a look at La Grande Maison's entry hall—big enough to skate in. We're in the wrong business, D."

"What's the right business?"

"Marry it young, spend the rest of your life pissing it away."

He looked back at the mansion, cast his eyes over the grounds. "Listen, Alex, it was good seeing you—little male pair-bonding, hostility release. How about we get together in a couple of weeks, shoot some pool at the Faculty Club, ingest some cholesterol?"

"Sounds great."

"Terrific. I'll call you."

"Look forward to it, Larry."

Buttressed by our lies, we left the party.

He was eager to get going but offered to drive me home. I said I'd rather walk, waited with him while the bearded valet fetched his keys. The Chevy station wagon had been repositioned for quick exit. And washed. The valet held the door open and expectorated a

mouthful of "sirs" as he waited for Larry to get comfortable. When
Larry put the key in the ignition, the valet shut the door gently and
held his palm out, smiling.

Larry looked over at me. I winked. Larry grinned, rolled up the
window, and started the engine. I strolled past the cars, heard the
wheeze of the Chevy's engine followed by curses muttered in some
Mediterranean language. Then, a clatter and squeal as the wagon
accelerated. Larry zipped past, stuck out his left hand and waved.

I'd walked several yards when I heard someone calling. Thinking
nothing of it, I didn't break step.

Then the call took on volume and clarity.

"Alex!"

I looked over my shoulder. Navy-blue dress. Swirl of black hair.
Long white legs running.

She caught up with me, breasts heaving, upper lip pearled with
sweat.

"Alex! It really is you. I can't believe it!"

"Hello, Sharon. How've you been?" Dr. Witty.

"Just fine." She touched her ear, shook her head. "No, you're
one person to whom I don't have to pretend. No, I haven't been fine,
not at all."

The ease with which she'd slipped into familiarity, the effortless
erasure of all that had passed between us, raised my defenses.

She stepped closer. I smelled her perfume—soap and water
tinged with fresh grass and spring flowers.

"I'm sorry to hear that," I said.

"Oh, Alex." She placed two fingers on my wrist. Let them rest
there.

I felt her heat, was jolted by a rush of energy below my waist. All
at once I was rock-hard. And furious about it. But alive, for the first
time in a long while.

"It's so good to see you, Alex." That voice, sweet and creamy.
The midnight eyes sparkled.

"Good to see you too." It came out thick and intense, nothing
like the indifference I'd aimed for. Her fingers were burning a hole in
my wrist. I dislodged her, put my hands in my pockets.

If she sensed rejection, she didn't show it, just let her arm fall to
her side and kept smiling.

"Alex, it's so funny we should run into each other like this—
pure ESP. I've been wanting to call you."

"About what?"

A triangle of tongue tip moved between her lips and licked away the sweat I'd coveted. "Some issues that have . . . come up. Now's not a good time, but if you could find some time to talk, I'd appreciate it."

"What issues would we have to talk about after all these years?"

Her smile was a quarter-moon of white light. Too immediate. Too wide.

"I was hoping you wouldn't be angry after all these years."

"I'm not angry, Sharon. Just puzzled."

She worried her earlobe. Her fingers flew forward and grazed my cheek before dropping. "You're a good guy, Delaware. You always were. Be well."

She turned to leave. I took hold of her hand and she stopped.

"Sharon, I'm sorry things aren't going well for you."

She laughed, bit her lip. "No, they really aren't. But that's not your problem."

Even as she said it, she came closer, kept coming. I realized I was pulling her toward me, but with only the faintest pressure; she was allowing herself to be reeled in.

I knew at that moment that she'd do anything I wanted, and her passivity touched off a strange mélange of feelings within me. Pity. Gratitude. The joy of being needed, at last.

The weight between my legs grew oppressive. I dropped her hand.

Our faces were inches apart. My tongue strained against my teeth like a snake in a jar.

A stranger using my voice said, "If it means that much to you, we can get together and talk."

"It means a lot to me," she said.

We made a lunch date for Monday.

5

The moment she disappeared behind the gates, I knew it had been a mistake. But I wasn't sure I regretted it.

Back home, I checked with my service, hoping for a call from Robin, something to make me regret it.

"Your board is clear, Dr. Delaware," said the operator. I thought I detected pity in her voice, told myself I was getting paranoid.

That night I went to sleep with a head full of erotic images. Some time during the early morning hours I had a wet dream. I woke sticky and cranky, and knew, without having to reason it out, that I was going to break the date with Sharon. Not looking forward to it, I went through the motions of a normal morning—showering, shaving, swallowing coffee, dictating reports, killed another couple of hours filing and skimming journals. At noon Mal Worthy called and asked me to reserve Wednesday for a deposition on the Darren Burkhalter case.

"Working on Sunday, Mal?"

"Brunch," he said. "Waiting for a table. Evil never rests; neither can the good guys. Going to be seven attorneys on the other side, Alex. Have your bullshit detector finely tuned."

"Why the army?"

"Multiple pockets. The other driver's insurance company has assigned two of their downtown hotshots; the estate's sending another. The drunk who rammed them was a fairly successful building contractor—there're some bucks involved. I told you about the brakes, which gives us the auto manufacturer's mouthpiece and the one representing the dealer who serviced the car. The restaurant that served him the drinks makes six. Add to that a county attorney because we're claiming inadequate lighting and insufficient cones around the ditch, and you've got seven *in toto*. Intimidated?"

"Should I be?"

"Nope. It's quality that counts, not quantity, right? We'll do it at my office, get a little home-base advantage. I'll start by reading off your qualifications, and as usual, one of them will cut it off before it gets too hoo-ha and stipulate to your expertise. You've done this before; you know the whole thing's supposed to be fact-finding, polite, but I'll be there to cover your ass if it starts to get nasty. The insurance guys will probably put up the biggest kick—their liability is clearest and they've got the most to lose. My hunch is that, rather than attack your information per se, they'll question the validity of early childhood trauma as a concept—is it scientific fact or just shrinky bullshit. And even if it is, how durable is the damage? Can you prove that a traumatic experience at eighteen months will warp poor little Darren for life."

"Never said I could."

"I know that and you know that, but please be more subtle on Wednesday. The important thing is *they* can't prove he'll be fine. And if it goes to trial, believe me, I'll make damn sure the burden of proof will be on *them*. A jury is going to feel mighty sorry for a cute little tyke who wakes up from a car nap only to see his father's head sailing over the back seat and landing right next to him. Videotaping your sessions was a beautiful touch, Alex. The kid comes across wonderfully vulnerable. In a trial situation, I'd get to show every second of footage—all that hyper stuff—along with the Polaroids from the accident. Nothing like a bloody head to get the old sympathy juices flowing, huh?"

"Nothing like it."

"A *jury* will fucking believe the concept, Alex. They'll see no way this kid could ever be normal again—and let's face it, can any of us guarantee something like that could ever heal? The other side knows that. They've already thrown out hints of settlement offers—penny-ante bullshit. So it's just a question of how much, how soon. Your job will be to tell it like it is, but don't get too academic. Just stick to the old 'to the best of my psychological knowledge' line and we'll be fine. I've got my actuary working overtime, want to hook these bastards so tight they'll be paying Darren's rent at the old-age home."

He paused, added, "It's only fair, Alex. Denise's life is shattered. It's the only way for someone like her to beat the system."

"You're a white knight, Mal."

"Something eating at you?" He sounded genuinely hurt.

"No, everything's fine. Just a little tired."

"You're sure?"

"I'm sure."

He said nothing for a moment. "All right, just as long as we're communicating."

"We're communicating perfectly, Mal. Quality, not quantity."

He was silent for a moment, then said, "Rest up and take care of yourself, doc. I want you in peak shape when you're dealing with the seven dwarfs."

I called Sharon just after noon. A machine answered—my year for them. ("Hello, this is Dr. Ransom. I'm not in right now, but I'm *very* interested in receiving your message. . . .")

Even on tape the sound of her voice brought back memories . . . the feel of her fingers on my cheek.

All at once I *had* to be rid of her, decided to do it *now*. I waited for the emergency beeper number that therapists typically include at the end of their tapes. But she didn't mention one.

Beep.

I said, "Sharon, this is Alex. Can't make Monday. Good luck."

Short and sweet.

Dr. Heartbreaker.

An hour later her face was still in my mind, a pale, lovely mask drifting in and out of my consciousness.

I tried to chase the image away, succeeded only in making it more vivid. I surrendered to reminiscence, told myself I was being a horny jerk, allowing my little head to think for my big one. Nevertheless, I sank deeper into time-buffered memories and began wondering if I'd done the right thing by breaking the date.

At one, hoping to exchange one lovely mask for another, I phoned San Luis Obispo. Robin's mother answered.

"Yes?"

"This is Alex, Rosalie."

"Oh. Hello."

"Is Robin there?"

"No."

"Do you know when she'll be back?"

"She's out. With friends."

"I see."

Silence.

"So, how's the baby, Rosalie?"

"Fine."

"Okay, then. Please tell her I called."

"All right."

" 'Bye."

Click.

The privilege of owning a mother-in-law without having to do the paperwork.

Monday, I struggled through the morning paper, hoping the venality and low-mindedness of international politics would cast my problems in a trivial light. It proved effective, until I finished the paper. Then that old empty feeling returned.

I fed the fish, did a wash, went down to the carport, started up the Seville, and drove into South Westwood to do some grocery shopping. Somewhere between frozen foods and canned goods I realized my basket was empty; I left the supermarket without buying a thing.

There was a multiplex theater up the block from the market. I chose a feature at random, paid the early-bird discount price and sat low in my seat along with giggling teenage couples and other solitary men. The show was a low-grade thriller graced by neither coherent dialogue nor plot. I walked out in the middle of a sweat-soaked love scene between the heroine and the dashing psychopath who was going to try to carve her up for postcoital dessert.

Outside, it was dark. Another day vanquished. I forced a fast-food burger down my throat, headed for home, then remembered that the newspaper had been temporarily therapeutic.

Evening. A new edition. A blind vendor was hawking it from a curb on Wilshire. I pulled over, bought a paper, paying with a dollar bill, not waiting for the change.

Back home, I called my service—no impersonal machine for old Alex. No messages either.

Stripping down to my undershorts, I took the *Times* and a cup of instant coffee to bed.

Slow news day; most of the evening special was a rehash of the morning edition. I stuffed myself on swindles and subterfuge. Found my eyes blurring. Perfect.

Then I was brought abruptly back to focus by a story on page 20.

Not even a story, just filler: a couple of column-inches next to a wire-service piece on the sociological structure of South American fire ants.

But the headline caught my eye.

PSYCHOLOGIST'S DEATH POSSIBLE SUICIDE
Maura Bannon
Staff Writer

(LOS ANGELES) Police sources said the death of a local psychologist, found this morning in her Hollywood Hills home, probably resulted from a self-inflicted gunshot wound. The body of Sharon Ransom, 34, was discovered this morning in the bedroom of her Nichols Canyon home. She had apparently died sometime Sunday night.

Ransom lived alone in the Jalmia Drive house, which also doubled as an office. A native of New York City, she was educated and trained in Los Angeles, received her Ph.D. in 1981. No next of kin have been located.

Sunday night. Just hours after I'd called her.

Something cold and rank as sewer gas rose in my gut and bubbled in my throat. I forced myself to read the article again. And again.

A couple of column inches. Filler . . . I thought of black hair, blue eyes, a blue dress, pearls. That remarkable face, so alive, so warm.

No, you're one person to whom I don't have to pretend. No, I haven't been fine, not at all.

A cry for help? The implied intimacy had angered me. Had it blocked me from seeing it for what it was?

She hadn't looked that upset.

And why me? What had she seen in that quick glance across the shoulders of strangers that had led her to think I was the right one to turn to?

Big mistake . . . old Alex fixated on his own needs, soft white thighs and pillowy breasts.

No, I haven't been fine. Not at all.

I'm sorry to hear that.

Dispensing vending-machine empathy.

I'd reeled her in, not giving half a shit. Enjoyed the feeling of power as she floated toward me, passive.

If it means that much to you, we can get together and talk . . . and let me fuck your ears off.

It means a lot to me.

I clawed the page free from the paper, crumpled it, and threw it across the room.

Closing my eyes, I tried to let myself cry. For her, for me, for Robin. For families that fell apart, a world falling apart. Little boys who watched their fathers die. Anyone in the world who goddam deserved it.

The tears wouldn't come.

Wait for the beep.

Pull the trigger.

6

Later, after some of the shock wore off, I realized that I'd rescued her once before. Perhaps she'd remembered it, had constructed a time-machine fantasy of her own.

The fall of '74. I was twenty-four, a brand-new Ph.D., caught up in the novelty of being addressed as Doctor but still as poor as a student.

I'd just returned to L.A. from the Langley Porter Institute in San Francisco to begin my fellowship at Western Pediatric Hospital. The position came with a jawbreaker of a title: National Institute of Mental Health Postdoctoral Scholar in Clinical Psychology and Human Development, jointly appointed to the hospital and its affiliated medical school. My job was to treat children, teach interns, do research, and come up with a paper or two the chief psychologist could co-author.

My pay was $500 a month, which the IRS had just declared taxable. There was barely enough left over to cover rent and utilities on a dingy Overland Avenue bachelor flat, plain-wrap food, discount clothing, thrift-shop books, and ongoing life support for a moribund Nash Rambler. Not covered was an eight-year accumulation of student loans and debts filed too long under Miscellaneous. A number of bank creditors delighted in dunning me monthly.

In order to earn extra money, I took on nighttime gigs playing guitar in dance bands, the way I'd scratched by in San Francisco. Irregular work with spotty pay and all the bar food I could get down between sets. I also let the University psych department know its illustrious graduate was available for free-lance teaching assignments.

The department ignored me until one afternoon in November when one of its secretaries had me paged at the hospital.

"Dr. Delaware, please."

"This is Dr. Delaware."

"Alice Delaware?"

"Alex."

"Oh. It says here Alice. I thought you were a woman."

"Not the last time I checked."

"Guess not. Anyway, I know it's short notice, but if you're available at eight tonight, we could use you."

"Use away."

"Don't you want to hear what it's about?"

"Why not?"

"Okay, we need someone to supervise Course 305A—the clinical practicum for first- and second-year graduate students. The professor who runs it was called out of town and none of the usual substitutes are available."

Barrel-scraping time. "Sounds fine to me."

"Okay. You're licensed, right?"

"Not until next year."

"Oh. Then I'm not sure . . . Hold on." A moment later: "Okay. Because you're not licensed the pay is eight dollars an hour instead of fifteen and subject to withholding. And there's some paperwork you'll have to fill out first."

"You've twisted my arm."

"Pardon?"

"I'll be there."

In theory, clinical practicum is a link between book learning and the real world, a way to introduce therapists-in-training to the practice of psychotherapy in a nurturant environment.

At my alma mater, the process started early: During their first semester clinical-psych graduate students were assigned patients—undergrads referred from the campus counseling service and poor people seeking free treatment at the University health clinic. The students diagnosed and treated under the supervision of a faculty member. Once a week they presented their progress, or lack thereof, to peers and instructors. Sometimes things stayed on an intellectual level. Sometimes they got personal.

Psych 305A was held in a windowless garret on the third floor of the Tudor mansion that housed the clinical program. The room was bare of furniture, painted a grayish blue, and carpeted in grubby gold shag. In one corner was a pair of foam-padded bats—the kind provided by marriage counselors for good clean fighting. In another were piled the remains of a disassembled polygraph.

I arrived five minutes late, "some paperwork" having turned out to be a mountain of forms. Seven or eight students were already in place. They'd removed their shoes and positioned themselves against the sloping walls, reading, chatting, smoking, catnapping. Ignoring me. The room smelled of dirty socks, tobacco, and mildew.

For the most part they were an older, seasoned-looking bunch— refugees from the sixties in serapes, faded jeans, sweat shirts, Indian jewelry. A few wore business clothes. Every one of them looked serious and burdened—straight-A students wondering if the grind was worth it.

"Hi, I'm Dr. Delaware." I let the title roll off my tongue with delight and some guilt, feeling like an impostor. The students looked me over, less than impressed. "Alex," I added. "Dr. Kruse can't make it, so I'm taking over tonight."

"Where's Paul?" asked a woman in her late twenties. She was short with prematurely gray hair, granny glasses, a tight, disapproving mouth.

"Out of town."

"Hollywood's not out of town," said a big, bearded man in plaid shirt and overalls, smoking a free-form Danish pipe.

"Are you one of his assistants?" asked the gray-haired woman. She was attractive but pinched-looking, with angry, nervous eyes; a Puritan in blue denim, she appraised me baldly, looked eager to condemn.

"No, I've never met him. I'm—"

"A new faculty member!" proclaimed the bearded man, as if uncovering a conspiracy.

I shook my head. "Recent grad. Ph.D. last June."

"Congratulations." The bearded man clapped his hands silently. A few of the others imitated him. I smiled, squatted, assumed a lotus position near the door. "What's your usual procedure?"

"Case presentation," said a black woman. "Unless someone's got a crisis to bounce around."

"Does anyone?"

Silence. Yawns.

"All right. Whose turn is it to present?"

"Mine," said the black woman. She was stocky, with a hennaed Afro haloing a round, chocolate face. She wore a black poncho, blue jeans, and red vinyl boots. An oversized carpetbag lay across her lap.

"Aurora Bogardus, second year. Last week I presented the case of a nine-year-old boy with multiple tics. Paul made suggestions. I've got some follow-up."

"Go ahead."

"For starters, nothing's worked. The kid's getting worse." She removed a chart from the carpetbag, flipped through it and gave a brief case history for my benefit, then described her initial treatment plan, which seemed well thought-out, though unsuccessful.

"That brings us up to date," she said. "Any questions, gang?"

Twenty minutes of discussion followed. The students' suggestions emphasized social factors—the family's poverty and frequent moves, the anxiety the child was probably experiencing due to lack of friends. Someone commented that the boy's being black in a racist society was a major stressor.

Aurora Bogardus looked disgusted. "I believe I'm well aware of that. Meanwhile, I've still got to deal with the damned tics on a *behavioral* level. The more he twitches, the angrier everyone gets at him."

"Then *everyone* needs to learn to deal with that anger," said the bearded man.

"Fine and dandy, Julian," said Aurora. "In the meantime, the kid's being ostracized, I need action."

"The operant conditioning system—"

"If you were paying attention, Julian, you would have just heard that your operant conditioning system didn't work. Neither did the role manipulation Paul suggested last week."

"What kind of role manipulation?" I asked.

"Change the programming. It's part of his approach toward therapy—Communication Dynamics. Shake up the family structure, get them to change their power positions so that they'll be open to new behaviors."

"Get them to change in what way?"

She gave me a weary look. "Paul had me instruct the parents and siblings to start twitching and shaking too. Exaggeratedly. He said once the symptom became part of the family norm, it would cease to have rebellion value for the boy and would drop out of his behavioral repertoire."

"Why's that?"

She shook her head. "It's his theory, not mine."

I said nothing, maintained a look of curiosity.

"Okay, okay," she said. "According to Paul, symptoms are communications. Because the tic communication wouldn't be unique anymore, the kid would have to find some other way of working through his rebellion."

It sounded ill-conceived, potentially cruel, and made me wonder about Dr. Paul Kruse. "I see."

"Hey, I thought it was bullshit too," said Aurora. "Going to tell Paul that, next week."

"Sure you will," said someone.

"Watch me." She closed the chart and put it back in her bag. "Meanwhile, this poor little boy's shaking and twitching and his self-esteem is going right down the tubes."

"Have you thought of Tourette's syndrome?" I asked.

She dismissed the question with a frown. "Of course. But he doesn't swear."

"Not all Tourette's patients do."

"Paul said the symptoms didn't conform to a typical Tourette's pattern."

"In what way?"

Another weary look. Her answer took five minutes and was seriously flawed. My doubts about Kruse grew.

"I still think you should consider Tourette's," I said. "We don't know enough about the syndrome to exclude atypical cases. My advice is, refer the boy to a pediatric neurologist. Haldol may be indicated."

"Ye olde medical model," said Julian. He tamped his pipe, relit it.

Aurora moved her jaws as if chewing.

"What are you feeling now?" one of the other men asked her. He was narrow-shouldered and thin, with rusty hair tied in a pony-tail, and a drooping, ragged mustache. He wore a wrinkled brown corduroy suit, button-down shirt, extra-wide rep tie, and dirty sneak-ers, and spoke in a soft, musical voice saturated with empathy. But unctuous, like a confessor or kiddie-show host. "Share your feelings with us, Aurora."

"Oh, Christ." She turned to me: "Yeah, I'll do what you say. If the medical model is what it takes, so be it."

"You sound frustrated," said the gray-haired woman.

Aurora turned on her. "Let's cut the shit and move on, okay?"

Before Gray Hair could reply, the door opened. All eyes drifted upward. All eyes hardened.

A beautiful black-haired girl stood in the doorway, holding an armful of books. Girl, not woman—she looked girlish, could have been an undergrad, and for a moment I thought she'd come to the wrong place.

But she stepped into the room.

My first thought was *time warp:* She had a dark, wounded beauty, like an actress in one of those black-and-white late-show *films noirs,* where good and evil blur, visual images vie for control with a sinuous jazz score, and everything ends ambiguously.

She wore a clinging pink knit dress piped with white and bisected by a white leather belt, pink pumps with medium heels. Her hair had been rolled and set, every strand in place, gleaming. Her face was powdered, mascaraed, her lips glossed a wet-looking pink. The dress reached her knees. The leg that showed was shapely, encased in sheer nylon. Her jewelry was real gold, her nails long and polished—the hue of the polish identical to that of the dress but precisely one shade deeper.

And perfume—the fragrance cut through the staleness of the room: soap and water, fresh grass, and spring flowers.

All curves and swells, porcelain whiteness and dusty rose, flawlessly put together. Almost painfully out of place in that sea of denim and deliberate drabness.

"Suzy Creamcheese," somebody muttered.

She heard it and winced, looked around for a place to sit. No empty spaces. No one moved. I shifted to one side, said, "Over here."

She stared at me.

"He's Dr. Delaware," said Julian. "*Alex.* He's endured the rites and rituals of this department and emerged seemingly unscathed."

She gave a fleeting smile, sat down next to me, folded her legs under. A stretch of white thigh showed. She tugged the dress down over her knees. It caused the fabric to go tight over her breasts and accentuate their fullness. Her eyes were wide and bright, midnight-blue, so dark the pupils blended with the irises.

"Sorry I'm late," she said. A sweet, creamy voice.

"So what else is new," said Gray Hair.

"Any more follow-ups to present?" I asked.

No one answered.

"Then I guess we can move on to new material."

"What about Sharon?" said Ponytail, grinning at the new arrival. "You haven't shared a thing with us all semester, Sharon."

The black-haired girl shook her head. "I really don't have anything prepared, Walter."

"What's to prepare? Just pick a case, give us the benefit of your wisdom."

"Or at least Paul's wisdom," said Julian.

Snickers, nods of assent.

She pulled at her earlobe, turned to me, seeking reprieve.

The crack about Kruse helped explain the tension that had accompanied her entrance. Whatever his therapeutic skills at manipulating roles, this supervisor had allowed his group to be poisoned by favoritism. But I was hired help, not the one to deal with it.

I asked her: "Have you presented at all this semester?"

"No." Alarmed.

"Do you have any case you could discuss?"

"I . . . I suppose so." She gave me a look more pitying than resentful: *You're hurting me but it's not your fault.*

Shaken a bit, I said, "Then go ahead, please."

"The one I could talk about is a woman I've been seeing for two months. She's a nineteen-year-old sophomore. Initial testing shows her to be within normal limits on every measure, with the MMPI Depression scale a little elevated. Her boyfriend is a senior. They met the first week of the semester and have been going together ever since. She self-referred to the Counseling Center because of problems in their relationship—"

"What kinds of problems?" asked Gray Hair.

"A communication breakdown. In the beginning they could talk to each other. Later, things started to change. Now they're pretty bad."

"Be more specific," said Gray Hair.

Sharon thought. "I'm not sure what you—"

"Are they *fucking*?" asked Ponytail Walter.

Sharon turned red and looked down at the carpet. An old-fashioned blush—I hadn't thought it still existed. A few of the students looked embarrassed for her. The rest seemed to be enjoying it.

"Are they?" pressed Walter. "Fucking?"

She bit her lip. "They're having relations, yes."

"How often?"

"I really haven't kept a record—"

"Why not? It could be an important parameter of—"

"Hold on," I said. "Give her a chance to finish."

"She'll never finish," said Gray Hair. "We've been through this before—terminal defensiveness. If we don't confront it, cut it off where it grows, we'll be spinning our wheels the whole session."

"There's nothing to confront," I said. "Let her get the facts out. Then we'll discuss them."

"Right," said Gray Hair. "Another protective male heard from— you bring it out in them, Princess Sharon."

"Ease up, Maddy," said Aurora Bogardus. "Let her talk."

"Sure, sure." Gray Hair folded her arms across her chest, sat back, glared, waited.

"Go ahead," I told Sharon.

She'd sat in silence, removed from the fray like a parent waiting out a spat between siblings. Now she picked up where she'd left off. Calm. Or on the edge?

"There's been a communication breakdown. The patient says she loves her boyfriend but feels they're growing distant from one another. They can no longer talk about things they used to be able to discuss."

"Such as?" asked Julian, through a cloud of smoke.

"Just about everything."

"*Everything?* What to have for breakfast? Stuffing versus potatoes?"

"At this point, yes. There's been a complete breakdown—"

"*Breakdown,*" said Maddy. "You've used that word three times without explaining what you mean. Try *clarifying* rather than *restating*. Operationalize the word *breakdown*."

"Things have deteriorated," said Sharon, making it sound like a question.

Maddy laughed. "Terrific. That makes it perfectly clear."

Sharon lowered her voice. "I don't really know what you're getting at, Maddy."

Maddy shook her head in disgust, said to no one in particular: "Why waste time on this shit?"

"Second the motion," someone said.

I said, "Let's stick to the case. Sharon, why does this girl feel things have broken down?"

"We've discussed that for several sessions. She claims she doesn't know. At first she thought he'd lost interest and was seeing another woman. He denies that—he spends all his free time with her, so she thinks he's telling the truth. But when they're together he won't talk and seems angry at her—or at least she feels that. It came on all of a sudden, got worse."

"Did anything else happen at that time?" I asked. "Some kind of stressful event?"

Another blush.

"Did they begin having sex at that time, Sharon?"

Nod. "Around then."

"Were there sexual problems?"

"It's hard to know."

"Bullshit," said Maddy. "It would be *easy* to know if you'd done your job properly."

I turned to her and asked, "How would *you* go about getting that kind of information, Maddy?"

"Be *real,* establish rapport." She ticked each phrase off with her finger. "Know the specific defenses of the client—be prepared for the defensive bullshit and roll with it. But if that doesn't work, *confront* and stay with it until the client knows you mean business. Then simply go for it—bring up the *subject,* for Christ's sake. She's been seeing this woman for two months. She should have done all of that by now."

I looked at Sharon.

"I have," she said, the blush still in force. "We've talked about her defenses. It takes time. There are problems."

"Sure are," said Julian.

"*Seck-shoo-all* problems," enunciated Maddy. "Say the 'S' word, honey. Next time it'll be easier."

Scattered laughter. Sharon seemed to be taking it calmly. But I kept my eye on her.

"Share the problems with us," Walter was urging, grinning and playing with his ponytail.

"They . . . she isn't satisfied," said Sharon.

"Is she *coming*?" asked Julian.

"I don't think so."

"Don't think so?"

"No. No, she isn't."

"Then what are you doing to *help* her come?"

She bit her lip again.

"Speak up," said Maddy.

Sharon's hands began to shake. She laced her fingers together to hide it. "We've . . . we've talked about . . . reducing her anxiety, relaxing her."

"Oh, Christ, blame the *woman,*" said Maddy. "Who says it's *her* problem? Maybe it's *him*? Maybe he's a bumbler. Or a preemie."

"She says he's . . . okay. She's the one who's nervous."

"Have you done any deep muscle relaxation?" asked Aurora. "Systematic desensitization?"

"No, nothing that structured. It's still hard for her to talk about it."

"Wonder why," said Julian.

"We're just working on trying to stay calm," said Sharon. It sounded like self-description.

"Hard to be calm about primal issues," soothed Walter. "Have they done oral sex?"

"Uh, yes."

"*Uh,* in what way?"

She looked back down at the carpet. "The usual."

"I don't know what that means, Sharon." He looked at the others. "Do any of you?"

Orchestrated smiles and shakes of the head. A predatory bunch. I pictured them as full-fledged therapists in a few years. Scary.

Sharon was looking at the floor, fighting a losing battle with her hands.

I thought of intervening, wondered whether that violated the norms of the group. Decided I didn't care if it did. But being too protective would harm her more, in the long run.

While I was deliberating, Walter said, "What kind of oral sex?"

"I think we all know what oral sex is," I said.

His eyebrows rose. "Do we? I wonder. Do any of you wonder?"

"This is bullshit," said Aurora. "Got too many things to do." She stood, hefted her carpetbag, and stamped out of the room. Three or four others followed quickly.

The door slammed. A tight silence followed. Sharon's eyes were moist and her earlobe had been tugged scarlet.

"Let's move on to something else," I said.

"Let's not!" shouted Maddy. "Paul says no holds barred—why the hell should she be the exception?" Her anger seemed to lift her from the floor. "Why the hell does she get saved every time she gets into her defensive mode and shuts us out!" To Sharon: "This is *reality,* honey, not some fucking sorority game."

"A *fucking* sorority game wouldn't be half-bad," mused Julian. He sucked on his pipe ostentatiously.

"Back off," I said.

He smiled as if he hadn't heard me, stretched and recrossed his legs.

"Sorry, Alex, no back-offs," Walter informed me. "Paul's rules."

A tear dribbled down Sharon's cheek. She wiped it away. "They do the usual."

"Meaning?"

"Sucking."

"Ah," said Walter. "Now we're getting somewhere." He held out his hands, palms up, fingers curled. "Come on, keep going."

The gesture seemed lecherous. Sharon sensed it too. She looked away from him and said, "That's all, Walter."

"Tsk, tsk," said Julian, raising a professorial pipe. "Let's operationalize. Does *she* suck *him*? Or does *he* suck *her*? Or have they advanced to *mutual* sucking, the old six-nine pretzel?"

Sharon's hands flew to her face. She coughed to keep from crying.

"Camille," said Maddy. "What bullshit."

"Enough," I barked.

Maddy's face darkened. "Another authoritarian father figure heard from."

"Easy," said someone. "Everyone mellow out."

Sharon got to her feet, scooping up her books, struggling with them, all white legs and rustling nylon. "I'm sorry, please excuse me." She made a grab for the doorknob, twisted it and ran out.

Walter said, "Catharsis. Could be a breakthrough."

I looked at him, at all of them. Saw vulture smiles, smugness. And something else—a flicker of fear.

"Class dismissed," I said.

I caught up with her just as she reached the sidewalk.

"Sharon?"

She kept running.

"Wait a second. Please."

She stopped, kept her back to me. I stepped in front of her. She stared down at the pavement, then up at the sky. The night was starless. Her hair merged with it so that only her face was visible. A pale, floating mask.

"I'm sorry," I said.

She shook her head. "No, it was my fault. I acted like a baby, totally inappropriate."

"There's nothing inappropriate about not wanting to be bludgeoned. They're some bunch. I should have kept a tighter rein on things, should have seen what was happening."

She finally made eye contact. Smiled. "That's all right. No one could have seen."

"Is it like that all the time?"

"Sometimes."

"Dr. Kruse approves?"

"Dr. Kruse says we have to confront our own defense systems

before being able to help others." Small laugh. "I guess I have a ways to go."

"You'll do fine," I said. "In the long run, this kind of stuff's irrelevant."

"That's nice of you to say, Dr. Delaware."

"Alex."

The smile widened. "Thanks for checking on me, Alex. I guess you'd better be heading back to class."

"Class is over. Are you sure you're okay?"

"I'm fine." She shifted her weight from one hip to the other, trying to get a firmer grip on the books.

"Here, let me help you with those." Something in her was bringing out the Lancelot in me.

She said, "No, no, that's okay," but didn't stop me from taking the books.

"Where's your car?"

"I'm walking. I live in the dorms. Curtis Hall."

"I can drive you to Curtis."

"It's really not necessary."

"It would be my pleasure."

"Well, then," she said, "I'd like that."

I dropped her off at the dorm, made a date for the following Saturday.

She was waiting at the curb when I came to pick her up, wearing a yellow cashmere sweater, black-and-yellow tartan skirt, black knee socks, and loafers. She let me open the car door for her. The second my hand touched the steering wheel, hers was upon it, warm and firm.

We had dinner at one of the smoky, noisy, beer-and-pizza joints that cling to every college campus—the best I could afford. Staking out a corner table, we watched Road Runner cartoons, ate and drank, smiled at each other.

I couldn't keep my eyes off her, wanted to know more about her, to forge an impossible, instant intimacy. She fed me nibbles of information about herself: She was twenty-one, had grown up on the East Coast, graduated from a small women's college, come west for graduate school. Then she steered the conversation to grad school. Academic issues.

Remembering the insinuations of the other students, I asked about her association with Kruse. She said he was her faculty adviser, made it sound unimportant. When I asked what he was like, she said he was dynamic and creative, then changed the subject, again.

I dropped it but remained curious. After that ugly session, I'd asked around about Kruse, had learned he was one of the clinical associates, a new arrival who'd already earned a reputation as a skirt-chaser and an attention-grabber.

Not the kind of mentor I would have thought right for someone like Sharon. Then again, what did I really know about Sharon? About what was right for her?

I tried to learn more. She danced nimbly away from my questions, kept shifting the focus to me.

I experienced some frustration, understood for an instant the anger of the other students. Then I reminded myself we'd just met; I was being pushy, expecting too much too soon. Her demeanor suggested old money, a conservative, sheltered background. Precisely the kind of upbringing that would stress the dangers of instant intimacy.

Yet there was the matter of her hand stroking mine, the open affection of her smile. Not playing hard-to-get at all.

We talked psychology. She knew her stuff but kept deferring to my superior knowledge. I sensed real depth beneath the Suzy Creamcheese exterior. And something else: agreeableness. A ladylike *niceness* that caught me by pleasant surprise in that age of four-letter female anger masquerading as liberation.

My diploma said I was a doctor of the mind, a sage at twenty-four, grand arbiter of relationships. But relationships still scared me. *Women* still scared me. Since adolescence I'd indentured myself to a regimen of study, work, more study, struggling to pull myself up out of blue-collar purgatory and expecting the human factor to fall into place along with my career goals. But new goals kept popping up and at twenty-four I was still pulling, my social life limited to casual encounters, mandatory, calisthenic sex.

My last date had been more than two months ago—a brief misadventure with a pretty blond neonatology intern from Kansas who asked me out as we stood in the cafeteria line at the hospital. She suggested the restaurant, paid for her own meal, invited herself to my apartment, immediately sprawled on the couch, popped a Quaalude, and got peevish when I refused to take one. A moment later the peevishness was forgotten and she was buck-naked, grinning and pointing to her crotch: "This is *L.A.,* Buster. Eat pussy."

Two months.

Now here I was, sitting opposite a demure beauty who made me feel like Einstein and wiped her mouth even when it was clean. I drank her in. In the candle-in-chianti-bottle light of that pizza joint, everything she did seemed special: spurning beer for 7-Up, laughing like a kid at the misfortunes of Wile E. Coyote, twirling strands of hot cheese around her finger before taking them between perfect white teeth.

A flash of pink tongue.

I constructed a past for her, one that reeked of high WASP sensibilities: summer homes, cotillions, deb balls, the hunt. Scores of suitors . . .

The scientist in me snipped my fantasies midframe: total conjecture, hotshot. She's left you empty spaces—you're filling them in with blind guesses.

I made another stab at finding out who she was. She answered me without telling me a thing, got me talking about myself again.

I surrendered to the cheap thrills of autobiography. She made it easy. She was a first-rate listener, propping her chin on her knuckles, staring up at me with those huge blue eyes, making it clear that every word I uttered was monumentally *important.* Playing with my fingers, laughing at my jokes, tossing her hair so that the light caught her earrings.

At that point in time I was God's gift to Sharon Ransom. It felt better than anything else I could recall.

Without all that, her looks might have snagged me. Even in that raucous place teeming with lush young bodies and heartbreaking faces, her beauty was a magnet. It seemed obvious that every passing man was stopping and caressing her visually, the women appraising her with fierce acuity. She was unaware of it, remained zeroed in on me.

I heard myself open up, talk about things I hadn't thought of in years.

Whatever problems she might have, she'd clean up as a therapist.

From the beginning I wanted her physically with an intensity that shook me. But something about her—a fragility that I sensed or imagined—held me back.

For half a dozen dates it remained chaste: hand-holds and goodnight pecks, a noseful of that light, fresh perfume. I'd drive home swollen but oddly content, subsisting on recollections.

As we headed toward the dorm after our seventh evening together, she said, "Don't drop me off yet, Alex. Drive around the corner."

She directed me to a dark, shaded side street, adjacent to one of the athletic fields. I parked. She leaned over, turned off the ignition, removed her shoes, and climbed over the seat and into the back of the Rambler.

"Come," she said.

I followed her over, glad I'd washed the car. Sat beside her, took her in my arms, kissed her lips, her eyes, the sweet spot under her neck. She shivered, squirmed. I touched her breast. Felt her heart pounding. We kissed some more, deeper, longer. I put my hand on her knee. She shivered, gave me a look that I thought was fear. I lifted my hand. She put it back, between her knees, wedged me in a soft, hot vise. Then she spread her legs. I went exploring, up columns of white marble. She was splayed, had thrown her head back, had her eyes closed, was breathing through her mouth. No underwear. I rolled her skirt up, saw a generous delta soft and black as sable fur.

"Oh, God," I said and started to pleasure her.

She held me back with one hand, reached for my zipper with the other. In a second I was free, pointing skyward.

"Come to me," she said.

I obeyed.

7

With Milo out of town, my only other police contact was Delano Hardy, a dapper black detective who sometimes worked as Milo's partner. A few years ago he'd saved my life. I'd bought him a guitar, a classic Fender Stratocaster that Robin had restored. It was clear who owed whom, but I called him anyway.

The desk man at West L.A. told me Detective Hardy wouldn't be in until the following morning. I debated trying him at home but knew he was a family man, always trying to scrounge more time for his kids, and left a message for him to call me.

I thought of someone who wouldn't mind being called at home. Ned Biondi was one of those journalists who lived for the story. He'd been a metro writer-reporter when I met him, had since progressed to associate editor but managed to squeeze in a story now and then.

Ned owed *me*. I'd helped reverse his daughter's descent to near-death from anorexia. He'd taken a year and a half to pay me, then added to his personal debt by profiting from a couple of big stories that I'd steered his way.

Just after 9:00 P.M. I reached him at his home in Woodland Hills.

"Doc. I was going to call you."

"Oh?"

"Yeah, just got back from Boston. Anne-Marie sends her love."

"How's she doing?"

"Still skinnier than we'd like, but otherwise great. She started social-work school this fall, got a part-time job, and found a new boyfriend to replace the bastard who dumped her."

"Give her my best."

"Will do. What's up?"

"I wanted to ask you about a story in today's final. Suicide of a psychologist, page—"

"Twenty. What about it?"

"I knew the woman, Ned."

"Oh, jeez. That's lousy."

"Is there anything more to it than what you printed?"

"No reason for there to be. It wasn't exactly a hot scoop. In fact I believe we got it over the phone from police communications—no one actually went out to the scene. Is there anything *you* know that I should?"

"Nothing at all. Who's Maura Bannon?"

"Just a kid—student intern. Friend of Anne-Marie's, in fact. She's doing a semester of work study, little here, little there. She was the one who pushed for the piece—kind of a naïve kid, thought the shri ... psychologist suicide angle was newsworthy. Those of us familiar with the real world were less impressed, but we let her stick it in the computer just to make her happy. Turns out Section One ends up using it as filler—the kid's thrilled. Want me to have her call you?"

"If she has anything to tell me."

"I doubt that she does." Pause. "Doc, the lady in question—did you know her well?"

My lie was reflexive. "Not really. It just came as a shock, seeing the name of someone I knew."

"Must have," said Ned, but his tone had turned wary. "You called Sturgis first, I assume."

"He's out of town."

"Aha. Listen, Doc, I don't want to be insensitive, but if there's something about the lady that would flesh out the story, I'd be open to hearing about it."

"There's nothing, Ned."

"Okay. Sorry for snooping—force of habit."

"That's all right. Talk to you soon, Ned."

At eleven-thirty I took a walk in the dark, trudging up the glen toward Mulholland, listening to crickets and night birds. When I got home an hour later, the phone was ringing.

"Hello."

"Dr. Delaware, this is Yvette at your service. I'm glad I caught you. A call came in for you twenty minutes ago from your wife up in

San Luis Obispo. She left a message, wanted to make sure you got it."

Your wife. Slap-on-a-sunburn. They'd been making the same mistake for years. Once upon a time it had been amusing.

"What's the message?"

"She's on the move, will be hard to reach. She'll get in touch with you when she can."

"Did she leave a number?"

"No, she didn't, Dr. Delaware. You sound tired. Been working too hard?"

"Something like that."

"Stay well, Dr. Delaware."

"Same to you."

On the move. Hard to reach. It should have hurt. But I felt relieved, unburdened.

Since Saturday I'd barely thought about Robin. Had filled my mind with Sharon.

I felt like an adulterer, ashamed but thrilled.

I crawled into bed and hugged myself to sleep. At two forty-five in the morning I woke up, wired and itchy. After throwing on some clothes I staggered down to the carport and started up the Seville. I drove south to Sunset, headed east through Beverly Hills and Boystown, toward the western tip of Hollywood and Nichols Canyon.

At that hour, even the Strip was dead. I kept the windows open, let the sharp chill gnaw at my face. At Fairfax, I turned left, traveled north, and swung onto Hollywood Boulevard.

Mention the boulevard to most people, and, inevitably, one of two images comes to mind: the good old days of Grauman's Chinese, the Walk of the Stars, black-tie premieres, a neon-flooded night scene. Or the street as it is today—slimy and vicious, promising random violence.

But west of that scene, just past La Brea, Hollywood Boulevard shows another face: a single mile of tree-lined residential neighborhood—decently maintained apartment buildings, old, stately churches, and only slightly tarnished two-story homes perched atop well-tended sloping lawns. Looking down on this smudge of suburbia is a section of the Santa Monica mountain range that meanders through L.A. like a crooked spine. In this part of Hollywood the mountains seem to surge forward threateningly, pushing against the fragile dermis of civilization.

Nichols Canyon begins a couple of blocks east of Fairfax, a lane and a half of winding blacktop feeding off the north side of the boulevard and running parallel to a summer-dry wash. Small, rustic houses sit behind the wash, concealed by tangles of brush, accessible only over homemade footbridges. I passed a Department of Water and Power terminal station lit by high arc lamps that gave off a harsh glare. Just beyond the terminal was flood-control district marshland fenced with chain link, then larger houses on flatter ground, sparsely distributed.

Something wild and swift scurried across the road and dived into the bush. Coyote? In the old days Sharon had talked about seeing them, though I'd never spotted one.

The old days.

What the hell was I expecting to gain by exhuming them? By driving past her house like some moony teenager hoping to catch a glimpse of his beloved?

Stupid. Neurotic.

But I craved something tangible, something to reassure me she'd once been real. That I was real. I drove on.

Nichols veered to the right. The straightaway turned into Jalmia Drive and compressed to a single lane, darkened even further under a canopy of trees. The road lurched, dipped, finally dead-ended without warning at a bamboo-walled cul-de-sac slotted with several steep driveways. The one I was looking for was marked by a white mailbox on a stake and a white lattice gate that sagged on its posts.

I pulled to the side, parked, cut the engine, and got out. Cool air. Night sounds. The gate was unlocked and flimsy, no more of a barrier than it had been years ago. Lifting it to avoid scraping the cement, I looked around, saw no one. Swung the gate open and passed through. Closing it behind me, I began climbing.

On both sides of the driveway were plantings of fan palm, bird of paradise, yucca, and giant banana. Classic fifties California landscaping. Nothing had changed.

I climbed on, unmolested, surprised at the absence of any kind of police presence. Officially, the L.A.P.D. treated suicides as if they were homicides, and the departmental bureaucracy moved slothfully. This soon after the death, the file would certainly be open, the paperwork barely begun.

There should have been warning posters, a crime-scene cordon, some kind of marker.

Nothing.

Then I heard a burst of ignition and the rumble of a high-performance car engine. Louder. I ducked behind one of the palms and pressed myself into the vegetation.

A white Porsche Carrera appeared from around the top of the drive and rolled slowly down in low gear with its headlights off. The car passed within inches, and I made out the face of the driver: hatchet-shaped, fortyish, with slit eyes and oddly mottled skin. A wide black mustache spread above thin lips, forming a stark contrast with blow-dried snow-white hair and thick white eyebrows.

Not a face easily forgotten.

Cyril Trapp. *Captain* Cyril Trapp, West L.A. Homicide. Milo's boss, a one-time hard-boozing high-lifer with flexible ethics, now born again into religious sanctimony and gut hatred of anything irregular.

For the past year Trapp had done his best to wear down Milo—a gay cop was as irregular as they come. Closed-minded but not stupid, he went about his persecution with subtlety, avoiding deliberate gay-bashing. Choosing instead to designate Milo a "sex crimes specialist" and assign him to every homosexual murder that came up in West L.A. Exclusively.

It isolated my friend, narrowed his life, and plunged him into a roiling bath of blood and gore: boy hookers, destroyed and destroying. Corpses moldering because the morgue drivers didn't show to pick them up, for fear of catching AIDS.

When Milo complained, Trapp insisted he was simply making use of Milo's specialized knowledge of "the deviant subculture." The second complaint brought him an insubordination report in his file.

Pushing the issue would have meant going up before hearing boards and hiring a lawyer—the Police Benevolent Association wouldn't go to bat on this one. And unremitting media attention that would turn Milo into The Crusading Gay Cop. That was something he wasn't—probably never would be—ready for. So he pushed his oars through the muck, working compulsively and starting to drink again.

The Porsche disappeared down the drive but I could still hear its engine pulsate in a chugging idle. Then the creak of the car door opening, padded footsteps, the scrape of the gate. Finally Trapp drove away—so quietly I knew he was coasting.

I waited a few minutes and stepped out of the foliage, thought about what I'd seen.

A captain checking out a routine suicide? A West L.A. captain, checking out a Hollywood Division suicide? It made no sense at all.

Or was the visit something personal? The use of the Porsche instead of an unmarked suggested just that.

Trapp and Sharon involved? Too grotesque to contemplate.

Too logical to dismiss.

I resumed my walk, climbed up to the house, and tried not to think about it.

Nothing had changed. The same high banks of ivy, so tall they seemed to engulf the structure. The same circular slab of concrete in lieu of a lawn. At the center of the slab, a raised circular bed rimmed with lava rock housed a pair of towering cocoa palms.

Beyond the palms a low-slung one-story house—gray stucco, the front windowless and flat-faced, shielded by a façade of vertically slatted wood and marked with oversized address numerals. The roof was pitched almost flat and coated with white pebbles. Off to one side was a detached carport. No car, no signs of habitation.

At first glance, an ugly piece of work. One of those "moderne" structures that spread over postwar L.A., aging poorly. But I knew there was beauty within. A free-form cliff-top pool that wrapped itself around the north side of the house and gave the illusion of bleeding off into space. Walls of glass that afforded a breathtakingly uninterrupted canyon view.

The house had made a big impression on me, though I didn't realize it until years later, when the time came to buy a home of my own and I found myself gravitating toward a similar ecology: hilltop remoteness, wood and glass, the indoor-outdoor blend and geologic impermanence that characterize canyon living in L.A.

The front door was unobtrusive—just another section of the slatted façade. I tried it. Locked. Looked around some more and noticed something different—a sign attached to the trunk of one of the palms.

I went over for a closer look and squinted. Just enough starlight to make out the letters:

FOR SALE.

A real estate company with an office on North Vermont, in the Los Feliz district. Below it another sign, smaller. The name and number of the salesperson. *Mickey Mehrabian.*

On the market before the body was cold.

Routine suicide notwithstanding, it had to be the fastest probate in California history.

Unless the house hadn't belonged to her. But she'd told me it did.

She'd told me lots of things.

I memorized Mickey Mehrabian's number. When I got back to the Seville, I wrote it down.

The following morning, I called the real estate office. Mickey Mehrabian was a woman with a Lauren Bacall voice, slightly accented. I made an appointment to see the house at eleven, spent the next hour thinking about the first time I'd seen it.

Something to show you, Alex.

Surprise, surprise. She'd been full of them.

I expected her to be flooded with suitors. But she was always available when I asked her out, even on the shortest notice. And when a patient crisis caused me to break a date, she never complained. Never pushed or pressured me for commitment of any sort—the least demanding human being I'd ever known.

We made love nearly every time we were together, though we never spent the night together.

At first she begged off going to my place, wanted to do it in the backseat of the car. After we'd known each other for several months she relented, but even when she did share my bed, she treated it as if it were a backseat—never completely disrobing, never falling asleep. After waking up several times from my own postcoital torpor to find her sitting on the edge of the bed, fully dressed, tugging her ear, I asked her what was bothering her.

"Nothing. I'm just restless—always have been. I have trouble sleeping anywhere but my own bed. Are you angry?"

"No, of course not. Is there anything I can do?"

"Take me home. When you're ready."

I accommodated myself to her needs: rut and run. Some of the edge was taken off my pleasure, but enough remained to keep me coming back for more.

Her pleasure—the lack of it—preyed on my mind. She went through passionate motions, moving energetically, fueled by an energy that I wasn't sure was erotic, but she never came.

It wasn't that she was unresponsive—she was easily moistened, always willing, seemed to enjoy the act. But climax wasn't part of her agenda. When I was finished, she was, having given something to me, but not her self.

I knew damn well that it wasn't right, but her sweetness and beauty—the thrill of possessing this creature I was sure everyone wanted—sustained me. An adolescent fantasy, to be sure, but a part of me wasn't that far past adolescence.

Her arm around my waist was enough to make me hard. Thoughts of her trickled into idle moments and filled my senses. I put my doubts aside.

But eventually it started to nag at me. I wanted to give as much as I was getting, because I really cared for her.

On top of that, of course, my male ego was crying out for reassurance. Was I too quick? I worked at endurance. She rode me out, tireless, as if we were engaged in some sort of athletic competition. I tried being gentle, got nowhere, switched and did the caveman bit. Experimented with positions, strummed her like a guitar, worked over her and under her until I dripped with sweat and my body ached, went down on her with blind devotion.

Nothing worked.

I remembered the sexual inhibitions she'd projected in practicum. The case that had stymied her: communications breakdown. *Dr. Kruse says we have to confront our own defense systems before being able to help others.*

The attack upon her defenses had brought her to tears. I struggled to find a way to communicate without breaking her. Mentally composed and discarded several speeches before finally coming up with a monologue that seemed minimally hurtful.

I chose to deliver it as we lay sprawled in the back of the Rambler, still connected, my head on her sweatered breast, her hands stroking my hair. She kept stroking as she listened, then kissed me and said, "Don't worry about me, Alex. I'm just fine."

"I want you to enjoy it too."

"Oh, I do, Alex. I love it."

She began rocking her hips, enlarging me, then wrapping her arms around me as I continued to swell inside of her. She forced my head down, smothered my mouth with hers, tightening the pressure of her pelvis and her arms, taking charge, imprisoning me. Arcing and swallowing, rotating and releasing, heightening the pace until the pleasure was squeezed out of me in long, convulsive waves. I cried out, gloriously helpless, felt my spine shatter, my joints come loose from their sockets. When I was still, she began stroking my hair, again.

I was still erect, began to move again. She rolled out from under me, smoothed her skirt, took out a compact and fixed her makeup.

"Sharon—"

She placed a finger on my lips. "You're so good to me," she said. "Wonderful."

I closed my eyes, drifted away for several moments. When I opened them she was gazing off in the distance, as if I weren't there.

From that night on, I gave up hope of perfect love and took her selfishly. She rewarded my compliance with devotion, subservience, though I was the one being molded.

The therapist in me knew it was wrong. I employed the therapist's rationalization to quell my doubts:

It did no good to push; she'd change when she was ready.

Summer came and my fellowship ended. Sharon had completed the first year of grad school with top grades in all her qualifying exams. I'd just passed my licensing exam and had a job lined up at Western Pediatric come autumn. Time to celebrate, but no income until autumn. The tone of the creditors' letters had turned threatening. When the opportunity to earn some real money presented itself I grabbed it: an eight-week dance-band gig back up in San Francisco, playing three sets a night, six nights a week at the Mark Hopkins. Four grand, plus room and board at a Lombard Street motel.

I asked her to come north with me, spun visions of breakfast in Sausalito, good theater, the Palace of Fine Arts, hiking on Mt. Tamalpais.

She said, "I'd love to, Alex, but I've some things to take care of."

"What kinds of things?"

"Family business."

"Problems back home?"

She answered quickly: "Oh, no, just the usual."

"That doesn't tell me a thing," I said. "I have no idea what the usual is, because you never talk about your family."

Soft kiss. Shrug. "They're just a family like any other."

"Let me guess: They want to haul you back to civilization so they can fix you up with the local scions."

She laughed, kissed me again. "*Scions?* Hardly."

I put my arm around her waist, nuzzled her. "Oh, yeah, I can see it now. In a few weeks I'll pick up the paper and see your picture in the society pages, engaged to one of those guys with three last names and a career in investment banking."

That made her giggle. "I don't think so, my dear."

"And why's that?"

"Because my heart belongs to you."

I took her face in my hands, looked into her eyes. "Does it, Sharon?"

"Of course, Alex. What do you think?"

"I think after all this time I don't know you very well."

"You know me better than anyone."

"That's still not very well."

She tugged her ear. "I really care about you, Alex."

"Then live with me when we get back. I'll get a bigger place, a better one."

She kissed me, so deeply I thought it signaled agreement. Then she pulled away and said, "It's not that simple."

"Why not?"

"Things are just . . . complicated. Please, let's not talk about this right now."

"All right," I said. "But consider it."

She licked the underside of my chin, said, "Yum. Consider this."

We began necking. I pressed her to me, buried myself in her hair, her flesh. It was like diving into a vat of sweet cream.

I unbuttoned her blouse, said, "I'm really going to miss you. I miss you already."

"That's sweet," she said. "We'll have fun in September."

Then she began unzipping my fly.

At ten-forty, I left to meet the real estate agent. The mild summer had finally begun to wilt, surrendering to high eighties' temperatures and air that smelled like oven exhaust. But Nichols Canyon still looked fresh—sun-washed, filled with country sounds. Hard to believe Hollywood—the grifters and geeks—was only yards away.

When I got to the house the lattice gate was open. Driving the Seville up to the house, I parked it next to a big burgundy Fleetwood

Brougham with chrome wire wheels, a phone antenna on the rear deck, and plates that said SELHOUS.

A tall dark brunette got out of the car. Mid-forties, aerobics-firm and shapely in tight acid-washed jeans, high-heeled boots, and a blousy, scoop-necked black suede top decorated with rhinestones. She carried a snakeskin purse, wore large onyx and glass costume jewelry and hexagonal, blue-tinted sunglasses.

"Doctor? I'm Mickey." A wide, automatic smile spread under the glasses.

"Alex Delaware."

"It is *Dr.* Delaware?"

"Yes."

She pushed the glasses up her forehead, eyed the coat of dirt on the Seville, then my clothes—old cords, faded workshirt, huaraches.

Running a mental Dun and Bradstreet on me: *Says he's a doctor, but the city's full of bullshit artists. Drives a Caddy, but it's eight years old. Another phony putting on the dog? Or someone who once had it and lost it?*

"Beautiful day," she said, one hand on the door handle, still scrutinizing, still wary. Meeting strange men up in the hills had to give a woman frequent pause.

I smiled, tried to look harmless, said, "Beautiful," and looked at the house. In the daylight, the *déjà vu* was even stronger. My personal patch of ghost town. Spooky.

She mistook my silent appraisal for displeasure, said, "There's a fabulous view from the inside. It's really a charmer, great bones—I think it was designed by one of Neutra's students."

"Interesting."

"It just came on the market, Doctor. We haven't even run ads—in fact, how did you find out about it?"

"I've always liked Nichols Canyon," I said. "A friend who lives nearby told me it was available."

"Oh. What kind of a doctor are you?"

"Psychologist."

"Taking a day off?"

"Half day. One of the few."

I checked my watch and tried to look busy. That seemed to reassure her. Her smile reappeared. "My niece wants to be a psychologist. She's a very smart little girl."

"That's terrific. Good luck to her."

"Oh, I think we make our own luck, don't we, Doctor?"

She pulled keys out of her handbag and we walked to the slatted front door. It opened to a small courtyard—a few potted plants, glass wind chimes that I remembered, dangling over the lintel, silent in the hot, static air.

We went inside and she began her spiel, all well-rehearsed pep.

I pretended to listen, nodded and said "Uh huh" at the right times, forced myself to follow, rather than lead; I knew the place better than she did.

The interior smelled of carpet cleaning fluid and pine disinfectant. Sparkly clean, expunged of death and disorder. But to me it seemed mournful and forbidding—a black museum.

The front of the house was a single open area encompassing living room, dining area, study, and kitchen. The kitchen was early deco-massacre: avocado-green cabinetry, round-edged coral-colored Formica tops, and a coral vinyl-covered breakfast nook tucked into one corner. The furniture was blond wood, synthetic pastel fabrics, and spidery black iron legs—the kind of postwar jet-streamed stuff that looks poised for takeoff. Walls, of textured beige plaster, were hung with portraits of harlequins and serene seascapes. Bracket bookshelves were crowded with volumes on psychology. The same books.

A bland, listless room, but the blandness projected the eye toward the east, toward a wall of glass so clean it seemed invisible. Panels of sheet glass, segmented by sliding glass doors.

On the other side was a narrow, terrazzo-tiled terrace rimmed with white iron railing; beyond the railing an eyeful—a mindful—of canyons, peaks, blue skies, summer foliage. "Isn't it something," said Mickey Mehrabian, spreading one arm, as if the panorama were a picture she'd painted.

"Really something."

We walked out on the terrace. I felt dizzy, remembered an evening of dancing, Brazilian guitars.

Something to show you, Alex.

Late September. I got back to L.A. before Sharon did, $4,000 more solvent, and lonely as hell. She'd left without leaving an address or number; we hadn't exchanged as much as a postcard. I should have been angry, yet she was all I thought about as I drove down the coast.

I headed straight for Curtis Hall. The floor counselor told me she'd checked out of the dorm, wouldn't be returning this semester. No forwarding address, no number.

I drove away, enraged and miserable, certain I'd been right: She'd been seduced back to the Good Life, plied with rich boys, new toys. She was never coming back.

My apartment looked dingier than ever. I avoided it, spent as much time as possible at the hospital, where the challenges of my new job helped distract me. I took on a full caseload from the waiting list, volunteered for the night shift in the Emergency Room. On the third day she showed up at my office, looking happy, almost feverish with delight.

She closed the door. Deep kisses and embraces. She made sounds about missing me, let my hands roam her curves. Then she pulled away, flushed and laughing. "Free for lunch, Doctor?"

She took me to the hospital parking lot, to a shiny red convertible— a brand new Alfa Romeo Spider.

"Like it?"

"Sure, it's great."

She tossed me the keys. "You drive."

We had lunch at an Italian place on Los Feliz, listened to opera and ate cannoli for dessert. Back in the car, she said, "There's something I want to show you, Alex," and directed me west, to Nichols Canyon.

As I pulled up the driveway to the gray, pebble-roofed house, she said, "So what do you think, Doc?"

"Who lives here?"

"Yours truly."

"You're renting it?"

"No, it's *mine!*" She got out of the car and skipped to the front door.

I was surprised to find the house furnished, even more surprised by the dated, fifties look of the place. These were the days when organic was king: earth tones, homemade candles, and batiks. All this aluminum and plastic, the flat, cold colors seemed déclassé, cartoonish.

She glided around exuding pride of ownership, touching and straightening, pulled open drapes and exposed the wall of glass. The view made me forget the aluminum.

Not a student's pad by a long shot. I thought: an arrangement. Someone had set the place up for her. Someone old enough to have bought furniture in the fifties.

Kruse? She'd never really clarified their relationship. . . .

"So what do you think, Doc?"

"Really something. How'd you swing it?"

She was in the kitchen, pouring 7-Up into two glasses. Pouting. "You don't like it."

"No, no, I do. It's fantastic."

"Your tone of voice tells me different, Alex."

"I was just wondering how you managed it. Financially."

She gave a theatrical glower and answered in a Mata Hari voice: *"I haf secret life."*

"Aha."

"Oh, Alex, don't be so glum. It's not as if I *slept* with anybody to get it."

That shook me. I said, "I wasn't implying you had."

Her grin was wicked. "But it did cross your mind, sweet prince."

"Never." I looked out at the mountains. The sky was pale aqua above a horizon of pinkish brown. More fifties color-coordination.

"Nothing crossed my mind," I said. "I just wasn't prepared. I don't see or hear from you all summer—now this."

She handed me a soda, put her head on my shoulder.

"It's gorgeous," I said. "Not as gorgeous as you, but gorgeous. Enjoy it."

"Thank you, Alex. You're so sweet."

We stood there for a while, sipping. Then she unlatched the sliding door and we stepped out onto the terrace. Narrow, white space cantilevering over a sheer drop. Like stepping onto a cloud. The chalky smell of dry brush rose up from the canyons. In the distance was the HOLLYWOOD sign, sagging, splintering, a billboard for shattered dreams.

"There's a pool, too," she said. "Around the other side."

"Wanna skinny-dip?"

She smiled and leaned on the railing. I touched her hair, put my hand under her sweater and massaged her spine.

She made a contented sound, leaned against me, reached around and stroked my jaw.

"I guess I *should* explain," she said. "It's just that it's involved."

"I've got time," I said.

"Do you really?" she asked, suddenly excited. She turned around, held my face in her hands. "You don't have to get back to the hospital right away?"

"Nothing but meetings until six. I'm due at the E.R. at eight."

"Great! We can sit here for a while and watch the sunset. Then I'll drive you back."

"You were going to explain," I reminded her.

But she'd already gone inside and turned on the stereo. Slow Brazilian music came on—gentle guitars and discreet percussion.

"Lead me," she said, back on the terrace. Snaking her arms around me. "In dancing the man's supposed to lead."

We swayed together, belly-to-belly, tongue-to-tongue. When the music ended she took my hand and led me through a short foyer into her bedroom.

More bleached, glass-topped furniture, a pole lamp, a low, wide bed with a square, bleached headboard. Above it, two narrow, high windows.

She removed her shoes. As I kicked off mine I noticed something on the walls: crude, childish drawings of apples. Pencil and crayon on oatmeal-colored pulp paper. But glass-framed and expensively matted.

Odd, but I didn't spend much time wondering about it. She'd drawn blackout drapes across the windows, plunged the room into darkness. I smelled her perfume, felt her hand cupping my groin.

"Come," she said—a disembodied voice—and her hands settled upon my shoulders with surprising strength. She bore down on me and lowered me to the bed, got on top of me, and kissed me hard.

We embraced and rolled, made love fully clothed. She, sitting, with her back against the headboard, legs spread and drawn up sharply, her hands clasping her knees. I, kneeling before her, as if in prayer, impaling her while gripping the top rim of the headboard.

A cramped, backseat position. When it was over she slid out from under me and said, "Now, I'll explain. I'm an orphan. Both of my parents died last year."

My heart was still pounding. I said, "I'm sorry—"

"They were wonderful people, Alex. Very glamorous, very gracious and *courant*."

A dispassionate way to talk about one's dead parents, but grief could take many forms. The important thing was that she was *talking,* opening up.

"Daddy was an art director for one of the big publishing houses in New York," she said. "Mummy was an interior designer. We lived in Manhattan, on Park Avenue, and had a place in Palm Beach and another on Long Island—Southampton. I was their only little girl."

The last sentence was uttered with special solemnity, as if lacking siblings were an honor of the first rank.

"They were active people, traveled a lot by themselves. But it didn't bother me because I knew they loved me very much. Last year they were in Spain, on holiday near Majorca. They were driving home from a party when their car went off a cliff."

I took her in my arms. She felt loose and relaxed, could have been talking about the weather. Unable to read her face in the darkness, I listened for a catch in her voice, rapid breathing, some evidence of sorrow. Nothing.

"I'm so sorry for you, Sharon."

"Thank you. It's been *very* hard. That's why I didn't want to talk about them—it was just too much to handle. Intellectually, I know that's not the optimal way to deal with it, that keeping it bottled up only leads to pathological grief and raises the risk of all kinds of symptoms. But affectively, I just couldn't talk about it. Every time I tried, I just couldn't."

"Don't pressure yourself. Everyone goes at their own pace."

"Yes. Yes, that's true. I'm just explaining to you why I didn't want to talk about them. Why I really still don't, Alex."

"I understand."

"I know you do." Deep kiss. "You're so right for me, Alex."

I thought of the constricted way we'd just made love. "Am I?"

"Oh, God, yes. Paul—" She stopped.

"Paul what?"

"Nothing."

"Paul approves of me?"

"It's not like that, Alex. But, yes. Yes, he does. I always talk about how wonderful you are and he says he's glad I've found someone so good for me. He likes you."

"We've never met."

Pause.

"He likes what I've told him about you."

"I see."

"What's the matter, Alex?"

"Sounds like you and Paul have lots to talk about."

I felt her hand reach around and take hold of me. She squeezed gently, kneaded. This time I didn't respond and she lowered her fingers, let them rest upon my scrotum.

"He's my faculty adviser, Alex. He supervises my cases. That means we have to talk." Gentle stroking. "Let's not discuss him or anyone else anymore, okay?"

"Okay. But I'm still curious about where the house came from."

"The house?" she said, surprised. "Oh. The house. Inheritance, of course. It belonged to them. My parents. They were both born in California, lived here before moving back East—before I was born. I was their only little girl, so it's mine now. It took time for the estate to clear, there was so much paperwork. That's the reason I couldn't go with you to San Francisco—I had to clear everything up. Anyway, now I have a house and some money—there's a trust fund, administered back East. That's how I got the Alfa. I know it's a little showy, but I thought it was cute. What do you think?"

"It's adorable."

She went on for a while, talking about the car, the places we could go in it.

But all I could think about was: a house. We could live here together. I was earning good money now, could pay the utilities—pay all the expenses.

"You've got a lot more room now," I said, nibbling her ear. "Enough for two."

"Oh, yes. After the dorm room, I'm looking forward to being able to stretch. And you can visit me up here, any time you want. We'll have fun, Alex."

". . . good-sized, especially by today's standards."

Mickey Mehrabian was hitting her stride.

"Tremendous decorator potential, fabulous flow, and the price includes all the furnishings. Some of these pieces are really deco classics—you could keep them or sell them. Everything's tiptop. The place is really a gem, Doctor."

We toured the kitchen and walked through the short foyer that led to the bedrooms. The first door was closed. She passed it by. I opened it and went in.

"Oh, yes," she said. "This was the master bedroom."

The shampoo/disinfectant smell was stronger here, mixed with other industrial scents: the ammonia of glass cleaner, the malathion bite of insecticide, lye soap. A toxic cocktail. The drapes had been removed; only a tangle of cords and pulleys remained. All the furniture was gone. The carpet had been pulled up, revealing hardwood flooring marred by tacks. The two high windows revealed a view of tree-tops and power lines. But no breeze, no dilution of the chemical bath.

No apple drawings.

I heard a buzz. She heard it too. Both of us looked around for the source, found it immediately:

A swarm of gnats circling the center of the room, an animate cloud, its borders shifting amoebically.

Pinpointing the spot.

Despite the attempts to wash away the aura of death, the insects knew—had sensed with their primitive little gnat brains—exactly what had taken place in this room. On that spot.

I remembered something Milo had told me. *Women kill in the kitchen and die in the bedroom.*

Mickey Mehrabian saw the look on my face and mistook it for squeamishness.

"The open windows, this time of year," she said. "No problem taking care of it. There's a motivated seller, extremely flexible. I'm sure you'll have no problem including any repairs or adjustments as contingencies during escrow, Doctor."

"Why is he or she selling?"

The wide smile reappeared. "Not he or she—an *it,* really. A corporation. They own lots of properties, turn them over regularly."

"Speculators?"

The smile froze. "That's a naughty word, Doctor. Investors."

"Who lives here now?"

"No one. The tenant moved out recently."

"And took the bed."

"Yes. Only the bedroom furniture belonged to her—I *believe* it was a woman." She lowered her voice to a conspiratorial whisper. "You know L.A., people coming and going. Now, let's take a look at the other bedrooms."

We left the death room. She asked, "Do you live alone, Dr. Delaware?"

I had to think before answering. "Yes."

"Then you can use one of the bedrooms for a study, or even to see your patients."

Patients. According to the newspaper, Sharon had seen *her* patients here.

I wondered about the people she treated. The impact her death could be having on them.

Then I realized there was someone else in her life. Someone upon whom the impact would be tremendous.

My mind went into overdrive. I wanted to be out of there.

But I let Mickey show me around, allowed her patter to pass through me for a while before consulting my watch and saying, "Oops, I've got to get going."

"Do you think you'll be putting in an offer, Doctor?"

"I need time to think about it. Thanks for showing it to me."

"If it's a view site you're after, I've got some other listings I could show you."

I tapped the watch. "Love to, but can't right now."

"Why don't we make an appointment for another day?"

"Not even time for that," I said. "I'll call you when I'm free."

"Fine," she said, coolly.

We left the house and she locked up. We walked silently to separate Cadillacs. Before she could open the door of her Fleetwood,

a hint of movement caught our attention. The rustle of foliage—
burrowing animals?

A man shot out of the greenery and began running away.

"Excuse *me!*" Mickey called out, struggling to stay calm, her
weirdo fantasies come to life.

The runner looked back, stared at us, stumbled, fell, and picked
himself up again.

Young. Disheveled hair. Wild-eyed. Mouth open as if in a silent
scream. Terrified, or mad, or both.

Patients . . .

"That gate," said Mickey. "It needs to be fixed. Better security—no
problem."

I was looking at the runner, called: "Hold on!"

"What is it? Do you know him?"

He picked up speed, disappeared around the curve in the driveway. I heard an engine start, began running myself, to the bottom of
the drive. Got there just as an old green pickup pulled away from the
curb. Gears grinding, swerving erratically, going too fast, weaving.
Some letters were painted in white on the door, but I couldn't make
them out.

I ran back to my car, got in.

"Who is that?" said Mickey. "Do you know him?"

"Not yet."

9

I managed to catch up to him, flashed my brights and honked. He ignored me, was all over the road, weaving, speeding. Then more gear-grinding as he tried to shift. The truck got stuck in neutral, slowed to a coast, the engine racing as he fed gas without disengaging the clutch. He hit the brakes suddenly, came to a full stop. I stayed back, could see him through the truck's rear window, struggling, tugging.

The truck stalled. Started, stalled again. He began coasting, picking up some speed on the downhill, then braking, sliding, reducing it to a crawl.

At the fenced marshland he let go of the wheel and threw his hands up. The truck skidded, veered, headed straight for the chain-link fence.

He hit it, but not hard—didn't even dent his fender. I pulled over behind him. The tires spun for a while; then the engine went dead.

Before I had a chance to get out of the car, he was out of the truck, lurching, arms hanging gorillalike, a bottle in one hand. I locked the car. He was right next to me, kicking the Seville's tires, pressing both hands on my door. The bottle was empty. Gatorade. He raised it as if to smash my window, lost his grip and let it spin out of his hand. He followed its descent, gave up, looked at me. His eyes were watery, swollen, rimmed scarlet.

"Gonna . . . kill your . . . ass, man." Slurred speech. Theatrical grimaces.

"The fuck . . . following me?"

He closed his eyes, staggered, fell forward, knocked his forehead on the roof of the car.

The brain-damaged stance of a lifelong boozehound. But his life hadn't been that long—what was he, twenty-two or three?

He kicked the car, grabbed the door handle, missed, and stumbled. Little more than a kid. Baby bulldog face. Short—five four or five—but strong-looking, with sloping shoulders and thick, sunburned arms. Red hair, shoulder-length, coarse, uncombed. Wispy mustache and beard the color of lint. Pimples on his brow and cheeks. He wore a sweat-stained T-shirt, cutoff shorts, tennis shoes without socks.

"Fuck, man," he said, and scratched an armpit. His hands were blunt-edged, scarred and scabbed, caked with grime.

He rocked on his heels, finally lost balance completely and landed on his rear.

He stayed that way for a while. I slid across the seat and exited the Seville on the passenger side. He watched me, not moving, let his eyes drop shut again, as if lacking the strength to keep them open.

I walked to his truck. Thirty-year-old Ford, poorly maintained. Wobbly white letters spelled out D.J. RASMUSSEN, CARPENTRY AND FRAMING on the door. Under that, a post office box in Newhall. In the truck bed were two ladders, a toolbox, a couple of blankets weighed down by metal parts.

The interior was littered with empty bottles—more Gatorade, Southern Comfort, several brands of wine cooler.

I pocketed the key, removed the distributor cap, and returned to where he still sat.

"You D.J.?"

Glazed look. Up close he smelled of ferment and vomit.

"What were you doing up there?"

No answer.

"Were you paying last respects? To Dr. Ransom?"

The glaze melted fast. Right track.

"Me too," I said.

"Fu-uck you." Followed by a putrid belch that made me step back. He mumbled, tried to move an arm, couldn't. Closed his eyes, seemed in pain.

I said, "I was a friend of hers."

Belch and a gurgle. He looked ready to throw up. I took another couple of steps back, waited.

An unproductive dry retch. His eyes opened, stared at nothing.

"I was her friend," I repeated. "How about you?"

He moaned. Dry-retched.

"D.J.?"

"Oh, man . . . you're . . ." He trailed off.

"What?"

"Fucking . . . with . . . my head."

"I'm not trying to," I said. "Just trying to understand why she's dead."

More moaning.

He ran his tongue over his lips, tried to spit and ended up drooling.

"If she was more than just a friend, it could be harder on you," I said. "Losing a therapist can be like losing a parent."

"Fuck you."

"Was she your doctor, D.J.?"

"Fuck you!" After several efforts he managed to get to his feet, came at me, fell upon me.

Limp as a bundle of rags, his arms bulky but booze-dead, carrying no punch. I stopped him easily with a hand to the chest. Took hold of his arm and sat him back down.

I showed him the cap and the keys.

"Hey, man . . . what the . . ."

"You're in no shape to drive. I'm holding on to these until you show me you've got it together."

"Fuck you." Less conviction.

"Talk to me, D.J. Then I'll be out of your hair."

"What . . . about?"

"About being Dr. Ransom's patient?"

Exaggerated shake of head. "Uh-uh . . . not . . . crazy."

"What's your connection to her?"

"Bad back."

"Lot of pain?"

"Hurt . . . fucking job." Remembering, he bit his lip.

"Dr. Ransom was helping you with the pain?"

Nod. "And . . . after—" He made a feeble try for the keys. "Gimme my shit!"

"After what?"

"Gimme my shit, man!"

"After she helped you with the pain, then what?"

"Fuck you!" he screamed. The cords on his neck swelled; he punched out wildly, missed, tried to get up, couldn't lift his butt from the ground.

I'd pushed a button. It set me thinking.

"Fuck *nothing* after! Fuck nothing!" He flapped his arms, swore, tried to get up and buckled.

"Who referred you to Dr. Ransom, D.J.?"

Silence.

I repeated the question.

"Fu-uck you-u."

"There may be other patients who are feeling as bad as you do, D.J."

He gave a sick smile, then a feeble head shake. "Uh-uh."

"If we can find out who referred them, we can track them down. Help them."

"No . . . fuck . . . ingway."

"Someone should get in touch with them, D.J."

"I'm . . . You're some . . . fucking Robin Hood?"

"A friend," I said. "A psychologist, like her."

He looked around, seemed to be noticing his surroundings for the first time. "Where am I?"

"Side of the road. Just down from Dr. Ransom's house."

"Who're you, some fucking . . . Robin Hood?"

"A friend. Who referred you to her, D.J.?"

"Doctor."

"Which doctor?"

"Carmen."

"Dr. Carmen?"

He giggled. "Carmen . . . doctor."

"Carmen's doctor?"

Nod.

"Who's Carmen?"

"Fuck you."

"What's the name of Carmen's doctor?"

A few more go-rounds before he said, "Bev . . . Hills Jew . . . Wein . . ."

I wasn't sure if he was giving me a name or asking for a drink. "Wine?"

"Dr. Weinfu-uck."

"Wein something? Wein*stein*? Wein*berg*?"

"Garden, grow grow grow."

"Weingarden? Dr. Weingarden?"

"Big . . . mouthed Jew."

He slumped and fell over, lay on his side.

I nudged him. Dead to the world. After copying down the post-office box number on the truck door, I searched among the bottles in the cab, found one that was half full, and emptied it. Then I let the air out of two of the tires, removed one of the blankets from the truck bed, hid the keys under the remaining two, stashed the distributor cap in the bottom compartment of his tool box. Figuring if he could work all that out, he'd be sober enough to drive. Then I spread the blanket over him and left him to sleep it off.

I drove away telling myself I'd use the post office box to reach him in a few days. Encourage him to get a new therapist.

God knew he needed the help. Through the booze haze there'd been heavy potential for violence—one of those tightly wound, pressure-cooked young bulls who let things build to an excruciating level, then blow it off without warning with fists, brass knuckles, blades, chains, and guns.

Not exactly your typical private-practice patient. Where had Sharon gotten him? How many others like him had she treated? And how many fragile personalities were on the verge of shattering be-cause she'd no longer be there to hold them together?

I recalled Rasmussen's sudden rage when I asked what had hap-pened after the pain treatment was over.

An ugly hunch that I couldn't justify, but one that refused to fade away, was that his relationship with Sharon had gone beyond treatment. Something strong enough to draw him back to her house. Searching? For what?

Following in Trapp's footsteps . . .

Could she have been sleeping with both of them? I realized I'd wondered the same thing about the old sheik at the party. About Kruse, years ago.

Maybe I was getting carried away—projecting. Assuming sexual links that didn't exist, because my own entanglement with her had been carnal.

As Milo would say: *Limited thinking, pal.*

But limited or not, I couldn't shake it.

I got home at one-thirty, found messages from Maura Bannon, the student reporter, and Detective Delano Hardy. Del was on an-other line when I called, so I pulled out the phone book and looked for a Dr. Weingarden in Beverly Hills.

There were two by that name, an Isaac on Bedford Drive and a Leslie, on Roxbury.

Isaac Weingarden answered his own phone. He sounded like an old man, with a soft, kindly voice and a Viennese accent. When I found out he was a psychiatrist, I was certain he was my man, but he denied knowing Sharon or Rasmussen.

"You sound upset, young man. Is there anything I can do?"

"No thanks."

I phoned Leslie Weingarden's office. The receptionist said, "Doctor's with a patient now."

"Could you please tell him it's about Dr. Sharon Ransom."

"*Him* is a *her.* Hold on."

I listened to Mantovani for several minutes. Then: "Doctor can't be disturbed. She said to take your number and she'll get back to you."

"Could you just tell me if Dr. Weingarden refers to Dr. Ransom?"

Hesitation. "I have no idea, sir. I'm only passing along what the doctor told me."

At two-fifteen Del Hardy called.

"Hi, Del. How's it going?"

"Busy. With this heat coming on, it's going to get busier. What can I do for you?"

I told him about Sharon, about seeing Cyril Trapp. About the quick sale of the house.

"Trapp, huh? Interesting." But he didn't sound interested. Though he was one of the few detectives cordial with Milo, that friendliness didn't stretch into friendship. Trapp was a burden he wasn't willing to share.

"Nichols Canyon is Hollywood Division," he said. "So I wouldn't even know who's on it. With the workload we've got, all the divisions are trying to clear the routine ones quickly, do lots of stuff over the phone."

"This quickly?"

"Not usually," he said, "but you never can tell."

I didn't say anything.

He said, "You say she was a friend of yours?"

"Yes."

"I suppose I could ask a few questions."

"I'd really appreciate that, Del. The paper said no family members had been located. But I know she has a sister—a twin. I met her six years ago."

I was their only little girl. Another surprise.

"Name?"

"Shirlee, with two e's. She was disabled, lived in a board-and-care out in Glendale. South Brand, about a mile past the Galleria."

"Name of the place?"

"I was only there once, never noticed."

"I'll check it out." He lowered his voice. "Listen, about the Trapp thing. Captain wouldn't be working some no-glory suicide. So his being up there was probably something personal—maybe a real estate thing. Some guys move in on properties, try to get 'em cheap. Not in good taste, but you know how it is."

"Donald Trump of the crime scene," I said.

He laughed. "You got it. One other possibility—was the victim rich?"

"She came from money."

"Then that could be it," he said, sounding relieved. "Someone pushed a few buttons; the word came down from on high to keep it quiet, clear it quickly. Trapp used to be with Hollywood Division— maybe someone remembered that, called in a favor."

"Personalized service?"

"Happens all the time. Main thing about being rich is having stuff no one else can have, right? Nowadays, anyone can buy a Mercedes on payments. Dope, clothes, same thing. But privacy— that's the ultimate luxury in this town."

"Okay," I said. But I was wondering who'd pushed the buttons. Thought, immediately, of the old sheik at the party. There was no way to pursue that with Del, so I thanked him again.

"Don't mention it," he said. "Hear from Milo recently?"

"No. Have you? I think he's due back Monday."

"Not a word. The duty roster says he's supposed to be back in the *office* Monday. Knowing Milo, that means he'll be in town Saturday or Sunday, pacing around, cussing. And none too soon, far as I'm concerned. The vermin are out in force."

After he hung up, I looked in the Yellow Pages for a rest home on South Brand, found nothing. A few minutes later Mal Worthy called to remind me of tomorrow's deposition. He seemed worried about my state of mind, kept asking me if I was okay.

"I'm fine," I told him. "Perry Mason couldn't get the better of me."

"Mason was a wimp. Watch out for these insurance guys. By the way, Denise says definitely no more sessions for Darren. She wants to handle things by herself. But that's off the record. As far as the other side's concerned, the kid will be in treatment for the rest of his life. And beyond."

"How's Darren doing?"

"About the same."

"Persuade her to continue treatment, Mal. If she wants someone else, I'll get her a referral."

"She's pretty resolute, Alex, but I'll keep trying. Meanwhile, I'm more concerned with helping her put food on the table. *Ciao.*"

I spent the next couple of hours preparing for the deposition, was interrupted by the phone.

"Dr. Delaware? Maura Bannon? *L.A. Times?*"

She sounded around thirteen, had a high voice with a slight lisp and a New England accent, and turned her statements into questions.

"Hello, Ms. Bannon."

"Ned Biondi gave me your number? I'm so glad I caught you—I wonder if we could meet?"

"For what purpose?"

"You knew Dr. Ransom, right? I thought maybe you could give me some background on her?"

"I don't think I can help you."

"Oh?" She sounded crestfallen.

"I haven't seen Dr. Ransom in years."

"Oh. I just thought ... Well, you know, I'm trying to give a well-rounded picture, establish some context? For the profile? It's such a strange thing, a psychologist killing herself like that—man bites dog, you know? People would be interested in finding out why."

"Have you learned anything more than what you put in your first article?"

"No, I haven't, Dr. Delaware. Is there anything more to find out? Because if there is, I'd surely appreciate knowing about it. I think the police have been holding back on me. I've put several calls in to them, but no one's returned them." Pause. "I don't think they're taking me seriously."

Privacy, the ultimate luxury.

"I'd like to help you," I said, "but I really have nothing to add."

"Mr. Biondi said—"

"If I led Mr. Biondi to believe any different, I'm sorry, Ms. Bannon."

"Okay," she said. "But if you find out anything, please let me know?"

"I'll do my best."

"Thanks, Dr. Delaware."

I sat back, stared out the window, and felt the loneliness coming on.

Misery loves company—the bigger the other guy's misery, the

better the company. I called Newhall information and asked for a number on D.J. Rasmussen. No listing. Thinking of my only other connection to the young drunk, I phoned Dr. Leslie Weingarden's office.

"I was just about to call you," said the receptionist. "Doctor can see you after her last patient, around six."

"I really don't need an appointment. Just wanted to talk to her over the phone."

"I'm telling you what she told me, Mr. Delaware."

"Six will be fine."

10

Leslie Weingarden's building was a three-story, red brick Federal structure with limestone cornice and forest-green awnings, situated in the heart of Beverly Hills' medical district. The interior was golden-oak raised paneling, green-and-rose carpeting. The directory listed several dozen tenants: M.D.'s, dentists, a handful of Ph.D.'s.

One of the Ph.D.'s caught my eye: KRUSE, P.P. SUITE 300. Made sense—this was couch row. But years before he'd had another address.

Leslie Weingarden's office was on the ground floor, toward the rear of the building. Her nameplate listed her specialties as Internal Medicine and Women's Health Issues. Her waiting room was small and decorated in budget good-cheer—white-and-gray miniprint paper, overstuffed white cotton chairs and Danish-modern tables, a scattering of art prints, a potted schefflera in a straw basket. No patients, but the remnants of the day's traffic were apparent: gum wrappers, an empty aspirin bottle and a used emery board on the coffee table, magazines splayed open on the chairs.

I knocked on the glass partition, waited several seconds before it slid open. A Hispanic woman in her fifties looked out. "Can I help you?"

"Dr. Delaware. I have an appointment with Dr. Weingarden."

"I'll let her know you're here."

I waited for half an hour, leafing through magazines, wondering if any of them had carried Paul Kruse's column. At six-thirty, the door to the inner office opened and a good-looking woman around thirty came out.

She was petite, very slender, with frosted short hair and a lean, alert face. She wore dangling silver earrings, a white silk blouse, pleated dove-gray gabardine slacks, and gray suede pumps. A stethoscope hung from around her neck. Under it was a heavy gold chain. Her features were delicate and regular, her eyes almond-shaped and dark brown. Like Robin's. She wore little makeup. Didn't have to.

I stood up.

"Mr. Delaware? I'm Dr. Weingarden." She held out her hand and I shook it. Her bones were tiny; her grip, firm and dry. She placed both hands on her hips. "What can I do for you?"

"You referred patients to a psychologist named Sharon Ransom. I don't know if you've heard, but she's dead, committed suicide on Sunday. I wanted to talk to you about her. About getting in touch with those patients."

No trace of shock. "Yes, I read the paper. What's your involvement with her and her patients?"

"Mostly personal, somewhat professional." I handed her my card.

She examined it. "You're a psychologist too. Then it's *Dr.* Delaware. Bea told me *Mr.*" She put the card in her pocket. "Were you her therapist?"

The question surprised me. "No."

"Because she sure needed one." Frown. "Why all the concern about her patients?"

"I ran into one of them today. D.J. Rasmussen. He gave me your name."

That made her flinch but she said nothing.

"He was drunk," I said. "Stoned drunk, really out of it. My hunch is that he was unbalanced to begin with, and is now at risk for some kind of breakdown. Maybe violence. Losing a therapist can be like losing a parent. I've been wondering how many of her other—"

"Yes, yes, of course. I understand all of that. But what I still don't get is *your* concern. What's your involvement in all of this?"

I thought about the best way to answer. "Some of it's probably guilt. Sharon and I knew each other well—back in graduate school. I hadn't seen her for years, ran into her by chance at a party last Saturday. She seemed upset about something, asked if she could talk to me. We made a date. I had second thoughts and canceled the next day. That night, she killed herself. I guess I'm still wondering if I could have stopped it. I'd like to prevent any more grief, if I can."

She fingered her stethoscope and stared at me. "This is for real, isn't it? You don't work for some shyster lawyer, do you?"

"Why would I?"

She smiled. "So you want me to contact any patients I might have referred to her?"

"And tell me about any other referral sources you're familiar with."

The smile got cold. "That would be difficult, Dr. Delaware. Not a good idea at all—not that there were that many referrals, anyway. And I have no idea who else referred to her. Though I sure feel sorry for them."

She stopped, seemed to be searching for words. "Sharon Ransom was a . . . She and I . . . Well, you tell me first. Why'd you break your date with her?"

"I didn't want to get involved with her. She's . . . She was a complicated woman."

"She sure was." She looked at her watch, removed the stethoscope. "All right, I'm going to make a call and check on you. If you're who you say you are, we'll talk. But I've got to eat first."

She left me in the waiting room, came back several moments later, and said, "Okay," without looking at me.

We walked a block to a coffee shop on Brighton. She ordered a tuna sandwich on rye and herb tea. I pushed rubbery scrambled eggs around on my plate.

She ate quickly, unceremoniously. Ordered a hot fudge sundae for dessert and finished half of it before pushing the dish away.

After wiping her mouth she said, "When they told me someone was calling about Sharon, frankly, I was uptight. She caused problems for me. We haven't worked together for a long time."

"What kinds of problems?"

"One second." She called the waitress over and asked for a refill of tea. I ordered coffee. The check came with the drinks.

I took it. "On me."

"Buying information?"

I smiled. "You were talking about the problems she caused."

She shook her head. "Boy. I don't know if I really want to get into this."

"Confidential," I promised.

"Legally? As in, you're my therapist?"

"If that makes you comfortable."

"Spoken like a true shrink. Yes, it makes me comfortable. We're talking hot potato here—*ethical* problems." Her eyes hardened. "There was no way for me to prevent it, but try telling that to a malpractice jury. When a shyster gets hold of something like that, he goes back in the chart, hits on every doc who's ever passed the patient in the hall."

"The last thing on my mind is fomenting a lawsuit," I said.

"Last thing on my mind, too." She slapped her hand on the table hard enough to make the salt shaker jump. "Darn it! She shafted me. Just thinking about her makes me mad. I'm sorry she's dead, but I just can't feel any grief. She used me."

She sipped her tea.

"I only met her last year. She walked in, introduced herself, and invited me out to lunch. I knew what she was doing—hustling referrals. Nothing wrong with that. I've only been in practice a little over a year, have done my share of brown-nosing. And my first impression of her was very positive. She was bright, articulate, seemed to have it all together. Her résumé looked terrific—lots of varied clinical experience. Plus, she was right here, in the building—it's always good business to cross-refer. Almost all my patients are women, most of them would be more comfortable with a female therapist, so I figured why not, give it a try. The only reservation I had was that she was so good-looking, I wondered if it mightn't threaten some women. But I told myself that was sexist thinking, began sending her referrals—not that many, thank God. It's a small practice."

"Was her office on the third floor? With Dr. Kruse?"

"That's the one. Only, he was never there, just her, by herself. She took me up there once—tiny place, just a postage-stamp waiting room and one consulting office. She was Kruse's psychological assistant or something like that, had a license number."

"An assistant's certificate."

"Whatever. Everything was kosher."

Psychological assistant. A temporary position, aimed at providing experience for new Ph.D.'s under supervision of a licensed psychologist. Sharon had earned her doctorate six years ago, had been long eligible for full licensure. I wondered why she hadn't gotten it. What she'd done for six years.

"Kruse wrote her this terrific letter of recommendation," she said. "He was a faculty member at the University, so I figured that counted for something. I really expected it to work out. I was blown away when it didn't."

"Do you still have that résumé?"

"No."

"Remember anything else from it?"

"Just what I told you. Why?"

"Trying to backtrack. How did she shaft you?"

She gave me a sharp look. "You mean you haven't figured it out?"

"My guess would be sexual misconduct—sleeping with her patients. But most of your patients are women. Was she gay?"

She laughed. "Gay? Yeah, I could see how you might think that. Frankly, I don't know *what* she was. I was raised in Chicago. Nothing about this city surprises me anymore. But no, she didn't sleep with women—as far as I know. We're talking *men*. Husbands of patients. Boyfriends. Men won't go into therapy without prodding. The women have to do everything—getting the referral, making the appointment. My patients asked me for referrals, and I sent half a dozen to Sharon. She thanked me by sleeping with them."

"How'd you find out?"

She looked disgusted. "I was doing my books, checking out bad debts and failure-to-shows and I noticed that most of the women whose husbands I'd sent her hadn't paid or kept their follow-ups. It stood out like a sore thumb, because other than those, my collections were excellent, my return rate close to perfect. I started calling around, to find out what had happened. Most of the women wouldn't speak to me—some even hung up on me. But two of them did talk. The first let me have it with both barrels. Seems her husband had seen Sharon for a few sessions—something to do with job stress. She taught him to relax; that was it. A few weeks later she called him and offered a follow-up session. Free of charge. When he showed up she tried to seduce him, really came on strong—she took her clothes off, for God's sake, right there in the office. He walked out on her, went home and told his wife. She was livid, screaming that I should be ashamed of myself for associating with a conniving, amoral bitch like that. The second one was worse. She just cried and cried."

She rubbed her temples, took an aspirin out of her purse, and swallowed it with tea.

"Unbelievable, isn't it? Free *follow-up visits*. I'm still waiting for the other shoe to drop—as in see-you-in-court. I've lost plenty of sleep over it."

"I'm sorry," I said.

"Not as sorry as I am. Now you tell me Rasmussen's all freaked out. Great."

"He was one of them?"

"Oh, yeah, a real prince. His girlfriend is the one who just cried. One of my walk-in patients, not too sophisticated, vague psychosomatic complaints—she needed attention. I got to know her a little and she started opening up about him—how he drank too much, took dope, pushed her around. I spent lots of time counseling her, trying to show her what a loser he was, get her to leave him. Of course she didn't. One of those passive types with an abusive father who keeps hooking up with papa surrogates. Then she told me the bum had injured himself on the job, was having back pain, and was thinking of suing. It was his lawyer who suggested he see a shrink—did I know one? I figured here was a chance to get him some help for his head and sent him to Sharon, told her all about his other problems. Boy, did *she* help him. How'd you meet him?"

"He was up at her house this morning."

"Up at her house? She gave a jerk like that her home address? What an idiot."

"She had an office there."

"Oh, yeah—the paper mentioned that. Makes sense, actually, because she moved out of this building right after I confronted her about the hanky-panky. Got a diagnosis on Rasmussen?"

"Some kind of personality disorder. Possible violent tendencies."

"In other words, a troublemaker. Terrific. He's the weakest link, a woman-hater with low impulse control. And he's already got a shyster. Wonderful."

"He won't sue for sexual harassment," I said. "Few men would. Too embarrassing."

"Frontal assault upon the old machismo? I sure hope you're right. So far, no one's made any moves. But that doesn't mean they're not going to. And even if I'm spared legal grief, she's already cost me plenty in terms of my reputation—one patient bad-mouthing to ten others. And none of the dropouts paid me for work I'd already done—we're talking solid four figures in lab fees alone. I'm not established enough to kiss off that kind of loss without pain—there's a doctor glut here on the West Side. Where do you practice?"

"Here on the West Side, but I work with kids."

"Oh." She drummed her nails along the rim of the teacup. "I probably sound pretty mercenary to you, huh? Here you are, talking altruism, debriefing patients, all that good Hippocratic stuff. And all I'm worried about is covering my butt. But I make no excuses for it, 'cause if *I* don't cover my butt, no one else will do it for me. When I came out from Northwestern to do my internship at Harbor General, I met the greatest guy in the world, married him three weeks later. A screenwriter, doing research at the hospital for a miniseries. Pow, love at first sight. All of a sudden I had a house in Playa Del Rey, till death do us part. He said he was turned on by my being a doctor, pledged he'd never leave me. Two years later he left me. Cleaned out our bank account and went to Santa Fe with some bimbo. It's taken me two years to climb out of it."

She looked inside the cup as if searching for gypsy leaves. "I've worked too darned hard to get this far and see some nymphomaniac ruin it all, so, no, I won't be calling to debrief any of the men she screwed. They're big boys—they can handle it. Probably turned it into a conquest by now, convinced themselves they're hot studs. You let it rest, too, Dr. Delaware. Keep her buried."

She'd let her voice rise. People were staring. She noticed and lowered it. "How does someone like that become a therapist anyway? Don't you people do any screening?"

"Not enough," I said. "How did she react when you confronted her?"

"Weirdly. Just looked at me with those big blues, all innocent, as if she didn't know what I was talking about, then started in with the uh-huhs, as if she were trying to play therapist with *me*. When I was through she said, 'Sorry,' and just walked away. No explanation, no nothing. The next day I saw her carrying boxes out of the office."

"As her supervisor, Kruse was legally responsible for her. Did you talk to him?"

"I tried to. Must have called him twenty times. I even slipped messages under the door. He never responded. I got pretty steamed, thought of filing a complaint. In the end I figured good riddance, just dropped it."

"His name's still on the office directory. Does he practice here?"

"Like I said, I've never seen him. And when I was looking for him, I spoke to the janitor and he said *he'd* never seen him. Ten to one Kruse set it up for *her*. She was probably screwing him too."

"Why do you say that?"

"Because screwing men was her thing, right? It was what she *did*. Probably screwed her way to that Ph.D."

I thought about that, got lost in thoughts.

She said, "You're not going to pursue this debriefing stuff any further, are you?"

"No," I said, making the decision at that moment. "What you've told me puts things in a different light. But we should do something about Rasmussen. He's a time bomb."

"Let him blow himself up—more good riddance."

"What if he hurts someone else?"

"What could you do to prevent that anyway?"

I had no answer.

"Listen," she said, "I want to make myself very clear. I want *out*—free of all the garbage, the worrying. Got that?"

"Got it."

"I sure hope you mean that. If you use anything I've said to connect me with her, I'll deny saying it. The files of all the patients she saw have been destroyed. If you mention my name, I'll sue you for breach of confidentiality."

"Take it easy," I said. "You've made your point."

"I certainly hope so." She snatched the check out of my hands and stood. "I'll pay my own way, thank you."

Free follow-up visits. That brought back something I'd worked hard at forgetting.

Driving home, I wondered how many men Sharon had victimized, how long it had been going on. It was impossible now for me to imagine a man in her life without assuming a carnal link.

Trapp. The sheik. D.J. Rasmussen. Victims all?

I wondered especially about Rasmussen. Had he still been involved with her at the time of her death? It could explain why the loss had hit him so hard. Why he'd drunk himself stuporous, made a pilgrimage to her house.

Meeting another pilgrim: me.

How does someone like that become a therapist anyway? Don't you people do any screening?

I hadn't screened her out of my life, had long rationalized it by telling myself I'd been young and naïve, too green to know any better. Yet three days ago I'd been jacked up and ready to see her again. Ready to start . . . what?

The fact that I'd broken the date was small comfort. What would have happened had she phoned, put a catch in her voice, told me what a wonderful guy I was? Would I have been able to resist being needed? Spurned the opportunity to hear about her "problem," maybe even solve it?

I didn't have an honest answer. Which said plenty about my judgment. And my mental health.

I lapsed into the esteem-sapping self-doubts I'd thought resolved during my training therapy: What gave me the right to mold other people's lives when I couldn't get my own life straight? What made me an authority on other people's kids when I'd never raised a child of my own?

Dr. Expert. Who the hell was I kidding?

I remembered the good-mother smile of my training therapist, Ada Small. Soft voice. Brooklyn accent. Soft eyes. Unconditional acceptance; even the tough messages sweetened by kindness . . .

. . . your strong need to always be in control, Alex. It's not a totally bad thing, but at some point we will need to examine it. . . .

Ada had taken me a long way; I'd been lucky to be assigned to her. Now we were colleagues, cross-referring, discussing patients; it had been a long time since I'd related to her as a patient. Could I ever go back to showing her my scars?

Sharon hadn't been so lucky with her assignment. Paul Peter Kruse. Power junkie. Pornographer. Equal opportunity flogger. I could only imagine what training therapy with him had been like. Yet she'd stayed with him long after graduating, remained his assistant instead of getting her license.

Doing her dirty work in space he leased. It said as much about her as about him, and I had to wonder who'd called the shots in their relationship.

Exploiters. Victims.

But her last victim had been herself. Why?

I forced myself to stop thinking about it, pushed Robin's face into my mind. No matter how things turned out, what we'd had once had been real.

The moment I got home I called San Luis Obispo.

"Hello."

"Hi, Robin."

"Alex? Mom said you called. I tried to reach you several times."

"Just got in. Mom and I had a charming conversation."

"Oh. Did she give you a hard time?"

"Nothing out of the ordinary. Main thing is, how's she treating you?"

She laughed. "I can handle her."

"You sure? You sound wiped out."

"I am wiped out, but that has nothing to do with her. Aaron's turned out to be a screamer—Terry's up all night. I've been relieving her—never been so exhausted in my life."

"Good. Maybe you'll yearn for the good old days and come back."

Silence.

"Anyway," I said, "I just thought I'd call and see how you're doing."

"I'm hanging in. How are you doing, Alex?"

"Just dandy."

"Really?"

"Would you believe semi-dandy?"

"What's the matter, Alex?"

"Nothing."

"You sound as if something's weighing on you."

"It's nothing," I said. "It just hasn't been a great week, so far."

"I'm sorry, Alex. I know you've been patient—"

"No," I said, "it has nothing to do with you."

"Oh?" she said, sounding more hurt than relieved.

"Someone I knew back in school committed suicide."

"How awful!"

"Yes, it is."

"Did you know this person well?"

That gave me pause. "No," I said, "not really."

"Still," she said, "that kind of thing's so upsetting to hear."

"How about we change the subject."

"Sure—did I say something wrong?"

"No, nothing. I just don't feel like getting into it."

"All right," she said.

"Anyway, I'll let you go now."

"I'm not rushing anywhere."

"Okay."

But we found little more to talk about and when I hung up I felt empty. I filled the void with memories of Sharon.

That second autumn, we remained lovers, of sorts. When I managed to reach her she always said yes, always had sweet things to say, stimulating bits of academic knowledge to share. She whispered in my ear, rubbed my back, spread her legs for me with the ease of applying her lipstick, insisting I was her guy, the only man in her life. But reaching her was the challenge. She was seldom home, never left a clue to her whereabouts.

Not that I was knocking myself out trying to find her. The hospital owned me fifty hours a week and I'd taken on private patients at night, in order to save up the down payment on a house of my own. I kept busy solving the problems of others and ignoring my own.

A couple of times I dropped in on her unannounced, making the drive up Jalmia only to find the gray house locked, the carport empty. I gave up trying, went without seeing her for a couple of weeks. But late one Saturday night, stuck in the stop-and-go on Sunset after a wrenching evening with the parents of a mercilessly deformed newborn baby, I found myself wanting a shoulder to cry on. Like a homing pigeon I veered north to Hollywood Boulevard, turned off at Nichols Canyon. When I pulled up the driveway, the Alfa Romeo was sitting there.

The front door was unlocked. I walked in.

The living room was brightly lit but empty. I called her name. No answer. Repeated it. Nothing.

I checked her bedroom, half expecting to find her with another man. Half wanting to.

But she was in there, alone, sitting cross-legged on the bed, stark naked, eyes closed, as if meditating.

I'd entered her body so many times, but this was the first time I'd seen it unclothed. She was flawless, unbelievably rich. I restrained myself from touching her, whispered, "Sharon."

She didn't budge.

I wondered if she was engaging in some kind of self-hypnosis. I'd heard Kruse was a master hypnotist. Had he been giving her private lessons?

But she looked stricken rather than entranced—frowning, breathing rapidly and shallowly. Her hands began to tremble. I noticed something in the right one.

A small black-and-white snapshot, the old-fashioned type, with sawtooth edges.

I came closer and looked at it. Two little beautiful black-haired girls, about two or three years old. Identical twins with Shirley Temple curls, sitting side by side on a wooden garden bench, clear skies and dark, brooding granite mountains in the background. Picture-postcard mountains, perfect enough to be a photographer's backdrop.

The twins looked solemn and posed. Too solemn for their age. They'd been dressed in identical cowgirl suits—chaps, fringes, rhinestones—and held identical ice cream cones. Carbon copies of each other except for one small detail: One girl clutched her cone in her right hand; the other, in her left.

Mirror-image twins.

Their features were set, hyper-mature.

Sharon's features, times two.

I was their only little girl.

Surprise, surprise.

I looked up at her, touched her bare shoulder, expecting the usual heat. But she felt cold and dry, strangely inorganic.

I leaned down and kissed the back of her neck. She jumped, cried out as if bitten. Striking out with her fists, she fell back on the bed, legs wide-flung in a helpless caricature of sexual welcome, panting, staring up at me.

"Sharon . . ."

She was looking at me as if I were a monster. Her mouth opened in a silent scream.

The snapshot fell to the floor. Picking it up, I saw something written on the back. A single sentence, in a strong hand.

S and S. Silent partners.

I turned the photo over, looked at the twins again.

"No!" she screamed as she sprang up and charged me. "No, no, no! Gimme, gimme! Mine, mine! Gimme!"

She clawed for the picture. Her fury was absolute, a hellish transformation. Stunned, I tossed it onto the bed.

She snatched it, clutched it to her chest, got up on all fours and crawled backward until she was up against the headboard. Her free hand struck out at the air between us, defining a no man's land. Her hair was tangled, Medusa-wild. She got to her knees, swayed and shook, big breasts bobbling.

"Sharon, what's the matter—"

"Go! Go!"

"Honey—"

"Go! Get out! Go! Go! Get out! Go!"

Sweat poured out of her, flowed down her body. Hot pink patches rose on the snow of her skin, as if she were burning from within.

"Sharon—"

She hissed at me, then whimpered and curled fetally, holding the snapshot to her heart. I watched it rise and fall with each labored breath. Took a step forward.

"No! Get out! Get out!"

The look in her eyes was murderous.

I backed out of the room, ran from the house, feeling dizzy, sick, sucker-punched.

Certain that whatever we had was over.

Not knowing if that was good or bad.

12

Wednesday morning I was back in Beverly Hills, in the penthouse offices of Trenton, Worthy and La Rosa. Waiting to give my deposition in a rosewood-paneled conference room slathered with abstract art and furnished with butter-colored leather chairs and a football-shaped smoked-glass table.

Mal sat next to me, grubbily trendy in an unstructured silver silk suit, five-day beard, and shoulder-length hair. Behind us was a blackboard on a rosewood easel, and a luggage rack holding a calfskin suitcase—Mal's one-up on briefcase toters. Across the table sat a legal reporter with a steno machine. Surrounding her were eight—not seven—attorneys.

"Insurance company sent three," Mal whispered to me. "Those first three."

I looked at the trio. Young, pin-striped, funereal.

Their spokesman was a big, prematurely bald fellow in his early thirties named Moretti. He had a meaty cleft chin, wide shoulders, and the charm of a drill instructor. One of Mal's secretaries served coffee and sweet rolls, and as we ate, Moretti made a point of letting me know he'd been a psych major at Stanford. He dropped the names of prominent professors, tried unsuccessfully to engage me in shoptalk, and watched me over the rim of his coffee cup with sharp brown eyes.

When I presented my report he moved to the edge of his chair. When I finished he was the first to speak. The other lawyers deferred to him. Like any wolf pack, they'd chosen their lead killer and were content to sit back and let him open the first wounds.

He reminded me that I was legally bound to tell the truth, just as if I were in court, that I was testifying under penalty of perjury. Then he removed a phone-book-thick pile of photocopied articles from his briefcase and made a show of stacking the papers on the table, shuffling and sorting and squaring off the corners. Lifting the top article, he said, "I'd like to read you something, Doctor."

"Sure."

He smiled. "I really wasn't asking permission, Doctor."

"I really wasn't granting it."

The smile disappeared. Mal nudged me under the table. Someone coughed. Moretti tried staring me down, then put on a pair of rimless octagonal glasses, cleared his throat, and began to read. He finished a paragraph before turning to me. "Familiar, Doctor?"

"Yes."

"Do you remember the source?"

"It's the introduction to an article I published in *The Journal of Pediatrics* in 1981. Summer of '81, I believe. August."

He examined the date but didn't comment on it. "Do you remember the gist of that article, Doctor?"

"Yes."

"Could you summarize it for us?"

"The article describes a study I did from 1977 through 1980, when I was at Western Pediatric Hospital. The research was funded by the National Institute of Mental Health and was designed to learn the effects of chronic disease upon the psychological adjustment of children."

"Was it a well-designed study, Doctor?"

"I believe so."

"You believe so. Tell us what you did in this well-designed study—be specific about your methodology."

"I administered several tests of psychological adjustment to a sample of sick children and a control group of healthy children. The groups were matched in terms of social class, parental marital status, and family size. There was no significant difference between the groups."

"No significant difference on any measure of psychological adjustment?"

"That's correct."

Moretti looked over at the legal reporter. "He talks fast. Do you have that down?"

She nodded.

Back to me: "For the sake of those of us who aren't familiar with psychological jargon, specify what *no significant difference* means."

"The groups were statistically indistinguishable. The average scores on these measures were similar."

"Average?"

"Median—the fifty percent mark. Mathematically, it's the best measure of typicality."

"Yes, of course, but what does all of that *mean?*"

"Chronically ill children may develop some problems but being sick doesn't inevitably make them neurotic or psychotic."

"Hold on for a moment," said Moretti, patting the stack of papers. "I don't see mention of any problems here, Doctor. Your basic finding was that the sick children were normal."

"That's true. However—"

"You spell it out right here, Doctor." He held up the article, flipped a page, and jabbed his finger at it. "Right here in Table Three. 'Spielberger State Anxiety scores, Rosenberg self-esteem scores, Achenbach Adjustment scores were all'—and I'm quoting verbatim—*'within normal limits.'* Put in simple English, these kids were no more nervous or insecure or maladjusted or neurotic than their healthy peers, were they, Doctor?"

"This is starting to sound argumentative," said Mal. "We're here to find facts."

"Quasi-facts, at best," said Moretti. "This is psychology, not science."

"*You* quoted the article, Counselor," said Mal.

"Your witness's report seems to be contradicting his own published work, Counselor."

"Would you like me to answer your question?" I asked Moretti.

He removed his glasses, sat back, and gave a quarter-smile. "If you can."

"Read the discussion section," I said. "The last three paragraphs specifically. I list several problem areas chronically ill children have to deal with throughout their lives—pain and discomfort, disruption of school due to treatment and hospitalization, body changes brought about by both disease and treatment, social rejection, overprotectiveness by parents. In general, children cope well with these problems, but problems still exist."

"The discussion section," said Moretti. "Aha. The place researchers dump their conjectures. But your own *data*—your *statistics* say otherwise. Really, Doctor—"

"In other words," Mal broke in, turning to me, "what you're saying, Dr. Delaware, is that sick children and traumatized children face a constant flood of challenges—life is *agonizing* for them—but some are able to handle it."

"Yes."

Mal swept his eyes up and down the table, avoiding Moretti, establishing momentary eye contact with each of the other lawyers. "No reason to penalize a child for coping well, is there, gentlemen?"

"Who's the witness here?" snapped Moretti, waving the reprint.

"No reason to penalize a child for dealing with his trauma," said Mal.

"Trauma?" said Moretti. "There's nothing in this article about *traumatized children,*" said Moretti. "These are chronically ill kids—*chronic*, as in long-term. Darren Burkhalter is a one-shot deal. He has no ongoing pain or physical change to deal with. He'd be even less vulnerable to problems than someone chronically disabled."

He allowed himself a full smile.

To him it was all a game. I thought of little boys engaging in back-alley pissing contests and said, "Good point, Mr. Moretti. Chronically ill and traumatized children are very different. That's why I was wondering why you quoted from the article in the first place."

A couple of the other lawyers smiled.

"Touché," Mal whispered in my ear.

One of the other insurance lawyers was whispering in Moretti's ear. The lead man wasn't pleased with what he was hearing but he listened impassively, then put the reprint aside.

"All right, Doctor, let's talk about the whole notion of early childhood *trauma.* Your conclusion, as I understand it, is that Darren Burkhalter will be scarred emotionally, for life, because of his presence during an automobile accident."

"You understand wrong," I said. Moretti reddened. Mal raised his eyebrows and gave a soft whistle.

"Now, Doctor—"

"What I *did* say, Mr. Moretti, was that during my examination of him, Darren Burkhalter exhibited classic symptoms of trauma for a child his age. Sleep problems, nightmares, phobias, aggressiveness, hyperactivity, tantrums, periods of increased clinginess. According to both his mother and his day-care teacher, he showed none of these behaviors prior to the accident. It's reasonable to assume they were related to the accident—though I can't prove that with hard *data.* Whether or not these problems will develop into chronic disabilities isn't clear, although the risk is high if psychotherapy doesn't continue. In addition, Darren is lagging in his speech and language development—his milestones are several months behind average. How much of that is due to the trauma is impossible to judge, but it's well worth thinking about when considering this child's future."

"It certainly *is* impossible to judge," said Moretti. "My reading of the literature in your field is that intelligence is primarily genetically determined. The best predictor of a child's IQ is his father's IQ—Katz, Dash, and Ellenberg, 1981."

"This father's IQ will never be tested again," said Mal.

"In lieu of that, I requested that Mrs. Burkhalter take an IQ test, but you refused that request, Mr. Worthy."

"She's had enough stress, Counselor."

"No matter," said Moretti. "Inferences may still be drawn from what we know of these people. Neither Mr. nor Mrs. Burkhalter finished high school. Both were *dropouts,* worked at menial jobs. That indicates a less than average genetic endowment for this family. I wouldn't *expect* Darren to be average. Would you, Dr. Delaware?"

"It's hardly that simple," I said. "Parental IQ predicts children's IQ better than most other factors, but it's still not a very *good* predictor, accounting for less than twenty percent of the variance. Katz, Dash, and Ellenberg emphasize that in their follow-up 1983 study. One out of five, Mr. Moretti. Not great odds for a bet."

"Are you a gambler, Doctor?"

"No. That's why I took this case."

The reporter smiled.

Moretti turned to Mal. "Counselor, I'd advise that you counsel this witness on appropriate demeanor."

"Consider yourself advised, Dr. Delaware," said Mal, fighting a grin. He flashed his cuffs and studied his Rolex. "May we proceed?"

Moretti put his glasses back on and scanned some papers. "Dr. Delaware," he said, then paused as if anticipating a punch line. "Come now, Dr. Delaware. You're not saying that except for the accident, Darren Burkhalter would have been expected to become a nuclear physicist, are you?"

"No one knows what Darren would have become or what he *will* become," I said. "Right now, the *facts* are that following an unusually severe psychological trauma, his language is below average and he's experiencing severe stress."

"What was his language like before the accident?"

"His mother reports he was starting to talk. However, after the traum—"

"His mother," said Moretti. "And you base your conclusions on what she tells you."

"Along with other input."

"Such as your interview with his day-care teacher."

"Such as."

"His teacher's *your* expert witness?"

"She seemed very credible and had a good understanding of Darren. She reported that the parents were very involved, very loving. His father, in particular, had taken an interest in his—"

"Yes, let's talk about his father. Gregory Joe Burkhalter had a criminal record. Are you aware of that, Doctor?"

"Yes I am. A conviction for petty theft, several years ago."

"Petty theft and larceny, Doctor. He did jail time."

"What's the point?" asked Mal.

"The point, Mr. Worthy, is that your *expert,* basing his opinion on an individual who would *not* qualify as an expert in court, wants to make a case for this father being a major source of intellectual stimulation for this child, hence major material and emotional loss due to paternal death. This father was a criminal, minimally educated . . ."

"Mr. Moretti," I said, "is it your position that only educated parents are worth grieving for?"

He ignored me. ". . . while, in point of fact, the *data* pertaining to the case in point indicate a socially and emotionally impoverished . . ."

He went on for a while, picking up volume and speed, fairly glowing with combat lust. Mal, too, was caught up in the joust, poised for the riposte.

More pissing. And the truth be damned. It started to really get to me and I broke in, raising my voice to be heard over the tide of legalese: "Mr. Moretti, you're a classic case of a little knowledge being dangerous."

Moretti rose half out of his seat, caught himself, then settled back down and bared his teeth. "Getting defensive, Doctor?"

"This was supposed to be a fact-finding meeting. If you want to hear what I have to say, fine. If you want to play ego games, I won't waste my time."

Moretti clucked his tongue. "Mr. Worthy, if this is a portent of his courtroom behavior, you're in a heap of trouble, Counselor."

Mal said nothing. But he scrawled on his note pad: *Have I created a monster?* then covered it with his hand.

Moretti didn't miss it: "Anything we should have on the record, Counselor?"

"Just doodling," said Mal and he began to sketch a naked woman.

"We were talking about childhood trauma," I said to Moretti. "Would you like me to address that issue or am I through?"

Moretti tried to look amused. "You may address it if you have something to add to your report."

"Since you drew faulty conclusions from my report, I have plenty to add. Darren Burkhalter is suffering a post-traumatic stress reaction that may convert to long-term psychological problems. Brief play therapy and counseling for the mother have brought about some symptom reduction but much more treatment is indicated." To the other lawyers: "I'm *not* saying long-term psychological problems are inevitable, but neither will I rule problems out. No reasonable expert would."

"Oh, for God's sake," said Moretti, "this child is two years old."

"Twenty-six months."

"Same difference. He was eighteen *months* at the time of the accident. You're telling me that you'll be willing to go into court and testify under oath that when he's twenty-six *years* old, he could be psychologically affected by an accident that took place when he was a baby?"

"That's exactly what I'm telling you. A traumatic scene that vivid and bloody, buried in his subconscious—"

Moretti snorted. "What does a *subconscious* look like, Doctor? I've never seen one."

"Nevertheless, you have one, Mr. Moretti. As do I and everyone else in this room. In simple terms, the subconscious is a psychic storage bin. The part of our mind where we put experiences and feelings we don't want to deal with. When our defenses are down, the bin tips over and some of the stored material spills out—dreams, fantasies, seemingly irrational or even self-destructive behaviors that we call symptoms. The subconscious is real, Mr. Moretti. It's what makes *you* dream of *winning*. A big part of what motivated you to become a lawyer."

That got to him. He took pains to be cool but his eyes twitched, his nostrils opened, and his mouth drew so tight it puckered.

"Thank you for that insight, Doctor. Send me a bill—though judging from what you're charging Mr. Worthy, I don't know if I can afford you. In the meantime, let's stick to the accident—"

"*Accident* doesn't begin to describe what Darren Burkhalter experienced. *Disaster* would be more accurate. The boy was napping in his car up until the moment of impact. The first thing he saw when he woke up was his father's decapitated head flying over the front seat and landing next to him, the features still twitching."

Several of the lawyers winced.

"It missed falling right in his lap by inches," I said. "Darren must have thought it was some kind of doll because he tried to pick it up. When he pulled away his hand and saw it covered with blood—saw what it really was—he went hysterical. And stayed hysterical for five full days, Mr. Moretti, screaming 'Dada!' totally out of control."

I paused to let the image sink in. "He knew what was happening, Mr. Moretti—he's played it out in my office every time he's been there. He's clearly old enough to form a durable memory. I'll quote you statistics on *that,* if you'd like. And that memory won't disappear simply because you want it to."

"A memory that you're keeping alive by making him go through it over and over again," said Moretti.

"So what you're asserting," I said, "is that psychotherapy is making him worse. That we should simply forget about it or pretend it didn't happen."

"Double touché," whispered Mal.

Moretti was bug-eyed. "It's *your* position that's under scrutiny, Doctor. I want to see you back up all this early trauma talk with *data.*"

"I'd be happy to."

I had my own stack of articles, pulled them out, cited references, tossed out numbers, and gave a somewhat manic lecture on the development of memory in children and their reactions to disaster and trauma. I used the blackboard to summarize my findings.

"Generalizations," said Moretti. "Clinical impressions."

"You'd prefer something more objective?"

He smiled. "It would be nice."

"Terrific."

A secretary rolled in the video monitor, slipped the tape into the VCR, dimmed the lights, and pushed the PLAY button.

When it was over, dead silence. Finally, Moretti smirked and said, "Planning a second career in the film business, Doctor?"

"I've seen and heard enough," said one of the other attorneys. He closed his briefcase and pushed his chair from the table. Several others did the same.

"Any more questions?" asked Mal.

"Nope," said Moretti. But he looked buoyant and I experienced a pang of self-doubt. He winked and saluted me. "See you in court, Doctor."

When they were all gone, Mal slapped his knee and did a little dance.

"Right in the *cojones,* absolutely beautiful. I should be getting their offers this afternoon."

"I made a stronger case than I'd intended," I said. "Bastard got to me."

"I know, you were beautiful." He began collecting his papers.

"What about Moretti's parting shot?" I asked. "He looked happy about going to court."

"Pure crapola. Saving face in front of his partners. He may be the last to settle, but believe me, he'll *settle.* Some asshole, eh? Has a rep as a real black-hearted litigator, but you slammed him good— your little jibe about the subconscious was right on the mark, Alex."

He shook his head with glee. "God knows how tight he had to hold his sphincter not to shit right then and there. *'And a big part of what motivated you to become a lawyer.'* I didn't tell you this, but Moretti's dad was a big-shot psychiatrist in Milwaukee, did a lot of forensics work. Moretti must have hated him because he really has a thing for shrinks—that's why they assigned him this one."

"Stanford psych major," I said. "Blah blah blah blah blah."

Mal raised his arm in mock terror. "Boy, you've really become a nasty bastard, haven't you."

"Just tired of the bullshit." I walked to the door. "Don't call me for a while, okay?"

"Hey, don't get me wrong, Alex. I'm not putting you down. I like it, I mean I really *like* it."

"Flattered," I said. And I left him to his triumphs and his calculations.

When I got back home the phone was ringing. I picked it up at the same time the service operator did, heard Del Hardy's voice asking for Dr. Delaware. I broke in and told the operator I'd take it.

"I found out a little," he said. "Couldn't get much help at Hollywood but spoke to one of the coroners. You in any mood to hear that kind of thing?"

"Go ahead."

"Okay, first off is time of death—between eight P.M. and three A.M. Sunday. Second is cause of death. Twenty-two caliber bullet to the brain. It passed right into the cerebral cortex and bounced around in there, the way a small-caliber bullet will, doing lots of damage. Third, there were heavy amounts of alcohol and barbiturates in her system—borderline lethal dosage. Coroner also found some old scars between her toes that looked like tracks. You ever know this lady to be into heavy drugs?"

"No," I said. "But it was a long time ago."

"Yeah. People change. It's what keeps us busy."

"OD and a bullet," I said.

"Seriousness of intent," said Del. "Especially for a female, though if she really wanted to be sure, eating the gun would have been the thing to do, straight into the medulla, wipes out the autonomic system and cuts off respiration. But most folks don't know that, they watch TV, think the temple shot . . ." He stopped. "Sorry."

"It's okay," I said. "With that much downer in her system, wouldn't she be too drowsy to shoot?"

"Not right away," said Del. "Now here's the interesting part: Coroner told me their office processed the case quickly, orders of the boss—their usual average is six to eight weeks this time of year. They got orders, also, not to discuss it with anyone."

"Why all the secrecy?"

"Pathologist got the clear impression it was a rich-folks case, grease the skids to the max, keep it hushed."

"The department released information to the press."

"Controlled info," said Del. "Strategic thinking. If you say *nothing* about something, and someone finds out you were holding back, they immediately start thinking conspiracy. Telling them what *you* want is safer, makes you look open and sincere. Not that there's much to tell on this one—straight suicide, no evidence of foul play. As far as the drug-gun combo, the pathologist had two scenarios: A, she cocktailed booze and dope to do herself in, then changed her mind and wanted to get it over faster or maybe more dramatically and went for the gun. Makes sense to me—suicide's a message, right? You guys taught us that—final statement to the world. People can get really choosy about how they phrase it, right?"

"Right. What's B?"

"She used the dope and the booze to lower her inhibitions, build up enough courage to shoot herself. When she was feeling sufficiently mellow, she pulled the trigger. Either way you look at it, the end result's the same."

"Did she leave a note?"

"No. Lots of people don't. Right?"

"Right."

"Like that Canadian guy, McWhatsisname said, the medium can be the message all by itself."

"Who's the detective in charge of the case?" I asked.

"Guy named Pinckley, just left yesterday for vacation in Hawaii."

"Convenient."

"I wouldn't get in an uproar over that," said Del. "Vacations are scheduled way in advance. Pinckley's a serious surfer—he used to compete nationally. He goes every year around this time, in order to catch the big ones at Wiamea. I called Hollywood and confirmed it—the duty roster'd been set months ago."

"Who took over from Pinckley?"

"Nothing to take over, Doc. The case is closed."

"What about Trapp being up at her house?"

He lowered his voice. "I said I found out *a little,* remember? That didn't include walking into my captain's office and giving him the third degree."

"Okay, sorry."

"No apology necessary. Just gotta be careful."

"Anything else, Del?"

Pause. "*How* well did you say you knew her?"

"It had been six years since I'd seen her."

"Well enough to know that she wasn't any nun?"

"Well enough."

"Okay. If you were next of kin or a husband, I wouldn't be telling you this. It's *strictly* off the record. My source at Hollywood says there's a rumor drifting around the station that when they went up to her place, one of the techs found a porn flick hidden under the mattress—nothing sophisticated, just a loop. But a loop with *her* in it. She might have been a doctor but she had other talents."

I sucked in my breath.

"Doc?"

"Is the loop still in the evidence room, Del?"

"Not everything makes it to the evidence room."

"I see."

"Case like this, it works out better for the lady. What's better, having the damned thing stored in some cop's underwear drawer, pulled out once in a blue moon for private screenings, or letting the papers get hold of it—'Doctor Had Secret Life'? You know what they'd do with that. I mean this loop wasn't Disney stuff."

"What was on it?"

"What you'd imagine."

"Could you be more specific, Del?"

"You really want to hear this?"

"Go ahead."

He sighed. "Okay. What I was told was that it was one of those doctor-patient things. You know, checkup turns to sex? She was the patient; some guy was the doc." Pause. "That's all I know. I did *not* see it."

"Did she leave anything else behind, like patient files?"

"I didn't ask."

"What about the quick sale on her house?"

"With the case closed there'd be no reason not to sell."

"Did she own the house?"

"I didn't check that."

"What about the twin sister? Has anyone located her?"

"No Shirlee Ransom on any of our files, which means nothing— she wasn't a criminal. But DMV didn't have her either."

"They wouldn't. She couldn't have driven a car."

"Whatever. Searching for heirs isn't our business, Doc. Which-ever lawyer's probating the will would have to hire someone private. And to answer your next question, no, I don't know who that is."

"Okay," I said. "Thanks for your time."

"No problem. Glad to give it. When I have it."

Which was a polite way of saying *Don't bother me anymore.*

A porn loop.

Kruse's "research."

Exploring the boundaries of human sexuality.

Larry had laughed about it, but self-consciously. Working for Kruse was a phase of his career he clearly wanted to forget. Now he was going to be reminded, again. I called his office in Brentwood, using the private line that bypassed his answering service.

"I'm with a patient," he said, sotto voce. "Call you back at a quarter to the hour?"

He did, at precisely 2:45, munching on something and talking between bites.

"Missed me already, D.? What's on your mind?"

"Sharon Ransom."

"Yeah, I read about it. Oh, God, I forgot—the two of you were an item way back when, weren't you?"

"She was at the party, Larry. I ran into her when you went to make your call. I talked to her the day before she died."

"Jesus. Did she look depressed?"

"A little down. She said things weren't going well. But nothing profound, nothing to set off any alarms. You and I both know how much that's worth, though."

"Yeah, ye olde professional intuition. Might as well use a ouija board."

Silence.

"Sharon Ransom," he said. "Unreal. She used to be gorgeous."

"Still was."

"Unreal," he repeated. "I haven't seen her since school, never ran into her at any meetings or conventions."

"She was living in L.A."

"Mystery lady. She always projected a bit of that."

"Did she work on the porn project, Larry?"

"Not when I was there. Why?"

I told him about her being Kruse's assistant. About the loop.

"Welcome to Hollyweird," he said. But he didn't sound surprised and I commented on it.

"That's 'cause I'm not surprised, D. Someone else, maybe, but not her."

"Why's that?"

"Truth be told, I always thought she was strange."

"In what way?"

"Nothing blatant, but something about her just wasn't set right—like a beautiful painting hung off kilter."

"You never said anything to me."

"If I'd told you I thought your girlfriend was iffy in the personality department, would you have listened to me calmly and said, 'Gee, thanks, Lar'?"

"Nope."

"Nope is right. *Au contraire*, you would have been highly pissed off, probably never spoken to me again. No, no, kiddies, Uncle Larry keeps his mouth shut. First rule of therapy: When you're not sure, say nothing. And I *wasn't* sure. It's not as if I was formally diagnosing her—this was just an impression. Besides, you seemed to be enjoying yourself with her, and I didn't see you marrying her."

"Why not?"

"She just didn't seem the marrying kind."

"What kind did she seem?"

"The kind you keep on the side and destroy your life over, D. I figured you were too smart for that. And I was right, wasn't I?"

Pause. He said, "Let me ask you a question and don't take offense: Was she any good in bed?"

"Not really," I said.

"Went through the moves but didn't really dig it?"

I was startled. "What makes you say that?"

"Talking about the loop made me realize who she reminded me of: the porn actresses Kruse used to have in his movies. I met them when I worked for him. Those girls all oozed sex appeal, came on as if they could suck blood out of a rock. But you got the feeling it was just a veneer, something that came off with their makeup. Sensuality wasn't integrated in their personalities—they knew how to split their feelings from their behavior."

"Split," I said. "As in borderline?"

"Exactly. But don't get me wrong. I'm not saying Sharon *was* a borderline, or even that all the actresses were. But she and they all had some of that borderline quality to them. Am I on target at all?"

"Bull's-eye," I said. "She had typical borderline qualities. All these years I never put it together."

"Don't shit on yourself, D. You were *sleeping* with her—afflicted with severe pussy-blindness. I especially wouldn't expect *you* to be diagnosing her. But I'm not surprised she made a fuck film."

Borderline personality disorder. If Sharon had deserved that diagnosis, I'd flirted with disaster.

The borderline patient is a therapist's nightmare. During my training years, before I decided to specialize in children, I treated more than my share of them and learned that the hard way.

Or, rather, I *tried* to treat them. Because borderlines never really get better. The best you can do is help them coast, without getting sucked into their pathology. At first glance they look normal, sometimes even supernormal, holding down high-pressure jobs and excelling. But they walk a constant tightrope between madness and sanity, unable to form relationships, incapable of achieving insight, never free from a deep, corroding sense of worthlessness and rage that spills over, inevitably, into self-destruction.

They're the chronically depressed, the determinedly addictive, the compulsively divorced, living from one emotional disaster to the next. Bed hoppers, stomach pumpers, freeway jumpers, and sad-eyed bench sitters with arms stitched up like footballs and psychic wounds that can never be sutured. Their egos are as fragile as spun sugar, their psyches irretrievably fragmented, like a jigsaw puzzle with crucial pieces missing. They play roles with alacrity, excel at being anyone but themselves, crave intimacy but repel it when they find it. Some of them gravitate toward stage or screen; others do their acting in more subtle ways.

No one knows how or why a borderline becomes a borderline. The Freudians claim it's due to emotional deprivation during the first two years of life; the biochemical engineers blame faulty wiring. Neither school claims to be able to help them much.

Borderlines go from therapist to therapist, hoping to find a magic bullet for the crushing feelings of emptiness. They turn to chemical bullets, gobble tranquilizers and antidepressants, alcohol and cocaine. Embrace gurus and heaven-hucksters, any charismatic creep promising a quick fix of the pain. And they end up taking temporary vacations in psychiatric wards and prison cells, emerge looking good, raising everyone's hopes. Until the next letdown, real or imagined, the next excursion into self-damage.

What they don't do is change.

Ada Small had once talked to me about it—the only time I can remember hearing anger in her voice:

Stay away from them, Alex, if you want to feel competent. They'll make you look stupid every time. You'll work on getting rapport for months, even years, finally think you've got it and are ready to do some insight work, maybe get some real change going, and they'll walk out on you in a minute. You'll find yourself wondering what you did wrong, questioning if you went into the right profession. It won't be you—it's them. They can look terrific one moment, be out on the ledge the next.

Out on the ledge.

More than any other psychiatric patient, borderlines could be counted on to attempt suicide. And to succeed.

"I used to sit around bullshitting with the actresses," Larry was saying. "Got to know some of them a little and began to understand them—their promiscuity, how they did what they did. From a borderline's point of view, promiscuity can be a halfway decent adaptation, the perfect split—one man for friendship, another for intellectual stimulation, another for sex. Split, split, split, neat and clean. If you can't achieve intimacy, it sure beats being lonely. Splitting's also a great way to cut yourself off from fucking on film and letting guys come all over your face. Just another job. I mean, how else could you do it, then go home and make macaroni and cheese and do the crossword puzzle? The girls admitted it, said when they were on camera it was like watching someone else."

"Dissociation," I said.

"Par excellence."

I thought of all the fragmentation in Sharon's life. The routinized, ultimately passionless way she made love. The refusal to live with me, with anyone. The detachment with which she'd spoken about her dead parents. Going into a helping profession and seducing her patients. Graduating but never getting her license. That horrible night I'd found her with the twin photo.

I'm their only little girl.

The lies.

The loop.

Hooking up with a sleaze like Kruse.

"Did Kruse ever film his students, Larry?"

"You think *he* made her do the film?"

"It's logical. He was her supervisor. He was into porn."

"I suppose so. Except his weren't loops—they were half-hour features, color, full sound. Supposed to be marital aids for couples with sexual dysfunction, pseudodocumentaries with a disclaimer at the beginning and some guy who sounds like Orson Welles doing a voice-over narration while the camera zooms in on insertion. Besides, Kruse used actors and actresses. Pros. I never saw a student in any of his stuff."

"There may have been stuff you didn't see."

"I'm sure there was. But do you have any indication he filmed her?"

"No. Just a gut feeling."

"What do you know about the loop besides the fact that she was in it?"

"Supposed to be a doctor-patient seduction thing. The person who described it to me never saw it himself, and it's since disappeared."

"So basically you're talking thirdhand information—the old telephone game. You know how that kind of thing improves with the telling. Maybe it wasn't even her."

"Maybe."

Pause. "Wanna try to find out?"

"How?"

"I *might* be able to get hold of a copy. Old contacts from the research project."

"I don't know," I said.

"Yeah," he said. "It *would* be kind of morbid—forget I mentioned it. Oops, my light just went on. Got a patient in the waiting room. Anything else on your mind?"

I wrestled with my feelings. Curiosity—no, tell it like it is, Delaware: voyeurism—locked in combat with fear of learning yet more repugnant truths.

But I said, "See if you can get hold of the movie."

"You're sure?"

I wasn't, but I heard myself say yes.

"Okay," he said. "I'll get back to you soon as I know."

Yesterday's conversation with Robin—my irritability, the way things had fizzled—still preyed on my mind. At four I phoned her. The last person I wanted to talk to answered.

"Yes?"

"It's me, Rosalie."

"She's not here."

"When are you expecting her back?"

"She didn't say."

"All right. Would you please tell her—"

"I'm not telling her anything. Why don't you just quit? She doesn't want to be with you. Isn't that plain to see?"

"It'll be plain when I hear it from her, Rosalie."

"Listen, I know you're supposed to be smart and all that but you're not as smart as you think. You and her think you're all grown up, got everything figured out, don't need to hear advice from no one. But she's still my kid and I don't like people pushing her around."

"You think I push her around?"

"If the shoe *fits,* mister. Yesterday, after she talked to you, she was all mopey for the rest of the day, the way she used to be when she was a kid and couldn't get her way. Thank God some friends called, so maybe she can finally have a good time. She's a good kid, doesn't need that kind of misery. So why don't you just forget it."

"I'm not about to forget anything. I love her."

"*Bullpuckey.* Words."

I gritted my teeth. "Just give her the message, Rosalie."

"Do your own dirty work."

Slam.

I sat there, tight with rage, feeling cut off and helpless. Grew angry at Robin for allowing herself to be protected like a child.

Then I cooled and realized Robin had no idea she was being protected, had no reason to expect her mother *would* protect her. The two of them had never had a close relationship. Daddy had seen to that. Now Rosalie was trying to reassert her maternal rights.

I felt sorry for Rosalie, but it only partially quelled my anger. And I still wanted to talk to Robin, to work things out. Why the hell was that turning out to be so difficult?

The phone was the wrong way to do it. We needed time alone, the right setting.

I called two airlines for flight schedules to San Luis. At both of them recorded messages put me on hold. When the doorbell rang, I hung up.

It rang again. I went to the door, looked through the peephole, and saw a familiar face: big and broad and lumpy, almost boyish except for the acne pits that blanketed the cheeks. Coarse black hair, slightly graying, cut unfashionably close around the ears and neck and left long up on top, with a Kennedyesque shock falling across a low, square brow and sideburns that reached to the bottom of fleshy earlobes. A big high-bridged nose, a pair of startling green eyes under shaggy black brows. Pallid skin now lacquered with a hot pink coat of sunburn. The nose, red and peeling. The entire ugly assemblage, scowling.

I opened the door.

"Four days early, Milo? Crave civilization?"

"Fish," he said, ignoring the question and holding out a metal ice chest. He stared at me. "You look terrible."

"Gee, thanks. You look like strawberry yogurt yourself. Stirred from the bottom."

He grimaced. "Itching all over. Here, take it. I have to scratch."

He shoved the chest at me. The weight made me step backwards. I carried it into the house and placed it on the kitchen counter. He followed me in and flopped down on a chair, stretching out long legs and running his hands over his face, as if washing without water.

"So," he said, spreading his arms. "What do you think? Pretty goddamned Abercrombie and Itch, huh?"

He had on a red-and-black plaid shirt, baggy khakis, rubber-soled lace-up boots, and a khaki fisherman's vest with about a dozen zippered compartments. Trout lures hung from one of the pockets. A fishing knife in a scabbard dangled from his belt. He'd put on some weight—had to be pushing 230—and the shirt was tight, the buttons straining.

"Stunning," I said.

He growled and loosened the laces on the boots. "Rick," he said. "He forced me to go shopping, insisted we had to outmacho everyone."

"Did you succeed?"

"Oh, yeah. We were so goddamned tough it scared the shit out of the fish. Little suckers jumped right out of the river, landing in our skillets, lemon slices in their mouths."

I laughed.

"Hey," he said, "man still remembers how. What's the matter, guy? Who died?"

Before I could answer, he was up and prying open the chest, removing two big trout wrapped in plastic.

"Give me a fry pan, butter, garlic, and onions—no, excuse me, this is an upscale household—*shallots*. Give me *shallots*. Got any beer?"

I got a Grolsch from the refrigerator, opened it, and gave it to him.

"Going temperate on me?" he asked, tilting his head back and drinking from the bottle. "Quaff, be social."

"Not right now." I gave him the pan and a knife and went back to rummage in the refrigerator, which was near empty. "Here's the butter. No shallots. No garlic either, just this."

He looked at the wilted half Bermuda onion in my hand. Took it and said, "Tsk, tsk, slipping, Dr. Suave. I'm reporting you to the Foodie Patrol."

He took the onion, sliced it down the middle, and immediately his eyes teared. Moving away and rubbing them, he said, "Better yet, we play hunters and gatherers. Me catch, *you* cook."

He sat down and worked on the beer. I lifted a trout and inspected it. It had been gutted and cleaned, expertly.

"Nice, huh?" he said. "Pays to take a surgeon along."

"Where is Rick?"

"Getting some shut-eye while he can. He's got a twenty-four-hour coming up at the E.R., then twenty-four off and back on again for the Saturday night shift—gunshots and malicious foolishness. After that he's started heading over to the Free Clinic to counsel AIDS patients. What a guy, huh? All of a sudden I'm living with Schweitzer."

He was smiling but his voice was heavy with irritation, and I wondered if he and Rick were going through another tough period. I hoped not. I had neither the energy nor the will to deal with it.

"How were the great outdoors?" I asked.

"What can I say? We did the whole Boy Scout camping bit—my daddy would have been heapum proud. Found a gorgeous place near the river, downstream from white water. Last day we were there a canoe full of executive types came coasting by: bankers, computer jockeys—you know the type. Play it so straight all year 'round, the moment they're away from home they freak and turn into blithering idiots? Anyway, these yahoos come barreling downstream, stinking drunk and louder than a sonic boom, spot us, lower their pants, and flash us the moon."

He gave an evil grin. "If they'd only known who they were shoving their asses at, huh? Panic time at the GOP convention."

I laughed and began frying the onions. Milo went to the refrigerator, got another beer, and came back looking serious.

"Nothing in here," he said. "What's going on?"

"I need to shop."

"Uh-huh." He reached under his shirt and scratched his chest. Paced the kitchen and said, "How's the lovely Ms. Castagna?"

"Working hard."

"Uh-huh." He kept pacing.

The onions turned translucent. I added more butter to the pan and put the trout in. They hissed and sizzled and the smell of fresh fish filled the room.

"Ah," he said. "Nothing like a friend at home in the kitchen. Do you do windows too?"

"Why'd you come back early?" I asked.

"Too much pristine, unspoiled beauty—couldn't take it. Amazing the things one learns about one's wretched self out in the wilds. Seems both of us are urban sleaze-junkies. All that clean air and calm and we were going through the shakes." He drank more beer, shook his head. "You know how we are, marriage made in heaven until we spend too much time together. But enough about the sweet agony of relationships. How're the trout?"

"Almost done."

"Be careful not to overcook."

"Want to do it yourself?"

"Touchy, touchy."

I gave him one and a half trout and put half a fish on my plate, then filled two glasses with ice water and brought them to the table. I had a bottle of white wine somewhere but it wasn't chilled. Besides, I didn't feel like drinking, and the last thing Milo needed was more alcohol.

He looked at the water as if it were polluted but drank it anyway. After finishing the trout in a few moments, he looked at my uneaten food.

"Want it?" I said.

"Not hungry?"

I shook my head. "I ate just before you dropped in."

He gave me a long look. "Fine, hand it over."

When the half-trout was gone, he said, "Okay, tell me what the hell is bothering you."

I considered telling him about Robin. Told him about Sharon instead, honoring my pledge to Leslie Weingarden and leaving out the patient seductions.

He listened without commenting. Got up and searched the refrigerator for dessert and found an apple that he demolished in four bites.

Wiping his face, he said, "Trapp, huh? You're sure it was him?"

"He's hard to miss with that white hair and that skin."

"Yeah, the skin," he said. "Some sort of weird disease. I described it to Rick and he gave me a name for it but I forgot it. Auto-immune condition—the body attacks itself by leeching pigment. No one knows what causes it, but in Trapp's case I've got a theory: Asshole's so full of poison, his own system can't stand him. Maybe we'll be lucky and he'll fade away completely."

"What do you think about his being at the house?"

"Who knows? I'd love nothing more than to get something on the scrote, but this one doesn't scream felony. Maybe he and your late friend were getting it on and he went back to make sure he hadn't left any evidence. Sleazy but not indictable." He shook his head. "If she was getting it on with him she *must* have been nuts."

"What about the quick sale on the house?" I asked. "And the twin sister? I know she exists—existed—because I met her six years ago. If she's still alive she'd be Sharon's heir."

"Six years is a long time, Alex. And who's to say she hasn't been found? Del was right—that's up to the lawyers. Sure, sure, it smells of cover-up, but that doesn't mean what's being covered up is anything juicy, pal. This kind of thing's routine when you're dealing with the pricey crowd. Just last month we had an art theft up in Bel Air. Thirteen million dollars' worth of French Impressionism, gone, like that." He snapped his fingers. "Private chef did it and split to Monaco. We filed the papers; family hired private help. They recovered the pictures; few months later the chef had an accident with scalding water.

"And speaking of accidents, last April the teenage daughter of a 'prominent manufacturer' up in the Palisades got pissed at the family maid for throwing out one of her magazines, stuck the poor lady's hand in a garbage disposal. Bye-bye five fingers, but the maid changed her mind about filing charges. Took early retirement—ten thousand per digit—and shipped back to Guatemala. Then there's a talk show host—everyone knows him, helluva witty and charming guy. His game is getting drunk and putting women in the hospital. The network adds two million a year to his salary for damage control. Ever read a word about any of it? Ever see it on the six o'clock news? Rich folk in awkward situations, Alex. Sweep it under the rug and keep it out of court. It happens all the time."

"So you're saying forget the whole thing."

"Not so fast, Lone Ranger. I didn't say I was going to *forget* it. I'll pursue it. But for selfish reasons—the chance of getting something on Trapp. And there's one thing about the film story that does snag my interest—Harvey Pinckley, the guy who caught the call. He was one of Trapp's boys when Trapp was at Hollywood. First-class ass-kisser."

"Del made it sound as if he was okay."

"Del didn't know him. I did. Besides, Del's a good guy, but our relationship's been a bit frosty of late."

"Departmental politics?"

"Marital problems—his wife's giving him grief. He's sure she's stepping out. It's turned him asocial."

"Sorry to hear that."

"Me too. He was the only one in the division who ever treated me human. And don't get me wrong—we're not ripping each other's throats out. But he's not going to extend himself—for anyone. Anyway, the timing's right for a little extracurricular info-gathering. I don't have to report till Monday, and Rick will either be working or sleeping it off all weekend."

He got up, walked around. "Idle hands make the devil's work, lad. Far be it from me to tempt Satan. Just don't expect anything dramatic, okay?"

I nodded, took the dishes to the sink and started washing.

He came over and placed a big, padded hand on my shoulder.

"You look down. 'Fess up, Doctor. This friend was more than just a friend."

"A long time ago, Milo."

"But from the way you look when you talk about her, it's not that ancient a history. Or is there something else on that scary thing you call your mind?"

"Nothing, Milo."

He removed his hand. "Do consider one thing, Alex. Are you ready to hear more dirt about her? 'Cause, from what we already know, once we start digging, it ain't gonna be buried treasure time."

"No problem," I said, trying to sound nonchalant.

"Uh-huh," he said. And went to get another beer.

14

When he was gone my nonchalance faded. How much more dirt did I really want to encounter, when I'd never made sense of what I knew already?

Free follow-up visits.

I'd been followed up too.

The scene with the twin photo left me addled, in pain, unable to concentrate on work. Three days later I started calling her, got no answer. Four days later I gathered my resolve and went back to the house on Jalmia. No one home. I inquired at the psych department, was informed she was on temporary leave. None of her professors was worried about her absence. She'd had to take leave before— "family business"—had always made up the work, was a top-notch student. They suggested I talk to her adviser, Dr. Kruse.

When Kruse didn't return a week's worth of phone calls, I looked up his office address and drove there. The building was five stories of anodized steel and bronzed glass on Sunset near Doheny, granite-lobbied and maroon-carpeted, with a noisy French restaurant that opened to a sidewalk café on the ground floor. The directory listed an odd mix of tenants: about a third psychologists and psychiatrists, the rest various film-related concerns—production companies, agents, publicists, personal managers.

Kruse's suite was on the top floor. His door was locked. I kneeled, opened the mail slot, and peeked in. Darkness. I got up and looked around. One other suite took up the rest of the floor—an outfit called Creative Image Associates. Its double doors were locked too.

I taped a note under Kruse's nameplate, leaving my name and number, and asking him to get in touch as soon as possible *re: S.R.* Then I drove up to the house on Jalmia again.

The oil stain in the carport was dry, the foliage wilting. The mailbox was crammed with at least a week's worth of correspondence. I skimmed the return addresses on the envelopes. All junk. Nothing indicating where she'd gone.

The following morning, before heading for the hospital, I went back to the psych department and got Kruse's home address out of the faculty files. Pacific Palisades. I drove there that evening and sat waiting for him.

The tail end of November, just before Thanksgiving. L.A.'s best time of year. The sky had just deepened from El Greco blue to a glowing pewter, swelling with rain clouds and sweet with electricity.

Kruse's house was big, pink, and Spanish, on a private road off Mandeville Canyon, just a short drive down to the coast highway and the high, battering tides of autumn. The street was narrow and quiet, the nearby properties estate-sized, but Kruse's layout was open, no high walls or gates.

Psychology had been good to him. The house was graceful, with two hundred feet of landscaped garden on each side, adorned with verandas, Monterey roofs, hand-turned wooden grillwork, leaded windows. Shading the south side of the lawn was a beautifully warped black pine—giant bonsai. A pair of Brazilian orchid trees had sprinkled the freshly sown rye grass with violet blossoms. A semicircular driveway inlaid with Moorish tile cut an inverted U through the grass.

At twilight, colored outdoor lights came on and highlighted the landscaping. No cars, not a sound. More canyon seclusion. Sitting there, I was reminded of the house on Jalmia—the master's influence?— thought about Sharon's inheritance story and wondered again if Kruse had set her up.

I wondered, too, about what had happened to the other little girl in the photo.

He showed up shortly after eight, driving a black, gold pin-striped Mercedes two-seater with the top down. He gunned up the driveway. Instead of opening the door, he swung his legs over it. His long yellow hair was perfectly windblown; a pair of mirrored sunglasses dangled from a gold chain around his neck. He carried no briefcase, just a small, purselike calfskin shoulder bag that matched his boots. He wore a gray cashmere sport coat, white silk turtleneck, and black slacks. A black silk handkerchief trimmed with scarlet spilled out of his breast pocket.

As he headed toward his front door I got out of the Rambler. The sound of my door slamming made him turn. He stared. I jogged toward him and stepped into the artificial light.

"Dr. Kruse, I'm Alex Delaware."

Despite all the messages, my name evoked no sign of recognition.

"I'm a friend of Sharon Ransom."

"Hello, Alex. I'm Paul." Half-smile. His voice was low, from the chest, modulated like that of a disc jockey.

"I'm trying to locate her," I said.

He nodded but didn't answer. The silence lengthened. I felt obligated to speak.

"She hasn't been home for over two weeks, Dr. Kruse. I was wondering if you knew where she is."

"You care about her," he said, as if answering a question I hadn't asked.

"Yes, I do."

"Alex Delaware," he said.

"I've called you several times. Left messages at your office."

Big smile. He gave his head a toss. The yellow hair whipped back, then settled across his forehead. He took his keys out of his purse.

"I'd love to help you, Alex, but I can't." He began walking to the door.

"Please, Dr. Kruse . . ."

He stopped, turned, looked over his shoulder, flicked his eyes at me, and smiled again. But it came out as a sour twist of his lips, as if the sight of me made him ill.

Paul likes you. . . . He likes what I've told him about you.

"Where is she, Dr. Kruse?"

"The fact that she didn't tell you implies something, doesn't it?"

"Just tell me if she's okay. Is she coming back to L.A. or gone for good."

"I'm sorry," he said. "I can't talk to you about anything. Therapeutic confidentiality."

"You're her therapist?"

"I'm her supervisor. Inherent in the supervisory relationship is more than a little psychotherapy."

"Telling me if she's all right won't violate confidentiality."

He shook his head. Then something odd happened to his face.

The upper half remained all hard scrutiny—heavy blond brows and pale-brown eyes flecked with green that bored into mine with Svengali-like intensity. But from the nose down he'd gone slack, the mouth curling into a foolish, almost clownish leer.

Two personalities sharing one face. Freaky as a carny show and twice as unsettling because there was hostility behind it, the desire to ridicule. To dominate.

"Tell her *I* care about *her*," I said. "Tell her whatever she does, that I still care."

"Have a good evening," he said. Then he went into his house.

An hour later, back in my apartment, I was furious, determined to flush her and her bullshit out of my life. A month later I'd settled down to solitude and a crushing workload, was managing to fake contentment well enough to believe it myself, when she called. Eleven P.M. I'd just gotten home, dog-tired and hungry. When I heard her voice, my resolve melted like old slush under a new sun.

"I'm back. I'm sorry—I'll explain everything," she told me. "Meet me at my house in an hour. I'll make it up to you, I promise."

I showered, put on fresh clothes, drove to Nichols Canyon prepared to ask hard questions. She was waiting for me at the door in a flame-red low-cut jersey dress that barely contained her. In her hand was a snifter of something pink and redolent of strawberries. It obscured her perfume—no spring flowers.

The house was brightly lit. Before I could speak she pulled me inside and pressed her mouth against mine, worming her tongue between my teeth and keeping us fastened by pressing one hand hard to the back of my head. Her breath was sharp with alcohol. It was the first time I'd seen her drink anything other than 7-Up. When I commented on it, she laughed and hurled the glass at the fireplace. It shattered and left pink snail-tracks on the wall.

"Strawberry daiquiri, darling. I guess I'm in a tropical mood." Her voice was husky, inebriated. She kissed me again, harder, began undulating against me. I closed my eyes, sank into the boozy sweetness of the kiss. She moved away from me. I opened my eyes, saw her peeling out of the red dress, shimmying and licking her lips. The silk caught on her hips, gave way after a tug, then fell to the floor, just a flimsy orange ribbon. She stepped away from me, gave me a look at her: braless, in black garter belt, mesh stockings, and high-heeled shoes.

She ran her hands over her body.

In the abstract it was X-rated comedy, Frederick's of Hollywood, a lampoon. But she was anything but abstract and I stood there, transfixed.

I let her strip me down in a practiced manner that excited and frightened me.

Too nimble.

Too professional.

How many other times?

How many other men? Who'd taught her—

To hell with that. I didn't care—I wanted her. She had me out, in her hand, kneading, nibbling.

We embraced again, naked. Her fingers traveled over my body, scratching, raising welts. She put my hand between her legs, rode my fingers, engulfed them.

"Yum," she said, stepping back once more, pirouetting and exhibiting herself.

I reached for the light switch. She said, "No. Keep it *bright*. I want to *see* it, see *everything*."

I realized that the drapes were open. We were standing before the wall of glass, top-lit, giving a free show to Hollywood.

I turned the light off.

"Party pooper," she said and kneeled before me, grinning. I put my fingers in her hair, was engulfed, spun backwards into a vortex of pleasure. She pulled away to catch her breath, said, "C'mon, the *lights*. I want to *see* it."

"In the bedroom," I gasped. Lifting her in my arms, I carried her down the hall as she continued to kiss me and stroke me. The bedroom lights were on, but the high windows afforded privacy.

I set her down on top of the covers. She opened like a book to a favorite page. I got on top.

She rounded her back and drew her legs up in the air. Put me in her and rocked her hips, holding me at arm's length so she could stare at the piston merger of our flesh.

Once, she'd been married to modesty; there'd been a quickie divorce. . . .

"You're *in* me, oh, God." She pinched her nipples, touched herself, made sure I watched.

She rode me, withdrew me, took me in hand, rubbed me over her face, slid me between her breasts, wrapped me in the soft tangle of her hair. Then got under me, pulled me down hard, and tongued my anus.

A moment later we were locked together standing, her back to the wall. Then she positioned me near the foot of the bed and sat on me, staring over my shoulder into the mirror above the dresser. Not satisfied with that, she pushed me off her and pulled me into the bathroom. I realized why right away—tall, mirrored medicine chests on two walls, mirrors that could be pulled out and angled, for side views, back views. After arranging her stage, she sat on the cold tile counter, shivering and goose-bumped, put me in her again, darted her eyes.

We ended up on the bathroom floor, she squatting over me, touching herself, tracing a vaginal trail up and down my chest, then impaling herself again.

When I closed my eyes she cried out, "No!" and pried them open. Finally she lost herself in the pleasure, opened her mouth wide, and panted and grunted. Sobbed and covered her face.

And came.

I exploded a second later. She extricated herself, licked me hard, and kept moving, slamming herself down on the tile, using me selfishly, climaxing a second time.

We staggered back to the bedroom and fell asleep in each other's arms, with the lights still on. I slept, woke up feeling drugged.

She wasn't in bed. I found her in the living room, hair pinned up, dressed in tight jeans and a tank top—another new look. Sitting in a sling chair drinking another strawberry daiquiri and reading a psych journal, unaware of my presence.

I watched her stick a finger in the drink, pull it out coated with pink foam, and lick it off.

"Hi," I said, smiling and stretching.

She looked up at me. Her expression was odd. Flat. Bored. Then it heated and turned ugly.

Contemptuous.

"Sharon?"

She placed the drink on the carpet and stood up. "Okay," she said. "You got what you wanted, you scummy prick. Now get the fuck out of here. Get the fuck out of my life—get *out*!"

I dressed hurriedly, carelessly, feeling as worthwhile as a scab. Rushed past her, out of the house and into the Rambler. Hands shaking, I started the car and hurtled down Jalmia.

Only when I was back on Hollywood Boulevard did I take the time to breathe.

But breathing hurt, as if I'd been poisoned. I wanted suddenly to destroy her. To leach her toxin from my blood.

I screamed.

Entertaining murderous thoughts, I sped along dark streets, as dangerous as a drunk driver.

I got onto Sunset, passed nightclubs and disco joints, smiling faces that seemed to mock my own misery. But by the time I reached Doheny, my rage had faded to gnawing sadness. Disgust.

This was it—no more mindfucks.
This was *it*.

Remembering had plunged me into a cold sweat.
Follow-up visits.
She'd followed herself up too. With pills and a gun.

15

On Thursday morning I called Paul Kruse's university office, not really knowing what I was going to say to him. He was out; the department secretary had no idea when he'd be back. I looked up his private office in the phone book. He had two: the one on Sunset and the one he'd leased for Sharon. No answer at either. Same old song—I'd become a virtuoso at playing it. I thought of calling the airlines again, didn't relish handling more phone abuse. My thoughts were interrupted by a knock on the door—a messenger with a check from Trenton, Worthy and La Rosa and two large, gift-wrapped packages, also from the law firm.

I tipped him and after he left I opened the packages. One held a case of Chivas Regal, the other a case of Moët & Chandon.

A tip for me. As I wondered why, the phone rang.

"Did it get there?" asked Mal.

"A minute ago."

"He-ey! Perfect timing or what? Don't drink it all in one place."

"Why the gratuity, Mal?"

"Seven-figure settlement is why. All that legal talent got together and decided to divvy up."

"Moretti too?"

"Moretti especially. Insurance company's putting in the biggest chunk. He called a couple of hours after your depo, didn't even bother to play hard to get. After he tumbled, the rest crashed like dominoes. Denise and little Darren have just won the lottery, Doctor."

"I'm happy for them. Try to see that both of them get some help."

"Being *rich* should help, but sure, I'll push her. By the way, after we settled on a figure, Moretti asked for your number. He was very impressed."

"Flattered."

"I gave it to him."

"He's wasting his time."

"That's what I figured. But it wasn't my place to tell him to shove it. Do it yourself. I imagine the new you will enjoy it."

At one o'clock I went out and made another try at grocery shopping. In the produce section my cart collided with one pushed by a tall auburn-haired woman.

"Oops, sorry." I disengaged, moved aside, and edged over to the tomatoes.

"Sorry myself," she said cheerfully. "Gets like the freeway in here sometimes, doesn't it?"

The market was nearly empty but I said, "Sure does."

She smiled at me with even white teeth and I took a closer look. Late thirties or well-preserved early forties, a thick shag of dark hair surrounding a roundish, pretty face. Snub nose and freckles, eyes the color of a choppy sea. She wore denim short shorts that advertised long, tan, runner's legs, and a lavender T-shirt that did the same for high, sharp breasts. Around one ankle was a thin gold chain. Her nails were long and silver; the ones on the index fingers had been inlaid with diamond chips.

"What do you think of this?" she asked, handing me a cantaloupe. "Too firm to be ripe?"

"No, I don't think so."

"Just right, huh?" Big grin, one leg bent and resting against the other. She stretched and the T-shirt rose up, exposing a flat, bronze tummy.

I turned the melon in my palms and knocked on it a couple of times. "Just right." When I handed it back, our fingers touched.

"I'm Julie."

"Alex."

"I've seen you here before, Alex. You buy lots of Chinese vegetables, don't you?"

A shot in the dark—and a miss—but why make her feel bad? "Sure do."

"Love that bok choy," she said as she hefted the cantaloupe. Placing it in her basket, she turned her attention to half a pineapple wrapped in plastic. "Mmm, everything looks so good and ripe today. Yum."

I bagged some tomatoes, selected a head of lettuce and a bunch of scallions, and began to wheel away.

"Lawyer, right?"

I smiled and shook my head.

"Um, let's see . . . architect."

"No, I'm a psychologist."

"Are you really? I *love* psychologists. Mine helped me so much."

"That's great, Julie." I began pushing my cart away. "Nice meeting you."

"Listen," she said. "I'm on this one-meal-a-day cleansing diet, just lunch—lots of complex carbohydrates—and I haven't had it yet. I'm famished. There's a pasta bar up the block. Would you care to join me?"

"Love to, Julie, but I can't. Thanks, though."

She waited for me to make a move. When I didn't, her face fell.

"Nothing personal," I said. "It's just a bad time."

"Sure," she said, and snapped her head away. As I left I heard her mutter, "All the cute ones are faggots."

At six Milo came by. Despite the fact that he wasn't due back at the station until Monday, he was dressed for work—wilted seersucker suit, wash-and-wear shirt, atrocious tie, desert boots.

"Spent all day detecting," he said, after getting himself a beer and remarking that I was a good boy for restocking my cupboards. "Hollywood Division, the coroner's, Hall of Records, Building and Safety. Your lady doc's a goddam phantom. I'd sure love to know what the hell's going on."

He sat down at the kitchen table. I settled across from him and waited for him to finish the beer.

"It's as if she never was processed through anyone's system," he said. "I had to skulk around at Hollywood, pretend to be looking at something else while I checked for any file on her. Nothing. Not on paper or in the central computer. I couldn't even find out who put the call in the night she died, or who took it. Zilch at the coroner's, too—no autopsy report, no cold-storage log, death certificate, release. I mean, there's cover-up and there's cover-up but this is twilight zone stuff."

He rubbed his hand over his face.

"One of the pathologists," he said, "is a guy Rick knew in med school. Usually I can get him to talk to me off the record, give me results before he writes up the final report, speculate about stuff that he can't put into writing. I thought he'd at least get me a copy of the report. No way. He made a big deal out of showing me there *was* no report, made it clear I shouldn't ask for any favors on this one."

"Same pathologist Del spoke to?"

"No. That was Itatani. I talked to him first, and it was the same thing. The fix has come down hard and heavy on this one. I confess to being intrigued."

"Maybe it wasn't suicide."

"Any reason to think that?"

"She made lots of people angry."

"Such as?"

I told him about the patient seductions, keeping Leslie Weingarden's name out of it.

"Beautiful, Alex. Why didn't you let me know about this in the first place?"

"Confidential source. I can't give you any more details."

"Jesus." He got up, walked around, sat back down. "You ask me to dig you a hole, but won't give me a shovel. Jesus, Alex." He went to get another beer. "It's bad enough being back in Realityville, without spinning my wheels all day."

"I didn't mean to send you on a wild-goose chase."

"Honk honk."

Then he waved his hand. "Nah, who am I kidding—I didn't do it for you. I did it for myself. Trapp. And I still don't think there's any big whodunit here. Ransom killed herself. She was a maladjust—what you just told me corroborates that."

Out on the ledge. I nodded. "Find out anything about the twin sister?"

"*Nada.* Another phantom. No Shirlee Ransom in any of our files or anyone else's. If you came up with the name of that hospital you saw her at, we could search the business transfer and bankruptcy files. But even then, tracing individual patients would be a very long shot."

"I can't come up with it, because I never knew it, Milo. What about checking the Medi-Cal files?"

"You said Ransom was rich. Why would her sister be on Medi-Cal?"

"The *parents* were rich, but that was years ago. Money runs out. Also . . ."

"Also," he said, "with all the lying she did, you don't know what to believe."

I nodded.

"Lie she did, pal. Like about owning the Jalmia house. The place is deeded to a corporation, just like the real estate agent said. A management company named Western Properties that's owned by a holding company that's owned by a savings-and-loan that's owned by the Magna Corporation. I think that's where it ends, but I wouldn't swear to it."

"Magna," I said. "Isn't that Leland Belding's company?"

"Was till he died. No idea who owns it now." He drank beer. "The old basket-case billionaire himself. Now a guy like that you could see putting on a big fix. But he's been buried for . . . what? Fifteen years?"

"Something like that. Wasn't his death disputed?"

"By who? The guy who wrote that hoax book? He killed himself after they exposed it, which is a pretty good indication he had something to be ashamed of. Even the conspiracy freaks didn't believe that one. Anyway, whoever owns it, the corporation lives on—clerk told me it's one of the biggest landowners west of the Mississippi, thousands of parcels. Ransom's house happened to be one of them. With that kind of landlord, you can see why there'd be a quick sale."

He finished his beer, got up to get a third.

"How's your liver?" I asked.

"Peachy. *Mom.*" He made a point of guzzling. "Okay, so where were we? Magna, Medi-Cal files on the sister. All right, I guess it might be worth a try in terms of finding her, though I don't know what the hell finding her's going to tell us. How disabled was she?"

"Very."

"Could she talk?"

"No."

"Terrific." He wiped foam from his lips. "I want to interview vegetables, I'll go to a salad bar. What I *am* going to do is drive up Jalmia and talk to the neighbors. Maybe one of them phoned in the call, knows something about her."

"About her and Trapp?"

"That would be nice."

He went into the living room, turned on the TV, put his feet up, and watched the evening news. Within moments he was asleep. And I was remembering a black-and-white snapshot and thinking, despite what he'd said, about Shirlee Ransom. I went into the library and called Olivia Brickerman.

"Hello, darling," she said, "I just got in and started tending to Prince Albert."

"If I'm catching you in the middle of something—"

"What? Prunes and oat bran is *something*? Just hold on one second and I'll be with you."

When she came back on the line, she said, "There, he's taken care of for the evening."

"How's Al doing?"

"Still the life of the party."

Her husband, a grandmaster and former chess editor for the *Times,* was a white-haired, white-bearded man who looked like an Old Testament prophet and had been known to go for days at a time without talking.

"I keep him around for torrid sex," she said. "So, how are *you,* handsome?"

"Just fine, Olivia. How about yourself? Still enjoying the private sector?"

"Actually, right now I'm feeling pretty abandoned by the private sector. You remember how I got into this hotshot group, don't you? My sister's boy, Steve, the psychiatrist, wanted to rescue me from civil service hell and set me up as benefits coordinator? It was fine for a while, nothing too stimulating, but the pay was good, no winos vomiting all over my desk, and I could walk to the beach during lunch. Then, all of a sudden, Stevie takes a position at some drug-abuse hospital out in *Utah.* He got hooked on skiing; now it's a religion with him. 'Gotta go with the snow, Aunt Livvy.' That's an M.D. talking. Yale. The guy who replaced him is a real yutz, very cold, thinks social workers are a notch below secretaries. We're already having friction. So if you hear I've retired permanently, don't be surprised. Enough about me. How've you been?"

"Fine."

"How's Robin?"

"Terrific," I said. "Keeping busy."

"I'm waiting for an invitation, Alex."

"One of these days."

"One of these days, eh? Just make sure you tie the knot while I'm still functioning and can enjoy it. Want to hear a terrible joke? What's the good thing about Alzheimer's disease?"

"What?"

"You get to meet new people every day. Isn't that *terrible*? The yutz told it to me. You think there was an underlying message?"

"Probably."

"That's what *I* think. The S.O.B."

"Olivia, I need a favor."

"And here I thought you were after my body."

I thought of Olivia's body, which resembled Alfred Hitchcock's, and couldn't help but smile.

"That too," I said.

"Big talk! What do you need, handsome?"

"Do you still have access to the Medi-Cal files?"

"You kidding? We've got Medi-Cal, Medicare, Short-Doyle, Workmen's Comp, CCS, AFDC, FDI, ATD—every file you can imagine, alphabet soup. These guys are serious billers, Alex. They know how to squeeze all the juice out of a claim. The yutz went back to school after his residency, and got an M.B.A."

"I'm trying to locate a former patient. She was disabled, needed chronic care, and was hospitalized at a small rehab place in Glendale—on South Brand. The place is no longer there and I can't remember the name. Ring any bells?"

"Brand Boulevard? No. Lots of places don't exist anymore. Everything's going corporate—these smart boys just sold out to some conglomerate from Minneapolis. If she's totally disabled, that would be ATD. If it's partial and she worked, she could be on FDI."

"ATD," I said. "Could she be on Medi-Cal too?"

"Sure. What's the name of this person?"

"Shirlee Ransom, with two e's. Thirty-four years old, with a birthday in May. May 15, 1953."

"Diagnosis?"

"She had multiple problems. The main diagnoses were probably neurological."

"Probably? I thought she was your patient."

I hesitated. "It's complicated, Olivia."

"I see. You're not getting yourself in trouble again, are you?"

"Nothing like that, Olivia. It's just that there are some confidentiality issues here. I'm sorry I can't get into it and if it's too much of a hassle—"

"Stop being such a Goody Two-shoes. It's not like you're asking me to commit a crime." Pause. "Right?"

"Right."

"Okay, in terms of getting hold of the data, our on-line access is limited to patients treated in California. If your Ms. Ransom is still being treated somewhere in the state, I should be able to get you the information immediately. If she moved out of state I'd have to tap into the master file in Minnesota, and that would take time, maybe even a week. Either way, if she's getting government money, I'll get you an address."

"That simple?"

"Sure, everything's on computer. We're all on someone's list. Some yutz with a giant mainframe has a record of what you and I ate for breakfast this morning, darling."

"Privacy, the last luxury," I said.

"You'd better believe it," she said. "Package it; market it; make a billion."

Friday morning I booked a Saturday flight to San Luis on Sky West. At 9:00 A.M. Larry Daschoff called and told me he'd located a copy of the porn loop.

"I was wrong. Kruse made it—must have been some kind of personal kick. If you still want to see it, I've got an hour and a half between patients," he said. "Noon to one-thirty. Meet me at this place and we'll watch a matinee."

He recited a Beverly Hills address. Turning-over-the-rock time. I felt queasy, unclean.

"D.?"

"I'll meet you there."

The address was on North Crescent Drive, in the Beverly Hills Flats—the pricey prairie stretching from Santa Monica Boulevard to Sunset, and from Doheny west to the Beverly Hilton Hotel. Houses in the Flats range from two-bedroom "tear-downs" that wouldn't stand out in a working-class tract to mansions big enough to corral a politician's ego. The tear-downs go for a million and a half.

Once a quiet, cushy neighborhood of doctors, dentists, and show-business types, the Flats has become a repository for very new, very flashy foreign money of questionable origin. All that easy cash has brought with it a mania for monument-building, unfettered by tradition or taste, and as I drove down Crescent half the structures seemed to be in various phases of construction. The final products would have done Disney proud: Turreted Gray-stone Castle *sans* moat but *cum* tennis court, Mock-Moorish Mini-Mosque, Italianate-Dutch Truffle, Haute Gingerbread Haunted House, Post-Moderne Free-form Fantasy.

Larry's station wagon was parked in front of a pea-green pseudo-French pseudo-Regency pseudo-townhouse with Ramada Inn overtones: glitter-flecked stucco walls, multiple mansards, green-and-gray striped awnings, louver windows, olive trim. The lawn was two squares of ivy, split by a concrete path. From the ivy sprouted whitewashed plaster statuary—naked cherubs, Blind Justice in agony, a copy of the Pietà, a carp taking flight. In the driveway was a fleet of cars: hot-pink '57 T-bird; two Rolls-Royce Silver Shadows, one silver, one gold; and a maroon Lincoln Town Car with red vinyl top and a famous designer's logo on its smoked windows.

I parked. Larry waved and got out of the Chevy. He saw me looking at the house and said, "Pretty recherché, huh, D.?"

"Who *are* these people?"

"Their name is Fontaine—Gordon and Chantal. They made their money in patio furniture somewhere out in the Midwest—the plastic strap and tubular aluminum stuff. Sold out for a fortune several years ago, moved to B.H., and retired. They give lots to charity, distribute Thanksgiving turkeys on Skid Row, come across like benevolent grandparents—which they are. But they love porn. Damn near worship it. They're the private donors I told you about, the ones who funded Kruse's research."

"Good simple folk, huh?"

"They really are, D. Not into S and M or kiddie stuff. Just good old-fashioned straight sex on celluloid—they claim it rejuvenated their marriage, can get downright evangelical about it. When Kruse was setting up his research, he heard about them and tapped them for funding. They were so happy someone was going to finally educate the world about the therapeutic benefits of erotica that they coughed up without a fuss—must have handed over a couple of hundred grand. You can imagine how they felt when he changed his tune and started playing to the pro-censorship crowd. And they're still steamed. When I called, Gordon remembered me as Kruse's R.A. and let me know that as far as they're concerned, Kruse is the scum of the earth. I mean he really *catharted.* When he stopped to take a breath, I made it clear I was no great Kruse fan myself, and told him what we were after. He calmed down and said sure, come on over. I think the idea of helping us really jazzed him. Like all fanatics, they love to show off."

"What reason did you give him for wanting to see the film?"

"That the star was dead, we were old friends, and we wanted to remember her for *everything* she'd done. They'd read about it, thought it would be a dandy memorial."

The grimy, Peeping Tom feeling returned.

Larry read my face, said, "Cold feet?"

"It seems . . . ghoulish."

"Sure it's ghoulish. So are eulogies. If you want to call it off, I'll go in there and tell them."

"No," I said. "Let's do it."

"Try not to look so tortured," he said. "One of the ways I gained entree was telling them you were sympatico to their hobby."

I crossed my eyes, leered, and did some heavy breathing. "How's that?"

"Oscar caliber."

We reached the front door, a solid slab painted glossy olive.

"Behind the green door," said Larry. "Very subtle."

"You're sure they have the loop?"

"Gordon said definitely. He also said they had something else we might be interested in."

He rang the bell and it chimed out the first few notes of "Bolero," then swung open. A Filipino maid in a white uniform stood in the doorway, petite, thirtyish, bespectacled, her hair in a bun.

"Yes?"

"Dr. Daschoff and Dr. Delaware to see Mr. and Mrs. Fontaine."

"Yes," said the maid. "Come in."

We stepped into a two-story rotunda with a pastoral mural: blue skies, green grass, fluffy sheep, hay bales, a shepherd playing the pipes in the shade of a spreading sycamore.

In front of all that agrarian bliss sat a naked woman in a deck chair—fat, middle-aged, gray-haired, lumpy legs. She held a pencil in one hand, a crossword puzzle book in the other, didn't acknowledge our entry.

The maid saw us staring, rapped her knuckles on the gray head.

Hollow.

Sculpture.

"An original Lombardo," she said. "Very expensive. Like that." She pointed upward. Dangling from the ceiling was what appeared to be a Calder mobile. Christmas bulbs had been laced around it—a do-it-yourself chandelier.

"Lots of money," said the maid.

Directly in front of us was an emerald-carpeted staircase that spiraled to the left. The space under the stairs terminated at a high Chinese screen. The other rooms were also blocked by screens.

"Come," said the maid. She turned. Her uniform was backless

and cut low, past the gluteal cleft. Lots of naked brown skin. Larry and I looked at each other. He shrugged.

She unfolded part of the Chinese screen, led us through twenty feet and yet another partition. Her walk took on a sashay and we followed her midway down the hall to a green metal door. On the wall was a keyhole and a key pad. She cupped one hand with the other, punched in a five-digit code, inserted a key, turned it, and the door slid open. We entered a small elevator with padded, quilted walls of gold brocade hung with ivory miniatures—scenes from the *Kama Sutra*. A button-press and we descended. The three of us stood shoulder to shoulder. The maid smelled of baby powder. She looked bored.

We stepped out into a small, dark anteroom and trailed her through japanned double doors.

On the other side was a huge, high-walled, windowless room—at least three thousand square feet paneled in black lacquered wood, silent and cool and barely lit.

As my eyes accommodated to the darkness, I was able to make out details: brass-grilled bookcases, reading tables, card catalogues, display cases, and library ladders, all in the same ebonized finish. Above us, a flat ceiling of black cork. Below, dark, carpeted floors. The only light came from green-shaded banker's lamps on the tables. I heard the hum of air conditioning. Saw ceiling sprinklers, smoke alarms. A large barometer on one wall.

A room designed to house treasures.

"Thank you, Rosa," said a nasal male voice from across the room. I squinted and saw human outlines: a man and woman sitting side by side at one of the far tables.

The maid bowed, turned, and wiggled away. When she was gone, the same voice said, "Little Rosie Ramos—she was a real talent in the sixties. *PX Mamas. Ginza Girls. Choose One From Column X.*"

"Good help's so hard to find," Larry whispered. Out loud he said, "Hello, people."

The couple stood and walked toward us. At ten feet away, their faces took on clarity, like cinema characters emerging from a dissolve.

The man was older than I'd expected—seventy or close to it, short and portly, with thick, straight white hair combed back and a jowly Xavier Cugat face. He wore black-framed eyeglasses, a white guayabera shirt over brown slacks, and tan loafers.

Even shoeless, the woman was half a foot taller. Late fifties, slender and fine-featured, with an elegant carriage, poodle-cut red hair with a curl that looked natural, and the kind of fair, freckled skin that bruises easily. Her dress was lime-colored Thai silk with a dragon print and mandarin collar. She wore apple jade jewelry, gauzy black stockings, and black ballet slippers.

"Thanks for seeing us," said Larry.

"Our pleasure, Larry," said the man. "Been a long time. Excuse me, it's *Doctor* Daschoff now, isn't it?"

"Ph.D.," said Larry. "Piled higher and deeper."

"No, no," said the man, wagging his finger. "You earned it—be proud." He shook Larry's hand. "Lots of therapists staking out L.A. You doing okay?"

"Oh, Gordie, don't be so direct," said the woman.

"I'm doing fine, Gordon," said Larry. Turning to her: "Hello, Chantal. Long time."

She curtsied and extended her hand. "Lawrence."

"This is Dr. Alex Delaware, an old friend and colleague. Alex, Chantal and Gordon Fontaine."

"Alex," said Chantal, curtsying again. "Charmed." She took my hand in both of hers. Her skin was hot and soft and moist. She had large hazel eyes and a jawline that had been tucked tight. Her makeup was thick, almost chalky, but couldn't conceal the wrinkles. And there was pain in the eyes—she'd been a knockout once, and was still getting used to thinking of herself in the past tense.

"Pleased to meet you, Chantal."

She squeezed my hand and released it. Her husband looked me over and said, "You've got a photogenic face, Doctor. Ever act?"

"No."

"I only ask because it seems everyone in L.A. has acted at one time or another." To his wife: "A good-looking boy, honey." He put his arm around her shoulder. "Your type, wouldn't you say?"

Chantal gave a cold smile.

Gordon told me: "She has a thing for men with curly hair." Running one hand over his own straight coiffure, he lifted it and revealed a bare scalp. "The way mine used to be. Right, honey?"

He put the hairpiece down and patted it into place. "So, did Larry tell you about our little collection?"

"Only in general terms."

He nodded. "You know what they say about the acquisition of art being an art itself? Now, that's pure bunkum, but it *does* take a certain determination and ... *panache* to acquire meaningfully, and we've worked like the dickens to do just that." He spread his arms as if blessing the room. "What you see here took two decades and I-won't-tell-you-how-many dollars to put together."

I knew my line: "I'd love to see it."

The next half hour was spent on a tour of the black room.

Every genre of pornography was represented, in astounding quantity and variety, catalogued and labeled with Smithsonian precision. Gordon Fontaine jounced along, guiding with fervor, using a hand-held remote-control module to switch lights on and off, lock and unlock cabinets. His wife hung back, insinuating herself between Larry and me, smiling a lot.

"Observe." Gordon rolled open a print drawer and untied several portfolios of erotic lithographs, recognizable without reading the signatures: Dali, Beardsley, Grosz, Picasso.

We moved on to an alarm-equipped glass case housing an old English manuscript handwritten on parchment and illuminated with copulating peasants and cavorting farm animals.

"Pre-Guttenberg," said Gordon. "Chaucerian apocrypha. Chaucer was a highly sexual writer. They never teach you that in high school."

Other drawers were filled with erotic sketches from Renaissance Italy, and Japanese art—watercolors of kimonoed courtesans entwined with stoic, top-knotted men lugging exaggerated sexual equipment.

"Overcompensation," said Chantal. She nudged my arm.

We were shown displays of fertility talismans, erotic woodblocks, marital aids, antique lingerie. After a while my eyes began to blur.

"Those were used by Brenda Allen's girls," said Gordon, pointing to a set of yellowed silk undergarments. "And those red ones are from the bordello in New Orleans where Scott Joplin played piano." He stroked the glass. "If only they could talk, eh?"

"We have edible ones, too," said Chantal. "Over there, in a refrigerated case."

We swept past still more sexual devices, collections of obscene party gags and novelties, raunchy record albums, and what Gordon proclaimed to be "the world's finest collection of dildoes. Six hundred and fifty-three pieces, gentlemen, from all over the world. Every medium imaginable, from monkeypod wood to scrimshawed ivory."

A hand brushed my rear. I did a quarter turn, saw Chantal smile.

"Our *bibliothèque*," said Gordon, pointing to a wall of bookshelves.

Oversized, gilt-edged treatises bound in leather; hard- and softcover contemporary books; thousands of magazines, some of them still shrink-wrapped and sealed, with covers that left nothing to the imagination—grandly tumescent men, semen-bathed, wide-eyed women. Titles like *Double-Fucked Stewardess* and *Orifice Supplies.*

The Fontaines seemed to know many of the models personally and discussed them with near-parental concern. ("That's Johnny Strong—he retired a couple of years ago and is selling securities up in Tiburon." "Look, Gordie, there's Laurie Ruth Sloan, the Milk Queen herself." To me: "She married money. Her husband's a real fascist and won't let her express herself anymore.")

I tried to look sympathetic.

"Onward," said Gordon, "to the *pièce de résistance.*"

A click of the remote module caused one of the bookcases to slide back. Behind it was a matte-black door that swung open at Gordon's prod. Inside was a large vault/screening room. Two walls were lined with racks of film reels in metal canisters and videocassettes. Three rows of black leather easy chairs, three chairs per row. Mounted on the rear wall was a gleaming array of projection equipment.

"These are the cleanest prints you'll ever see," said Gordon. "Every important explicit film ever made, all converted to videotape duplicate. We're also trying really hard to preserve the originals. Our restorer is top-notch—twenty years at one of the studio archives, another ten at the American Film Institute. And our curator is a well-known film critic who must remain unnamed"—he cleared his throat—"due to lack of spine."

"Impressive," I said.

"We hope," said Chantal, "to donate it to a major university. One day."

"What she means by 'one day,'" said Gordon, "is after I'm gone."

"Oh, hush, Gordie. I'm going first."

"No way, hon. You're not leaving me alone with my memories and my hand." He waved a fleshy palm.

"Oh, go on, Gordie. You'll do just fine for yourself."

Gordon patted her hand. The two of them exchanged affectionate glances.

Larry looked at his watch.

"Of course," said Gordon. "I'm retired—I've forgotten about time pressure. You wanted to see Shawna's loop."

"Shawna who?" I asked.

"Shawna Blue. That's the name Pretty Sharon used on the loop."

"We always called her Pretty Sharon," said Chantal, "because she was such a lovely thing, virtually flawless. Shawna Blue was her *nom d'amour.*" She shook her head. "How sad that she's gone—and a suicide."

"Do you find that surprising?" I asked.

"Of course," she said. "To destroy oneself—how awful."

"How well did you know her?"

"Not well at all. I believe we just met her once—am I right, Gordie?"

"Just once."

"How many films did she make?"

"Same answer," said Gordon. "Just one, and it wasn't a commercial endeavor. It was supposed to be for educational purposes."

The way he said *supposed* made me say, "Sounds like you have your doubts."

He frowned. "We put up the money based on its being educational. The actual production was handled by that first-class cockroach P. P. Kruse."

"Peepee," said Chantal. "How apropos."

"He claimed it was part of his research," said Gordon. "Told us that one of his students had agreed to act in an erotic film as part of her course work."

"When was this?"

"Seventy-four," he said. "October or November."

Not long after Sharon began grad school. The bastard had been a fast worker.

"It was supposed to be part of her research," said Gordon. "Now we weren't born yesterday, we thought that was pretty thin, but Kruse assured us it was all on the up-and-up, showed us forms approved by the University. He even brought Sharon to meet us, here in our home—that was the one time. She seemed very vivacious, very Marilyn—down to the hair. She verified it was all part of her course work."

"Marilyn," I said. "As in Monroe."

"Yes. She projected that same innocent yet erotic quality."

"She was a blonde?"

"Platinum," said Chantal. "Like sunshine on clear water."

"The Sharon we knew had black hair," said Larry.

"Well, I don't know about that," said Gordon. "Kruse may have been lying about who she was. He lied about everything else. We opened our home to him, gave him free access to our collection, and he turned around and used it to pander to the bluenoses."

"He gave a speech in front of church groups," said Chantal, stamping her foot. "Stood there and said terrible things about us—called us perverted, sexist. If there's one man who isn't sexist it's my Gordie.

"He didn't use our names," added Chantal, "but we knew he was referring to us."

"His own wife was a porn star," I said. "How'd he explain that to the church groups?"

"Suzy?" said Gordon. "I wouldn't call her a star—adequate style, but strictly second drawer. I suppose he could always claim he saved her from a life of sin. But he probably never had to explain. People have short memories. After she married him, Suzy stopped working, disappeared from view. He probably turned her into a docile little hausfrau—he's the type, you know. Obsessed with power."

It echoed something Larry had said at the party. *Power junkie.*

"Onward," said Gordon. He went to the back of the room and began fiddling with the projection equipment.

"Kruse has just been appointed head of the psychology department," I said.

"Scandalous," said Chantal. "You'd think someone would know better."

"You'd think," I said.

"All cued," Gordon called from the back. "Everyone get comfortable."

Larry and I took the front end seats; Chantal got between us. The room went black; the screen, dead white.

"Checkup," he announced. "Starring the late Miss Shawna Blue and the late Mr. Michael Starbuck."

The screen filled with dancing lint followed by flickering count-down numbers. I sat rigid, holding my breath, told myself I'd been an idiot to come. Then, black-and-white images floated in front of me and I lost myself in them.

There was no sound track, only the whir of projection breaking the silence. Lettering that resembled white typescript over a grainy black background proclaimed:

CHECKUP

STARRING

SHAWNA BLUE

MICKEY STARBUCK

A CREATIVE IMAGE ASSOC. PRODUCTION

Creative Image. A name on a door. Kruse's neighbors in the Sunset Boulevard office. Not a neighbor after all, but the two faces of Dr. K. . . .

DIRECTED BY

PIERRE LE VOYEUR

A jumpy black-and-white sweep of a doctor's examining room—the old-fashioned kind, with enameled fixtures, wooden examining table, eye chart, chintz drapes, a square of six framed diplomas on the wall.

The door opened. A woman walked in.

The camera pursued her, spending a long time on the sway of her buttocks.

Young and beautiful and well-endowed, with long, wavy platinum-blond hair. She wore a clinging, low-cut jersey dress that barely contained her.

Black-and-white film, but I knew the dress was flame-colored.

A flickering close-up magnified a beautiful, pouting face.

Sharon's face. Despite the wig, no doubt about it.

I felt sick and regretful. Stared at the screen like a child at a squashed bug.

The camera pulled back. Sharon pirouetted, gazed into the mirror, and fluffed her hair. Then a quick zoom—more pout, big eyes gazing out at the viewer.

Boring into mine.

A full body shot, shift to buttocks, a series of quick bounces from mouth to hands to bosom.

Shoddy, the cheapest of the cheap. But perversely magical—*she* had come back to life, was up there, smiling and beckoning—immortality conceived in light and shadow. I had to restrain myself from reaching out to touch her. Wanted, suddenly, to yank her out of the screen, to pull her back in time. Rescue her.

I gripped my armrests. My heart was pounding, filling my ears like a winter tide.

She stretched languidly and licked her lips. The camera got so close her tongue resembled some kind of giant sea slug. More close-ups: wet white teeth. A purposeful bend forward, flashing cleavage. Moon-cratered nipplescape. Hands stroking breasts, pinching.

She was twisting, exhibiting, clearly enjoying center stage.

Keep it bright. I want to see it. See everything.

I thought of angled mirrors, started sweating. Finally, concentrating on the choppiness and relentless zooming helped restore her to something two-dimensional.

I exhaled, closed my eyes, determined to maintain a sense of detachment. Before my breath had been totally expelled, something dropped on my knee and settled there. Chantal's hand. I looked at her out of the corner of my eye. She stared straight ahead, mouth slightly parted.

I did nothing, hoped she wouldn't explore. Let my eyes settle back on the screen.

Sharon was performing a slow, sinuous striptease, peeling down to black garter belt, mesh stockings, and high-heeled shoes—a Frederick's of Hollywood parody—touching herself, bending, spreading, and kneading, playing for the camera.

I watched her hands move. *Felt them.*

But something was wrong. Something about the hands—off-kilter.

The more I tried to figure out what it was, the further it receded: Chinese finger-puzzle time. I stopped trying, told myself it would come to me.

The camera got gynecologic, moved upward, inch by inch.

Sharon, on the examining table now, fondled herself, looked down at her crotch.

The camera swung to the doorknob as it rotated. The door opened. A tall, dark, broad-shouldered man walked in carrying a clipboard. Late thirties, long white coat, headlamp and stethoscope. A narrow, hungry face—down-slanted eyes, broken nose, thin wide lips, five o'clock shadow. The eyes were jumpy, those of a hustler on full burn. He'd greased his hair to shoe-polish sheen and parted it in the center. A pencil-line mustache traveled the length of his upper lip.

Classic Gigolo meets Dumb Blonde.

He stared at Sharon, raised his eyebrows, mugged for the camera.

She pointed to her crotch, gave a pained expression.

Scratching his head, he consulted his clipboard, then put it down and removed the stethoscope. He stood over her, bent his knees, and put his head between her legs, poking, probing. Looked up, shrugged.

She winked at the camera, pushed his head down, writhed on cue.

He came up, pretended to be gasping for breath. She pushed him down again. The rest was predictable—close-up of his trousered erection, she forcing him down, sucking the fingers of one of her hands.

She pushed him off, worked his zipper. His pants fell to his ankles. She removed the coat. He was shirtless, wore only a tie. She pulled the tie until he hovered. Took him orally, wide-eyed and gulping.

As he got up on the table and mounted her, Chantal's fingers began spider-walking up my thigh. I placed my hand over them, preventing further progress, gave a friendly squeeze, and deposited them gently in her lap. She made no sound, didn't move a muscle.

Comically rapid shifts in positions. Close-ups of both their faces, contorted. He saying something—cuing her—a series of rapid thrusts, withdrawal, the milky proof of climax flying through the air.

She retrieved some from her belly, licked her fingers. Winked at the camera again.

Blank screen.

A checkup turned carnal. Follow-up visits . . .

I felt suffocated, angry. Sad.

The room stayed mercifully dark.

"Well," said Gordon finally, "there it is."

Chantal got up fast, smoothed her dress. "Excuse me, I have something to attend to."

"Everything all right, hon?"

"Just fine, dearie." She kissed his cheek, curtsied, and said, "Nice to see you again, Lawrence. Nice meeting you, Dr. Delaware." She left the vault.

"The late Mickey Starbuck," I said. "How'd he die?"

Gordon was still staring at his wife's exit route. I had to repeat the question.

"Cocaine overdose, several years ago. Poor Mickey wanted to break into straight films but couldn't—there's terrible discrimination against explicit stars. He ended up driving a cab. A sensitive soul, really a fine young man."

"Two actors, two suicides by overdose," said Larry. "Sounds like a jinx."

"Nonsense," said Gordon sharply. "Explicit films are like any other aspect of show business. Fragile egos, instability, big ups, big downs. Some people can't cope."

"The production company?" I said. "Creative Image Associates—a shadow for Kruse?"

Gordon nodded. "Protection. Foolish of me not to smell something rotten when he set it up—if he'd really gotten University approval, why the need for a shadow? When I saw the finished product I knew precisely what he'd done, but I didn't call him on it—he was the doctor, the expert. At the time I thought he was brilliant, visionary. I figured he had a reason."

"What had he done?"

"Sit back down and I'll show you." He returned to the rear of the vault, the room returned to darkness, and another movie came on the screen.

This one had no title, no actors' credits, just grainy, jumpy action, the camera work even more amateurish than the first, but clearly its inspiration.

The setting: a doctor's office, same kind of furniture, same square of framed diplomas.

The stars: a gorgeous woman with wavy blond hair, long-legged, stacked, but several inches shorter than Sharon, the bones smaller, the face slightly fuller. Similar enough to be Sharon's twin.

Twin. Shirlee. No, that was impossible. The Shirlee I'd met had been crippled in childhood. . . .

If Sharon had told the truth.

Big if.

Film number two was barreling along at a Keystone Kops pace: striptease, hair-fluffing, a tall dark man entering through the door.

Close-up on him: fortyish, shiny hair, pencil mustache. White coat, stethoscope, clipboard.

A crude resemblance to the late Mickey Starbuck, but nothing striking.

And no leer. This doctor seemed to be showing genuine surprise at the sight of the naked blonde lying spread-legged on the table.

No shifts of context, either. A stationary camera, full-view long shots and occasional close-ups that seemed less concerned with eroticism than identification of the actors.

Of him.

The blonde got up and rubbed herself against the doctor. Showed herself, pinched her nipples, stood on tiptoes and licked his neck.

He shook his head, pointed to his watch.

She held him to her, ground her hips.

He started to pull away again, then loosened—like something thawing. Allowed himself to be caressed.

She moved in.

Then the same progression as in Sharon's film.

But different.

Because this one wasn't staged. This doctor wasn't acting.

No mugging for the camera, because he didn't know there *was* a camera.

She knelt before him.

The camera concentrated on his face.

Real passion.

They were up on the table.

The camera concentrated on his face.

He was lost in her, she in control.

The camera concentrated on his face.

Hidden camera.

A documentary—real peep-through-the-window stuff. I closed my eyes, thought of something else.

The blond beauty working like a pro.

Sharon's twin—but from another time. His Alfalfa hairdo and pencil mustache authentic.

Contemporary . . .

"When was this made?" I called back to Gordon.

"1952," he said in a choked voice, as if resenting the interruption.

The doctor was bucking and gritting his teeth. The blond woman waved him like a flag. Winked at the camera.

Blank screen.

"Sharon's mother," I said.

"I can't prove it," said Gordon, returning to the front of the room. "But with that resemblance she'd have to be, wouldn't she? When I met Pretty Sharon, she reminded me of someone. I couldn't remember who, hadn't seen this film in a long time—years. It's quite rare, a real collector's item. We try to avoid exposing it to unnecessary wear and tear."

He stopped, expectant.

"We appreciate your showing it to us, Mr. Fontaine."

"My pleasure. When I saw Kruse's finished product, I realized who she'd reminded me of. Kruse must have realized it too. We gave him full access to our entire collection, and he spent a lot of time in the vault. He discovered Linda's film and set out to ape it. Mother and daughter—an intriguing theme, but he should have been truthful about it."

"Did Sharon know about the first film?"

"That I can't tell you. As I said, I only met her once."

"Linda who?" said Larry.

"Linda Lanier. She was an actress—or at least wanted to be. One of the pretty young things who flooded Hollywood after the war—still do, for that matter. I believe she got a contract at one of the studios, but she never actually worked."

"Wrong kind of talent?" said Larry.

"Who knows? She didn't stick around long enough for anyone to find out. That particular studio was owned by Leland Belding. She ended up being one of his party girls."

"The basket-case billionaire," I said. "The Magna Corporation."

"You're both too young to remember," said Gordon, "but he was quite a guy in his day, Renaissance man—aerospace, armaments, shipping, mining. And the movies. He invented a camera that they still use today. And a no-shimmy girdle based on aircraft design."

I said, "By party girl, you mean hooker?"

"No, no, more like hostesses. He used to throw lots of parties. Owning the studio gave him easy access to beautiful girls and he hired them as hostesses. The bluenoses tried to make a thing of it, but they never could prove a thing."

"What about the doctor?"

"He was a *real* doctor. The film was real, too—the *vérité* is almost overwhelming, isn't it? This is the original print, the only remaining one."

"Where'd you get it?"

He shook his head. "Trade secret, Doctor. Suffice it to say I've had it for a long time and it cost me plenty. I could make copies and recoup all my original investment plus, but that would open the floodgates for multiple reproduction and dilute the historical value of the original, and I refuse to bend my principles."

"What was the name of the doctor?"

"I don't know."

A lie. Fanatic and voyeur that he was, he wouldn't have rested before gleaning every last detail about his treasure.

I said, "The film was part of a blackmail ploy, wasn't it? The doctor was the victim."

"Ridiculous."

"What else, then? He didn't know he was being filmed."

"Hollywood practical joke," he said. "Old Errol Flynn bored peepholes in the walls of his bathrooms, used a hidden camera to film his lady friends on the commode."

"Tacky," muttered Larry.

Gordon's face darkened. "I'm sorry you feel that way, Dr. Daschoff. It was all in the spirit of fun."

Larry said nothing

"Never mind," said Gordon, walking to the door of the vault and holding it open. "I'm sure you gentlemen have to get back to your patients."

He ushered us through the black room and to the elevator.

"What happened to Linda Lanier?" I asked.

"Who knows?" he said. Then he began to prattle about the relationship between cultural norms and erotica, and continued the lecture until we left his house.

17

"Never saw him like that," said Larry, when we were back on the sidewalk.

"His belief system's under assault," I said. "He likes to think of his hobby as something benign, like stamp collecting. But you don't use stamps to blackmail."

He shook his head. "It was weird enough watching Sharon, but the second one was something else—really evil. That poor guy humping away, all the while he's making his cinematic debut."

Another shake of the head. "Blackmail. Shit, this is getting curiouser and curiouser, D. To make things worse I got a call this morning from an old fraternity brother. A guy Brenda and I both knew in college, also ended up a shrink—behavior therapist, had a huge practice out in Phoenix. Screwed his secretary, she gave him the clap; he passed it on to his wife and *she* kicked him out, started bad-mouthing him all around town, destroyed the practice. Couple of days ago he walks into the house, blows her brains out and then his own. Doesn't say much for our profession, does it? Know how to take tests, write a dissertation, and you graduate. Send in your check, renew your license. No one checks for psychopathology."

"Maybe the psychoanalysts have the right idea," I said. "Making their candidates go through long-term analysis before being allowed to qualify."

"Come on, D. Think of all the analysts you've met who are total weirdos. And all of us had our training therapies. Someone can be therapized up the ying-yang and still be a rotten human being. Who knows, maybe we're suspect from the beginning. I just read this article, study of psychologists' and psychiatrists' family histories. A whole bunch of us had severely depressed mothers."

"I read it too."

"Sure fits me," he said. "How about you?"

I nodded.

"You see, that's it. As kids we had to take care of our mommies so we learned to be hyper-adult. Then, when we grow up we look for other depressives to take care of—that in itself isn't bad, if we've worked through all our personal shit. But if we don't . . . Nah, there ain't no simple answer, D. Let the buyer goddam beware."

I walked him to the station wagon. "Larry, could Sharon's film have had anything to do with Kruse's research?"

"Doubt it."

"What about the University forms Gordon saw?"

"Bogus," he said. "And illogical—even back then, no university would put itself out on a limb like that. Kruse showed him some piece of bullshit; Gordon believed it because he wanted to. Besides, Kruse never bothered to use any forms for anything—he and the department had a mutual apathy going. They took the bread he brought in, gave him a basement lab no one was using, didn't want to know what he was up to. Compared to all the deception experiments the social psychologists were doing, his stuff seemed benign." He stopped, looked troubled. "What the hell was he after, filming her like that?"

"Who knows? The only thing I can think of is some sort of radical therapy. Working through the sins of the mothers."

He thought about that. "Yeah. Maybe. That kind of weirdness would be right up his alley: total control of the patient's life, marathon sessions, regression hypnosis—break down the defenses. If in the process she found out that her mom was a bimbo, he'd have her vulnerable."

"What if *she* found out because Kruse told her?" I said. "He had access to the Fontaines' film vault, could have been looking through it and discovered Linda Lanier's loop. Her resemblance to Sharon was striking—he put it together. Then he researched Lanier, learned some nasty details—maybe even about blackmail. Sharon told me some bogus story about rich, sophisticated parents. Looks like she was hiding from reality. Kruse could have shown her the film when she was under hypnosis, used it to break her down completely, put her completely under his control. Then he suggested a way she could work through the trauma by making a film of her own— cathartic role-playing."

"Fucking bastard," he said. Then: "She was a smart girl, D. How could she fall for it?"

"Smart, but screwed up—those borderline characteristics we talked about. And you yourself told me how persuasive Kruse was— he had radical libbers believing whipping his wife was something noble. Those were women he knew *casually.* He was Sharon's supervisor, *her* training therapist, and she stayed with him after she got her doctorate, as his assistant. I never really understood the relationship between them, but I knew it was intense. The film was made soon after she came to L.A., which means he was monkeying with her head right from the beginning."

"Or maybe," he said, "he knew her from before."

"Maybe."

"Therapy plus cum shots." He looked grim. "Our esteemed department head's a real prince."

"Do you think the University should be apprised of his methods?"

"A little fling at whistle-blowing?" He worried his mustache. "Brenda tells me the slander laws are pretty damned convoluted. Kruse's got money—he could keep us in court for years—and no matter how it turned out, we'd be raked over in the process. Are you ready for something like that?"

"I don't know."

"Well, I'm not. Let the University do its own damned detective work."

"Let the buyer beware?"

He put his hand on the door handle, looked peeved. "Look, D., you're semi-retired, your own man, got plenty of time to run around looking at dirty movies. I've got five kids, a wife in law school, high blood pressure, and a mortgage to match. Forgive me for not wanting to play Crusader Rabbit, okay?"

"Okay," I said. "Take it easy."

"I try to, believe me, but reality keeps squeezing my nuts."

He got in the car.

"If I do anything," I said, "I'll keep you out of it."

"Good idea." He looked at his watch. "Got to roll. Can't say it's been a yuck a minute but it certainly has been different."

Two films. Another link to a dead billionaire.

And one amateur movie producer, masquerading as a healer.

I drove home determined to reach Kruse before I left for San Luis the next day. Determined the bastard was going to talk to me, one way or the other. I tried his offices again. Still no answer. I was about to phone his University exchange when the phone rang.

"Hello."

"Dr. Delaware, please."

"Speaking."

"Dr. Delaware, this is Dr. Leslie Weingarden. I've got a crisis on my hands that I thought you might be able to help me with."

She sounded tightly strung.

"What kind of crisis, Dr. Weingarden?"

"Related to our previous conversation," she said. "I'd rather not discuss it over the phone. Could you see your way clear to come down to my office sometime this afternoon?"

"Give me twenty minutes," I said.

I changed shirts, put on a tie, called my service, and was told Olivia Brickerman had called.

"She said to tell you the system's down, Doctor," said the operator. "Whatever that means. She'll try to get you what you want as soon as it's up again."

I thanked her and hung up. Back to Beverly Hills.

Two women sat reading in the waiting room. Neither appeared in good humor.

I rapped the glass partition. The receptionist came around and let me in. We passed several examining rooms, stopped at a door marked PRIVATE, and knocked. A second later it opened partially and Leslie slipped out. She was perfectly made up, every hair in place, but she looked haggard and frightened.

"How many patients out there, Bea?"

"Just a couple. But one's a nagger."

"Tell them an emergency came up—I'll be with them soon as I can."

Bea left. Leslie said, "Let's get away from the door."

We moved down the hall. She leaned against the wall, blew out her breath, knitted her hands.

"Wish I still smoked," she said. "Thanks for coming."

"What's up?"

"D.J. Rasmussen. He's dead. His girlfriend's inside, totally coming apart. She walked in half an hour ago, just as I got back from lunch, and broke down in the waiting room. I hustled her in here fast, before the other patients arrived, and I've been tied up with her ever since. I gave her a shot of IM Valium—ten milligrams. That seemed to calm her down for a while but then she started falling apart again. Still want to help? Think you can do anything by talking to her?"

"How did he die?"

"Carmen—the girlfriend—said he'd been drinking heavily for the last few days. More heavily than usual. She was frightened he was going to get rough with her, because that was his usual pattern. But instead he got weepy, deeply depressed, started talking about what a bad person he was, all the terrible things he'd done. She tried to talk to him but he just got lower, kept drinking. Early this morning she woke up and found a thousand dollars in cash on his pillow, along with some personal snapshots of the two of them and a note that said 'Goodbye.' She jumped out of bed, saw he'd taken his guns out of the cabinet but couldn't find him. Then she heard his truck starting and ran out after him. The truck was full of guns and he'd already started drinking—she could smell it on him. She tried to stop him but he shoved her away and drove off. She got in her car and followed him. They live out in Newhall—apparently there are lots of canyons and winding roads there. He was speeding and weaving, going over ninety. She couldn't keep up and missed a turn. But she retraced, stayed with him, and saw him go over an embankment. The truck rolled around, landed at the bottom, and exploded. Just like TV, she said."

Leslie chewed on a fingernail.

"Do the police know about this?"

"Yes. She called them. They asked her a few questions, took her statement, and told her to go home. According to her, they didn't seem very concerned. D.J. was known locally as a troublemaker, history of driving under the influence. She claims she heard one of them mutter, 'Fucking streets are safer now.' That's all I know. Can you help?"

"I'll try."

We entered her private office—small, book-lined, furnished with a pine writing desk and two chairs, decorated with cute posters, plants, souvenir mugs, photo cubes. In one of the chairs sat a chubby young woman with a poor complexion. She wore a white blousy shift, brown stretch pants, and flat sandals. Her hair was long and black, blond-streaked and disheveled; her eyes, red-rimmed and puffy. When she saw me she turned away and buried her face in her hands.

Leslie said, "Carmen, this is Dr. Delaware. Dr. Delaware, Carmen Seeber."

I sat in the other chair. "Hi, Carmen."

"Carmen, Dr. Delaware's a psychologist. You can talk to him."

And with that, Leslie left the room.

The young woman kept her face hidden, didn't move or speak. After a while, I said, "Dr. Weingarden told me about D.J. I'm very sorry."

She started to sob, humped shoulders heaving.

"Is there anything I can do for you, Carmen? Anything you need?"

More sobs.

"I met D.J. once," I said. "He seemed a very troubled person."

A rush of tears.

"It must have been hard for you, living with him, all the drinking. But even so, you miss him terribly. It's hard to believe he's gone."

She began swaying, clutching her face.

"Oh, God!" she cried out. "Oh, God! Oh, God, help me! Oh, God!"

I patted her shoulder. She shuddered but didn't move away.

We sat that way for a while, she calling out for divine help, me absorbing her grief, feeding her small bites of empathy. Providing tissues and a cup of water, telling her none of it was her fault, that she'd done the best she could, no one could have done better. That it was okay to feel, okay to hurt.

Finally she looked up, wiped her nose, and said, "You're a nice man."

"Thank you."

"My papa was a nice man. He ya know died."

"I'm sorry."

"He left a long time ago, when I was in ya know kindergarten. I came home with stuff we made for Thanksgiving—ya know paper turkeys and Pilgrim hats—and I saw them take him away in the ambulance."

Silence.

"How old are you, Carmen?"

"Twenty."

"You've dealt with a lot in twenty years."

She smiled. "I guess so. And now Danny. He was ya know nice, too, even though he was a mean one when he drank. But deep down, nice. He didn't ya know give me no hassles, took me places, got me ya know all kinds of stuff."

"How long did you know each other?"

She thought. " 'Bout two years. I was driving this catering

truck—ya know, the roach wagon. Used to drive by all these ya know construction sites and Danny was working at one, framing."

I nodded encouragement.

"He liked burritos," she said. "Ya know meat and potato but no beans—beans made him toot which made him ya know mean. I thought he was kinda cute so I gave him freebies, the boss never knew. Then we started ya know living together."

She gazed at me, childlike.

I smiled.

"I never, ever thought he'd really ya know do it."

"Kill himself?"

She bobbed her head. Tears ran down her pimpled cheeks.

"Had he talked about suicide, before?"

"When he drank and got all p.o.'d, ya know, he'd go on about how ya know life sucked, it was better to be dead, ya know, he was gonna do it some day, tell everyone the f-word off. Then when he hurt his back—ya know the pain, out of work—he was real low. But I never thought . . ." She broke down again.

"There was no way to know, Carmen. When a person makes up his mind to kill himself, there's no way to stop him."

"Yeah," she said, between gulps of air. "Ya couldn't stop Danny when he made his mind up, that's fer sure. He was a real hardbutt, real ya know stubborn. I tried to stop him this morning but he just kept going, like he wasn't ya know hearing me, just all juiced and ya know shootin' ahead like a bat out of . . . hell."

"Dr. Weingarden said he talked about some bad things he'd done."

She nodded. "He was pretty broke up. Said he was a ya know grievous sinner."

"Do you know what he was broken up about?"

Shrug. "He used to ya know get in fights, beat people up in bars—nothing really heavy, but he did hurt some people." She smiled. "He was little but ya know real tough. Scrappy. And he liked to smoke weed and drink, which made him real scrappy—but he was a good dude, ya know. He didn't do nothing real bad."

Wanting to know her support system, I asked her about family and friends.

"I don't got no family," she said. "Neither did Danny. And we didn't have no ya know friends. I mean I didn't mind but Danny didn't like people—maybe 'cause his papa beat him up all the time and it turned him ya know angry at the world. That's why he . . ."

"He what?"

"Offed him."

"He killed his father?"

"When he was a kid—self-defense! But the cops did a number on him—they sent him to ya know CYA till he was eighteen. He got out and did his own thing but he didn't like no friends. All he liked was me and the dogs—we got two Rottweiler mixes, Dandy and Paco. They liked him a lot. They been crying all day, going to miss him something bad."

She cried for a long time.

"Carmen," I said, "you're going through hard times. It will help to have someone to talk to. I'd like to hook you up with a doctor, a psychologist like me."

She looked up. "I could talk to you."

"I'm . . . I don't usually do this kind of work."

She pursed her lips. "It's the bread, right. You don't take no Medi-Cal, right?"

"No, Carmen. I'm a child psychologist. I work with children."

"Right, I understand," she said with more sadness than anger. As if this were the latest injustice in a life full of them.

"The person I want to refer you to is very nice, very experienced."

She pouted, rubbed her eyes.

"Carmen, if I talk to her about you and get you her number, will you call?"

"A her?" She shook her head violently. "No way. I don't want no lady doctor."

"Why's that?"

"Danny had a lady doctor. She messed with him."

"Messed with him?"

She spit on the floor. "Ya know *ballin'* him. He always said, bullshit, Carmen, we never done it. But he'd come back from ya know seein' her and have that ya know look in his eyes and he'd smell all of lovin'—disgustin'. I don't want to talk about it. Don't want no lady doctor in any case."

"Dr. Weingarden's a lady."

"That's different."

"Dr. Small, the person I want to send you to, is different too, Carmen. She's in her fifties, very kind, would never do anything dishonest."

She looked unconvinced.

"Carmen, I've seen her myself."

She didn't understand.

"Carmen, she was my doctor."

"You? What for?"

"Sometimes I need to talk too. Everyone does. Now promise me to go see her once. If you don't like her, I'll get you someone else." I pulled out a card with my exchange number on it and gave it to her.

She closed one hand over it.

"I just don't think it's right," she said.

"What isn't?"

"Her balling him. A doctor should, ya know, know better."

"You're absolutely right."

That surprised her, as if it were the first time anyone had ever agreed with her.

"Some doctors shouldn't be doctors," I said.

"I mean," she said, "I could sue or something."

"No one to sue, Carmen. If you're talking about Dr. Ransom, she's dead. She killed herself too."

Her hand flew to her mouth. "Oh, my God, I didn't . . . I mean, I ya know *wished* it to happen, but I didn't . . . Now it's . . . oh, my God."

She crossed herself, squeezed her temples, stared at the ceiling.

"Carmen, none of this is your fault. You're a victim."

She shook her head.

"A victim. I want you to understand that."

"I—I don't understand nothing." Tears. "This is all too ya know . . . too . . . I don't understand it."

I leaned forward, smelled her anguish. "Carmen, I'll stay here with you as long as you need me to. All right? All right, Carmen?"

Nod.

A half hour passed before she'd composed herself, and when she dried her eyes she seemed to have regained some dignity as well.

"You're very nice," she said. "I'm okay. You can go now."

"What about Dr. Small—the therapist I want you to see?"

"I dunno."

"Just one time."

Wan smile. "Okay."

"Promise?"

"Promise."

I took her hand, held it for a moment, then went to the front desk and told Bea to watch her. I used a phone in an empty examining room to call Ada. The operator at her service told me she was about to go into session.

"It's an emergency," I said, and was patched through.

"Alex," said Ada. "What's wrong?"

"I've got a young woman in crisis that I'd like you to see as soon as possible. It's not a choice referral, Ada—she's on Medi-Cal and is anything but insightful. But when I tell you the details I think you'll agree it's important that she be seen."

"Tell me."

When I was through, she said, "How terrible. You were right to call, Alex. I can stay and see her at seven. Can she get here by then?"

"I'll see that she does. Thanks so much, Ada."

"My pleasure, Alex. I've got a patient waiting, so I can't linger."

"I understand. Thanks again."

"No problem. I'll call you after I've seen her."

I went back to the private office and gave the number to Carmen.

"It's all arranged," I said. "Dr. Small will see you at seven tonight."

"Okay."

I squeezed her hand and left, caught Leslie between examining rooms, and told her what I'd arranged.

"How's she look to you?" she asked.

"Pretty fragile and she's still cushioned by shock. The next few days could get really bad. She doesn't have any support system. It's really important for her to be seeing someone."

"Makes sense. Where's this therapist's office?"

"Brentwood. San Vicente near Barrington." I gave her the address and the time of the appointment.

"Perfect. I live in Santa Monica. I'll be leaving the office around six-thirty. I'll take her there myself. Until then, we'll babysit her." A moment's hesitation. "This person you're referring to is good?"

"The best. I've seen her myself."

That bit of self-disclosure had reassured Carmen but it irritated her doctor.

"California honesty," she said. Then: "Jesus, I'm sorry. You've really been nice, coming here on no notice—it's just that I've become a total cynic. I know it's not healthy. I've got to get myself to where I can trust people again."

"It's tough," I said, thinking of my own crumbling sense of trust.

She fiddled with an earring. "Listen, I really do want to thank you for coming down here. Tell me what your fee is and I'll write a check right now."

"Forget it," I said.

"No, I insist. I like to pay as I go."

"No way, Leslie. I never expected to get paid."

"You're sure? I just want you to know I'm not into exploitation."

"I never suspected you were."

She looked uncomfortable. Removed her stethoscope and passed it from hand to hand.

"I know the first time you were here I sounded pretty mercenary, just out for myself. All I can say is, that's really not me. I did want to call those patients, kept batting it back and forth in my mind. I don't blame myself for Rasmussen's death—he was a time bomb. It was only a matter of when. But it has made me realize I have to take responsibility, start acting like a physician. When I left you with Carmen, I went to the phone and started calling. I got through to a couple of the women. They sounded okay, said their men are okay, too, which I hope is true. Actually, it went better than I thought— they were less hostile than the first time. Maybe I got through, I don't know. But at least I made contact. I'll try until I reach all of them, let the darned chips fall where they may."

"For what it's worth, you're doing the right thing."

"It's worth plenty," she said, with sudden intensity. Then she looked embarrassed and glanced at the door of one of the examining rooms. "Well, I've got to be going, try to hang on to the patients I have. Thanks again."

Hesitation.

She stood on tiptoes, kissed me on the cheek. Caught by surprise, I moved my head and our lips brushed.

"That was stupid," she said.

Before I could tell her it hadn't been, she went in to see her next patient.

It was close to five by the time I reached the University. The psych building was emptying and only one secretary remained in the department office. I headed straight for the faculty roster and thumbed through it without her commenting. Maybe it was the corduroy jacket. Kruse was already listed in the directory as chairman; his office number was 4302. I took note of his home address—same place in Pacific Palisades.

I ran up the four flights, aware, suddenly, that my energy had returned; for the first time in a long while I felt imbued with purpose, righteous with anger.

Nothing like an enemy to cleanse one's soul.

His office was at the end of a long white hall. Carved mahogany double doors had replaced the usual departmental plywood. The floor in front of the doorway was tarped with sawdust-coated canvas. From inside came the sound of sawing and banging.

The doors were unlocked. I walked into an outer office and found workmen laying parquet tile and hammering in mahogany molding, others on ladders painting the walls a rich, glossy burgundy. Brass wall sconces instead of overhead fluorescence, a leather armchair still wrapped in plastic. The air smelled of scorched wood and glue and paint. A transistor radio on the floor blared out country music.

One of the workmen saw me, turned off his skill-saw, and stepped down from his footstool. He was in his late twenties, medium-sized but burly, with enormous shoulders. A bandanna flowed out of the rear pocket of his filthy jeans and he wore a bent-visored baseball cap over black curly hair. His black beard was whitened by dust, as were his hairy Popeye arms. His utility belt was crammed with tools and rode low on narrow hips, clanking, as he swaggered over.

"Professor Kruse?" he said in a high, boyish voice.

"No, I'm looking for him."

"Damn, aren't we all. You know where he can be reached, tell him to get over here, pronto. Some fixtures came in that don't match the specs. I don't know if they changed their mind again or what, but we can't go much further till someone clears it up, and the boss is out of the office, scoping another job."

I said, "When's the last time you saw him?"

He pulled out the bandanna and wiped his face.

"Last week, when we were laying out the plans, doing the rough work and the bathroom. We didn't come back till yesterday, 'cause the materials weren't in. Everyone was getting bent out of shape 'cause this was supposed to be a rush job. Now there're other problems. They keep changing their minds about what they want."

"Who's *they*?"

"Kruse and his wife. She was supposed to meet us an hour ago and go over everything, but she never showed. They're not answering their phone, either. The boss comes back from Palm Springs he's gonna be steamed, but I don't know what the hell we're supposed to do without the client showing up."

"You don't work for the University?"

"Us? Hell, no. Chalmers Interiors, Pasadena. This is a custom job—retile the bathroom, coffered ceiling in the big office, lots of wood, antique furniture, Persian rugs, fake fireplace with a marble mantle." He rubbed his forefinger against his thumb. "Big money."

"Who's paying?"

"They are—the Kruses. Cost plus, by the hour. You'd think they'd show up."

"You'd think."

He stuffed the bandanna back in his pocket. "Easy come, easy go, huh? Didn't know professors did so good. You one, too?"

"Yes, but not here. Crosstown."

"Better football team Crosstown," he said. He removed his hat and scratched his head, gave a broad smile. "You here spying for the other side?"

I smiled back. "Just looking for Dr. Kruse."

"Well, if you see him, tell him to get in touch, or tomorrow we'll be somewhere else. Only got a half-day's work for a two-man crew. Boss won't want to commit."

"I'll do that, Mr. . . . ."

"Rodriguez. Gil Rodriguez." He picked up a piece of scrap wood from the floor and used a stubby pencil to scratch his name and number on it. "I free-lance, too—dry wall, painting, plastering. Can fix anything that don't have a computer in it. And if you got any football tickets you want to sell, I'll be happy to take them off your hands."

Traffic on Sunset was thick. The Stone Canyon entry to Bel Air was barricaded by roadwork, making things even worse, and the sun was sinking over the Palisades when I got to Kruse's house. Same time of day as the first time I'd been there, but no teal sky; this one was baby-blue innocence melting to sea clouds.

After what Rodriguez had told me, I'd expected an empty driveway. But three cars were parked in front of the house: the customized white Mercedes with the PPK PHD plates I'd seen at the party, a restored blue Jaguar E-type with SSK plates and an old Toyota the color of split-pea soup. I walked past them, knocked on the front door, waited, knocked again, louder, then used the bell.

I could hear the chimes; anyone inside had to hear them too. But no one answered. Then I looked down and noticed the pile of mail on the front steps, wet and warped. Saw the wrought-iron mail slot stuffed with magazines and correspondence.

I rang again, looked around. To one side was the semienclosed courtyard, planted with perennials and climbing bougainvillea. It ended in a round-topped gate of weathered wooden planks.

I went to the gate, pushed it. It opened. I stepped through and walked toward the back of the property, along the south side of the house, passed under a wooden arbor, and found myself in a large backyard— gentle roll of lawn, borders of tall trees, freeform flower beds, rock pool with spa, backed by a waterfall that fell in a glassy sheet.

I heard a click. The yard was bathed in soft, colorful light and the pool glowed sapphire. Timers.

No light shone from inside the house, but a rose-colored bulb wired to a birch tree highlighted a patio with a shade-cloth awning and a floor of Mexican tile. Several groupings of stylish teak furniture. Suntan lotion on a table, crumpled bath towels on some of the chairs, looking as if they'd been there for a while. I sniffed mildew. Then something stronger. A swim interrupted . . .

One of the French doors was open. Wide enough for the stench to stream out. Wide enough to enter.

I put my handkerchief over my nose and mouth, stuck my head in far enough to see a rose-colored nightmare. Using the handkerchief, I fumbled for a light switch, found one.

Two bodies, sprawled across a desert of Berber carpet, barely recognizable as human but for the clothing that covered what remained of their torsos.

I gagged, looked away, saw high, beamed ceilings, overstuffed furniture. Tasteful. Good decorator.

Then back down again to the horror . . .

I stared at the carpet. Tried to lose myself in the damn thing. Good weave. Immaculate. Except for the blackening stains . . .

One of the bodies wore a pink-flowered maillot bathing suit. The other, a once-white pair of Speedo shorts and a peacock-blue Hawaiian shirt patterned with red orchids.

The bright cloth stood out against glutinous, brownish green flesh. Faces replaced by lumps of oily, cratered meat. Meat thatched with hair—blond hair. On both. The hair on the bikinied corpse lighter, much longer. Tipped with brown crust.

I gagged again, pressed the handkerchief over my mouth and nose, held my breath, felt myself strangling, and backed away from the corpses.

Outside again, back onto the patio.

But even as I backed away my eye was drawn through the French doors, to the end of the room, up a flight of tiled stairs.

Rear staircase. Curving iron bannister.

On the top stair another decaying heap.

Pink housedress. What looked like dark hair. More putrefaction, more black stain, oozing down the steps like some malignant Slinky toy.

I turned and ran, past the pool, across springy grass to a bed of night-lit flowers, all unearthly blues and mauves. Bent low and smelled their perfume.

Sweet. Too sweet. My gut churned. I tried to vomit but couldn't.

I ran along the side of the house, back to the courtyard, across the front lawn.

Empty road, silent road. All that horror, but no one to share it with.

I got back in the Seville, sat in the car smelling death. Tasting it.

Finally, though the stink remained with me, I felt able to drive and headed south down Mandeville, then east on Sunset. Wanting a time machine, anything that could turn back the clock.

Turn it way back . . .

But willing to settle for a strong cigar, a telephone, and a friendly voice.

I found a pharmacy and a phone booth in Brentwood. Milo picked up on the first ring, listened to what I had to say, and said, "I knew there was a reason I came home early."

Twenty minutes later he came driving up to Mandeville and Sunset and followed me back to the murder house.

"Stay right there," he said, and I waited in the Seville, drawing on a cheap panatela, while he went around to the back. A while later he reappeared, wiping his forehead. He got into the passenger seat, took a cigar out of my shirt pocket, and lit up.

He blew a few smoke rings, then began taking my statement, coolly professional. After leading me through my discovery of the bodies, he put down his pad and asked, "Why'd you come up here, Alex?"

I told him about the porn loops, D.J. Rasmussen's fatal accident, the resurfacing of Leland Belding's name.

"Kruse's hand runs through most of it."

"Not much hand left," he said. "Bodies been there for a while." He put the note pad away. "Any working guesses about whodunit?"

"Rasmussen was an explosive type," I said. "Killed his father. For the last few days he'd been talking about being a sinner, doing something terrible. This could have been it."

"Why would he snuff Kruse?"

"I don't know. Maybe he blamed Kruse for Sharon's death—he was pathologically attached to her, sexually involved."

Milo thought for a while. "What'd you touch in there?"

"The light switch—but I used a handkerchief."

"What else?"

"The gate . . . I think that's it."

"Think harder."

"That's all I can think of."

"Let's retrace your steps."

When we were through, he said, "Go home, Alex."

"That's it?"

Glance at his Timex. "Crime scene boys should be here any minute. Go on. Disappear before the party begins."

"Milo—"

"Go on, Alex. Let me do the damned job."

I drove away, still tasting decay through the bite of tobacco.

Everything Sharon had touched was turning to death.

Ever the mind-prober, I found myself wondering what had made her that way. What kind of early trauma. Then something hit me: the way she'd acted that terrible night I'd found her with the twin photo. Thrashing, screaming, collapsing, and ending up in a fetal curl. So similar to Darren Burkhalter's behavior in my office. The reactions to the horror in his life that I'd captured on videotape, then played for a roomful of attorneys without noticing the connection.

Early childhood trauma.

Long ago, she'd explained it to me. Followed it up with a display of tender, loving kindness. Looking back, a well-staged display. Another act?

It was the summer of '81, a hotel in Newport Beach, swarming with psychologist conventioneers. A cocktail lounge overlooking the harbor—tinted picture windows, red-flocked walls, chairs on rollers. Dark and empty and smelling of last night's party.

I'd sat at the bar gazing out at the water, watching dagger-sharp yachts etch the surface of a blown-glass marina. Nursing a beer and eating a dry club sandwich while lending half an ear to the bartender's gripes.

He was a short, potbellied Hispanic with quick hands and a coppery Indian face. I watched him clean glasses like a machine.

"Worst I've ever seen, without a doubt, yessir. Now, your salesmen—insurance, computers, whatever—your salesmen are serious drinkers. Your pilots too."

"Comforting thought," I said.

"Yeah, your salesmen and your pilots. But you psycho guys? Forget it. Even the teachers we had last winter were better and they weren't any great shakes. Look at this place. Dead."

Twisting open a bottle of baby onions, he drained the juice and poured the pearly balls into a tray. "How many of you guys at this shebang, anyway?"

"Few thousand."

"Few thousand." He shook his head. "Look at this place. What is it, you all too busy analyzing other people, not allowed to have fun?"

"Maybe," I said, reflecting on how dull the convention had been. But conventions always were. The only reason I'd attended this one was because I'd been asked to deliver a paper on childhood stress.

The paper having now been read, the inevitable picayune questions fielded, I was grabbing a bit of solitude before heading back to L.A. and a night shift on the adolescent ward.

"Maybe you guys should study yourselves, pal. Analyze why you don't like to have fun."

"Good idea." I put some money down on the bar and said, "Have one on me."

He stared at the bills. "Sure, thanks." Lighting a cigarette, he poured himself a beer and leaned forward.

"Anyway, I'm for live and let live. Someone don't want to have fun, okay. But at least come in and order something, know what I mean? Hell, don't drink it—*analyze* it. But order and leave a tip. Leave something for the working man."

"To the working man," I said and raised my glass. I put it down empty.

"Refill, Doc? On the house."

"I'll take a Coke."

"Figures. One rum and Coke coming up, hold the rum, hold the fun."

He put the drink on the bar and was about to say something else when the door to the lounge opened and let in lobby noise. His eyes shifted to the back of the room and he said, "My, my."

I looked over my shoulder and saw a woman in white. Long-legged, shapely, a cloud of black hair. Standing near the cigarette machine, head moving from side to side, as if scouting foreign territory.

Familiar. I turned to get a better look.

Sharon. Definitely Sharon. In a tailored linen suit, matching purse and shoes.

She saw me, waved as if we'd had an appointment.

"Alex!"

All at once she was at my side. Soap and water, fresh grass . . .

She sat down on the stool next to mine, crossed her legs, and pulled her skirt down over her knees.

The bartender winked at me. "Drink, ma'am?"

"Seven-Up, please."

"Yes, ma'am."

After he handed her the drink and moved down, she said, "You look great, Alex. I like the beard."

"Saves time in the morning."

"Well, I think it's handsome." She sipped, toyed with her stirrer. "I keep hearing good things about you, Alex. Early tenure, all those publications. I've read quite a few of your articles. Learned a lot from them."

"Glad to hear it."

Silence.

"I finally graduated," she said. "Last month."

"Congratulations, Doctor."

"Thanks. It took me longer than I thought it would. But I got involved in clinical work and didn't apply myself to writing the dissertation as diligently as I should have."

We sat in silence. A few feet away, the bartender was whistling "La Bamba" and tinkering with the ice crusher.

"It's good to see you," she said.

I didn't answer.

She touched my sleeve. I stared at her fingers until she removed them.

"I wanted to see you," she said.

"What about?"

"I wanted to explain—"

"There's no need to explain anything, Sharon. Ancient history."

"Not to me."

"Difference of opinion."

She moved closer, said, "I know I blew it," in a choked whisper. "Believe me, I know it. But that doesn't change the fact that after all these years, you're still with me. Good memories, special memories. Positive energy."

"Selective perception," I said.

"No." She inched closer, touched my sleeve again. "We did have some wonderful times, Alex. I'll never let go of that."

I said nothing.

"Alex, the way we . . . it ended. I was horrible. You had to think

I was psychotic—what happened *was* psychotic. If you only knew how many times I've wanted to call you, to explain—"

"Then why didn't you?"

"Because I'm a coward. I run away from things. It's my style—you saw that the first time we met, in practicum." Her shoulders drooped. "Some things never change."

"Forget it. Like I said, ancient history."

"What we had was special, Alex, and I allowed it to be destroyed."

Her voice stayed soft but got tighter. The bartender glanced over. My expression sent his eyes back to his work.

"*Allowed* it?" I said. "That sounds pretty passive."

She recoiled as if I'd spit in her face. "All right," she said. "*I* destroyed it. *I* was crazy. It was a crazy time in my life—don't think I haven't regretted it a thousand times."

She tugged at her earlobe. Her hands were smooth and white. "Alex, meeting you here today was no accident. I never attend conventions, had no intention of going to this one. But when I got the brochure in the mail I happened to notice your name on the program and wanted suddenly to see you again. I attended your lecture, stood at the back of the room. The way you spoke—your humanity. I thought I might have a chance."

"A chance for what?"

"To be friends, bury the hard feelings."

"Consider them buried. Mission accomplished."

She leaned forward so that our lips were almost touching, clutched my shoulder, whispered, "Please, Alex, don't be vindictive. Let me show you."

There were tears in her eyes.

"Show me what?" I said.

"A different side of me. Something I've never shown anyone."

We walked to the front of the hotel, waited for the parking valets.

"Separate cars," she said, smiling. "So you can escape any time you want."

The address she gave me was on the south side of Glendale, the down side of town, filled with used-car lots, splintering, by-the-day rooming houses, thrift shops, and greasy spoons. Half a mile north on Brand, the Glendale Galleria was under construction—a polished brick tribute to gentrification—but down here, *boutique* was still a French word.

She arrived before me, was sitting in the little red Alfa in front

of a one-story brown stucco building. The place had a jaillike quality—
narrow, silvered windows bolted and barred, the front door a slab of
brushed steel, no landscaping other than a single thirsty liquidambar
tree which cast spindly shadows on the tar-paper roof.

She met me at the door, thanked me for coming, then pushed
the buzzer in the center of the steel door. Several moments later it
was opened by a stocky, coal-black man with short hair and a
corkscrew chin beard. He wore a diamond stud in one ear, a light-
blue uniform jacket over a black T-shirt and jeans. When he saw
Sharon he flashed a gold-jacketed smile.

"Afternoon, Dr. Ransom." His voice was high-pitched, gentle.

"Afternoon, Elmo. This is Dr. Delaware, a friend of mine."

"Pleased to meet you, sir." To Sharon: "She's all prettied up
and ready for you."

"That's great, Elmo."

He stood aside and we entered a waiting room floored with
oxblood linoleum and furnished with orange plastic chairs and green
tables. To one side was an office labeled RECEPTION and windowed
with a square of yellowed Lucite. We walked past it and up to another
steel door, marked NO ENTRY. Elmo selected a key from a heavy ring
and sprung the latch.

We stepped into brightness and pandemonium: a long, high
room with steel-shuttered windows and a fluorescent ceiling that
radiated a cold, flat imitation daylight. The walls were covered with
sheets of emerald-green vinyl; the air was hot and rancid.

And everywhere, movement. A random ballet.

Scores of bodies, twitching, rocking, stumbling, brutalized by
Nature and the luck of the draw. Limbs frozen or trapped in endless,
athetoid spasm. Slack, drooling mouths. Hunched backs, shattered
spines, nubbed and missing limbs. Contortions and grimaces born of
ravaged chromosomes and derailed neural pathways and made all the
more cruel by the fact that these patients were young—teenagers and
young adults who'd never know the pleasures of youth's false
immortality.

Some of them clutched walkers and measured their progress in
millimeters. Others, contracted stiff as plaster statues, bucked and
fought the confines of wheelchairs. The saddest among them slumped,
flaccid as invertebrates, in high-sided wagons and metal carts that
resembled oversized baby strollers.

We made our way past a sea of glazed eyes as inert as plastic
buttons. Past witless faces gazing up from the leather sanctuary of

protective headgear, an audience of blank faces unperturbed by the merest flicker of consciousness.

A gallery of deformity—a cruel display of all that could go wrong with the box that humans come in.

In a corner of the room a rabbit-eared console TV blasted a game show at top volume, the shrieks of contestants competing with the wordless jabber and inchoate howls of the patients. The only ones watching were half a dozen blue-jacketed attendants. They ignored us as we passed.

But the patients noticed. As if magnetized, they swarmed toward Sharon, began flocking around her, wheeling and hobbling. Soon we were surrounded. The attendants didn't budge.

She reached into her purse, took out a box of gumdrops, and began distributing candy. One box emptied, another appeared. Then another.

She dispensed another kind of sweetness, too, kissing misshapen heads, hugging stunted bodies. Calling patients by name, telling them how good they looked. They competed for her favors, begged for gumdrops, cried out in ecstasy, touched her as if she were magic.

She looked happier than I'd ever seen her—complete. A storybook princess reigning over a kingdom of the misshapen.

Finally, gumdrops depleted, she said, "That's all, people. Gotta go."

Grumbles, whines, a few more minutes of pats and squeezes. A couple of the attendants came forward and began corralling the patients. Finally we managed to pull away. Resumption of chaos.

Elmo said, "They sure love you." Sharon didn't seem to hear.

The three of us walked to the end of the big room, up to a door marked INPATIENT UNIT and shielded by an iron accordion grille, which Elmo unlocked. Another key twist, the door opened and closed behind us, and all was quiet.

We walked through a corridor covered in the same lurid green vinyl, passed a couple of empty wards reeking of illness and despair, a door with a mesh glass window that afforded a view of several stout Mexican women laboring in a steamy industrial kitchen, another green hallway, and finally a steel slab marked PRIVATE.

On the other side a new ambience: plush carpeting, soft lighting, papered walls, perfumed air, and music—the Beatles, as interpreted by a somnolent string orchestra.

Four rooms marked PRIVATE. Four oak doors, fitted with brass peepholes. Elmo unlocked one and said, "Okay."

The room was beige and hung with French Impressionist lithos.

More plush carpeting and soft lighting. Oak wainscotting and oak crown molding rimmed the ceiling. Good furniture: an antique chiffonier, a pair of sturdy oak chairs. Two generous, arched windows, barred and filled with opaque glass block, but curtained with chintz pull-backs and lace. Vases of fresh-cut flowers strategically placed. The place smelled like a meadow. But I wasn't paying attention to decorator touches.

In the center of the room was a hospital bed covered by a pearly pink quilt, which had been pulled to the neck of a dark-haired woman.

Her skin was gray-white, her eyes huge and deep-blue—the same color as Sharon's, but filmed and immobile, aimed straight up at the ceiling. Her hair was black and thick, spread over a plump, lace-trimmed pillow. The face it framed was emaciated, dust-dry, still as a plaster cast. Her mouth gaped—a black hole studded with peg teeth.

Faint movement nudged the quilt. Shallow breathing, then nothing, then re-ignition heralded by a squeeze-toy squeak.

I studied her face. Less a face than a sketch of one—anatomic scaffolding, stripped of the adornment of flesh.

And somewhere amid the ruins, resemblance. A hint of Sharon.

Sharon was holding her, cradling her, kissing her face.

Squeak.

A swivel table next to the bed held a pitcher and glasses, a tortoise-shell comb and brush set with matching manicure tools. Lipstick, tissues, makeup, nail polish.

Sharon pointed to the pitcher. Elmo filled the glass with water and handed it to her, then left.

Sharon tipped the rim of the glass to the woman's mouth. Some of the water dribbled down. Sharon wiped the pale flesh, kissed it.

"It's so good to see you, darling," she said. "Elmo says you're doing just fine."

The woman remained blank as eggshell. Sharon cooed to her and rocked her. The covers slipped down, revealing a limp wisp of a body wrapped in a pink flannel nightgown, contracted, pathetic—too fragile to be viable. But the breathing continued. . . .

"Shirlee, we have a visitor. His name is Dr. Alex Delaware. He's a nice man. Alex, meet Miss Shirlee Ransom. My sister. My twin. My silent partner."

I just stood there.

She stroked the woman's hair. "Clinically, she's deaf and blind—minimal cortical functioning. But I know she senses people, has some subliminal awareness of her surroundings. I can *feel* it—she gives off small vibrations. You have to be tuned in to them, have to be actually making contact with her to feel them."

She took my hand, put it on a cold, dry brow.

Turning to Shirlee: "Isn't that true, darling? You *do* know what's going on, *don't* you? You're fairly *humming* today."

"Say something to her, Alex."

"Hello, Shirlee."

Nothing.

"There," said Sharon. "She's humming."

She hadn't stopped smiling, but there were tears in her eyes. She let go of my hand, spoke to her sister: "Alex *Delaware,* darling. The one I've told you about, Shirl. So handsome, isn't he? Handsome and good."

I waited as she talked to a woman who couldn't hear. Sang, prattled on about fashion, music, recipes, current events.

Then she folded back the covers, rolled up the pink nightgown, exposing chicken-carcass ribs, stick legs, spiky knees, loose, putty-gray skin—the remnants of a female form so pathetically wasted I had to look away.

Sharon turned her sister gently, searching for bed sores. Kneading and stroking and massaging, flexing and unflexing arms and legs, rotating the jaw, examining behind the ears before covering her up again.

After tucking her back under the quilt and propping the pillow, she gave Shirlee's hair a hundred strokes with the tortoise-shell brush, wiped her face with a damp washcloth, dusted the collapsed cheeks with makeup and blush.

"I want her to be as ladylike as possible. For her morale. Her feminine self-image."

She lifted one limp hand, inspected nails that were surprisingly long and healthy. "These are looking beautiful, Shirl." Turning to me: "Hers are so healthy! They grow faster than mine do, Alex. Isn't that funny?"

Later, we sat in the Alfa and Sharon cried for a while. Then she started to speak, in those same flat tones she'd used years ago, to tell me about her parents' deaths:

"We were born absolutely identical. Carbon copies of each other—I mean, no one could tell us apart." She laughed. "Sometimes we couldn't tell ourselves apart."

Remembering the photograph of the two little girls, I said, "One difference: mirror-image identical."

That seemed to jolt her. "Yes. That—she's a lefty; I'm a righty. And our hair whirls go in opposite directions."

She looked away from me, tapped the Alfa's wooden steering wheel. "Strange phenomenon, mirror-image monozygotes—from a scientific point of view. Biochemically, it makes no sense at all. Given an identical genetic structure in two individuals, there should be no differences at all, right? Let alone reversal of the cerebral hemispheres."

She got a dreamy look in her eyes and closed them.

"Thank you so much for coming, Alex. It really means a lot to me."

"I'm glad."

She took my hand. Hers was shaking.

I said, "Go on. You were talking about how similar the two of you were."

"Carbon copies," she said. "And inseparable. We loved each other with a gut intensity. Lived for each other, did everything together, cried hysterically when anyone tried to separate us, until finally no one tried. We were more than sisters—more than twins. Partners. Psychic partners—sharing a consciousness. As if each of us could only be whole in the presence of the other. We had our own languages, two of them: a spoken one, and one based on gestures and secret looks. We never stopped communicating—even in our sleep we'd reach out and touch each other. And we shared the same intuitions, the same perceptions."

She stopped. "This probably sounds strange to you. It's hard to explain to someone who's never had a twin, Alex, but believe me, all those stories you hear about synchrony of sensation are true. They were certainly true for us. Even now, sometimes I'll wake in the middle of the night with an ache in my belly or a cramp in my arm. I'll call Elmo and find out Shirlee had a rough night."

"It doesn't sound strange. I've heard it before."

"Thanks for saying that." She kissed my cheek. Tugged her earlobe. "When we were little, we had a wonderful life together. Mummy and Daddy, the big apartment on Park Avenue—all those rooms and cupboards and walk-in closets. We loved to hide—loved to hide from the world. But our favorite place was the summer house in Southampton. The property had been in our family for generations. Acres of grass and sand. A big old white-shingled monstrosity with creaky floors, wicker furniture that was coming apart, dusty old hooked rugs, a stone fireplace. It sat on top of a bluff that overlooked the ocean and sloped down to the water in a couple of places. Nothing elegant—just a few tortured old pines and tarry dunes. The beach hooked around in a crescent shape, all wide and wet and full of clam spouts. There was a dock with rowboats moored to it—it danced in the waves, slapped against all that warped wood. It scared us, but in a nice way—we loved to be scared, Shirl and me.

"In autumn, the sky was always this wonderful shade of gray with silvery-yellow spots where the sun broke through. And the beach was full of horseshoe crabs and hermit crabs and jellyfish and strings of seaweed that would wash up in huge tangles. We'd throw ourselves into the tangles, wrap ourselves in it, all slimy, and pretend we were two little mermaid princesses in silken gowns and pearl necklaces."

She stopped, bit her lip, said, "Off to the south side of the property was a swimming pool. Big, rectangular, blue tiles, sea horses painted on the bottom. Mummy and Daddy never really decided whether they wanted an indoor or outdoor pool, so they compromised and built a pool house over it—white lattice with a retractable roof and devil ivy running through the lattice. We used it a lot during the summer, getting all salty in the ocean, then washing it off in fresh water. Daddy taught us to swim when we were two and we learned quickly—took to it like little tadpoles, he used to say."

Another pause to catch her breath. A long stretch of silence that made me wonder if she'd finished. When she spoke again, her voice was weaker.

"When summer was over, no one paid much attention to the pool. The caretakers didn't always clean it properly and the water would get all green with algae, give off a stench. Shirl and I were forbidden to go there, but that only made it more appealing. The moment we were free we'd run straight there, peek through the lattice, see all that gooky water and imagine it was a lagoon full of monsters. Hideous monsters who could rise from the muck and attack us at any moment. We decided the smell was monsters filling the water with their excretions—monster poop." She smiled, shook her head. "Pretty repulsive, huh? But exactly the kind of fantasies children get into, in order to master their fears, right?"

I nodded.

"The only problem, Alex, was that *our* monsters materialized."

She wiped her eyes, stuck her head out the window and breathed deeply.

"Sorry," she said.

"It's okay."

"No, it's not. I promised myself I'd maintain." More deep breathing. "It was a cold day. A gray Saturday. Late autumn. We were three years old, wore matching wool dresses with thick, knitted leggings and brand-new patent-leather shoes that we'd pleaded with Mummy to let us wear on condition that we wouldn't scratch them on the sand. It was our last weekend on the Island until spring. We'd stayed longer than we should have—the house had poor heating and the chill was seeping right up from the ocean, that kind of sharp East Coast chill that gets right into your bones and stays there. The sky was so clogged with rain clouds it was almost black—had that old-penny smell a coastal sky gives off before a storm.

"Our driver had gone into town to fill the car with gas and have it tuned before the drive back to the city. The rest of the help was busy closing up the house. Mummy and Daddy were sitting in the sun-room, wrapped in shawls, having a last martini. Shirl and I were off gallivanting from room to room, unpacking what had been packed, unfastening what had been fastened, giggling and teasing and just getting generally underfoot. Our mischief level was especially high because we knew we wouldn't be back for a while and were determined to squeeze every bit of fun out of the day. Finally, the help and Mummy had enough of us. They bundled us in heavy coats and put galoshes over our new shoes and sent us with a nanny to collect shells.

"We ran down to the beach, but the tide was rising and it had washed away all the shells, and the seaweed was too cold to play with. The nanny started flirting with one of the gardeners. We snuck away, headed straight for the pool house.

"The gate was closed but not locked—the lock lay on the ground. One of the caretakers had begun to drain and clean the pool—there were brushes and nets and chemicals and clumps of algae all around the deck—but he wasn't there. He'd forgotten to lock it. We snuck in. It was dark inside—only squares of black sky coming in through the lattice. The filthy water was being suctioned through a garden hose that ran out to a gravel sump. About three quarters of it remained—acid-green and bubbling, and stinking worse than it ever had, sulfur gas mixed in with all the chemicals the caretaker had dumped in. Our eyes started burning. We began to cough, then broke out into laughter. This was *really* monstrous—we loved it!

"We began pretending the monsters were rising from the gook, started chasing each other around the pool, shrieking and giggling, making monster faces, going faster and faster and working ourselves up into a frenzy—a *hypnotic* state. Everything blurred—we saw only each other.

"The concrete decking was slippery from all the algae and the suds from the chemicals. Our galoshes were slick and we started skidding all over the place. We loved that, too, pretended we were at an ice rink, tried deliberately to skid. We were having a great time, lost in the moment, focused on our inner selves—as if we *were* one self. Round and round we went, hooting and slipping and sliding. Then all at once I saw Shirl take a big skid and *keep* skidding, saw a terrible look come on her face as she threw up her arms for balance. She called out for help. I knew this was no game and ran to grab her, but I fell on my butt and landed just as she let out a horrible scream and plunged, feet-first, into the pool.

"I got up, saw her hand sticking out, her fingers flexing, unflexing, threw myself at her, couldn't reach her, started crying and screaming for help. I stumbled again, went down on my butt again, finally got to my feet and ran to the edge. The hand was gone. I screamed her name—it brought the nanny. How she'd looked—the surprise, the terror as she'd gone under—stayed with me and I kept screaming as the nanny asked me where she was. I couldn't answer. I'd *absorbed* her, become her. I *knew* she was drowning, could feel myself choking and suffocating, taste the putrid water clogging my nose and my mouth and my lungs!

"The nanny was shaking me, slapping my face. I was hyperventilating, but somehow I managed to point to the pool.

"Then Mummy was there and Daddy, some of the help. The nanny jumped in. Mummy was screaming 'My baby, oh, my baby!' and biting her fingers—they bled all over her clothes. The nanny was thrashing around, coming up gasping, covered with muck. Daddy kicked off his shoes, tore off his jacket, and dove in. A graceful dive. A moment later he surfaced with Shirlee in his arms. She was limp, all covered with filth, pale and dead-looking. Daddy tried to give her artificial respiration. Mummy was still panting—her fingers were *running* with blood. The nanny was lying on the ground, looking dead herself. The maids were sobbing. The caretakers were staring. At me, I thought. They were blaming me! I started to howl and claw at them. Someone said, 'Take her out,' and everything went black."

Telling the story had made her break out in a sweat. I gave her my handkerchief. She took it without comment, wiped herself, said, "I woke up back on Park Avenue. It was the next day; someone must have sedated me. They told me Shirlee had died, had been buried. Nothing more was ever said about her. My life was changed, empty—but I don't want to talk about that. Even now, I can't talk about that. It's enough to say I had to reconstruct myself. Learn to be a new person. A partner without a partner. I came to accept, lived in my head, away from the world. Eventually I stopped thinking about Shirlee—consciously stopped. I went through the motions, being a good girl, getting good grades, never raising my voice. But I was empty—missing something. I decided to become a psychologist, to learn why. I moved out here, met you, started to really live. Then, everything changed—Mummy and Daddy dying. I had to go back East to talk to their lawyer. He was nice. A handsome, fatherly man—I remembered him vaguely from parties. He took me out to the Russian Tea Room and told me about my trust fund, the house, talked a lot about *new responsibilities,* but wouldn't come out and say what they were. When I asked him what he meant, he looked uneasy, called for the check.

"We left the restaurant, took a walk down Fifth Avenue, past all the fine shops that Mummy had always loved. We walked in silence for several blocks and then he told me about Shirlee. That she'd never died, had been comatose when Daddy pulled her out of the pool, remained that way—damaged, with minimal cerebral functioning. All the time I'd thought her dead, she'd been living in an institution in Connecticut. Mummy was a perfect lady, very genteel, but she wasn't strong, couldn't cope with adversity.

"The lawyer said he knew it had to come as a shock, he was sorry I'd been lied to, but Mummy and Daddy had felt it best. Now, however, they were gone, and since I was next of kin, Shirlee was my legal responsibility. Not that that had to burden me. He—the law firm—would assume her guardianship, handle all the finances, administer her trust fund so that her medical expenses would continue to be paid. There was absolutely no need for me to disrupt my life. He had papers for me to sign and it would all be taken care of.

"I filled with an anger I didn't know I was capable of, started yelling at him right there on Fifth Avenue, demanding to see her. He tried to talk me out of it, said I should wait until the shock subsided. But I insisted. I had to see her right now. He called for a limousine. We drove to Connecticut. The place was big and nice-looking—an old stone mansion, well-kept lawns, a big sun porch, nurses in starched uniforms, doctors with German accents. But she needed more than that—she needed her partner. I told the lawyer she'd be returning with me to California, to have her ready for travel within a week.

"He tried again to talk me out of it. Said he'd seen this kind of thing before—survivor guilt. The more he talked, the angrier I got, the poor man. And since I'd reached my majority, he had no choice. I returned to L.A. feeling righteous with purpose—no longer just another grad student caught up in the grind, I was a woman with a mission. But the moment I stepped into my dorm room, the enormity of everything hit me. I realized my life would never be the same, never be normal. I dealt with it by staying busy, ordering the lawyer around, moving into the house, signing papers. Convincing myself, Alex, that I was in control. I found *this* place—it doesn't look that great on the outside, but they really treat her special. Elmo is fantastic, totally oriented toward one-on-one care."

She lifted my hand to her cheek, then placed it in her lap and held it tight.

"Now you, Alex. Your entree to this mess. The night you found me holding the snapshot was soon after Shirlee had been flown out—what a job, just getting her off the plane and into a van. I hadn't slept for days, was wired *and* fatigued. The photo had come in a box with other family papers; it had been in Mummy's purse the day she died.

"I started staring at it, fell into it, like Alice down the hole. I was trying to integrate everything, remember the good days. But so angry that I'd been deceived, that my whole life had been a deceit—every moment colored by lies. I felt sick, Alex. Nauseous. My stomach was heaving. As if the photo was capturing me—eating me up, the way the pool had eaten Shirlee. I freaked out, stayed freaked for days—I was hanging by a thread when you came in.

"I never heard you, Alex. Not until you were standing over me. And you seemed angry—judging me. Disapproving. When you picked the picture up off the floor and examined it, it was as if you'd *invaded* me—forced your way into my private pain. I wanted the pain all to myself—wanted *something* all to myself. I just blew. I'm so sorry."

I returned the pressure of her hand. "It's all right."

"The next couple of weeks were horrible, just a nightmare. I worried what I'd done to you and me, but frankly, I was too drained to do anything about it and guilty because I couldn't get myself to care more about it. I had so much to deal with: my rage at my parents for lying to me, my grief at losing them, my rage at Shirlee for coming back so damaged, for being unable to respond to my love. At the time I didn't realize that she was vibrating, trying to communicate with me. So many changes all at once, Alex. Like a jumble of crisscrossing live wires burning into my brain. I got help."

"Kruse."

"Despite what you think of him, he *helped* me, Alex. Helped put me back together again. And he told me you'd come looking for me, which let me know you cared. I cared about you—that's why I finally forced myself to get together with you, even though Paul said I wasn't ready. And he was right. I came on like a nympho because I was feeling worthless, out of control, felt I owed you something. Acting like a sexpot made me feel in charge, as if I were stepping out of my personality and adopting a new one. But just for a short while. Later, while you slept, I despised what I'd done, despised you. I dumped on you because you were there."

She looked away. "And because you were good. I ruined what we had because I was unable to tolerate goodness, Alex. I didn't feel I deserved goodness. And after all these years, I still regret that."

I sat there, trying to take it all in.

She leaned over and kissed me. Gradually, the kiss took on heat and depth and we were pressed against each other, groping, our tongues dancing. Then we both pulled away.

"Sharon—"

"Yes, I know," she said. "Not again. How could you ever know you'd be safe?"

"I—"

She placed a finger over my lips.

"No reason to explain, Alex. Ancient history. I just wanted to show you that I'm not all bad."

I kept quiet, didn't say what had passed through my mind. That maybe we could start again—slowly. Carefully. Now that both of us had grown up.

She said, "I'll let you go now."

We drove away in separate cars.

Back from Kruse's house, I sat in my living room with the lights out and turned it over, again and again. Park Avenue, Southampton summers. Mummy and Daddy. Martinis in the sun-room. Genteel cardboard cutouts.

But a nasty little scrap of celluloid said Mummy had been anything but genteel. A rich man's party girl who'd made love on film, probably used it for blackmail.

My whole life had been a deceit—every moment colored by lies.

I thought about Shirlee Ransom. Vegetative. *Squeaking.* Wondered if any part of the story had been true.

If she loved her twin, how could she kill herself, abandon a helpless cripple?

Unless Shirlee was dead too.

S and S, silent partners.

A pair of little girls, beautiful, black-haired. Mountains in the background. Ice cream cones in opposite hands.

Mirror-image twins. *She's a lefty; I'm a righty.*

Suddenly I realized what had bothered me about the porn loop—the tip-of-the-mind incongruity that stayed under my skin.

Sharon was right-handed but in the film—stroking, kneading— she'd favored her left.

Being a sexpot made me feel in charge. As if I were stepping out of my personality and stepping into someone else's.

Switching? Trying on a new identity?

The left hand. *Sinestra.* Sinister. Some primitive cultures considered it evil.

Putting on a blond wig and becoming a bad girl . . . a left-handed *sinister* girl.

Suddenly something about the drowning story bothered me— something that hadn't troubled me six years ago, when I'd wanted to believe her:

The details, the vivid imagery.

Too complex for a three-year-old. Too much for a toddler to remember.

Practiced detail. Or a well-rehearsed lie? Had she been coached? Had her memory enhanced?

As in hypnosis.

As in Paul Kruse, master hypnotist. Amateur film-maker. Professional sleaze.

I was certain, now, that he'd known enough to fill in lots of blanks. Had died with that knowledge. Horribly, bloodily, taking two other people with him.

I wanted, more than ever, to know why.

20

Feeling infected, the carrier of some dread disease, I canceled my flight to San Luis, turned on the TV, and created some electronic companionship.

The Kruse murders were the lead item on the eleven o'clock news, complete with sweeping live minicam shots of the murder house and inset photos of Paul and Suzanne in better days. The third victim was identified as Lourdes Escobar, age twenty-two, a native of El Salvador who'd worked as the Kruses' maid. Her picture portrayed an open-faced young woman with plaited black hair and dark, melting eyes.

Innocent victim, pronounced the reporter, lowering his voice and oozing irony. She'd fled the turmoil and poverty of her native land, fueled by the dream of a better life, only to encounter violent death amid the seductive luxury of the City of the Angels. . . .

That kind of philosophizing meant he didn't know much.

I switched back and forth between channels, hungry for facts. All three newscasts were identical in style and lack of substance: reporters addressing the anchors instead of the audience, wondering out loud if one of Kruse's patients had turned homicidal, or if this was just another random L.A. bloodletting.

I absorbed predictions of runs on gun shops, starved attack dogs. The reporter cupped one ear and said, "One moment. We're about to have a statement from the police."

The camera shifted to Cyril Trapp, clearing his throat. His shirt was TV blue. His white hair gleamed like a steel helmet. Under the spotlights his mottled skin was the color of dirty sheets. His mustache wriggled as he chewed his cheek. Establishing eye contact with the camera, he read a prepared statement pledging that the full investigative resources of the Los Angeles Police Department would be marshaled to solve these vicious slayings. A tight smile and head shake. He said, "That's all I'm at liberty to divulge at this time," and walked away.

The reporter said, "There you have it, Keith and Kelly. Reporting live at the scene of . . ."

I turned off the set, wondered about Trapp's presence at the crime scene, waited for Milo to call and clue me in. When he hadn't phoned by one, I undressed and slipped beneath the covers, drymouthed and so tense my palate ached. I tried deep breathing but, instead of relaxing, worked myself into a state of wide-eyed hyperawareness. Embracing the pillow like a lover, I tried to fill my head with pleasant images. None came. Finally, some time before dawn, I managed to sink into sleep.

The next morning I called Milo at the station and was told he was still on vacation. No one answered at his house.

I took in the morning paper. Unlike Sharon's death, the Kruse murders were being treated as serious news—a headline shouting DOCTOR AND SPOUSE SLAIN bannered over the top half of page 3. The byline was that of a staff writer named Dale Conrad, a name I recognized because he'd covered behavioral science stories in the past, generally doing a slipshod job.

The Kruse piece was no exception. Despite all those column inches, Conrad had come up with nothing about the murders that hadn't been covered on last night's broadcasts. The bulk of the article was biographical information on Kruse. He'd been sixty at the time of his death, twice the age of his wife—whom the article described only as a former actress. His birthplace was New York City; his origins, moneyed. He'd been commissioned as an officer in Korea attached to a psychological warfare unit, received his doctorate from a university in south Florida and, aided by society connections and his advice column, built up a lucrative Palm Beach practice before moving to California. His recent appointment to head the department was noted, and his predecessor, Professor Milton Frazier, was quoted as being shocked by the senseless death of an esteemed colleague.

The death of Lourdes Escobar was a last-paragraph afterthought: "Also found was the body of the housekeeper . . ."

I put the paper down. New York, old money, society connections— reminiscent of the phony background Sharon had created for herself.

Had it been a total fabrication? Failed starlet mother or not, she'd lived like a rich girl—the clothes, the car, the house. Perhaps Linda Lanier had married money—the call girl's fantasy come true.

Or perhaps she'd gotten it another way. Passing along to her daughter a choice chunk of hillside real estate once owned by a dead billionaire who'd employed her. Still deeded to that billionaire's corporation and put up on the market the day after Sharon died.

Too many questions. My head was starting to hurt.

I dressed, found a legal pad and a couple of pens, and left the house. Walking down the glen, I crossed Sunset and entered the north end of the University campus. It was eleven-twenty when I passed through the doors of the research library.

I headed straight for the reference section, played with the MELVYL computerized index, and found two books on Leland Belding in the library's holdings.

The first was a 1949 volume entitled *Ten Tycoons.* The second was *The Basket-Case Billionaire* by Seaman Cross. Surprised, because I'd thought all copies of the book had been recalled, I jotted down the call numbers, began looking for anything on Lanier, Linda, but found nothing.

I left the computer and did a little low-tech research—two hours spent turning the pages of volume after volume of the Periodicals Index. Nothing on Linda Lanier here either, but over a hundred articles on Leland Belding, stretching from the mid-thirties to the mid-seventies. I selected what I hoped was a representative dozen references, then took the elevator up to the stacks and began seeking out the sources. By two-thirty I was ensconced in a reading cubicle on the fourth floor, surrounded by stacks of bound magazines.

The earliest pieces on Belding were in aerospace-industry journals, written while the tycoon was still in his early twenties. In them, Leland Belding was hailed as a technical and financial prodigy, a master designer of aircraft and collateral equipment with three patents for every year of his life. The same photograph was used in each, a publicity shot credited to L. Belding Industries: the young inventor sitting in the cockpit of one of his planes, goggled and helmeted, his attention fixed upon the instrument panel. A handsome man, but cold-looking.

Belding's enormous wealth, precocity, boyish good looks, and shyness made him a natural media hero, and the tone of the earliest popular magazine pieces was worshipful. One article designated him the Most Eligible Bachelor of 1937. Another called him the closest America had come to producing a crown prince.

A prewar profile in *Collier's* summed up his rise to fame: He'd been born to wealth, in 1910, the only child of an heiress from Newport, Rhode Island, and a Texas oil wildcatter turned gentleman rancher.

Another official corporate photo. Belding appeared frightened of the camera, standing, shirtsleeves rolled to the elbows, a large lug wrench in one hand, next to a gargantuan piece of cast-iron machinery. By age thirty he'd attained a monkish look—high forehead, sensitive mouth, thick eyeglasses that couldn't hide the intensity of round, dark eyes. A modern-day Midas, according to the article, representing the best of American ingenuity combined with good old-fashioned hard work. Though born with a silver spoon in his mouth, Belding had never allowed it to tarnish; he'd favored twenty-hour days, and wasn't afraid of getting his hands dirty. He had a photographic memory, knew his hundreds of employees by name, but didn't suffer fools gladly, had no patience for the frivolity of the "cocktail crowd."

His idyllic life as an only son had been cut cruelly short when both his parents perished in a car crash—returning, after a party, to their rented villa on the Spanish island of Ibiza, just south of Majorca.

Another layer. I stopped reading, tried to make some sense of that. When I couldn't, I resumed reading.

At the time of the accident, Belding had been nineteen, a senior at Stanford, majoring in physics and engineering. He dropped out of college, returned to Houston to run the family petroleum business, and expanded immediately into the manufacture of oil-drilling equipment, using designs that he'd developed as student projects. A year later he diversified into heavy farm machinery, took flying lessons, proved to be a natural, and qualified easily as a pilot. He began devoting himself to airplane construction. Within five years he dominated the aerospace industry, flooding the field with technical innovations.

In 1939 he consolidated his holdings as the Magna Corporation (corporate press release: "... had Mr. Belding graduated Stanford, he would have received his degree *magna cum laude*."), and moved from Texas to Los Angeles, where he built corporate headquarters, an aircraft assembly plant, and a private airstrip on a 1,500-acre tract in the suburb of El Segundo.

Rumors of a public stock offering made bulls and bears take note. But the offering never materialized and Wall Street regretted that out loud, calling Lee Belding a cowboy who'd eventually bite off more than he could chew. Belding had no comment, continued branching out—to shipping, railroads, real estate, construction.

He obtained the contract for a Department of Labor annex in Washington, D.C., built low-cost housing in Kentucky, an army base in Nevada, then bucked the mob and the unions in order to create the Casbah—the largest, most ostentatious casino ever to blot out the Las Vegas sun.

By his thirtieth birthday he'd increased his inheritance thirty times over, was one of the five richest men in America, and definitely its most secretive, refusing interviews and shunning public events. The press forgave him; playing hard to get only made him better copy and gave them more latitude.

Privacy, the last luxury . . .

It wasn't until after World War II that the honeymoon between America and Leland Belding began to sour. As the nation buried its dead, and working people faced an uncertain future, left-leaning journalists began to point out that Belding had used the war to become a billionaire while ensconced in his penthouse at Magna headquarters.

Subsequent snooping revealed that between '42 and '45, the assets of the Magna Corporation had quadrupled, due to successful bidding for thousands of government defense contracts: Magna had been the armed forces' prime supplier of bombers, aircraft guidance systems, antiaircraft weapons, tanks and halftracks, even K-ration kits and servicemen's uniforms.

Terms like *robber baron, profiteer,* and *exploiter of the working man* began to crop up in editorials, commentators asserting that Lee Belding was all take, no give, a self-obsessed tightwad devoid of the slightest shred of patriotic spirit. One writer pointed out that he never donated to charity, hadn't given a penny to the War Bond drive.

Rumors of corruption soon followed—intimations that all those contracts hadn't been won by putting in the lowest bid. By early 1947 the intimations became accusations and took on enough substance for the U.S. Senate to pay heed. A subcommittee was created, charged with investigating the genesis of Leland Belding's war profits and dissecting the inner workings of the Magna Corporation. Belding ignored the furor, turned his talents to movies, bought a studio, and invented a hand-held motion picture camera that promised to revolutionize the industry.

In November of '47, the Senate subcommittee held public hearings.

I found a summary of the proceedings in a business magazine— conservative point of view, no pictures, all small print and dry prose.

But not dry enough to camouflage the racy nature of the main accusation against Belding:

That he was less captain of industry than high-class pimp.

Committee investigators claimed Belding had shifted the odds on contract bids by throwing "wild parties" for War Board officials, government purchasing agents, legislators. These bashes took place in several secluded Hollywood Hills houses purchased by the Magna Corporation expressly as "party pads," and featured "stag movies," flowing booze, indulgence in "marijuana reefers," as well as nude dancing and swimming displays by legions of "young women of loose morals."

These women, described as "professional party girls," were aspiring actresses chosen by the man who ran Belding's studio, a "former management consultant" named William Houck "Billy" Vidal.

The hearings went on for more than six months; then, gradually, what had promised to be a juicy story began to shrivel. The subcommittee proved unable to produce witnesses to the notorious parties, other than Belding's business competitors, who testified from hearsay and crumpled in cross-examination. And the billionaire himself refused subpoenas to testify, on the grounds of endangering the national security, and was backed up by the Defense Department.

Billy Vidal did show up—in the company of high-priced legal talent. He denied his major role was to procure women for Leland Belding, described himself as a successful Beverly Hills-based management consultant to the film industry prior to meeting Belding, and produced documents to prove it. His friendship with the young tycoon had begun when the two of them were students at Stanford, and he admired Lee Belding. But he denied involvement in anything illegal or immoral. A legion of character witnesses backed him up. Vidal was dismissed.

When subpoenas for Magna's accounting records were rejected by the company, once again on the basis of national security, and both Defense and State backed up Belding, the committee reached an impasse and died.

The senators saved face by delivering a mild reprimand to Leland Belding, noting his invaluable contributions to the national defense but suggesting he be more careful in the future with his record keeping. Then they assigned staffers to compile a report of their findings and voted the committee out of existence. Cynics suggested that in view of the charge that members of Congress had been on Belding's party list, the entire process had been just another example of the foxes guarding the henhouse. But by this time no one really cared; now the country was ripe with optimism, intent on rebuilding, and determined to have a damned good decade. If a few hearty rascals had indulged in a little high living, so be it.

Party pads. A film connection. Stag films. I wanted to know more about Bashful Belding's conduit to the fast life.

Before I could return to the index section to look for anything on William Houck Vidal, the announcement that the library was closing in fifteen minutes came blaring out of a ceiling speaker. I collected my two books and as many unread periodicals as I could carry, made a beeline for the photocopy machines, and spent the next ten minutes feeding dimes. Then I went downstairs and used my faculty card to check out the books. Armed with my treasures, I headed home.

21

A white VW Rabbit was parked in front of my carport, blocking the Seville. A young woman slouched against it, reading a book.

When she saw me she sprang up.

"Hi! Dr. Delaware?"

"Yes."

"Dr. Delaware? I'm Maura Bannon? From the *Times*? The Dr. Ransom story? I wondered if I could talk to you—just for a minute?"

She was tall and stick-skinny, about twenty, with a long, freckled face that needed finishing. She wore yellow sweats and white running shoes. Her pageboy hairdo was dyed orange with pink overtones, the same color as the lashes around her light-brown eyes. She had a marked overbite with a toothpick-wide gap between the upper incisors.

The book in her hand was Wambaugh's *Echoes in the Darkness* and she'd flagged it in several places with yellow tags. Her nails were gnawed stubby.

"How'd you find out where I live, Ms. Bannon?"

"We reporters have our ways." She smiled. It made her look around twelve.

When she saw I wasn't smiling back, she said, "There's a file on you at the paper. From a few years ago? When you were involved in catching those child molesters?"

Privacy, the last luxury. "I see." At least Ned Biondi hadn't played fast and loose.

"I could tell from reading the clippings on you that you're a dedicated person," she said. "Someone who doesn't like bullshit? And bullshit is what they're giving me."

"Who is?"

"My bosses. Everyone. First they tell me to forget the Ransom story. Now, when I ask to cover the Kruse murders, they give it to that dweeb Dale Conrad—I mean the guy never leaves his desk. He has about as much drive as a sloth on Quaaludes. When I tried to reach Mr. Biondi, his secretary told me he was out of town—off to *Argentina,* taking some *Spanish* course. Then she handed me an assignment to follow up a trained horse story—out in *Anaheim*?"

A mild, warm breeze blew in from somewhere across the glen. It ruffled the tags in her book.

"Interesting reading?" I said, holding my own books in a way that obscured their titles.

"Fascinating. I want to be a crime writer—get into the core of good and evil? So I need to immerse myself in life-and-death issues. I figured I'd go with the best—the man was a cop, has a real solid experiential base. And the people in this one were so weird—outwardly respectable but totally crazed. Like the people in this case?"

"Which case?"

"*Cases,* actually. Dr. Ransom? Dr. Kruse? Two psychologists dying in the same week—two psychologists who were connected to each other. If they were connected in life, maybe in death too? Which means Ransom may have been murdered, don't you think?"

"How were they connected?"

She made a naughty-naughty gesture. "Come on, Dr. Delaware, you know what I'm talking about. Ransom was one of Kruse's students. More than that—a prize student. He was her doctoral committee chairman."

"How do you know that?"

"Sources. C'mon, Dr. Delaware, stop being coy. You're a graduate of the same program. You knew *her,* so chances are you knew *him,* too, right?"

"Very thorough."

"Just doing the job. Now could you please talk to me? I'm not giving up on this story."

I wondered how much she actually knew and what to do with her.

"Want some coffee?" I said.

"Do you have tea?"

Once inside the house, she said, "Camomile, if you've got it," and immediately began inspecting the decor. "Nice. Very L.A."

"Thanks."

Her gaze shifted to the pile of papers and unopened mail on the table and she sniffed. I realized the place had taken on a stale, unlived-in smell.

"Live alone?" she asked.

"For the moment." I went into the kitchen and stashed my research materials in a cupboard, fixed her a cup of tea and myself a cup of instant coffee, put all of it on a tray with cream and sugar, and brought it into the living room. She was half-sitting, half-lying on the sofa. I sat down facing her.

"Actually," I said, "I was off campus by the time Dr. Kruse came to the University. I graduated the year before."

"Two months before," she said. "June of '74. I found *your* dissertation too." She flushed, realized she'd given away her "sources," and tried to recover by looking stern. "I'm still willing to bet you knew him."

"Have you read the Ransom dissertation?"

"Skimmed it."

"What was it about?"

She bobbed her tea bag, watched the water in her cup darken. "Why don't you answer some of my questions before I answer yours?"

I thought of the way the Kruses had looked in death. Lourdes Escobar. D.J. Rasmussen. Bodies piling up. Big-money connections. Grease the skids.

"Ms. Bannon, it's not in your best interests to pursue this case."

She put the cup down. "What's *that* supposed to mean?"

"Asking the wrong questions could be dangerous."

"Oh, wow," she said, rolling her eyes. "I don't believe this. Sexist protectionism?"

"Sexism has nothing to do with it. How old are you?"

"That's not relevant!"

"But it is, in terms of experience."

"Dr. Delaware," she said, standing, "if all you're going to do is patronize me, I'm out of here."

I waited.

She sat. "For your information, I've worked as a reporter for *four years.*"

"On your college paper?"

She flushed, deeper this time. Bye-bye, freckles. "I'll have you know the college beat had plenty of tough stories. Because of one of my investigations, two bookstore clerks were fired for embezzling."

"Congratulations. But we're talking about a whole other level now. It wouldn't do to have you sent home to Boston in a box."

"Oh, come *on*," she said, but there was fear in her eyes. She masked it with indignation. "I guess I was wrong about you."

"Guess so."

She walked to the door. Stopped and said, "This is rotten, but no matter."

Primed for action. All I'd done was whet her appetite.

I said, "You may be right—about there being a connection between the deaths. But at this point all I've got is guesses—nothing worth discussing."

"Guesses? You've been snooping *yourself*! Why?"

"That's personal."

"Were you in love with her?"

I drank coffee. "No."

"Then what's so personal?"

"You're a very nosy young lady."

"Goes with the territory, Dr. Delaware. And if it's so dangerous, how come it's okay for *you* to snoop?"

"I've got police connections."

"Police connections? That's a laugh. The cops are the ones covering up. I found out—through *my* connection—that they've done a total Watergate on Ransom. All the forensic records have disappeared—it's as if she never existed."

"My connection's different. Outside the mainstream. Honest."

"That gay guy from the molester case?"

That caught me by surprise.

She looked pleased with herself. A minnow swimming happily among the barracudas.

I said, "Maybe we can cooperate."

She gave me something intended to be a hard, knowing smile. "Ah, back-scratching time. But why would I want to deal?"

"Because without dealing, you'll get nowhere—that's a promise. I've uncovered some information you'll never be able to get hold of, stuff that's useless to you in its present form. I'm going to follow it up. You'll have exclusive rights to whatever I come up with—*if* going public's not hazardous to our health."

She looked outraged. "Oh, that's just great! It's okay for big strong brave to go hunting but squaw must stay in teepee?"

"Take it or leave it, Maura." I began clearing the cups.

"This stinks," she said.

I waved goodbye. "Then go do your own thing. See what you come up with."

"You're boxing me in and pulling a power trip."

"You want to be a crime writer? I'm offering you a chance—not a guarantee—to get a crime story. And live long enough to see it come to print. Your alternative is to barrel ahead like Nancy Drew, in which case you'll either end up being fired and sent home on a supersaver flight, or *shipped* back in the baggage hold in the same physical state as the Kruses and their maid."

"The maid," she said. "No one talks about her."

"That's 'cause she's *expendable,* Maura. No money, no connections—human garbage, straight to the compost heap."

"That's crude."

"This is no teenage sleuth fantasy."

She tapped her foot, chewed a thumbnail.

"Put it in writing?" she said.

"Put what in writing?"

"That we have a deal? A contract? I have first dibs on your info?"

"I thought you were a journalist, not an attorney."

"Rule one: cover your ass."

"Wrong, Maura. Rule one is never leave tracks."

I carried the tray into the kitchen. The phone rang. Before I could get to it, she'd picked up the living room extension. When I came back she was holding the phone and smiling. "She hung up."

"Who's 'she'?"

"A woman. I told her to hold on, I'd get you. She said forget it, sounded angry." Cute smile. "Jealous." Shrug. "Sorry."

"Very classy, Maura. Is total lack of manners part of your job training?"

"Sorry," she said, looking, this time, as if she meant it.

A woman. I pointed to the door. "Goodbye, Ms. Bannon."

"Listen, that really *was* rude. I *am* sorry."

I went to the door and held it open.

"I *said* I was sorry." Pause. "Okay. Forget about the contract. I mean if I can't trust you, a piece of paper would be worthless, wouldn't it? So I'll trust you."

"I'm touched." I turned the doorknob.

"I'm *saying* I'll go along."

I said, "Back-scratching time?"

"Okay, okay, what do you want in return?"

"Three things. First, a promise to back off."

"For how long?"

"Until I tell you it's safe."

"Unacceptable."

"Have a nice day, Maura."

"Shit! What do you want!"

"Before we go on, let's be clear," I said. "No drop-ins, no eavesdropping, no cute stuff."

"I got it the first time."

"Who's your contact at the coroner's? The person who told you about the missing file."

She was shocked. "What makes you think he—or she—is at the coroner's?"

"You mentioned forensic data."

"Don't assume too much from that," she said, struggling to look enigmatic. "Anyway, no way will I divulge my sources."

"Just make sure he—or she—cools it. For personal safety."

"Fine."

"Promise?"

"*Yes!* Was that Two?"

"One-B. Two is tell me everything you've learned about the connection between Ransom and Kruse."

"Just what I've told you. The dissertation. He was her supervisor. They had an office together in Beverly Hills."

"That's it?"

"That's *it*."

I studied her long enough to decide I believed her.

She asked, "What's Three?"

"What was the dissertation about?"

"I told you I've only skimmed it."

"From what you've skimmed."

"It was something on twins—twins and multiple personalities and, I think it was, *ego integrity*. She used a lot of jargon."

"Three is make me a photocopy."

"No way. I'm not your secretary."

"Fair enough. Return it where you found it—probably the ed-psych library at the University—and I'll make my own copy."

She threw up a hand. "Oh, what the hell, I'll drop off a Xerox tomorrow."

"No drop-ins," I reminded her. "Mail it—express it."

I wrote down my Fed-Ex number and gave it to her. She stuck it between the pages of the Wambaugh book.

"Shit," she said. "Are you this authoritarian with your patients?"

I said, "That's it. We're in business."

"At least *you* are. I haven't gotten a damned thing but promises."

She scrunched up her face. "You'd better come through for me,

Dr. Delaware. Because one way or the other, I'm going to get a story."

"When I learn something reportable, you'll be the first person I call."

"And one more thing," she said, half out the door. "I'm no damned teenager. I'm twenty-one. As of yesterday."

"Happy birthday," I said. "And many more."

After she drove off I called San Luis Obispo. Robin answered.

"Hi, it's me," I said. "Was that you a few minutes ago?"

"How'd you ever guess?"

"The person who picked up said there was an angry woman on the other line."

"The person?"

"Some kid reporter who's bugging me about an interview."

"Kid as in twelve?"

"Kid as in twenty-one. Buckteeth, freckles, a lisp."

"Why do I believe you?"

"Because I'm saintly. It's great to hear from you. I wanted to call—each time I hang up I regret the way the conversation turned out. Think of all the right things to say, but it's too late."

"That's the way I feel, too, Alex. Talking to you has been like walking a mine field. As if we're lethal ingredients—can't mix without exploding."

"I know," I said. "But I've got to believe it doesn't have to be that way. It wasn't always that way."

She said nothing.

"Come on, Robin, it used to be good."

"Of course it did—a lot was wonderful. But there were always problems. Maybe they were all mine—I kept it all inside. I'm sorry."

"Blame is useless. I want to make it better, Robin. I'm willing to work at it."

Silence.

Then she said, "I went into Daddy's shop yesterday. Mom has it preserved just the way it was at the time he died. Not a tool out of place, like a museum. The Joseph Castagna Memorial. She's that way—never lets go, never *deals* with anything. I locked myself in, just sat there for hours, smelling the varnish and the sawdust, thinking of him. Then of you. How similar the two of you are: well-meaning, warm, but dominant—so strong you take over. Alex, he would have liked you. There would have been conflict—two bulls scratching and snorting—but eventually the two of you would have been able to laugh together."

She laughed herself, then cried.

"Sitting there, I realized that part of what attracted me to you was that similarity—how much you were like Daddy. Even physically: the curly hair, the blue eyes. When he was younger he was handsome, the same type of good looks as yours. Pretty profound insight, huh?"

"Sometimes it's hard to see that kind of thing. God knows I've missed plenty of obvious things."

"Guess so. But I can't help feeling stupid. I mean, here I've been going on and on about independence and establishing my identity, resentful of you for being strong and dominating, and all along I've *wanted* to be taken care of, wanted to be *daddied*. . . . God, I miss him so much, Alex, and I miss *you,* too, and it's all meshing into one big hurt."

"Come back home," I said. "We can work it out."

"I want to but I don't. I'm afraid everything will go back to being just like it was before."

"We'll make it different."

She didn't answer.

A week ago I would have pushed. Now, with ghosts tugging at my heels, I said, "I want you back right now, but you've got to do what's right for yourself. Take your time."

"I really appreciate your saying that, Alex. I love you."

"Love you too."

I heard a creak, turned and saw Milo. He saluted and retreated hastily from the kitchen.

"Alex?" she said. "Are you still there?"

"Someone just walked in."

"Little Miss Buckteeth?"

"Big Mr. Sturgis."

"Give him my love. And tell him to keep you out of trouble."

"Will do. Be well."

"You too, Alex. I mean it. I'll call soon. 'Bye."

" 'Bye."

He was in the library, thumbing through my psych books, pretending to be interested.

"Hello, Sergeant."

"Major league oops," he said. "Sorry, but the goddamned door was open. How-many-times-have-I-told-you-about-that."

He resembled an old sheepdog that had wet the rug. Suddenly all I wanted to do was alleviate his embarrassment.

"No secret," I said. "Temporary separation. She's up in San Luis Obispo. We'll work it out. Anyway, you probably figured it out, right?"

"I had my suspicions. You've been looking stepped-on. And you haven't been talking about her the way you usually do."

"Thus spake the detective." I walked over to my desk, began straightening papers without purpose.

He said, "Hope you guys work it out. The two of you were good."

"Try to avoid the past tense," I said sharply.

"Oops again. Mea culpa. Mia Farrow." He beat his breast but looked genuinely abashed.

I went up to him and patted his back. "Forget it, big guy. Let's talk about something more pleasant. Like murder. I went digging today, came up with some interesting stuff."

"Dr. Snoop?" he said, adopting the same protective tone I'd used on Maura.

"The library, Milo. Not exactly combat duty."

"With you, anything's possible. Anyway, you tell me yours, I'll tell you mine. But not on a dry mouth."

We went back into the kitchen, popped a couple of beers, and opened a package of sesame breadsticks. I told him about Sharon's fantasy childhood—the East Coast society background that resembled Kruse's, the orphanhood that echoed Leland Belding's.

"It's as if she's collecting fragments of other people's histories in order to build one of her own, Milo."

"Okay," he said. "Other than her being a stone liar, what does that mean?"

"Probably a serious identity problem. Wish fulfillment—maybe her own childhood was filled with abuse or abandonment. Being a twin played a part in it too. And the Belding connection is more than coincidence."

I told him about the War Board parties. "Secluded Hollywood Hills houses, Milo. The one on Jalmia fits that bill. Her mother works the party pad circuit. Thirty-five years later, Sharon's living in a pad."

"So what are you saying? Old Basket Case was her daddy?"

"It would sure explain the high-level cover-up, but who knows? The way she twisted the truth has me doubting everything."

"Cop-thinking," he said.

"I checked out a couple of books on Belding—including *The Basket-Case Billionaire*. Maybe something in there will be useful."

"The book was a scam, Alex."

"Sometimes scams are laced with a bit of truth."

He chewed a breadstick, said, "Maybe. How'd you find it, anyway? I thought the damn thing was recalled."

"I asked the librarian about that. Apparently, large libraries get advance copies; the recall order only applied to bookstores and commercial distributors. Anyway, it's been buried there since '73, very few checkouts."

"Rare show of good taste on the part of the reading public," he said. "Anything else?"

I recounted my meeting with Maura Bannon.

"I think I convinced her to back off, but she's got a source at the coroner's."

"I know who it is."

"You're kidding."

"Nope. Your telling me clears something up. Few days ago there was this third-year med student from S.C. rotating through the coroner's office. Asking too many questions about recent suicides, seemed to be snooping around the files. *My* source told me about it. He was worried it was someone from the city, spying around."

"Is he still snooping?"

"Nah, rotation's over, kid's outta there. Probably just a boyfriend angling for some white-knight sex from Lois Lane Junior. Anyway, you did right to cool her off. This whole thing keeps getting weirder and weirder and the fix *is* in heavy. Yesterday, at the Kruse place, Trapp shows up before the crime scene crew arrives, all evil smiles, wanting to know how I caught the call when I'm still officially on vacation. I told him I'd come in early to the squad room, was working at my desk clearing some paperwork when an anonymous call came through reporting foul play at the Kruse address. Total crap, wouldn't have fooled a rookie. But Trapp didn't pursue it, just thanked me for my initiative and said he'd take over from here."

Milo growled, cracked his knuckles. "Asshole *co-opted* me."

"I saw him on the news."

"Wasn't that a display? Bullshit augmented by horseshit. And more to follow: Word has it Trapp's pushing the sex maniac angle. But those women weren't positioned like any sex murder victims I've ever seen—no spread legs or sexual posing, no rearranged clothing. And, as far as my coroner source can tell, given the state of the bodies, no strangulation or mutilation."

"How did they die?"

"Beaten and shot—no way to tell which came first. Hands tied behind the backs, single bullet to the back of the head."

"Execution."

"That would be *my* working guess."

He took his anger out on a breadstick, crunching and wiping crumbs off his shirt. Then he finished his beer and went to get another one from the fridge.

"What else?" I said.

He sat down, tilted his head back and poured brew down his throat. "Time of death. Putrefaction's no exact science, but for that much rot to go down in an air-conditioned room, even with the door open, those bodies had to be lying there for a while. There was gas bloat, skin peel, and fluid loss, meaning days, not hours. Four to ten days is my source's theoretical range. But we know the Kruses were alive last Saturday, at that party, so that narrows it to four to six days."

"Meaning they could have been killed either after Sharon died, or before."

"That's right. And if it was *before,* a certain scenario rears its ugly head confirming your theory about Rasmussen. I called the Newhall sheriffs station about him. They knew him well: ugly drunk, chronic troublemaker, very short fuse, multiple assault busts, and he did kill his dad—beat him to death, then shot him. Now we know he was getting it on with Ransom, but not as an equal, right? He was a major maladjust, probably had half her IQ. She was manipulating him, playing with his head. Let's say she had some major beef against Kruse and mentioned it to Rasmussen. She wouldn't even have had to be direct—as in *go and kill the bastard.* Just hint around, complain about how Kruse had hurt her—maybe use hypnosis. You said she knew hypnosis, right?"

I nodded.

"So she could have used it to soften Rasmussen up. Angling for some white-knight pussy of his own, he went and played Lord High Executioner."

"Killing his father all over again," I said.

"Ah, you shrinks." His smile faded. "The maid and the wife died because they were in the wrong place at the wrong time."

He stopped talking. The silence put me somewhere else.

"What's the matter?"

"Seeing her as a murder contractor."

"Just a scenario," he said.

"If she was that cold, why'd she kill herself?"

He shrugged. "Thought you might be able to fill in that one."

"I can't. She had problems, but she was never cruel."

"Fucking all those patients wasn't an act of charity."

"She was never overtly cruel."

"People change."

"I know that but I just can't see her as a killer, Milo. It doesn't sit right."

"Then forget it," he said. "It's all theoretical bullshit, anyway. I can spin you ten like it in as many minutes. And it's about as far as we're gonna go, given the state of the evidence—too many unanswerable questions. Like are there phone records tying Rasmussen to Ransom between the time the Kruses died and the time she died? Newhall to Hollywood is a toll call. Normally, that would be easy to trace, except when I tried, the records had been pulled and sealed, courtesy of my employers. And who reported Ransom's death in the first place? Normally, if I wanted to know that, I'd just take a peek in her file, but there ain't no goddam file. Courtesy, my employers."

He got up, rubbed his hand over his face, and paced the kitchen.

"I drove up to her house this morning, wanted to talk to her neighbors, see if any of them had made the call. I even figured out who lived across the canyon and visited them to see if they'd seen anything, heard anything, maybe a peeper with a telescope. Zilch. Two of the four houses in her cul-de-sac were unoccupied—owners out of town. The third's owned by this free-lance artist, old gal who does children's books, shut-in, bad arthritis. She wanted to help. Problem is, from her place you can't see what's going on in Ransom's—just the driveway. No good view from any of them, matter of fact."

"Party pad architecture," I said.

"Hmm," he said. "Anyway, from her garden, the artist could see some comings and goings. Occasional visitors—women and men, including Rasmussen—in and out after about an hour's time."

"Patients."

"That's what she assumed. But all that stopped about half a year ago."

"The same time she was caught sleeping with her patients."

"Maybe she decided to retire. Except for Rasmussen—she held on to him. He kept coming, not often, but up until a month ago, the artist remembered seeing the green truck. She also described a guy who sounded like Kruse—he stayed longer, several hours at a time, but she only saw him once or twice. Which doesn't mean much. She can't get around too well—it might have been more often. Other interesting thing is that a photo of Trapp didn't register. Which means he probably wasn't one of Ransom's boyfriends. And if the bastard was investigating the case, he never bothered to talk to the next-door neighbor—didn't even do the basics. Sum total: Slimeball's involved in the cover-up. And I'm off the case. Goddammit, Alex, it makes my adrenals hurt."

"There are other question marks," I said. "Your scenario's based on some kind of hostility between Sharon and Kruse. She *was* having problems—she told me so at the party. But nothing indicates they were with Kruse. At the time of her death she was still registered as his assistant. She showed up at a party to *honor* him, Milo. I did see her arguing with that older guy I told you about. But I have no idea who he is."

"What else?" he said.

"There's lots of other factors to consider: Belding, Linda Lanier, the blackmailed doctor, whoever he is. And Shirlee, the missing twin—I called Olivia Brickerman, tried to get into the Medi-Cal files. The computer was down. I'm hoping for something soon."

"Why're you still pushing that? Even if you find her, you won't be able to talk to her."

"Maybe I can find someone who knows her—knew both of them. I don't believe we'll ever understand Sharon without knowing more about Shirlee, about the relationship between the two of them. Sharon perceived Shirlee as more than a sister—they were psychological partners, halves of a whole. Twins can develop identity problems. Sharon chose that topic—or something like it—for her doctoral dissertation. Ten to one she was writing about herself."

That gave him pause.

"Air your dirty laundry and get a Ph.D.? That's considered kosher?"

"Not at all. But she managed to get around lots of things."

"Well," he said, "you go ahead, look for your twin. Just don't expect too much."

"What about you?" I said.

"I've got another day and a half left before Trapp locks me into some new plum assignment. Seeing as we're dealing with thirty-five-year-old stuff, there comes to mind someone who might be able to educate us. Someone who was around in those days. Problem is he's unpredictable, and we're not exactly good buddies."

He got up, slapped his thigh. "What the hell, I'll give it a try, call you tomorrow morning. Meantime, keep reading those books and magazines. Uncle Milo will be giving you a pop quiz when you least expect it."

22

I spent the rest of the day getting a master's degree in Leland Belding, starting where I'd left off—the demise of the Senate hearings.

Immediately following his reprimand, the billionaire threw himself into the movie business, renaming his studio Magnafilm, scripting, directing, and producing a string of combat sagas featuring rugged individualist heroes who bucked the establishment and emerged victorious. All were panned by the critics as mechanical and bland. Audiences stayed away.

In 1949 he purchased a Hollywood trade paper, fired the film critic, and installed his own yes man. Bought a string of movie houses and filled them with his product. More losses. In 1950 he went into deeper seclusion than ever and I found only one reference covering the next two years: Magna's patent application for an aluminum-reinforced girdle that suppressed bulges but heightened jiggle. The device, developed for an actress with a tendency to corpulence, was marketed as the Magna-Corsair. American women didn't go for it.

In late 1952 he emerged, suddenly a new man—a public Leland Belding, attending premieres and parties, squiring starlets to Ciro's, Trocadero, the Mocambo. Producing a new string of films—vapid comedies heavy with double entendre.

He moved from his "monastic" apartment at Magna headquarters to an estate in Bel Air. Built himself the world's most powerful private jet, upholstered in leopard skin and paneled with antique walnut stripped from a centuries-old French chateau that he reduced to rubble.

He bought Old Masters by the truckload, outbid the Vatican for religious treasures plundered from Palestine. Snapped up race horses, jockeys, trainers, an entire racecourse. A baseball team. An entire passenger train which he converted to a moving party pad. He acquired a fleet of custom-made cars: Duesies, Cords, Packards, and Rolls-Royces. The world's three largest diamonds, auction houses full of antique furniture, more casinos in Vegas and Reno, an assortment of domiciles stretching from California to New York.

For the first time in his life he began contributing to charity— hugely, ostentatiously. Endowing hospitals and scientific research institutions, on condition that they be named after him and staffed by him. He threw lavish balls supporting the opera, the ballet, the symphony.

All the while, he was assembling a harem: actresses, heiresses, ballerinas, beauty queens. The most eligible bachelor had finally come into his own.

On the surface, a radical personality shift. But a *Vogue* writer, reporting on a bash Belding threw for the Metropolitan Museum of Art, described the billionaire as "standing on the sidelines, unsmiling and fidgety, observing the festivities rather than participating in them. He looked, to these admittedly cynical eyes, like a little lost boy locked in a room full of candy—so much candy that he's lost his appetite for sweets."

Given all the partying, I expected to find something about William Houck Vidal. But there was nothing, not even a snapshot, to suggest that the former "management consultant" had participated in the metamorphosis of his boss. The sole mention of Vidal during the early fifties was a quote in a business journal regarding early development of a new fighter bomber. A quote attributed to "W. Houck Vidal, Senior Vice-President and Head of Operations for Magna."

One man going from businessman to playboy. The other reversing the process. It was as if Belding and Vidal were perched on a psychic teeter-totter.

Switching identities.

Then, in early '55, all of it stopped.

Belding canceled a gala for the Cancer Society, dropped completely from sight. Then commenced what one magazine called "the greatest rummage sale in history." The mansions, cars, jewels, and other trappings of princely consumption were sold—at great profit. Even the movie studio—nicknamed Magnaflop—earned millions in real estate appreciation.

The press wondered what Belding's new "phase" would be. But there was none, and when it became clear that the disappearing act was permanent, coverage grew progressively sketchier until, by the mid-sixties, neither Belding nor Magna was mentioned other than in financial and technical journals.

The sixties: Oswald. Ruby. Hoffman and Rubin. Stokely and Rap. No shortage of actors willing to strip for the camera. No one cared about a rich hermit who'd once made bad movies.

In 1969, Leland Belding's death was reported "somewhere in California, following a prolonged illness." In accordance with the bachelor billionaire's will, a group of former Magna executives assumed leadership of Magna, with the chairman of the board position going to William Houck Vidal.

And that was it. Until 1972, when a former reporter and hack ghostwriter named Seaman Cross produced a book claiming to be the unauthorized biography of Leland Belding. According to Cross, the billionaire had faked his death in order to achieve "true peace." Now, having meditated in solitude for seventeen years, he'd decided he had something to say to the world and had chosen Cross as his Pepys, granting hundreds of hours of interviews for a proposed book before abruptly changing his mind and calling off the project.

Cross went ahead and completed the book anyway, titling it *The Basket-Case Billionaire* and obtaining a "strong six-figure advance." During its very brief life, it had caused a furor.

Not my kind of stuff. I hadn't paid much attention to it at the time. But I ate it up now, didn't put it down until I finished.

Cross's thesis was that a personal tragedy during the early fifties—a tragedy Belding refused to discuss but which Cross guessed was romantic—had plunged the young billionaire into a manic playboy phase, followed by serious mental collapse and several years of convalescence in a private mental hospital. The man who emerged was "a phobic, paranoid, self-obsessed devotee of a bizarre personal philosophy combining Eastern religion, militant vegetarianism, and Ayn Randish individualism taken to the extreme."

Cross claimed numerous visits to Belding's home, a hermetically sealed geodesic dome, somewhere out in the desert, which the billionaire never left. The mode of transport was dramatic: Cross was driven, always blindfolded, always in the middle of the night, to a heliport less than an hour out of L.A.—the implication was El Segundo—then flown to the dome for about two hours and whisked home before dawn.

The dome was described as equipped with a computerized communications panel by which Belding could monitor his international business interests, regulate air and water purification systems (developed by the Magna Corporation for NASA), automatic vacuuming and ambient chemical disinfection, and a convoluted network of pipes, valves, tubes, and chutes through which mail, messages, sterile food and drink entered and waste material exited.

No one but Belding was allowed inside the dome; no photos or sketches were permitted. Cross had been forced to conduct his interviews from a booth on wheels, positioned so that it abutted a speaker panel on the dome.

"We communicated," he wrote, "by a two-way microphone system that Belding controlled. When he wanted me to see him, he afforded me a view through a clear plastic window—a panel that he could blacken with the touch of a button. He used this blackout panel, not infrequently, to punish me for asking the wrong question. He would withhold his attention until I apologized and promised to be good."

Bizarre as that was, the strangest part of the story was Cross's description of Belding:

> Emaciated to near-Auschwitzian dimensions, full-bearded, with long, matted gray hair reaching halfway down his back, tangles of crystal necklaces hanging from his wattled neck, and huge crystal rings on every finger. The nails of those fingers were polished a glossy black, sharpened into points, and appeared nearly two inches long. The color of his skin was an eerie greenish-white. His eyes, behind thick rose-tinted lenses, bulged exophthalmically and never ceased to move, darting from side to side and blinking like those of a toad hunting flies.
>
> But it was his voice that I found most unsettling—flat, mechanical, completely stripped of emotion. A voice devoid of humanity. Even now I shiver when I think of it.

Cross's posture throughout the book was one of morbid fascination. He couldn't conceal his antipathy toward the billionaire, but neither could he tear himself away.

> At regular intervals [he wrote] Belding would interrupt our sessions to nibble on raw vegetables, drink copious amounts of sterilized water, then squat to urinate and defecate, in full view of this writer, into a brass pot that he kept atop an altarlike platform. Once the pot had sat on the altar for precisely fifteen minutes, he'd remove it and expel it

through an evacuation chute. During the process of excretion, a self-satisfied, near-religious expression would settle upon his gaunt, raptorish features, and though he refused to discuss this ritual, my reflexive impression was: self-worship, the logical culmination of a lifetime of unbridled narcissism and power.

The latter half of the book was fairly dull stuff: Cross pontificating about the weakness of a society that could create a monster like Belding, transcripts of Belding's ramblings on the meaning of life—a barely intelligible amalgam of Hinduism, nihilism, quantum physics, and social Darwinism, including indictments of the "mental and moral dwarfs who deify weakness."

The biography ended with a final burst of editorializing:

> Leland Belding represents everything wrong with the capitalist system. He is the grotesque result of the concentration of too much wealth and too much power in the hands of one eminently fallible and twisted man. He is the emperor of self-indulgence, a fanatical misanthrope who views other life forms as nothing more than potential sources of bacterial and viral infection. He is preoccupied with his own body on a corpuscular level and would like nothing more than to live out his day on a planet denuded of all animal and plant life, other than those organisms required to sustain what remains of the wretched life of one Leland Belding.

The Basket-Case Billionaire had been a well-kept publishing industry secret, catching even the Magna Corporation by surprise, garnering massive post-publication attention, and shooting immediately to the top of the nonfiction best-seller list. A record paperback sale was made. Magna lost no time in suing Cross and his publishers, claiming the book was a hoax and libelous, producing medical and legal documents proving Leland Belding had indeed died, years before Cross claimed to have spoken with him. Reporters were taken to a gravesite at company headquarters; a body was exhumed and verified as Belding's. Cross's publisher got nervous and asked the writer to produce *his* data.

Cross reassured them and held a defiant news conference, his editor at his side, in front of a public storage vault in Long Beach, California, where he'd stashed thirty cartons of notes, many of them supposedly signed and dated by Leland Belding. Cameras whirring, he unlocked the vault, opened box after box, only to find each stuffed with notes unrelated to Belding. Frantic, he continued searching, produced old college essays, tax returns, stacks of bound newspapers, shopping lists—the detritus of a life soon to be ruined.

Not a word on Belding. Cross's horror was captured in close-up as he shrieked conspiracy. But when a police investigation concluded that no one but the writer had entered the vault, and his editor admitted she'd never actually seen the alleged notes, Cross's credibility vanished.

His publishers, faced with public humiliation and a legal adversary rich enough and tough enough to bankrupt them, settled quickly: They ran full-page ads in major newspapers featuring apologies to the Magna Corporation and the memory of Leland Belding. Immediately ceased further publication, and recalled all volumes shipped to stores and wholesalers. Refunded the record paperback advance to the soft-cover house.

The publishers then sued Cross, demanding return of *his* advance plus interest plus punitive damages. Cross refused, hired attorneys, countersued. The publishing house filed a criminal complaint for fraud and misrepresentation in New York District Court. Cross was arrested, fought extradition and lost, was shipped back East and imprisoned for five days at Riker's Island. During that time he claimed to have been beaten and homosexually raped. He tried to sell his account of the ordeal to several magazines but none was interested.

Released on bail, he was found one week later in a tenement room on Ludlow Street in New York's Lower East Side, head in the oven, a note on the floor admitting the book had been fiction, an audacious scam. He'd taken the risk, believing Magna would be too publicity-shy to challenge him, hadn't meant to harm anyone and was sorry for any pain he'd caused.

More death.

I turned to the magazines, looking for coverage of the hoax, found a long feature in *Time,* complete with a picture of Cross, shackled, in police custody. Next to that was a shot of William Houck Vidal.

The chairman of Magna had been photographed walking down courtroom steps, a wide smile on his face, the fingers of one hand held in a victory V.

I knew that face. Big and square and deeply tanned. Narrow pale eyes, a few blond hairs remaining in the brush-cut hair.

A country club face.

The face, fifteen years younger, of the man I'd seen with Sharon at the party. The old sheik she'd been trying to convince of something.

23

I reached Milo the next morning and told him what I'd learned.

He said nothing for a moment, then: "I've got us a history lesson lined up at eleven. Maybe we can tie up some more loose ends."

He arrived at ten after ten. We got in the Seville and he directed me east on Sunset. The boulevard was Sunday-empty even on the Strip. Only a thin gathering of brunchers and featherheaded rockers hunched at sidewalk cafés, mixing with coke whores, call girls, and call boys trying to shake off the night before.

"Wholesome," said Milo. He pulled out a cigar, said, "You got me started on these again," lit up, and blew soapy-looking smoke out the window.

"What is that? Panamanian?"

"Transylvanian." He puffed with enthusiasm. Within seconds the car was fogged.

We cruised past La Brea, past Western. No more café scene, just fast-food stands, pawnshops, discount outlets, and darker skin tones. Through the window came laughter and transistor music seasoned with bursts of Spanish. Families strolled the boulevard—parents young enough to be kids themselves, marshaling broods of black-haired cherubs.

"Now that's wholesome," I said.

He nodded. "Cream of the crop—I mean it. Poor devils ransom everything they own to the goddam *coyotes,* get raped, robbed, and ripped off trying to make it over the fence. Then we treat 'em like vermin and send 'em back, as if the goddam country wasn't built on immigration—hell, if my forebears hadn't stowed away on a steamer and snuck in through Canada, I'd be digging potatoes somewhere out in County Cork." He thought about that. "Seen postcards of County Cork. Maybe better off?"

We passed through the Hospital Row that stretched between Edgemont and Vermont, rode past Western Peds, where I'd spent so much of my life.

"Where're we going?" I asked.

"Just keep driving." He ground the cigar out in the ashtray. "Listen, there's something else I should tell you. After I left you yesterday, I took a drive out to Newhall and spoke to Rasmussen's old lady—Seeber."

"How'd you find her? I never gave you her name."

"Don't worry, your virtue's intact. Newhall sheriffs took her statement on the accident. I got the address from that."

"How's she doing?"

"Seems to have made a good recovery—already has another guy shacking up with her. Skinny Casanova with junkie eyes and dirty arms, thought I was raiding and was halfway out the window before I calmed him down."

He stretched, yawned. "Anyway, I asked her if Rasmussen had been working much recently. She says no, his temper had gotten him into too many scrapes. Nobody wanted him on their crew. She's been supporting the both of them for the past six months with the roach wagon gig. Then I popped the matter of the thousand bucks he left her on the pillow, and she almost wet her pants. Even though the sheriffs released the money to her, she's scared I'm gonna confiscate it—what's left of it. Chances are Junkie's shoveled most of it up his arm.

"I calm her down, tell her if she cooperates she can keep it, keep all the *rest* of it too. She gives me this look that says 'How'd *you* know about all the rest of it?' Bingo. I say, how much was it, Carmen? Fess up. She hems and haws, tries to play hard-to-get—gives it her best shot, but she really doesn't have much will and finally she just blurts everything out: D.J. had come into lots of money recently, was throwing it around, buying expensive parts for his truck. She's not really sure of the exact amount—ya know? But she found ya know forty-four hundred more in one of his ya know socks."

"How long ago was recently?"

"Couple of weeks ago. At least one week before everyone started dying."

I kept driving, past the Silverlake district and Echo Park, toward the western edge of downtown, where skyscrapers rose out of a tangle of freeway loops and back streets, glinting silver and bronze against a mud-bottomed sky.

"If it was cash for kill," he said, "you know what that means. Premeditation—someone'd been planning that contract. Setting it up."

He told me to turn left on an unmarked alley that climbed north of Sunset and tunneled between two building-supply lots. We passed dumpsters stuffed to the rim, graffiti'd rear walls, piles of plywood discards, damaged window screens, and hacked-up packing crates. Another quarter mile and we were weaving on cracked asphalt through weed-choked lots. At the back of some of the lots were lean-to shacks that looked ready to crumble. The alley angled and turned to dirt. Fifty yards later it terminated at a cinder-block wall. To the left, more dead grass; to the right of it a crow's-eye view of the freeway.

"Park," said Milo.

We got out. Even this high up, the traffic roared from the interchange.

The block wall was topped by barbed wire. Cut into the block was a round-topped wooden door scraped raw by time and the elements. No lock, no handle. Just a rusty metal spike imbedded in the wood. Looped around it was a leather thong. Hanging from the thong was an old, corroded cowbell. A tile sign over the door said: RUE DE OSCAR WILDE.

I looked up at the barbed wire, said, "Where are the gun turrets?"

Milo frowned, picked up a rock, and hit the cowbell. It gave off a dull clunk.

All at once, from the other side of the wall came a rising tide of animal sounds. Dogs, cats—lots of them. And barnyard clatter: poultry clucks. Goat bleats. The animals got closer, louder—so loud that they almost blocked out the sound of the freeway. The goats were the loudest. They made me think of voodoo rites, and the back of my neck tingled.

"Don't say I never took you anywhere interesting," said Milo.

The animals were scratching at the other side of the wall. I could smell them.

Milo called out, "Hello."

Nothing. He repeated the greeting, pounded the cowbell several times.

Finally a whiny, crackling voice of indeterminate gender said, "Hold your frigging water. Who's there?"

"Milo."

"So? What do you want me to do? Break open the frigging Mouton Rothschild?"

"Opening the door would be a good start."

"Wouldn't it just."

But the door did push open. An old man stood in the doorway, wearing only a baggy pair of white boxer shorts, a red silk scarf around his neck, and a long puka-shell necklace that rested on a hairless chest. Behind him an army of quadrupeds bounced and squealed and churned up the dust: dozens of dogs of uncertain pedigree, a couple of battle-scarred tomcats, and in the background, chickens, geese, ducks, sheep, several black Nubian goats, which licked the dust and tried to chomp our cuffs.

"Cool it," said Milo, swatting.

The old man said, "Down, quiet," without enthusiasm. He walked through the opening, closed the door behind him.

He was midsized and very thin, but flabby, with stringy arms and knobby, varicosed legs, narrow, sagging, grandmother's breasts, and a protuberant belly. His skin had been sun-baked the color of bourbon and had an oily sheen. The hair on his head was skimpy white fuzz, as if he'd coated his bare pate with glue, then dipped it in cotton wool. He had a weak chin, big beak nose, and narrow-set eyes that squinted so tightly they appeared sealed shut. A shaggy white Fu Manchu mustache ran down the sides of his mouth, continuing past the jawline and dangling an inch.

He looked us over, frowned, spat on the ground.

Gandhi with gastritis.

"Afternoon, Ellston," said Milo. "Nice to see you're in your usual good cheer." The sound of his voice set the dogs howling.

"Quiet. You're upsetting them—way you always do." The old man came up to me and stared, running his tongue along the inner wall of one cheek, scratching his head. He gave off a strange blend of odors: children's zoo, French cologne, mentholated unguent.

"Not bad," he said finally, "but Rick was cuter."

He touched my shoulder. I stiffened involuntarily. His stare hardened and he spat again.

Milo stepped closer to me. "This is Dr. Alex Delaware. He's a friend."

"Another doctor?" The old man shook his head and turned to me. "Tell me one thing, Curly: What the hell you upscale medico studs see in an ugly, uncouth lump like him?"

"Friend," said Milo. "As in *friend*. He's straight, Ellston."

The old man raised a limp wrist, adopted a mincing pose.

"Sure he is, darling." The old man looped his arm in mine. "What kind of *doctor* are you, Dr. Alex?"

"Psychologist."

"Ooh," he drew away quickly, stuck out his tongue and made a raspberry. "I don't *like* your type, always analyzing, always judging."

"Ellston," said Milo, "you gave me enough shit over the phone, I have no appetite for any more. If you want to help, fine. If not, that's fine, too, and we'll leave you to play Farmer John."

"Such a rude lump," said the old man. To me: "He's a frigging rude lump. Full of anger. Because he still hasn't accepted what he is, thinks he can deal with all of it by playing *po-lice-man.*"

Milo's eyes flashed.

The old man's opened wide in response. The left iris was blue; the right, milky gray with cataract.

"Tsk, tsk, our poor gendarme is upset. Hit a nerve, Lump? Good. The only time you look half-human is when you're pissed off. When you get frigging *real.*"

" 'I don't like your type,' " mimicked Milo. " 'Always analyzing, always judging.' " To me: "Enough of this crap. Let's split."

"Suit yourself," said the old man, but there was worry in his voice. A headstrong kid who'd pushed his parents too far.

We headed back to the car. Every step we took made the dogs bark louder.

The old man cried out, "Stupid Lump! No patience! Never had any."

Milo ignored him.

"Just so happens, Lump, that the subject of your inquiry is one with whom I'm well versed. I actually *met* the rat bastard."

"Right," said Milo over his shoulder. "And you fucked Jean Harlow."

"Well, maybe I did that too." An instant later: "What's in it for me, anyway?" The old man was raising his voice to be heard over the animals.

Milo stopped, shrugged, turned. "Good will?"

"Ha!"

"Plus a hundred for your time. But forget it."

"Least you could have frigging done," shouted the old man, "was to be civil!"

"I tried, Ellston. I always try."

The old man was standing with his hands on his hips. His boxer shorts flapped and his hair flew out like strands of cotton candy.

"Well, you didn't try hard enough! Where was the introduction? A proper, civil introduction?" He shook one fist and his loose flesh danced.

Milo growled and turned. "An introduction will make you happy?"

"Don't be an ass, Sturgis. I haven't aimed for happy in a long, long time. But it might frigging *placate* me."

Milo swore under his breath. "C'mon," he told me. "One more try."

We retraced our steps. The old man looked away from us, worked his jaws and tried hard to maintain dignity. The boxer shorts interfered.

"Ellston," said Milo, "this is Dr. Alex Delaware. Alex, meet Mr. Ellston Crotty."

"Incomplete," huffed the old man.

"*Detective* Ellston Crotty."

The old man held out his hand. "Detective *First Grade* Ellston J. Crotty, Junior. Los Angeles Police Department, Central Division, retired." We shook. He thumped his chest. "You're looking at the Ace of Central Vice, Dr. Curly. A pleasure to make your frigging acquaintance."

The animals followed us as if heading for the Ark. A homemade pathway of railroad ties and cement squares bordered by unkempt hedges and sick-looking dwarf citrus trees took us to a small, asphalt-shingled house with a wide front porch littered with boxes and old machine parts. Next to the house an ancient Dodge coupe sat on blocks. The structure looked out on a flat half-acre of dirt yard fenced with chicken wire. More goats and poultry paced the yard. To the rear of the property was a ramshackle henhouse.

The barnyard smell had grown intense. I looked around. No neighbors, only sky and trees. We were atop a hill. To the north were smog-glazed hints of mountaintop. I could still hear the freeway, providing a bass line to the treble clucks of the chickens.

Leaning against one of the fence posts was a bag of feed corn. Crotty stuck his hand in, tossed a handful of grain into the yard, and watched the birds scramble.

"Frigging greedy bastards," he said, then gave them some more.

Old MacDonald's farm on the edge of the urban jungle.

We climbed onto the porch.

"This is all frigging illegal," Crotty said with pride. "Breaks every frigging zoning law in the books. But my *compadres* down the hill are all illegals living in noncode shacks. Love my fresh eggs and hate the authorities—hell if *they're* going to rat. I pay their little kids to clean up the coop, two bucks an hour—more greenback than they're ever gonna see otherwise. They think I'm some kind of frigging great white father."

"Great white shark," muttered Milo.

"What's that?"

"Some of those little kids are pretty sharp."

"Well, I wouldn't know about that, but they do know how to work their little tushies off, so I pay 'em. All of them think I'm the greatest frigging thing since sliced bread. Their *mamacitas* are so grateful, they bring me food all wrapped in aluminum foil—they love aluminum foil. Good stuff, too, no fast-food shit—menudo and sweet tamales like you used to be able to get over on Alvarado before the corporate frigs took over."

He pushed open a screen door, walked into the house, and let it slam shut. Milo caught it. We entered.

The house was small and unlit, crammed so full of junk there was barely room to walk. We inched our way past stacks of old newspapers, towers of cardboard boxes and raw-wood fruit crates, jumbles of clothing, an upright piano painted with gray primer, three ironing boards bearing a collection of clock radios in various stages of disassembly. The furniture that managed to coexist with the clutter was cheap, dark wood and overstuffed chairs sleeved with antimacassars and doilies. Thrift shop fare.

The floor was pine, trodden gray, splintered in several places by dry rot. A mantel above the bricked-in fireplace bore porcelain figurines, most of them chipped or missing limbs. The clock on the mantel wall said Coca-Cola. It was frozen at seven-fifteen.

"Sit," said Crotty. He brushed newspapers off an easy chair and sank down. A cloud of dust rose and settled like dew.

Milo and I cleared a sofa with broken springs, created our own dust storm.

Crotty cleared his throat. Milo pulled out his wallet and handed him several bills. The old man counted it, fanned it out, closed his fingers over it. "Okay, let's make this quick. Belding. Leland, A. Capitalist pig, too much money, no morals, a latent fag."

I said, "Why do you say that?" and heard Milo groan.

Crotty turned on me. "Because I'm a frigging expert on latency is why, Dr. Psychology. *You* might have the diploma, but I've got the experience." He grinned and added, "Hands-on experience."

"Let's stick to Belding," said Milo.

Crotty ignored him: "Let me tell you, Curly, one thing I know, it's latents. For thirty years I frigging lived that trip."

Milo yawned, closed his eyes.

"*He's* frigging bored," said Crotty. "If anyone should be listening it's him. Hell, you'd think someone in his position would seek me out, kneel at my feet and beg for my accumulated wisdom. But no, how do I meet the lump in the first place? Half-dead in the Emergency Room, sweet Rick massaging my heart, bringing me back to life. And then this lump shows up all Dragnet-butch, checking his watch and wanting to know when Rick's going off-shift. Frigging Beauty and the Beast."

He turned to Milo, shook one finger. "You were always insensitive. There I was fading away and all you could think of was your cock."

"Don't make it sound life-threatening, Ellston. You had an upset stomach. Gas. Too much menudo, not enough fiber."

"So *you* say." To me: "Got your work cut out for you, shrink. That is one big frigging piece of work sitting next to you—take you years just to get through the top layer of denial."

"Belding," said Milo. "Or give back the bread."

"Belding," repeated Crotty. "A capitalist. Vicious. *Because* he was a latent. I know what that does to a person." He got up, looked over a group of boxes on the floor, went down on his knees in front of one of them and pawed through it with both hands.

"Here we go," said Milo.

Crotty pulled out a brown cloth scrapbook, flipped pages, wiped his forehead, then sat down next to me and pointed.

"There."

His fingertip rested next to a snapshot of a young man in police uniform. Black-and-white, sawtooth edges, just like the one of Sharon and Shirlee.

The young man wore a police uniform, stood next to a patrol car on a palm-lined street. His features were delicate, almost girlish, his eyes big and round. Innocent. Thick, wavy dark hair parted in the middle, a dimple on his right cheek. A pretty boy—the easily bruised countenance of a young Monty Clift.

"Glom this," said Crotty and pointed to another photo on the page. Same man in civilian attire, standing next to the Dodge I'd just seen in the driveway. He wore sports clothes and had his arm around the waist of a girl. She wore a halter and shorts, was shapely. Her face had been scratched out with a ballpoint pen.

"I was some piece of beef back then," said Crotty. He yanked the book away, snapped it shut, and tossed it on the floor.

"Those were taken in '45. I was just out of Uncle Sam's Navy, earned ribbons in the Pacific, thought I was God's gift to women and kept telling myself that those little shipboard episodes with the cook—sweaty Swedish meatball—had been just a bad dream. No matter that doing it with him had felt the way love should feel, and all the frails I nailed had a better time than I did."

He tapped his chest. "I was as sweet as Mary Pickford but trying to convince myself I was frigging Gary Cooper. So what better job for an overcompensating macho buck than to wear blue and carry a big stick?"

He laughed. "Day I got my discharge papers, I applied to the force. Day I finished the academy I thought I was King Hetero Stud. Being Butch Blue was going to solve all my problems. The brass took one look at me and knew exactly where to send me. Toilet decoy in MacArthur Park till all the local queers made me, then gay-bar detail over in Hollywood. I was great, busted more faggots than any other piece of bait. Got promoted, assigned to Vice, spent the next ten years of my life busting *more* faggots—busting *myself,* drinking it off every night. I made detective in record time but was nothing more than a frigging lure—kissed up to so many sad suckers my lips started to callous. Vice loved me. I was their frigging secret weapon, batting my lashes, breaking up private parties up in the hills, rousting raucous black-and-tans out in the colored districts—*that* gave the other pigs the chance to break some nappy heads."

He reached over, took hold of my collar, opened his good eye wide. He was sweating and seemed to have gone pale, though in the dim light it was hard to be sure.

"Know the reason I was so frigging good, Curly? 'Cause deep down inside I wasn't acting. Slam, bam, out in the alley, then here come the other Vice pigs with their saps and their sticks. Another meat wagon full of faggots expressed to County Lockup, black-and-blue, puking blood. Once in a while one of them would hang himself in his cell. The Vice boys would say good riddance, less paperwork. I'd laugh the loudest, chug-a-lug the fastest."

His mustache quivered. "For ten years I was an accessory to the assault and murder of gay men, never stopped to wonder why I was going home each night, puking my own guts out and drinking gin until I could feel my liver sizzling."

He let go of my collar. Milo was looking the other way, staring off into space.

"I was eating myself up is why," said Crotty. "Until I took a vacation down south—Tijuana. Crossed the border looking for action, got stoned drunk in a *cantina* watching a donkey mount a woman, stumbled outside and asked a cabbie to take me to a whore-house. But the cabbie wasn't fooled. Drove me to a crappy little place on the outskirts of town. Cardboard walls painted turquoise, chick-ens outside the door and in. Twenty-four hours later I *knew* who I was, knew I was trapped. What I didn't know was how to get out of it."

He folded and unfolded the money, finally crumpled it in his fist. "No guts for quick suicide, I kept pouring the sauce down. Wasn't till a year later—February—that opportunity knocked. Some-one tipped Vice to a big soiree out on Cahuenga—absinthe drinkers and dancing boys, an all-sweet jazz band, things in drag smoking reefer. I sailed in wearing a boatnecked sailor shirt, red scarf—*this* frigging scarf. Inside of thirty seconds I'd snagged a fish—good-looking blond kid, Ivy League get-up, rosy cheeks. Took him outside, made sure to unlock the door, let him kiss me, then stood there fighting not to cry as he got beat up. They broke the whole place open, tore the frigging house *apart,* but I just sat on the sidelines, only got credit for the blond kid's bust."

He stopped, wiped his brow again. "Early the next morning I showed up to process the paper on him but they were gone and so was he. I got pissed, checked it out, found out he was the son of a city councilman, champion athlete, high school valedictorian, Har-vard sophomore, BMOC. *Leverage.* I got off the force with honorable discharge, full pension plus another chunk of cash for *'disability'* settlement. The blond kid went back to Boston, married money, had four kids, ran a bank. I bought El Rancho Illegalo, here, learned about myself, tried to undo ten years by helping others—giving wisdom to those who take it." He glared at Milo, who ignored him, then turned back to me. "Happy ending, right, Dr. Psychology?"

"Guess so."

"Then you guess *wrong,* because at this very moment that blond kid is stretched out on a sanitarium bed out in Altadena, dying of AIDS, frigging skeleton. Dying alone because wifey and the four kids have cut him off like an obscene phone call. I found out through the network, been seeing him. Saw him yesterday, in fact, and changed his frigging *diapers.*"

Milo cleared his throat. Crotty turned on him.

"God forbid *you* should get involved with the network, Lump. Maybe reach out to help someone. Perish the thought *you* should admit to sizzling *your* liver 'cause you don't know who you are."

"Belding," said Milo, taking out his note pad. "That's what we're here to talk about."

"Ah," said Crotty disgustedly.

No one spoke for a while.

"Mr. Crotty," I said, "why do you think Belding was latent?"

The old man coughed, waved his hand. "Ahh, who the hell knows. Maybe he wasn't. Maybe I'm full of shit. One thing I can tell you, he was no stud, despite how the papers played up his dating all those actresses. I did meet him. At a party. He used to hire off-duty cops for security. And sometimes not so off-duty—the department was in to him in a big way, kissing his rich ass until it sparkled."

"Be specific," said Milo.

"Yeah, right. Okay, one time, must have been back in '49 or '50, I got pulled off a child-molesting case and assigned to one of his bashes out in Bel Air—priorities, eh? Big charity thing, full orchestra, all the best folks tooting and shuffling, lots of female flesh, plenty of cloakroom clinches. But all Stud Belding did was watch everyone else. That's what he was—a watcher. Like some frigging camera on legs. I remember thinking what a cold bastard he was—repressing. Latent."

"That's what you meant by meeting him?"

"Yeah. We shook frigging hands, okay?"

"Why'd you call him vicious?" I said.

"I call killing vicious."

"Who'd he kill?" asked Milo.

Crotty wiped his brow and coughed. "Thousands of people, Lump—all the ones his frigging planes bombed."

Milo looked disgusted. "Thanks for the political commentary. Anything more you want to tell us about Belding?"

"I told you plenty."

"How about his sidekick, Vidal?"

"Billy the Pimp? He was at that party too. Very suave. Good teeth. Excellent-looking teeth."

"Anything else besides his dental health?"

"He was supposed to be the one who supplied Belding with the girls."

"What about the War Board parties?" asked Milo. "The ones Belding got investigated for. Did the department do guard duty on those?"

"Wouldn't surprise me. Like I said, the department was in to him."

"Name names," said Milo, pencil poised.

"It was a frigging long time ago, Lump."

"Listen, Ellston, I didn't pay a hundred to get stuff I can get in the locker room."

Crotty smiled. "Guy in your situation, Lump, doesn't get anything in the locker room."

Milo ran his hand over his face. A knot swelled his jawline.

"Okay, okay," said Crotty. "The two I'm sure were in Belding's pocket were a couple of shits named Hummel and DeGranzfeld. Working Ad-Vice when I came on—as head crackers. Soon after, Hummel was transferred out to be the chief's chauffeur. A year later he was a lieutenant out at Newton Division, which was a hell of a match because he was a racist pig, used to go down to Main Street and beat colored whores to a pulp. Wore pigskin gloves—said he wanted to avoid infection."

"How do you know he and the other guy were Belding's boys?"

"It was obvious from the way they moved up fast without earning it—they were connected. And both of them always dressed good, ate good. DeGranzfeld had a big house out in Alhambra, horses, orchard land. You didn't have to be Sherlock to see they were in somebody's pocket."

"Lots of pockets besides Belding's."

"Let me frigging finish, Lump. Later, both of them quit the force and went to work for Belding at probably six times the salary, all the graft they could eat."

"First names," said Milo, writing.

"*Royal* Hummel. *Victor* DeGranzfeld—Sticky Vicky we used to call him. He was a twerp and a sneak, too yellow-bellied to get physical but just as sadistic as Hummel. When he worked Vice he was head bagman, coordinated collections from all the downtown bookies and pimps. When Hummel moved to Newton he had DeGranzfeld transferred over there as day-watch commander. Bosom buddies, probably a couple of latents themselves. Later both of them were picked to head Metro Narcotics—this was in the early fifties, there was a big dope panic, and the department knew it could get funding increases by making big busts."

"All right," said Milo. "Let's talk about the houses Belding owned—the party pads. Know where any of them were located?"

Crotty laughed. "Party pads? Isn't that sweet? Where'd you come up with that, Lump? *Party* pads. They were *fuck* pads—everyone called 'em that, 'cause that's what Mr. Leland Belding used 'em for. Brought bigwigs there, had a stable of bimboes all set to clean their pipes until they were ready to sign on any frigging dotted line. And no, I don't know any locations. Never got invited to *those* soirees."

He got up, sidestepped a wall of boxes, and went through a doorway into what I assumed was the kitchen.

Milo said, "Sorry you had to hear his life story."

"It's okay. It was interesting."

"Not after the thousandth time."

"You bad-mouthing me?" Crotty had come out of the kitchen, was glaring at us, a glass of water in one hand, the other balled up in a fist.

"No," said Milo. "Just admiring the decor."

"Hah!" The old man opened his free hand, revealing a palmful of pills.

"Vitamins," he said and swallowed some of them. He washed them down, grimaced, swallowed some more, and rubbed his abdomen. "I'm getting tired. Get the hell out of here and let me get some rest."

"Tab's not run yet," said Milo.

"Make it snappy."

"Got a couple more names for you. Actress named Linda Lanier, rumored to be one of Belding's bimboes. And some doctor she screwed on a stag film—give him the physical description, Alex."

As I did, Crotty lost color and put the glass down on a crate. Wiped his forehead, seemed to lose balance, and rested his hands on the back of a moth-eaten settee. He puffed out his cheeks.

Milo said, "Let's have it, Ellston."

"Why're you poking around in the dead-letter pile, Lump?"

Milo shook his head. "You know the rules."

"Sure, sure. Come here and squeeze me, then throw me a few crumbs."

"A hundred buys a lot of squeeze," said Milo, but he pulled out his wallet and gave the old man more money.

Crotty looked surprised. He stared at the bills.

"Linda Lanier," said Milo. "And the doctor in the film."

"In reference to Belding?" asked Crotty.

"In reference to anything. Spit it out, Ellston. Then we'll leave you to dream of your Swede."

"You should know such dreams," said Crotty. He looked at the floor, rubbed his mustache, crossed his legs. "Linda Lanier. Well, well, well. Everything comes around in a circle, doesn't it? Like my little blond banker and everything else in this frigging world."

He straightened, stood, made his way to the gray piano, sat down and picked off a couple of notes. The instrument was badly out of tune. He extracted a dissonant boogie-woogie with his left hand, random high notes with his right.

Then, as abruptly as he'd begun, he stopped and said, "This is terribly weird, Lump. If I didn't know better, I'd start using words like *destiny*—not that I'd want you in my destiny." He played several bars of slow blues, let his hands fall to his sides. "Lanier and the doctor—you say they did it on film?"

Milo nodded and pointed to me. "He saw it."

"She was beautiful, wasn't she?"

I said, "Yes, she was."

"C'mon," said Milo, "spit it *out*."

Crotty gave a weak smile. "I fibbed, Lump. When you asked me about Belding being a killer. I fudged with that political shit because I didn't know what alley cat you were chasing. Actually I meant it literally, but I didn't want to get into it—nothing I could ever prove."

"You don't have to prove a goddam thing," said Milo. "Just tell me what you know." He peeled off more bills. Crotty snatched them.

"Your doctor," he said, "sounds exactly like a guy named Neurath. Donald Neurath, M.D. You described him to a T, Curly, and I know he and Linda Lanier had a thing going."

"How do you know that?" said Milo.

Crotty looked ill-at-ease.

"C'mon, Ellston."

"Okay, okay. One of my assignments, when I wasn't snaring faggots, was working the Scraper Club detail—illegal abortions. Back in those days there were three ways for a girl in trouble to go: coat hanger in the alley, some butcher in a white coat, or a bona fide medico moonlighting for big bucks. Neurath was one of the bona fides—plenty of doctors did it. But it was still a Class A felony, meaning excellent payoff potential for the department.

"There was an approved group of abortionists—we used to call it the Scraper Club—maybe twenty or so doctors, spread all over the city, respectable guys with established practices. They kicked back a percentage of their fees in return for protection by Vice and a guarantee that anyone not in the club would get busted hard and fast. And it worked. There was this one guy, osteopath out in the Valley, tried to muscle in on one of the approved guys' business by charging half as much for a scrape. A week after he started, they busted him—using a female cop who just happened to be pregnant. Bail denied, stuck in a county cell with hardcases. While he was in lockup, his office got torched and someone scared his daughter while she was walking home from school."

"Pretty," said Milo.

"That's the way it was back then, Lump. Are you sure it's that much better now?"

"You're positive this Neurath was a member of the club."

"I know it for a fact because I picked up moolah from his office. Big fancy suite on Wilshire near Western." He stopped, stared at Milo. "That's right, I played bagman too. Not my favorite frigging assignment, but I had enough on my mind without worrying about some penny-ante payoff for something that was gonna happen anyway. Hell, today a kid can walk into a clinic and leave scraped, half-hour later. So what's the big deal, right?"

Milo said, "Keep talking."

Crotty gave him a sour look. "We conducted our business after hours, no one around. I'd ride the elevator up to his office, make sure I was alone, give a coded knock on the door. Once I was in, neither of us would talk—pretending it wasn't happening. He'd hand me a manila envelope; I'd do a superficial count and be off."

"What kind of doctor was he?"

"Obstetrician. Nice little irony there, eh? Neurath giveth, Neurath taketh away."

"What about him and Lanier?"

"One evening, after I picked up the loot, I went down the block to this Chinese place to have a little moo-goo and rice wine before heading back. I was sitting in a back booth when in walks Neurath with this platinum-blond dish. It was dark; they didn't notice me. She had her arm in his—they were looking pretty cozy. They took a table across the room, sat close together, talking pretty intense. The old piece-on-the-side routine, except this dish was really elegant-looking, no tramp. Few minutes later she got up to go to the ladies' room and I got a good look at her face. It was then that I recognized her—from Belding's party. She'd been wearing a black dress—no back, very little front, lots of mink trim. Because of the mink, I'd figured her for a rich brat. She'd stuck in my mind because she was gorgeous, really gorgeous. Perfect face, delicious body. But elegant. Classy."

He shifted his glance to me. "I'm not without feeling for females, Dr. Psychology. Probably appreciate the species a lot more than most hetero studs."

"What else?" said Milo.

"Nothing else. They had a couple of drinks, coochy-cooed, then left—no doubt for some motel. No big deal. Then, about a year later, the dish's face is all over the papers. And the more I learn about it the more curious I get."

He coughed again, scratched his midriff. "There was this dope bust, lots of shooting. She got killed, along with some guy who turned out to be her brother. The papers made both of them out to be big-time pushers. She was a contract player with Belding's studio— never made a single film and supposedly that was strong evidence it was just a cover. No matter that most of the players never worked, and she'd been a party girl—not a word of that in print. The brother worked at the studio, too, as a grip. Both of them small potatoes. Yet they managed to pay the rent on this very ritzy pad on Fountain—ten rooms—owned a fancy car, were living frigging high. Papers made a big deal about that, going into detail about her furs and jewelry, about how the two of them had come a long way for a couple of Texas crackers—'cause that's what they were. Her real name was Eulalee Johnson. The brother was a nasty little punk named Cable, used to strong-arm small-time bookies, lean on streetwalkers, but never got too far—small-time all the way. Not exactly your big-time pushers, huh, Lump? But the department fed it to the papers, and the papers ate it like candy. Three hundred grand worth of H found on the premises—hell of a lot in those days. John Q. Public bought it."

"You didn't."

"Hell, no. No one pushing that much smack south of Fresno was doing it without mob connections—Cohen or Dragna. Certainly not a couple of Texas crackers who'd come out of nowhere. I checked the brother's sheet—drunk and disorderly, lewd conduct, larceny, the strong-arm stuff. Penny ante. No connections with anyone—no one on the street had ever seen him with a reefer in his pocket. The whole thing smelled bad. And the fact that Hummel and DeGranzfeld did the shooting made it stink to high heaven."

"Why were you checking, Ellston?"

Crotty smiled. "Always searching for leverage, Lump, but this was too scary. I didn't want to touch it. Still, it stuck in my craw. Now here you are stirring it up again—ain't that sweet."

"How'd it go down?" asked Milo.

"Supposedly someone phone-tipped Metro Narc to a huge stash in the Fountain pad. Hummel and DeGranzfeld took the call, brought a couple of black-and-whites along for backup, but had the uniforms wait outside while they checked out the premises. All's quiet on the western front, then bang bang bang. The uniforms rush in. Both Johnsons are shot to pieces on the living room floor; Hummel and

DeGranzfeld are tallying up this giant dope stash. Department's version is they knocked on the door, were met with unfriendly fire, smashed the door down and jumped in, guns ablazin'. Cute, eh? A party girl and a small-time drifter taking on Narco bulls."

"Any board of inquiry into the shooting?" said Milo.

"Very funny, Lump."

"Even with a woman getting shot? John Q.'s usually squeamish about that."

"This was '53, McCarthy fever, height of the dope panic. John Q. was paranoid about pushers in every schoolyard. And the department made Lanier out to be a big-time bad girl, Satan's frigging *bride*. Not only weren't Hummel and Sticky Vicky investigated, they were instant heroes—the mayor pinned ribbons on them."

This was '53. Just before Leland Belding had turned into a playboy.

The year of Sharon and Shirlee's birth.

"Did Linda Lanier leave any children?" I asked.

"No," said Crotty. "I'd remember that. That kind of thing would have made it into the papers—human interest and all that. Why? You got family members out for revenge?"

"Revenge against who?" asked Milo.

"Belding. That phony bust had his name written all over it."

"Why do you say that?"

"Hummel and DeGranzfeld were his boys; Lanier was his party girl—supporting that place on Fountain woulda been like you and me springing for lunch. In the process of asking around, I learned Lanier might have been more than just a party girl—she'd been known to enter Belding's private office on the studio lot, stay in for a couple of hours, leave happy. This is stuff *office boys* knew, but it never got a line of print. I figure they had something or other going, she offended Belding in some serious way, and he had to get rid of her."

"Offended how?" said Milo.

"Who knows? Maybe she got pushy about something. Maybe her stupid brother put the arm on the wrong guy."

"The doctor—Neurath—could have been her sugar daddy," said Milo.

Crotty shook his head. "Neurath had money problems. His wife was a compulsive gambler; he was into the sharks on and off—it's why he started moonlighting in the first place. And one more thing: Lanier's building on Fountain was owned by Belding."

Milo and I looked at each other.

Crotty said, "Bastard owned half of L.A. at one time."

"Neurath was an obstetrician," I said. "Maybe Linda Lanier was seeing him professionally."

"Pregnant?" said Crotty. "Putting the paternal squeeze on Belding? Sure, why not?"

Milo said, "How soon after the shooting did Hummel and DeWhatsisname quit?"

"Not long after, maybe a couple of months. And this with both of them commended and promoted. Now tell me more about the film Lanier and Neurath were on."

"Doctor and nurse skit," I said. "The doctor didn't know he was on camera."

"More strong-arm," said Milo. "The brother?"

"Could be," said Crotty.

"What would they be strong-arming Neurath about?"

"Who knows? Maybe the Scraper Club, maybe the wife's gambling problem. Either could have screwed up his reputation—he had a society practice, nice plump Hancock Park matrons waiting for stirrup time."

"Is he still around?"

"Who knows?"

"What about Hummel and DeGranzfeld?"

"DeGranzfeld died a couple of years after moving to Nevada. Affair with a married woman, husband had a temper. Far as I know, Hummel's still in Vegas. One thing for sure, he's still got pull in the department, or at least he did a couple of years ago."

"How so?" said Milo.

"He had this nephew, real fascist fuckup, liked the booze, almost flunked out of the academy, the bullying son of a bitch—frigging chip off the old block. He was involved in that Hollywood Division robbery scandal a few years back, eminently qualified for a Board of Rights or worse. But nothing, except a transfer to Ramparts. Then all of a sudden, guy's a born-again Christian, promoted to captain, West L.A.—" He stopped, stared at Milo, grinned like a kid on Christmas morning.

"So that's what this is about."

"What?" said Milo, innocently.

"Lump, you crafty badger. Gonna get that scum, aren't you? Finally do a good deed, after all."

24

After that, Crotty got solicitous, offering us coffee and cake, but we thanked him and declined, left him standing in the doorway, under the cowbell, surrounded by his animals.

"Feisty old guy," I said when we were back in the car.

"Bluster," said Milo. "He's been pouring it on since he tested positive."

"Oh."

"Yeah. Those pills weren't vitamins—they're some kind of immune strengthening regimen he got through his network. He beat hepatitis a few years back, thinks if he's mean enough he'll beat this too." Pause. "That's why I humored him."

It took a while to turn the Seville around in the alley. When we'd gone a couple of miles on Sunset, Milo said, "Trapp. Paying off old debts to his uncle." A moment later: "Got to find out what he's fixing."

"Maybe a murder made to look like suicide?"

"You keep coming back to that and wouldn't it be nice. But where's the evidence?"

"Belding and Magna were old hands at camouflaging murder."

"Belding's dead."

"Magna lives on."

"What? Some corporate conspiracy? The old chrome-and-glass bogeyman."

"No," I said, "it's always people. It always comes down to people."

Several blocks later he said, "The Kruse killings weren't made to look like anything but murder."

"Hard to do that with three bodies, so Trapp's using the sex murder thing instead. And maybe killing Kruse wasn't part of the plan—if Rasmussen did it, the way we theorized."

Milo's face got hard. We passed Vine. Hollywood was finally getting out of bed. The Cinerama Dome was showing a Spielberg movie and the lines stretched around the block. A few blocks farther it was all by-the-hour motels and jumpy-looking streetwalkers banking on loneliness and clean blood.

Milo stared at them, turned away, leaned back against the seat and said, "I could use a drink."

"Early for me."

"I didn't say I *wanted* one. I said I could *use* one. Descriptive statement."

"Oh."

When we stopped for a red light at La Cienega, he said, "What do you think of Crotty's theory? Lanier and her brother squeezing Belding and Neurath?"

"The loop sure seemed to be setting Neurath up."

"The loop," he said. "Where'd those porn freaks say they got it?"

"They didn't. Just said it was expensive."

"I'll bet," he said. Then: "Let's take a side trip, see if we can get them to be a little more forthcoming."

I drove to Beverly Hills and turned left at Crescent. The streets were empty; people who tear down $2 million houses in order to build $5 million houses tend to stay inside to play with their toys.

We pulled up in front of the Fontaines' green monstrosity and got out of the car.

The windows were shuttered. Empty driveway. No answer to Milo's ring. He tried again, waited several minutes before heading back toward the car.

I said, "Last time there were four cars here. They're not just out to brunch."

Before he could answer, a rattling noise from the neighboring house drew our attention. A heavyset dark-haired boy of around eleven was riding his skateboard up and down the driveway, dodging between a trio of Mercedes.

Milo waved at him. The boy stopped, turned off his Walkman, and stared at us.

Milo flashed his gold badge and the kid gave his board a kick and skated our way. He turned a handle on the front gate, rolled through, and sped over.

"Hi," said Milo. The boy peered at the badge.

"Beverly Hills cop?" he said, with a thick accent. "Yo, dude."

He had a black spiky hairdo and a buttery round face. His teeth were banded with plastic braces. A bit of black down clouded his cheeks. He wore a red nylon tank top emblazoned with the legend SURF OR DIE and red-flowered shorts that reached below his knees. His board was black graphite and plastered with decals. He spun its wheels and kept smiling at us.

Milo put away the badge, said, "What's your name, son?"

"Parvizkhad, Bijan. Six grade."

"Good to meet you, Bijan. We're trying to find the people next door. See them lately?"

"Mr. Gordon. Sure."

"That's right. And his wife."

"They gone."

"Gone where?"

"Trip."

"A trip where?"

The boy shrugged. "They take suitcase—Vuitton."

"When was this?"

"Sat-day."

"Saturday—yesterday?"

"Sure. They go away, have cars take away. On big truck. Two Rolls-Royce, gangster whitewalls Lincoln, and radical T-Bird."

"They put all the cars on a big truck?"

Nod.

"Was there a name on the truck?"

Uncomprehending look.

"Letters," said Milo. "On the side of the truck. The name of the tow company?"

"Ah. Sure. Red letters."

"Do you remember what the letters said?"

Shake of the head. "What's their case? Coke burn? Hit man?"

Milo stifled a smile, bent, and put his face close to the boy's. "Sorry, son, I can't tell you that. It's classified."

More puzzlement.

"Classified information, Bijan. Secret."

The boy's eyes lit up. "Ah. Secret Service. Walther PPK. Bond. Chames Bond."

Milo looked at him gravely.

The boy took a closer look at me. I bit my lip to keep a straight face.

"Tell me, Bijan," said Milo. "What time Saturday were the cars taken away?"

The boy gestured with his hand, seemed to be struggling for phrasing. "Zero seven zero zero hour."

"Seven in the morning?"

"Morning, sure. Father go to office, I bring him Mark Cross."

"Mark Cross?"

"His briefcase," I suggested.

"Sure," said the kid. "Napa leather. Executive styling."

"You brought your father his briefcase at seven in the morning and saw Mr. Gordon's cars being taken away on a truck. So your father saw it too."

"Sure."

"Is your father home now?"

"No. Office."

"Where's his office?"

"Century City."

"What's the name of his business?"

"Par-Cal Developers," said the boy, volunteering a phone number, which Milo wrote down.

"What about your mother?"

"No, she don't see. Sleeping. Still sleeping."

"Did anyone but you and your father see?"

"No."

"Bijan, when the cars were taken away, were Mr. Gordon and his wife there?"

"Just Mr. Gordon. Very angry about cars."

"Angry?"

"Always, about cars. One time I throw Spalding, hit Rolls-Royce, he get angry, scream. Always angry. About cars."

"Did someone damage one of his cars while they were taking it away?"

"No, sure not. Mr. Gordon jump around, scream to red men, say careful, careful, idiot, don't scratch. Angry always about cars."

"Red men," said Milo. "The men who took the cars away were wearing red clothing?"

"Sure. Like pit crew. Indy Five Hundred."

"Coveralls," muttered Milo as he scrawled.

"Two men. Big truck."

"Okay, good. You're doing great, Bijan. Now, after the cars were taken away on the truck, what happened?"

"Mr. Gordon go in house. Come out with Missus and Rosie."

"Who's Rosie?"

"The maid," I said.

"Sure," said the boy. "Rosie carry the Vuittons."

"The vweet—the suitcases."

"Sure. And one long bag for airplane. Not Vuitton—maybe Gucci."

"Okay. Then what happened?"

"Taxi come."

"Do you remember the color of the taxi?"

"Sure. Blue."

"Beverly Hills Cab Company," said Milo, writing.

"All get in taxi," said the boy.

"All three of them?"

"Sure. And Vuittons and one maybe-Gucci in trunk. I go out and wave, but they don't wave back."

Milo autographed one of the boy's Nikes, gave him a business card and a sheet of paper from his L.A.P.D. note pad. We returned his wave and left him skating up and down the empty block.

I got back into traffic on the east side of Sunset Park. The park was filled with tourists, milling around the arcing fountains, shading themselves under the floss trees. I said, "Saturday. They split the day after the Kruse murders were discovered. They knew enough to be scared, Milo."

He nodded. "I'm gonna call the taxi company, try to find who moved the cars—see if I can trace them that way. Check the post office in the event they left a forwarding—unlikely, but you never know. Call the kid's father, too, though I doubt he noticed as much as old Bijan. Kid was sharp, wouldn't you say?"

"You bet your Ralph Laurens," I said. And for the first time in a long time, we laughed.

But it faded quickly and by the time we reached home, both of us were morose.

"Fucking case," said Milo. "Too many dead people, too long ago."

"Vidal's still alive," I said. "Looking damned robust, in fact."

"Vidal," said Milo, grunting. "What did Crotty call him—Billy the Pimp? From that to chairman of the board. Steep climb."

"Sharp spikes would lend traction," I said. "Along with a few heads to step on."

25

My plan, Monday morning, was to return to the library and search for more on Billy Vidal and the Linda Lanier dope bust. But the Fed-Ex man came to the door at 8:20 bearing a single parcel. Inside was a dictionary-size book bound in dark-green leather. A note rubber-banded to the cover said: "Here. I kept my side of it. Hope you do ditto. M.B."

I took the book into the library, read the title page:

THE SILENT PARTNER: IDENTITY CRISIS AND EGO DYSFUNCTION IN A CASE OF MULTIPLE PERSONALITY MASQUERADING AS PSEUDO-TWINSHIP. CLINICAL AND RESEARCH RAMIFICATIONS.

by

Sharon Jean Ransom

———

A Dissertation Presented to the

FACULTY OF THE GRADUATE SCHOOL

In Partial Fulfillment of the

Requirements for the Degree

DOCTOR OF PHILOSOPHY

(Psychology)

June 1981

I turned to the dedication page.

> To Shirlee and Jasper, who have meant more to me than
> they could ever imagine, and to Paul, who has guided
> me, adroitly, from darkness to light.

Jasper?

Friend? Lover? Another victim?

In the Acknowledgments section, Sharon reiterated her thanks to Kruse, following it with cursory appreciation for the other members of her committee: Professors Sandra J. Romansky and Milton F. Frazier.

I'd never heard of Romansky, supposed she could have come to the department after I'd left. I pulled out my American Psychological Association Directory and found her listed as a consultant in public health at a hospital in American Samoa. Her bio cited a one-year visiting lectureship at the University during the academic year 1981–1982. Her appointment had been in women's studies, out of the anthropology department. In June of '81 she'd been a brand new Ph.D. Twenty-six years old—two years younger than Sharon.

The "outside member" permitted on each committee, usually chosen by the candidate for easygoing personality and lack of deep knowledge in the field of research.

I could try to trace her, but the directory was three years out of date and there was no guarantee she hadn't moved on.

Besides, there was a better source of information, closer to home.

Hard to believe the Ratman had agreed to sit on the committee. A hard-nosed experimentalist, Frazier had always despised anything vaguely patient-oriented and regarded clinical psychology as "the soft underbelly of behavioral science."

He'd been department chairman during my student days and I recalled how he'd pushed for the "rat rule"—requiring all graduate students to conduct a full year of animal research before advancing to candidacy for the Ph.D. The faculty had voted that down, but a requirement that all doctoral research feature experimentation—control groups, manipulation of variables—had passed. Case studies were absolutely forbidden.

Yet that was exactly what this study sounded like.

My eye dropped to the last line on the page:

> And deep thanks to Alex, who,
> even in his absence, continues to
> inspire me.

I turned the page so hard it nearly tore. Began reading the document that had earned Sharon the right to call herself doctor.

The first chapter was very slow going—an excruciatingly complete review of the literature on identity development and the psychology of twins, flooded with footnotes, references, and the jargon Maura Bannon had mentioned. My guess was that the student reporter hadn't gotten past it.

Chapter Two described the psychotherapy of a patient Sharon called J., a young woman whom she'd treated for seven years and whose "unique pathology and ideative processes possess structural and functional, as well as interactive, characteristics that traverse numerous diagnostic boundaries heretofore believed to be orthogonal, and manifest significant heuristic and pedagogic value for the study of identity development, the blurring of ego boundaries, and the use of hypnotic and hypnagogic regressive techniques in the treatment of idiopathic personality disorders."

In other words, J.'s problems were so unusual, they could teach therapists about the way the mind worked.

J. was described as a young woman in her late twenties, from an upper-class background. Educated and intelligent, she'd come to California to pursue a career in an unspecified profession, and presented herself to Sharon for treatment because of low self-esteem, depression, insomnia, and feelings of "hollowness."

But most disturbing of all were what J. called her "lost hours." For some time, she'd awakened, as if from a long sleep, to find herself alone in strange places—wandering the streets, pulled to the side of a road in her car, lying in bed in a cheap hotel room, or sitting at the counter of a dingy coffee shop.

Ticket stubs and auto rental receipts in her purse suggested she'd flown or driven to these places, but she had no memory of doing so. No memory of what she'd done for periods that calendar checks revealed to be three or four days. It was as if entire chunks had been stolen out of her life.

Sharon diagnosed these time warps correctly as "fugue states." Like amnesia and hysteria, fugue is a dissociative reaction, a literal splitting-off of the psyche from anxiety and conflict. A dissociative patient, confronted with a stressful world, self-ejects from that world and flies off into any number of escapes.

In hysteria, the conflict is transferred to a physical symptom— pseudoparalysis, blindness—and the patient often exhibits a *belle indifférence*: apathy about the disability, as if it were happening to someone else. In amnesia and fugue, actual flight and memory loss take place. But in fugue the erasure is short-term; the patient remembers who he or she was before the escape, is fully in touch when he comes out of it. It's what happens in between that remains the mystery.

Abused and neglected children learn early to cut themselves off from horror and, when they grow up, are susceptible to dissociative symptoms. The same is true of patients with fragmented or blurred identities. Narcissists. Borderlines.

By the time J. showed up in Sharon's office, her fugues had become so frequent—nearly one a month—that she was developing a fear of leaving her house, was using barbiturates to calm her nerves.

Sharon took a detailed history, probing for early trauma. But J. insisted she'd had a storybook childhood—all the creature comforts, worldly, attractive parents who'd cherished and adored her up until the day they died in an automobile crash.

Everything had been wonderful, she insisted; there was no rational reason for her to be having these problems. Therapy would be brief—just a tune-up and she'd be in perfect running order.

Sharon noted that this type of extreme denial was consistent with a dissociative pattern. She thought it unwise to confront J., suggested a six-month trial period of psychotherapy and, when J. refused to commit herself for that long, agreed to three months.

J. missed her first appointment, and the next. Sharon tried to call her but the phone number she'd been given was disconnected. For the next three months she didn't hear from J., assumed the young woman had changed her mind. Then one evening, after Sharon had seen her last patient, J. burst into the office, weeping and numbed by tranquilizers, begging to be seen.

It took a while for Sharon to calm her down and hear her story: Convinced that a change of scenery was all she really needed ("a willful flight," commented Sharon), she'd taken a plane to Rome, shopped on the Via Veneto, dined at fine restaurants, had a wonderful time until she woke up, several days later, on a filthy Venice side street, clothing torn, half-naked, bruised and sore, her face and body caked with dried semen. She assumed she'd been raped, but had no memory of the attack. After showering and dressing, she booked the next flight back to the States, drove from the airport to Sharon's office.

She realized now that she'd been wrong, that she seriously needed help. And she was willing to do whatever it took.

Despite that flash of insight, treatment didn't proceed smoothly. J. was ambivalent about psychotherapy and alternated between worshipping Sharon and verbally abusing her. Over the next two years it became clear that J.'s ambivalence represented a "core element of her personality, something fundamental to her makeup." She presented two distinct faces: the needy, vulnerable orphan begging for support, endowing Sharon with godlike qualities, flooding her with flattery and gifts; and the rage-swollen, foul-mouthed brat who claimed, "You don't give a shit about me. You're only into this in order to lay some giant fucking power trip on me."

Good patient, bad patient. J. grew more facile at switching between the two, and by the end of the second year of therapy, shifts were occurring several times during a single session.

Sharon questioned her initial diagnosis and considered another:

Multiple personality syndrome, that rarest of disorders, the ultimate dissociation. Though J. hadn't exhibited two distinct personalities, her shifts had the feel of "a latent multiple syndrome," and the complaints that had brought her into therapy were markedly similar to those exhibited by multiples unaware of their condition.

Sharon checked with her supervisor—the esteemed Professor Kruse—and he suggested using hypnosis as a diagnostic tool. But J. refused to be hypnotized, shied away from the loss of control. Besides, she insisted, she was feeling great, was sure she was almost completely cured. And she did look much better; the fugues had lessened, the last "escape" taking place three months earlier. She was free of barbiturates, had higher self-esteem. Sharon congratulated her but confided her doubts to Kruse. He advised waiting and seeing.

Two weeks later J. terminated therapy. Five weeks after that she returned to Sharon's office, ten pounds lighter, back on drugs, having experienced a seven-day fugue that left her stranded in the Mojave Desert, naked, her car out of gas, her purse missing, an empty pill vial in her hand. Every bit of progress seemed to have been wiped out. Sharon had been vindicated but expressed "profound sadness at J.'s regression."

Once again, hypnosis was suggested. J. reacted with anger, accusing Sharon of "lusting for mind control . . . You're just jealous because I'm so sexy and beautiful and you're a dried-up spinster bitch. You haven't done me a fucking bit of good, so where do you come off telling me to hand you my mind?"

J. stomped out of the office, proclaiming she was through with "this bullshit—going to find myself another shrink." Three days later she was back, stoned on barbiturates, scabbed and sunburned, tearing at her skin and weeping that she'd "really fucked up this time," and was willing to do anything to stop the inner pain.

Sharon began hypnotic treatment. Not surprisingly, J. was an excellent subject—hypnosis itself is a dissociation. The results were dramatic, almost immediate.

J. was indeed suffering from multiple personality syndrome. Under trance, two identities emerged: J. and Jana—identical twins, precise physical replicas of each other but psychological polar opposites.

The "J." persona was well-mannered, well-groomed, a high achiever, though tending toward passivity. She cared about other people and, despite the unexplained absences due to fugue, managed to perform excellently in a "people-oriented profession." She had an "old-fashioned" view of sex and romance—believed in true love, marriage, and family, absolute fidelity—but admitted to being sexually active with a man she'd cared deeply about. That relationship had ended, however, because of intrusion by her alter ego.

"Jana" was as blatant as J. was reticent. She favored tinted wigs, revealing clothing, and heavy makeup. Saw nothing wrong with "tooting dope, popping the occasional downer," and liked to drink . . . strawberry daiquiris. She boasted of being a "live-for-today bitch, queen of the hop-to, a total Juicy Lucy wrapped up in a fucking Town and Country ribbon, which makes what's inside all the more hot." She enjoyed promiscuous sex, recounted a party during which she'd taken Quaaludes and had intercourse with ten men, consecutively, in one night. Men, she laughed, were weak, primitive apes, governed by their lusts. A "sexy snatch is everything. With one of *these,* I can get as many of *those* as I want."

Neither "twin" acknowledged the other's existence. Sharon regarded their existence as a pitched battle for the patient's ego. And despite Jana's flair for drama, it was the mannerly J. who appeared to be winning.

J. occupied about 95 percent of the patient's consciousness, served as her public identity, carried her name. But the 5 percent claimed by Jana was the root of the patient's problems.

Jana stepped in, Sharon theorized, during periods of high stress, when the patient's defense system was weak. The fugues were brief periods of actually "being" Jana. Doing things that J. couldn't reconcile with her self-image as a "perfect lady."

Gradually, under hypnosis, Jana reappeared more and more, and eventually began describing what had happened during the "lost hours."

The fugues were preceded by a pressing drive for complete physical escape, an almost sensual pressure to bolt. Impulsive travel soon followed: The patient would put on a wig, get in her "party clothes," jump in her car, get onto the nearest freeway, and drive aimlessly, often for hundreds of miles, without itinerary, "not even listening to music, just the sound of my own hot blood pumping."

Sometimes the car "took" her to the airport, where she used a credit card to book a flight at random. Other times she stayed on the road. In either case, the jaunts usually ended in debauchery: an excursion to San Francisco that climaxed with a three-day orgy of "meth sniffing and righteous group gropes with a bunch of Angels in Golden Gate Park." Pill-eating in a Manhattan disco, followed by skin-popping heroin in a South Bronx shooting gallery. Orgies in various European cities, assignations with derelicts and "head-case street pickups."

And a "righteous skin groove." Making a pornographic movie "somewhere out in Florida. Fucking and sucking like a superstar."

The "parties" always ended in drug-induced blackout during which Jana retreated and J. woke up, oblivious to everything her "twin" had done.

This ability to split was the crux of the patient's problem, Sharon decided, and she targeted it for therapeutic assault. J.'s ego had to be integrated, the "twins" drawn closer and closer, eventually confronting each other, reaching some sort of rapprochement, and merging into one fully functioning identity.

A potentially traumatic process, she acknowledged, unsupported by much clinical data. Very few therapists claimed to have actually integrated multiple personalities, so the prognosis for change was poor. But Kruse encouraged her, supporting her theory that, since these multiples were identical "twins," they shared a "psychic core" and would be amenable to fusion.

During hypnosis she began introducing J. to small bites of Jana: brief glimpses of drives down a highway, a signpost or hotel room that Jana had mentioned. Camera-shutter exposures of neutral material that could be easily withdrawn if the patient's anxiety rose too high.

J. tolerated this well—no outward signs of anxiety, though she didn't respond to any of the Jana material and disobeyed Sharon's post-hypnotic suggestion that she recall these details. The following session was identical: no memory, no response at all. Sharon tried again. Nothing. Session after session. Blank wall. Despite the patient's previous suggestibility, she was completely noncompliant. Determined, apparently, that the "twins" would never meet.

Surprised at the strength of the patient's resistance, Sharon wondered if she'd been wrong about twinship making integration easier. Perhaps just the opposite was true: The fact that J. and Jana were physically identical, but psychological mirror opposites, had *intensified* their rivalry.

She began researching the psychology of twins, especially identicals, consulted Kruse, then took another tack: continuing to hypnotize the patient but backing away from attempts at integration. Instead, she adopted a more chummy role, simply chatting with the patient about seemingly innocuous topics: female siblings, twins, identicals. Leading J. through dispassionate discussions—was there really a special bond between twins, and if so, what was its nature? What was the best way to raise twins as children? How much of the behavioral similarity between identicals was due to heredity, how much to genetics?

"Riding with the resistance," she termed it. Taking careful note of the patient's body language and speech tones, synchronizing her own movements with them.

Exploiting the hidden message, in accordance with Dr. P. P. Kruse's theory of communication dynamics.

This went on for several more months; at a casual glance, nothing more than two friends gabbing. But the patient responded to the shift in strategy by slipping deeper than ever into hypnosis. Showing such profound suggestibility that she developed total skin anesthesia to a lit match, eventually adjusting her breathing to the cadence of Sharon's speech. Appearing ready for direct suggestion. But Sharon never offered one, just kept on chatting.

Then, during the fifty-fourth session, the patient slipped spontaneously into the Jana role and began describing a wild night that had taken place in Italy—a party at a private villa in Venice, peopled by weird, grinning characters and fed by flowing booze, abundant dope.

At first just another Jana orgy tale, every prurient detail recounted with relish. Then, halfway into the story, something else.

"My sister's there," Jana said, amazed. "A fucking wallflower over in that corner, in that ugly unvarnished chair."

Sharon: "What's she feeling?"

"Terrified. Scared shitless. Men are sucking her nipples—naked, hairy. Baboons—they're swarming over her, sticking things into her."

Sharon: "Things?"

"Their things. Their scummy things. They're hurting her and laughing and there's the camera."

Sharon: "Where's the camera?"

"There, on the other side of the room. I'm—oh, no, I'm holding it, I want to see everything, the lights are all on. But she doesn't like it. But I'm filming her anyway. I can't stop."

As she continued to describe the scene, Jana's voice faltered and quivered. She described J. as "exactly like . . . *looking* exactly like me, but, you know, more innocent. She was always more innocent. They're really going at her. I feel . . ."

Sharon: "What?"

"Nothing."

Sharon: "What did you feel, Jana? When you saw what was happening to your sister?"

"Nothing." Pause. "Bad."

Sharon: "Very bad?"

"A . . . a little bad." Angry expression. "But it was her own fucking fault! Don't do the crime if you can't do the time, right? She shouldn't have gone if she didn't want to play, right?"

Sharon: "Did she have a choice, Jana?"

Pause. "What do you mean?"

Sharon: "Did J. have a choice about going to the party?"

Long silence.

Sharon: "Jana?"

"Yeah. I heard you. First I thought yeah, sure she did—everyone has a choice. Then, I . . ."

Sharon: "What, Jana?"

"I don't know—I mean I really don't know her. I mean we're exactly the same but there's something about her that . . . I don't know. It's like we're—I don't know—more than sisters. I don't know what the right word is, maybe part— Forget it."

Pause.

Sharon: "Partners?"

Jana, startled: "I said forget it, enough of this shit! Let's talk about fun stuff, what *I* was doing at the fucking party."

Sharon: "All right. What *were* you doing?"

Jana, baffled; after a long silence: "I don't . . . remember. Aw, it was probably boring anyway—any party *she'd* go to had to be."

A door had been opened; Sharon restrained herself from nudging it further. She let Jana ramble on, waited until all her anger dissipated, then ended the session, certain that a breakthrough had taken place. For the first time in more than three years, J. had allowed the twins to coexist. And had offered a new clue: The word *partner* seemed to have strong emotional loading. Sharon decided to pursue that, brought it up the next time she hypnotized J.

"What's that, doctor? What did you just say?"

Sharon: "Partners. I suggested that you and Jana are something more than just sisters. Or even twins. Perhaps you're partners. Psychological partners."

J. is thoughtful, silent, starts to smile.

Sharon: "What's funny, J.?"

"Nothing. I suppose you're right—you usually are."

Sharon: "But does it make sense to *you*?"

"I suppose so, though if she is my partner, she's certainly a silent one. We never talk. She refuses to talk to me." Pause. Her smile widens. "Silent partners. What business are we in?"

Sharon: "The business of living."

J., amused: "I suppose so."

Sharon: "Would you like to talk more about that? About being a silent partner?"

J.: "I don't know. I guess so . . . Maybe not. No. She's so rude and unpleasant, I really can't tolerate being around her. Let's change the subject, if you don't mind."

J. didn't show up for the next session, or the next. When she finally reappeared, two months later, she seemed composed, claimed her life was going great, she just needed a tune-up.

Sharon resumed hypnotherapy, continued her attempt to get the "twins" to meet. Five more months of frustration, during which Sharon began thinking of herself as a failure, wondered if J.'s needs couldn't be better served by another therapist, "one with more experience, perhaps a male."

But Kruse encouraged her to continue, advising still more reliance on nonverbal manipulation.

Another month of status quo and J. disappeared once again. Five weeks later she materialized, bursting into the office while Sharon was seeing another patient, calling that woman a "fucking wimp," telling her, "your problems don't mean diddly," and ordering her out of the office.

Despite Sharon's attempt to take charge of the situation, the other patient ran out crying. Sharon told J. never to do that again. J. became Jana and accused Sharon of being "an evil and selfish cunt. You're a fucking manipulating cunt out to get everything I own, everything I am. All you want to do is bleed me fucking dry!" After threatening to sue Sharon and ruin her, she stormed out of the office.

And never returned.

End of treatment. Time for the failing therapist to ruminate.

A hundred-page discussion section. A hundred pages of Monday-morning quarterbacking. The end point: Sharon's realization that her attempt to, reconcile J. and Jana had been doomed to failure at the outset because the "twins" were "intractable psychic enemies; the triumph of one necessitated the death of the other—a psychological death, but one that had to be so vivid, so decisive that it might have been a literal demise."

Instead of seeking integration, she realized now, she should have worked at strengthening good J.'s identity, teamed up with the good twin to destroy the "destructive, flagrantly disturbed Jana."

"There's no room," she concluded, "in this young woman's psyche for any type of partner, let alone the conflictual, *silent partners* represented by the splits of her personality. The nature of human identity is such that the business of living is, must be, a solitary process. Lonely at times, but enriched by the strength and satisfaction that comes from self-determination and a fully integrated ego.

"Alone, we're born; alone, we die."

One hell of a case. If there had ever *been* a case.

I knew J. I'd made love to her, danced with her out on a terrace.

I knew Jana, too, had watched her throw strawberry daiquiris against a fireplace, wiggle out of a flame-colored dress and do with me what she wanted.

A chapter on the psychology of twins, yet never once had Sharon acknowledged in print that she had a twin. Her own silent partner.

Denial? Deceit?

Autobiography.

She'd delved into her own tormented psyche, created a phony case history and passed it off as doctoral research.

Working it through. Some sort of avant-garde therapy?

Just like the porn loop.

Kruse had been her chairman.

It stank of Kruse.

But what of Shirlee? The real silent partner. Had Sharon abandoned her to a silent, dark world?

And who the hell was "Jasper"?

And deep thanks to Alex, who, even in his absence, continues to inspire me.

Demure, passive, ladylike "J." Old-fashioned views about sex and romance ... though she'd been sexually active with a man she cared deeply about ... the relationship ending after intrusion by Jana.

I hefted the dissertation. Four hundred-plus pages of soul-dredging, pseudoscholarship. Lies.

How the hell had she gotten away with it?

I thought I knew a way to find out.

26

Before I left, I called Olivia's office.

"Sorry, darling, system's still down. Maybe by the end of the day."

"Okay, thanks. I'll call you later."

"One more thing—that hospital you were looking for in Glendale? I spoke to a friend of mine, used to work at Glendale Adventist. She said there was a place on Brand named Resthaven Terrace that closed down just recently. She used to consult to them, doing their Medi-Cal management."

"Closed down completely?"

"That's what Arlene said."

"Where can I reach Arlene?"

"St. John's, in Santa Monica. Assistant director of social services. Arlene Melamed."

She gave me the number and said, "You're really hot to find this Shirlee gal, aren't you?"

"It's complicated, Olivia."

"It always is with you."

I called Arlene Melamed's office and used Olivia's name to get through her secretary. Seconds later, a woman with a strong voice said, "Mrs. Melamed."

I introduced myself, told her I was trying to trace a former patient who'd been at Resthaven Terrace.

"Treated when, Doctor?"

"Six years ago."

"That's before my time. I didn't start there until a year ago."

"This patient had multiple disabilities, needed chronic care. She could very well have been there a year ago."

"Name?"

"Shirlee Ransom, two e's in Shirlee."

"Sorry, doesn't ring a bell—not that that means much. I wasn't doing any casework, just paper shuffling. What ward was she in?"

"One of the private rooms—back of the building."

"Then I certainly can't help you, Doctor. I worked only with the Medi-Cal cases, trying to get the billing system in shape."

I thought for a moment. "She had an attendant, a man named Elmo. Black, muscular."

"Elmo Castelmaine."

"You know him?"

"After Resthaven closed he came to work for me at Adventist. A very fine man. Unfortunately we had budgetary problems and had to let him go—he didn't have enough formal education to satisfy Personnel."

"Do you have any idea where he's working now?"

"After the layoff he got a job at an old-age home in the Fairfax area. I have no idea if he's still there."

"Do you recall the name of *that* place?"

"No, but hold on. He's in my Rolodex. He was such a nice man, I'd planned to keep in touch with him in case something came up. Ah, here it is: Elmo Castelmaine, King Solomon Gardens, Edinburgh Street."

I copied down the address and number and said, "Mrs. Melamed, when did Resthaven close?"

"Six months ago."

"What kind of a place was it?"

"I'm not sure what you mean."

"Who ran it?"

"A corporation. National outfit called ChroniCare—they owned a string of similar places all over the West Coast. Fancy-looking operation, but they never got their act together running Resthaven."

"Clinically?"

"Administratively. Clinically they were adequate. Not the best, but far from the worst. Business-wise, the place was a disaster. Their billing system was a complete mess. They hired incompetent clerical help, never even came close to recovering most of the money the state owed them. I was brought in to straighten it out, but it was an impossible assignment. There was no one to talk to—the home office was out in El Segundo; nobody ever returned calls. It was as if they really didn't care about turning a profit."

"After it closed, where did the patients go?"

"Other hospitals, I suppose. I quit before that."

"El Segundo," I said. "Do you know if they were owned by a larger corporation?"

"Wouldn't surprise me," she said. "Nowadays everything is."

I thanked her, called my broker, Lou Cestare, in Oregon, and confirmed that ChroniCare was a subsidiary of the Magna Corporation.

"But forget about buying in, Alex. They never went public. Magna never does."

We chatted a while; then I signed off and phoned King Solomon Gardens. The receptionist confirmed that Elmo Castelmaine still worked there. But he was busy with a patient, couldn't come to the phone right then. I left a message for him to call me regarding Shirlee Ransom and set out for campus.

I got to Milton Frazier's office by two. The Office Hours card on the door was blank. A knock produced no response, but the door was unlocked. I opened it to find the Ratman, wearing a stiff tweed suit and rimless half-glasses, hunched over his desk, using a yellow felt-tip pen to underline sections of a manuscript. The window shades were partially drawn, giving the room a sallow cast. Frazier's beard was disheveled, as if he'd been picking at it.

My "Hello, Professor" produced a scowl and a wave of his hand that could have meant anything from Come In to Get the Hell Out of Here.

A stiff-backed chair faced the desk. I sat down and waited as Frazier continued to underline, using graceless slashing movements. The desk was stacked high with more manuscripts. I leaned forward and read the title of the one on top. A textbook chapter.

He edited; I bided my time. The office had beige walls, a dozen or so diplomas and certificates, double-stacked metal bookshelves over cracked vinyl flooring. No custom interior design for this department head. Lined up on one of the shelves was a collection of glass beakers—animal brains floating in formaldehyde. The place smelled of old paper and wet rodent.

I waited for a long time. Frazier finished with one manuscript, lifted another from the stack, and began working on it. He made more yellow marks, shook his head, twisted his beard hairs, showed no intention of stopping.

"Alex Delaware," I said. "Class of '74."

He sat up sharply, stared at me, straightened his lapels. His shirt bagged; his tie was a hand-painted horror just ancient enough to have come back into fashion.

He studied me. "Hmm. Delaware. Can't say that I remember."

A lie, but I let it pass.

"I thought you were a student," he said. As if that explained his ignoring me. Eyes back on the manuscript, he added, "If it's an associateship you're after, it will have to wait. I'm not seeing anyone without an appointment. Publisher's deadline."

"New book?"

Headshake. "Revised edition of *Paradigms*." Slash, flip.

Paradigms of Vertebrate Learning. For thirty years, his claim to fame.

"Tenth edition," he added.

"Congratulations."

"Yes, well, I suppose congratulations are in order. However, one almost regrets obligating oneself to a new edition when the onerousness of the task becomes apparent—strident demands by commercially motivated publishers to include new chapters, regardless of the lack of rigor with which they are obtained or the coherence with which they are presented."

He slapped the stack of chapters. "Enduring all this rubbish has shown me just how low standards have sunk. The American psychologist trained after 1960 hasn't a clue about proper research design, nor the ability to construct a grammatical sentence."

I nodded. "Damned shame when standards sink. All sorts of strange things start to happen."

He looked up, annoyed, but listening.

I said, "Strange things like an unqualified attention-seeker making department head."

The marker froze, midair. He tried to stare me down but his eye contact was spotty. "Given the circumstances, that's an exceptionally rude remark."

"Doesn't change the facts."

"Exactly what's on your mind, Doctor?"

"How Kruse managed to bend all the rules."

"This is in exceedingly poor taste. What's your concern with all this?"

"Call me a concerned alumnus."

He sucked his teeth. "Any complaints you may have had against Professor Kruse have been rendered moot by his untimely death. If, as you contend, you're truly concerned about the department, you won't occupy my time or anyone else's on trivial personal matters.

We're all frightfully busy—this whole horrid affair has greatly disrupted the scheme of things."

"I'll bet it has. Especially for those members of the faculty who'd counted on all that Blalock money. Kruse's death has put all of you in jeopardy."

He put the marker down, fought to keep his hand steady.

I said, "With the rug pulled out from under you, I can see why you'd have to get that tenth edition rolling."

Moving stiffly, robotically, he leaned back in his chair, trying to look casual but coming across deflated. "You think you're such a bright boy, don't you? Always did. Always barreling your way through everything—'doing your own thing.'"

"And here I thought you didn't remember."

"Your rudeness jogged my memory, young man. I recall you quite clearly now—the precocious *three-year man*. In case you don't know, I was opposed to letting you finish early, even though you completed your requirements. I sensed that you needed seasoning. Maturity. Obviously the passage of time alone hasn't solved that problem."

I moved to the edge of my chair, picked up the yellow marker and put it down. "The issue, Professor, isn't my maturity. It's the sorry state of *your* ethics. Selling the department to the highest bidder. How much did Kruse pay to have you step down and let him take over? Was it in a lump sum or monthly installments? Check or credit card? Or did he bring you cash in a plain brown bag?"

He paled, started to rise from his chair, sank back down and shook a wobbly finger at me. "Watch your tongue! Don't be crass!"

"Crass," I said, "is a quick-buck, mail-order stop-smoking scheme targeted at the sucker market. What kind of scientific rigor did you muster to come up with that one?"

He opened his mouth and closed it, moved his head and shoulders in a way that made his clothing seem to swallow him up. "You've no comprehension of the situation, Delaware. Not a whit."

"Then educate me. What was the payoff?"

He swiveled away, stared at a thousand books, pretended to be studying the spine on one of the volumes.

"If you're clogged," I said, "let me prime your pump. Kruse funded your little stab at free enterprise—all the ad money, the printing, the manufacture of the tapes. Either his own money or he tapped Mrs. Blalock. What did it come out to—ten thousand? Fifteen? He spent more on his summer wardrobe. But for you it would be major venture capital."

He said nothing.

"No doubt he was the one who suggested the con in the first place," I said. "Ads in the back of the magazine that ran his column."

More silence, but he'd gone pale.

"Add to that the nonstop flow of Blalock money for your academic research and it was a sweet deal for both of you. No more brown-nosing for grants or pretending to be relevant for you. And Kruse got tenure, instant respectability. In order to avoid wagging tongues and petty jealousies, he probably arranged some funding for the other faculty members too. All you rigorous researchers would be coasting—doing *your* own thing. Though I suspect the rest of the senior staff would be surprised to learn how much extra Kruse kicked back to you—make for a terrific staff meeting, wouldn't it, Professor?"

"No," he said feebly. "There's nothing to be ashamed of. My regimen for smokers is based on sound behavioral principles. Obtaining private endowments for research is a time-honored tradition. Given the state of our national economy, it's certainly the wave of the future."

"You were never one for the future, Frazier. Kruse shoved you into it."

"Why are you doing this, Delaware? Attacking the department? We made you."

"I'm not talking about the department. Just you. And Kruse."

He made cud-chewing motions with his lips, as if trying to bring up the right word. When he finally spoke, his voice was weak. "You'll find no scandal here. Everything's been done through proper channels."

"I'm willing to test that hypothesis."

"Delaware—"

"I spent the morning reading a fascinating document, Frazier. 'The Silent Partner. Identity Crisis and Ego Dysfunction in a Case of Multiple Personality,' et cetera. Ring a bell?"

He looked genuinely blank.

"The doctoral dissertation of Sharon Ransom, Ph.D. Submitted to the department in partial fulfillment. And approved—by you. A single case study, not a shred of empirical research—a clear violation of every rule *you* pushed through. You signed your name to the damn thing. How'd she get away with it? How much did Kruse pay you to bend that far?"

"Sometimes," he said, "allowances are made."

"This went beyond allowances. This was fraud."

"I fail to understand just what—"

"She wrote about *herself*. About her own *psychopathology*. Camouflaged it as a case history and palmed it off as research. What do you think the Board of Regents would make of that? Not to mention APA's ethics committee. *Time* and *Newsweek*."

Whatever remained of his composure crumbled and his color got bad. I remembered what Larry had said about a heart attack and wondered if I'd pushed too hard.

"Jesus God," he said. "Don't pursue this. I didn't know—an aberration. I assure you it will never happen again."

"True. Kruse is dead."

"Let the dead *rest,* Delaware. Please!"

"All I want is information," I said softly. "Give me some truth and the matter's dropped."

"What? What do you want to know?"

"The connection between Ransom and Kruse."

"I don't know much about that. That's the Lord's truth. Only that she was his protégée."

I remembered how soon it was after Sharon arrived that Kruse had filmed her.

"He brought her with him, didn't he? Sponsored her application."

"Yes, but—"

"Where did he bring her from?"

"Wherever he was from, I assume."

"Where was that?"

"Florida."

"Palm Beach?"

He nodded.

"Was she from Palm Beach too?"

"I have no idea—"

"We could find out by checking her application records."

"When did she graduate?"

" '81."

He picked up the phone, called the department, and mouthed a few orders. A moment later he was frowning, saying, "Are you sure? Double-check." Silence. "All right, all right." He hung up and said, "Her file is gone."

"How convenient."

"Delaware—"

"Call the registrar's office."

"All they'd have would be her transcript."

"Transcripts list prior institutions attended."

He nodded, dialed a number, pulled rank with a clerk, and waited. Then he used the yellow marker to write something in a column of the manuscript and hung up. "Not Florida. Long Island, New York. A place called Forsythe Teachers College."

I used his paper and pen to copy that down.

"By the way," he said, "her grades were superb—undergraduate and graduate. Unblemished A's. No indication of anything other than exceptional scholarship. She might very well have gotten in without his help."

"What else do you know about her?"

"Why do you need to know all of this?"

I stared at him, said nothing.

"I had nothing to do with her," he said. "Kruse was the one with a personal interest in her."

"How personal?"

"If you're assuming something . . . corrupt, I wouldn't know about that."

"Why would I assume that?"

He hesitated, looked queasy. "It's no secret that he was known for certain . . . proclivities. Drives."

"Were those drives directed toward Sharon Ransom?"

"No, I . . . That's not the kind of thing I pay much attention to."

I believed him. "Think those drives helped her get straight A's?"

"Absolutely not. That's simply—"

"How'd he manage to get her in?"

"He didn't *get* her in. He sponsored her. Her grades were *perfect.* His sponsorship was simply an additional factor in her favor—nothing unusual. Faculty members have always been allowed to sponsor applicants."

"Tenured faculty," I said. "When have clinical associates ever had that kind of clout?"

A long silence. "I'm sure you know the answer to that."

"Tell me anyway."

He cleared his throat, as if ready to spit. Expelled a single word: *"Money."*

"Blalock money?"

"As well as his own—he came from a wealthy family, ran in the same social circle as Mrs. Blalock and her ilk. You know how rare those kinds of contacts are among academics, especially at a public university. He was regarded as more than just another clinical associate."

"A clinical associate with training in psychological warfare."

"I beg your pardon?"

"Never mind," I said. "So he was your bridge between town and gown."

"That's correct. Nothing shameful about that, is there?"

I remembered what Larry had said about Kruse treating one of the Blalock children. "Was his only connection with Mrs. Blalock a social one?"

"As far as I know. Please, Delaware, don't make something ominous out of all this and get *her* involved. The department was in dire financial straits; Kruse brought substantial funds with him and promised to use his connections to obtain an ample endowment from Mrs. Blalock. He made good on that promise. In return we offered him an unpaid appointment."

"Unpaid in terms of salary. He got lab facilities. For his pornography research. Real academic rigor."

He flinched. "It wasn't that simple. The department did not simply yield like a harlot. It took *months* to confirm his appointment. The senior faculty debated it heavily—there was significant opposition, not least of which was my own. The man was sorely lacking in academic credentials. His column in that crass magazine was positively offensive. However . . ."

"However, in the end, expediency won out."

He twisted beard hairs, made them crackle. "When I heard about his . . . research, I realized letting him in had been an error in judgment—but one impossible to undo without creating adverse publicity."

"So instead you made him department head."

He continued playing with his beard. Several brittle white hairs rained down on the desk.

"Back to the Ransom dissertation," I said. "How'd it get through departmental scrutiny?"

"Kruse came to me requesting that the experimental rule be waived for one of his students. When he told me she planned to submit a case study, I immediately refused. He was persistent, pointed out her perfect academic record. Said she was an unusually skillful clinician—for what that's worth—and that the case she wanted to present was unique, had major research ramifications."

"How major?"

"Publishable in a major journal. Nevertheless, he failed to sway me. But he kept pressing, buttonholing me daily, coming into my office, interrupting my work in order to argue his case. Finally, I relented."

Finally. As in fill the coffers. I said, "When you read the dissertation, did you regret your decision?"

"I thought it was rubbish, but no different from any other clinical study. Psychology should have remained in the laboratory, true to its scientific roots, never been allowed to venture out into all that poorly defined treatment rubbish. Let the psychiatrists muck around in that kind of silliness."

"You had no idea it was autobiographical?"

"Of course not! How could I? I never met her, except once, at her oral exam."

"Must have been a tough exam. Kruse, you as his rubber stamp. And an outside member: Sandra Romansky. Remember her?"

"Not in the slightest. Do you know how many committees I sit on? Had I the smallest inkling of any impropriety, I would have put my foot down—you can count on that."

Reassuring.

He said, "I was only tangentially involved."

"How thoroughly did you read it?" I asked.

"Not thoroughly at all," he said, as if seizing on extenuating evidence. "Believe me, Delaware, I barely skimmed the blasted thing!"

I went down to the department office, told the secretary I was working with Professor Frazier, verified that the file was missing, and called Long Island information to find the number of Forsythe College. Administration there confirmed that Sharon Jean Ransom had attended the school from 1972 through 1975. They'd never heard of Paul Peter Kruse.

I called my service for messages. Nothing from Olivia or Elmo Castelmaine. But Dr. Small and Detective Sturgis had phoned.

"The detective said don't call him, he'll get back to you," the operator told me.

She giggled. "*Detective.* You getting involved in something exciting, Dr. Delaware?"

"Hardly," I said. "Just the usual."

"Your usual's probably a major rush compared to mine, Dr. Delaware. Have a nice day."

One forty-three. I waited seven minutes and called Ada Small, figuring to get her between patients. She picked up the line, said, "Alex, thanks for getting back so quickly. That young woman you referred, Carmen Seeber? She came for two sessions, then didn't show up for the third. I called her several times, finally managed to reach her at home, and tried to talk to her about it. But she was pretty defensive, insisted she was fine, didn't need any more therapy."

"She's fine, all right. Shacked up with a drug addict, probably giving him every penny she owns."

"How do you know that?"

"From the police."

"I see." Pause. "Well, thank you for the referral anyway. I'm sorry it didn't work out."

"I'm the one who should be apologizing. You did me the favor."

"That's all right, Alex."

I wanted to ask her if Carmen had shed any light on D.J. Rasmussen's death, but knew better than to try to breach confidentiality.

"I'll try calling her next week," she said, "but I'm not optimistic. You and I both know about the power of resistance."

I thought of Denise Burkhalter. "All we can do is try."

"True. Tell me, Alex, how are *you* doing?"

I answered too quickly: "Just dandy. Why?"

"If I'm out of line, please forgive me. But both times we've spoken recently, you've sounded . . . tight. Tense. On full burn."

The phrase I'd used, in therapy, to describe the fast-track mindset that overtook me during periods of stress. What Robin had always called *hyperspace.* And managed to soothe me out of . . .

"Just a little tired, Ada. I'm fine. Thanks for asking."

"I'm glad to hear that." Another pause. "If you ever *do* need to toss things around, you know I'm here for you."

"I do, Ada. Thanks and take care."

"You, too, Alex. Take *good* care of yourself."

I walked toward the north end of campus, stopping for a cup of vending-machine coffee before entering the research library.

Back to the Periodical Index. I found nothing on William Houck Vidal, other than business quotes prior to the *Basket-Case Billionaire* lawsuit. I backtracked and found a *Time* piece on the War Board Senate hearings, entitled "Hollywood Meets D.C. Amid Rumors of Scandal"—a piece I'd missed while culling Belding material.

Vidal had just made his first appearance before the committee and the magazine was trying to flesh out his background.

A headshot photo showed him with fewer wrinkles, thick blond hair. A blinding smile—the good teeth Crotty had remembered. And wise-guy eyes. Vidal was described as a "socialite who'd parlayed shrewdness, connections and more than a soupçon of charm into a lucrative motion picture consulting position." Hollywood sources suggested it was he who'd persuaded Leland Belding to enter the movie business.

Both men had attended Stanford. As a sophomore Vidal had served as the president of a men's club that Belding also belonged to. But their association was thought to have been casual: The future billionaire had shunned organizations, never attending a single club function.

Their working relationship was cemented in 1941: Vidal served as the "middleman" in a business deal between Belding and Blalock Industries, which supplied wartime steel to the Magna Corporation at a discount rate. Vidal introduced Leland Belding to Henry Abbot Blalock; he was perfectly positioned to do so because Blalock was his brother-in-law, married to Vidal's sister, the former Hope Estes Vidal.

The Vidals were described as the last descendants of an old, venerable family—*Mayflower* lineage but dwindled fortunes. Henry Blalock, London-born, son of a chimney sweep, had been admitted to the Blue Book set after his 1943 marriage to Hope; the Vidal name still dripped with social status. *Time* wondered if brother Billy's current problems with the Senate would change all that.

Billy and Hope, brother and sister. It explained Vidal's presence at the party, but not his relationship to Sharon. Not what they'd been talking about . . .

I searched for further mention of the Blalocks, found nothing on Hope, some business-related references to Henry A. His fortune had been made in steel, railroads, and real estate. Like Leland Belding, he owned it all, had never gone public. Unlike Belding, he'd stayed out of the headlines.

In 1953 he died, age fifty-nine, of a stroke, while on safari in Kenya, leaving a grieving widow, the former Hope Estes Vidal. Contributions to the Heart Foundation in lieu of flowers . . .

No mention of offspring. What of the child Kruse had treated? Had the widow remarried? I kept thumbing the index, found a single item, dated six months after Henry Blalock's death: the sale of Blalock Industries to the Magna Corporation, for an unspecified sum, rumored to be a bargain. The decline of Blalock's holdings was noted and attributed to failure to adapt to changing realities, particularly the growing importance of cross-continental air shipping.

The implication was clear: Belding's planes had helped antiquate Blalock's trains. Then Magna had swooped down and made off with the pickings.

Though from the looks of Hope Blalock's lodgings, those pickings had been substantial. I wondered if brother Billy had played "middleman" again, seen to it that her interests were protected.

Another hour of thumbing brought nothing more. I thought of somewhere else to look, went down to the ground floor and asked the reference librarian if the stack holdings included social registers. She looked it up, told me the Los Angeles Blue Book was kept in Special Collections, which had closed for the day.

My thoughts slid down to the lower rungs of the social ladder, another brother-sister story. I remained in the reference section, tried to find newspaper accounts of the Linda Lanier dope bust.

It was harder than I thought. Of all the local papers, only the *Times* was indexed, and that only from 1972. The *New York Times* index went back to 1851 but contained nothing on Linda Lanier.

I went to the newspaper stacks on the second floor—banks of drawers and rows of microfiche machines. Showed my faculty card, filled out forms, collected spools.

Ellston Crotty had dated the bust 1953. Assuming Linda Lanier had been Sharon's mother, she'd had to have been alive at the time of Sharon's birth—May 15—which narrowed it further. I spun my way through the spring of '53, starting with the *Times* and keeping the *Herald, Mirror,* and *Daily News* in reserve.

It took more than an hour to find the story. August 9. The *Times,* never one for crime stories, relegated it to the middle of Part One, but the other papers had given it front-page treatment, complete with purple prose, photographs of the slain "pushers" and the cops who'd killed them.

The articles jibed with Crotty's account, minus his cynicism. Linda Lanier/Eulalee Johnson and her brother, Cable Johnson, major "heroin traffickers," had fired at raiding Metro Narc detectives and been killed by return fire. In a single "lightning operation," Detectives Royal Hummel and Victor DeGranzfeld had put an end to one of the most predatory drug rings in L.A. history.

The detectives' photos showed them grinning and kneeling beside bindles of white powder. Hummel was wide and beefy, in a light suit and wide-brimmed straw hat. I thought I detected a hint of Cyril Trapp in the hatchet jaw and narrow lips. DeGranzfeld was pear-shaped, mustachioed, and slit-eyed, and wore a chalk-striped double-breasted suit and dark Stetson. He looked ill-at-ease, as if smiling were an imposition.

I didn't have to study the picture of Linda Lanier/Eulalee Johnson to recognize the blond bombshell I'd watched seduce Dr. Donald Neurath. The photo was high-quality, a professional studio job—the kind of windswept, glossy three-quarter-face pose favored by would-be actresses for publicity portfolios.

Sharon's face, in a platinum wig.

Cable Johnson was memorialized in a county jail mug shot that showed him to be a mean-looking, poorly shaven loser with drooping eyes and a greasy duck's-ass hairdo. The eyes were lazy but managed to project a hard-edged scrap-for-survival brightness. Shrewdness rather than abstract intelligence. The kind who'd make out in the short term, get tripped up, over and over again, by an inflated sense of self and inability to delay gratification.

His criminal record was termed "extensive" and included arrests for extortion—trying to squeeze money out of some small-time East L.A. bookies—public drunkenness, disorderly conduct, larceny, and theft. A sad but petty litany, nothing that supported the papers' labeling of him and his sister as "major-league dope pushers, ruthless, sophisticated, but for their deaths, destined to flood the city with illegal narcotics."

Anonymous police sources were quoted claiming the Johnsons were associated with "Mexican mob elements." They'd grown up in the South Texas border town of Port Wallace, "a tough hamlet known to law enforcement officials as an entry point for brown heroin," had clearly moved to L.A. with intentions of pushing that substance to the schoolchildren of Brentwood, Pasadena, and Beverly Hills.

As part of their plan, they obtained jobs at an unnamed film studio, Cable as a grip, Linda as a contract player trawling for bit parts. This provided a cover for "narcotics trafficking within the film community, a segment of the population long known to be enamored of illicit drugs and nonconformist personal habits." Both were known as hangers-on at "left-leaning parties also attended by known Communists and fellow travelers."

Dope and Bolshevism, prime demons of the fifties. Enough to make shooting a beautiful young woman to death palatable—admirable.

I ran a few more spools through the machine. Nothing linking Linda Lanier to Leland Belding, not a word about party pads.

And nothing about children. Singly or in pairs.

27

Old stories, old connections, but the strands were tangling even as they knitted, and I was no closer to understanding Sharon—how she'd lived and why she, and so many others, had died.

At 10:30 P.M. Milo called and added to the confusion.

"Bastard Trapp lost no time snowing me under," he said. "Reorganizing the dead-case file—pure scutwork. I played hooky, wore out my phone ear. Your gal Ransom had a severe allergy to the truth. No birth records in New York, no Manhattan Ransoms—not on Park Avenue or any of the other high-priced zip codes—clear back to the late forties. Same for Long Island: Southampton's a tight little community; the local gendarmes say no Ransoms in the phone book, no Ransoms ever lived in any of the big estates."

"She went to college there."

"Forsythe. Not right there—nearby. How'd you find out?"

"Through her university transcript. How'd *you* find out?"

"Social Security. She applied in '71, gave the college as her address. But that's the first time her name shows up anywhere—as if she didn't exist until then."

"If you have any contacts in Palm Beach, Florida, try there, Milo. Kruse practiced there until '75. When he moved out to L.A. he brought her with him."

"Uh-uh. I'm ahead of you. *Him* I did find plenty of paper on. Born in New York—Park Avenue, as a matter of fact. Big apartment that he sold in '68. The real estate transfer listed a Palm Beach address and I called down there. These rich-town departments aren't easy to deal with—very protective of the locals. I told them Ransom had been a burglary victim—we recovered her stuff, wanted to give it back to her. They looked her up. *Nada,* not even a whisper, Alex. So Kruse hooked up with her somewhere else. And speaking of Kruse, he was *not* the hotshot psychotherapist you described. I stroked my source at the IRS, accessed the guy's tax returns. His practice only produced income of thirty thou a year—at a hundred bucks an hour, that's only five or six hours a week. Not exactly your busy shrink. Another five G's came from writing. The rest, another half *mil,* was investment income: blue-chip stocks and bond dividends, real estate, and a little business venture called Creative Image Associates."

"Blue movies."

"He listed it as a 'producer and manufacturer of health education materials.' He and his wife were sole shareholders, declared a loss for five years, then folded."

"What years?"

"Let me see, I've got it right here: '74 through '79."

Sharon's last year in college, her first four years in grad school.

"What it boils down to, Alex, is a rich guy living off inheritance. Dabbling."

"Dabbling in people's lives," I said. "The army taught him psychological warfare."

"For what that's worth. When I was a medic I caught an eyeful of the army's psychological warfare. For the most part, worthless bullshit. The Viet Cong laughed at it—ad agencies do it better. Anyway, bottom line is, Ransom emerges as your basic phantom lady with a rich patron. For all practical purposes she could have dropped out of the sky in 1971."

"Martinis in the sun-room."

"What's that?"

"Nothing important," I said. "Here's another possibility. I looked up the newspaper coverage of the Lanier/Johnson drug bust. Linda and her brother were from South Texas—place called Port Wallace. Maybe there are records down there."

"Maybe," he said. "Anything in the papers that Crotty didn't tell us?"

"Just that in addition to the dope thing, the Red Scare was raised—supposedly the Johnsons went to parties with subversives. Given the mood of the country, that would have guaranteed public support for the shootout. Hummel and DeGranzfeld were treated like Most Valuable Players."

"Uncle Hummel," he said. "I called Vegas. He's still alive, still working for Magna—chief of security at the Casbah and two other casinos the company owns there. Lives in a big house in the best part of town. Wages of sin, huh?"

"One more thing to chew on," I said. "Billy Vidal and Hope Blalock are brother and sister. Vidal set up deals between Blalock's husband and Belding. After Blalock's husband died, Magna bought her out cheap. After Belding died, Vidal ended up chairman of Magna. Mrs. Blalock was bankrolling Kruse—supposedly because he'd treated one of her kids. But she doesn't seem to have any kids."

"Jesus," he said. "Ever get the feeling, Alex, we're playing somebody else's game by somebody else's rules? In somebody else's goddam stadium?"

He agreed to run a Texas trace and told me to watch my back before hanging up.

I wanted to call Olivia again, but it was close to eleven, past her and Albert's bedtime, so I waited until nine the next morning, phoned her office, and was told Mrs. Brickerman was up in Sacramento on business this morning and was expected back shortly.

I tried to reach Elmo Castelmaine at King Solomon Gardens. He was on shift again, busy with a patient. I got in the Seville and drove to the Fairfax district, to Edinburgh Street.

The old-age home was one of dozens of boxy two-story buildings lining the narrow, treeless street.

King Solomon Gardens had no gardens, just one pudgy-trunked, roof-high date palm to the left of the double glass entry doors. The building was white texture-coat trimmed in electric blue. A ramp carpeted in blue Astroturf served in place of front steps. Cement had been laid down where the lawn should have been, painted hospital green and furnished with folding chairs. Old people sat, sun-visored, kerchiefed, and support-hosed, fanning themselves, playing cards, just staring off into space.

I found a parking space halfway down the block and was headed back when I spotted a chunky black man across the street, pushing a wheelchair. I quickened my pace and got a better look. White uniform tunic over blue jeans. No corkscrew beard, no earring. The crown of the head yielding to near-total baldness; the stocky body, softer. The face looser, double-chinned, but the one I remembered from Resthaven.

I crossed the street, caught up. "Mr. Castelmaine?"

He stopped, looked back. An old woman was in the wheelchair. She didn't pay any notice. Despite the heat, she wore a sweater buttoned to the neck and an Indian blanket across her knees. Her hair was thin and brittle, dyed black. The breeze blew through it, exposing white patches of scalp. She appeared to be sleeping with her eyes open.

"That's me." The same high-pitched voice. "Now, who might you be?"

"Alex Delaware. I left you a message yesterday."

"That doesn't help me much. I still don't know you any better than I did ten seconds ago."

"We met years ago. Six years ago. At Resthaven Terrace. I came with Sharon Ransom. Visited her sister, Shirlee?"

The woman in the chair began to sniffle and whimper. Castelmaine bent down, patted her head, pulled a tissue out of his jeans and dabbed at her nose. "Now, now, Mrs. Lipschitz, it's okay, he's gonna come get you."

She pouted.

"Come on now, Mrs. Lipschitz, honey, your beau's gonna come, don't you worry."

The woman lifted her face. She was sharp-featured, toothless, wrinkled as a discarded shopping bag. Her eyes were pale-brown and heavily mascaraed. A bright-red patch of lipstick had been smeared over a puckered fissure of a mouth. Somewhere behind the crease and corrugation, the mask of cosmetics, shone a spark of beauty.

Her eyes filled with tears.

"Aw, Mrs. Lipschitz," said Castelmaine.

She drew the blanket up to her mouth, began chewing on the coarse fabric.

Castelmaine turned to me and said softly, "They reach a certain age, they can never get warm, no matter what the weather. Never get full satisfaction of any kind."

Mrs. Lipschitz cried out. Her lips worked around a word for a while and finally formed it: "Party!"

Castelmaine kneeled beside her, eased the blanket away from her mouth, and tucked it around her. "You're gonna go to that party, hon, but you've got to be careful not to ruin your makeup with all those tears. Okay?"

He placed two fingers under the old woman's chin and smiled. "Okay?" She looked up at him, nodded.

"Goo-ood. And we *are* looking pretty today, honey. All spiffed up and raring to go."

The old woman held up one shriveled hand. A thick black one wrapped around it.

"Party," she said.

"Sure, there's gonna be a party. And you're so pretty, Clara

Celia Lipschitz, that you're gonna be the belle of that party. All the handsome boys are gonna line up to dance with you."

A rush of tears.

"Now c'mon, C.C., no *more* of that. He's gonna come, take you to that party—you've got to be looking your best."

More struggle to enunciate: "Late."

"Just a little late, Clara Celia. He probably hit some heavy traffic—you know, all that gridlock I've been telling you about. Or maybe he stopped off at a flower shop to get you a nice corsage. Nice pink orchid corsage, like he knows you love."

"Late."

"Just a little," he repeated, and resumed pushing the chair. I tagged along.

He began singing, softly, in a sweet tenor so high it verged on falsetto. "Now C., C.C. Rider. C'mon *see,* baby, what you have *done . . .*"

The music and the repetitive rub of the chair's tires against the sidewalk set up a lullaby rhythm. The old woman's head began to loll.

". . . C.C. Lipschitz, see what *you* have done . . ."

We stopped directly across the street from King Solomon. Castelmaine looked both ways and nudged the chair over the curb.

". . . you made all the handsome boys *love* you . . . and now your man has *come.*"

Mrs. Lipschitz slept. He pushed her across the green cement, exchanging greetings with some of the other old people, got to the bottom of the ramp and told me: "Wait here. I'll be with you soon as I'm through."

I stood around, got drawn into conversation with a thick-waisted old man with one good eye and a VFW cap who claimed to have fought with Teddy Roosevelt at San Juan Hill, then waited, belligerently, as if expecting me to doubt him. When I didn't he launched into a lecture on U.S. policy in Latin America and was going strong, ten minutes later, when Castelmaine reappeared.

I shook the old man's hand, told him it had been educational.

"A smart boy," he told Castelmaine.

The attendant smiled. "That probably means, Mr. Cantor, that he didn't disagree with you."

"What's to disagree? *Emes* is *emes,* you got to keep those pinkos in line or they eat your liver."

"The *emes* is, we gotta go, Mr. Cantor."

"So who's stopping you? Go. *Gey avek.*"

We walked back across the green cement.

"How about a cup of coffee," I said.

"Don't drink coffee. Let's walk." We turned left on Edinburgh and strolled past more old people. Past sweating windows and cooking smells, dry lawns, musty doorways.

"I don't remember you," he said. "Not as a specific person. I do remember Dr. Ransom visiting with a man, because it only happened once." He looked me over. "No. I can't say that I remember it being you."

"I looked different," I said. "Had a beard, longer hair."

He shrugged. "Could be. Anyway, what can I do for you?"

Unconcerned. I realized he hadn't heard about Sharon, gritted my teeth and said:

"Dr. Ransom died."

He stopped, put both hands alongside his face. "Died? When?"

"A week ago."

"How?"

"Suicide, Mr. Castelmaine. It was in the papers."

"Never read the papers—get enough bad news just from living. Oh, no—such a kind, wonderful girl. I can't believe it."

I said nothing.

He kept shaking his head.

"What pushed her so low she had to go and do something like that?"

"That's what I'm trying to find out."

His eyes were moist and bloodshot. "You her man?"

"I was, years ago. We hadn't seen each other for a long time, met at a party. She said something was bothering her. I never found out what it was. Two days later she was gone."

"Oh, Lord, this is just terrible."

"I'm sorry."

"How'd she do it?"

"Pills. And a gunshot to the head."

"Oh, God. Doesn't make any sense, someone beautiful and rich doing something like that. All day I wheel around the old ones—fading away, losing the ability to do anything for themselves, but they hang on, nothing but memories to keep them going. Then someone like Dr. Ransom throws it all away."

We resumed walking.

"Just doesn't make sense," he repeated.

"I know," I said. "I thought you might be able to help me make some sense of it."

"Me? How?"

"By telling me what you know about her."

"What I know," he said, "isn't much. She was a fine woman, always looked happy to me, always treated me well. She was devoted to that sister of hers—you don't see a lot of that. Some of them start out all noble, guilty for putting the loved one away, swearing to God they're gonna be visiting all the time, taking care of *everything*. But after a while of getting nothing back, they get tired, start coming less and less. Lots of them disappear completely. But not Dr. Ransom— she was always there for poor Shirlee. Every week, like clockwork, Wednesday afternoon, two to five. Sometimes two or three times a week. And not just sitting—feeding and fixing and loving that poor girl and getting nothing in return."

"Did anyone else ever visit Shirlee?"

"Not a one, excepting the time she came with you. Only Dr. Ransom, like clockwork. She was the best family to one of those people I ever saw, giving, not getting. I watched her do it steadily up until the day I quit."

"When was that?"

"Eight months ago."

"Why'd you quit?"

" 'Cause they were gonna let me go. Dr. Ransom tipped me off that the place was going to shut down. Said she appreciated all I'd done for Shirlee, was sorry she couldn't take me with her, but that Shirlee would continue to get good care. She said I'd made a big difference. Then she gave me fifteen hundred dollars cash, to show she meant it. That shows you what she was like. Makes no sense for her to get that low."

"So she knew Resthaven was going to close."

"And she was correct. Couple of weeks later, everyone else got form letters, pink slips. *Dear employee.* A friend of mine was working the wards—I warned her but she didn't believe me. When it happened she didn't get any notice, no severance, just bye-bye, Charlie, we're bankrupt. Out of business and so are you."

"Do you have any idea where Dr. Ransom took Shirlee?"

"No, but believe me, it had to be somewhere fine—she loved that girl, treated her like a queen." He stopped, turned grim. "With her dead, who's gonna take care of the poor thing?"

"I don't know. I have no idea where she is. No one does."

"Oh, Lord. This is starting to sound mournful."

"I'm sure she's all right," I said. "The family has money—did she talk much about them?"

"Not to me she didn't."

"But you knew she was rich."

"She was paying the bills at Resthaven, she had to be. Besides, anyone could tell she had money just by looking at her—the way she dressed and carried herself. Being a doctor."

"Dr. Ransom was paying the bills?"

"That's what it said right at the top of the chart: *All financial correspondence to be directed to Dr. Ransom.*"

"What else was in the chart?"

"All the therapy records—PT, OT. For a while Dr. Ransom even had a speech therapist come in but that was a waste of time—Shirlee was nowhere near talking. Same with a Braille teacher. Dr. Ransom tried everything. She loved that girl—I just can't see her destroying herself and abandoning the poor thing."

"Was there a medical history in the chart?"

"Just some early stuff and a summary of all the problems written out by Dr. Ransom."

"Any birth records?"

He shook his head.

"Were any other doctors involved in Shirlee's care?"

"Just Dr. Ransom."

"No physicians?"

"What do you think *she* was?"

"She was a psychologist. Did she tell you she was an M.D.?"

He thought for a while. "Come to think of it, no, she didn't. But the way she took charge of Shirlee's case, writing orders for the therapists, I just took it for granted."

"Shirlee must have had physical complaints. Who handled those?"

"You'd think she would have, but funny thing was, except for all her problems, she was really healthy, had a good strong heart, good blood pressure, clear lungs. All you had to do was turn her, feed her, change her, give her postural drainage, and she'd go on forever." He gazed up at the sky, shook his head. "Wonder where she is, poor thing."

"Did Dr. Ransom ever talk about the accident?"

His eyebrows arched. "What accident is that?"

"The drowning that caused all of Shirlee's problems."

"Now you lost me."

"She drowned when she was a small child. Dr. Ransom told me about it, said it was what caused Shirlee's brain damage."

"Well, I don't know about that, because what she told me was something totally different—the poor girl was born that way."

"Born blind and deaf and crippled?"

"That's right, all of it. 'Multiple congenital deformities.' Lord knows I saw it often enough, staring up from Dr. Ransom's summary."

He shook his head. " 'Multiple congenital deformities.' Poor thing started out that way, never any chance at all."

It was close to noon. I drove to a gas station nearby and used the pay phone to call Olivia's office. Mrs. Brickerman, I was informed, had returned from Sacramento but wasn't expected back in the office today. I phoned her home number, let it ring ten times, and was just ready to hang up when she picked it up, breathless.

"Alex! I just got in. Literally. From the airport. Spent the morning taking a power breakfast with Senate aides and trying to get them to give us more money. What a bunch—if any of them had ever owned an idea, they sold it a long time ago. Cheap."

"Hate to bother you," I said, "but I was wondering if—"

"The system was back up. Yes, it is, as of this morning. And just to show you how much I love you, I used Sacramento Division's mainframe to run your Shirlee Ransom through. Sorry, nothing. I did find a person by that name, same spelling. But on the Medi-Cal files. Date of birth 1922, not '53."

"Do you have an address on her?"

"No. You told me '53, I didn't figure you'd be interested in a senior citizen."

"Makes sense," I said.

"You *are* interested?"

"I might be . . . if it's not too much of a—"

"All right, all right. Let me change out of this business suit and I'll call the office, try and get my assistant to overcome her computerphobia. It'll take a while. Where can I get back to you?"

"I'm calling from a pay phone."

"Cloak and dagger nonsense? Alex, what *are* you up to?"

"Digging up bones."

"Ugh. What's your number?"

I read it off to her.

"That's *my* neighborhood. Where are you calling from?"

"Gas station on Melrose near Fairfax."

"Oh, for God's sake, you're two minutes away! Come over and watch me play high-tech detective."

The Brickermans' house was small, newly painted white, with a Spanish tile roof. Narrow beds of petunias had been planted along the driveway, which was filled with Olivia's mammoth Chrysler New Yorker.

She'd left the door unlocked. Albert Brickerman was in the living room, in a bathrobe and slippers, staring at the chessboard. He grunted in response to my greeting. Olivia was in the kitchen, scrambling eggs, wearing a white ruffled blouse and size 18 navy skirt. Her hair was a henna'd frizz, her cheeks plump and rosy. She was in her early sixties but her skin was smooth as a girl's. She hugged me, crushed me to an upholstered bosom.

"What do you think?" She ran her hands over the skirt.

"Very board-room."

She laughed, turned down the fire under the eggs. "If my socialist papa could see me now. Do you believe, at my age, being dragged kicking and screaming into the whole yuppie puppie thing?"

"Just keep telling yourself you're working *within* the system to change it."

"Oh, sure." She motioned me to the kitchen table. Spooned out eggs, set out plates of rye toast and sliced tomatoes, filled mugs with coffee. "I figure I've got one more year, maybe two. Then goodbye to all the nonsense and set out for some serious traveling—not that Prince Albert would ever budge, but I've got a friend, lost her husband last year. We plan to do Hawaii, Europe, Israel. The works."

"Sounds great."

"Sounds great, but you're antsy to get into the computer."

"Whenever it's convenient."

"I'll call now. It'll take a while for Monica to get into the system."

She phoned her assistant, gave instructions, repeated them, hung up. "Cross your fingers. Meanwhile, let's eat."

Both of us were hungry and we wolfed in silence. Just as I'd started on my second serving of eggs, the phone rang.

"Okay, Monica, that's okay. Yes. Type in SRCH, all capitals. Good. Now type capital M dash capital C capital R, then the RETURN button twice. CAL. C-A-L, also all in caps, four three five six dash zero zero nine. Good. Then capital LA dash capital W dash one dash two three six. Okay? Try again. I'll wait . . . good. Now press RETURN one more time, then the HOME button. . . . Under the seven . . . No, hold down the control button while you do it—over on the left side of the keyboard, CTRL. Yes, good. Now what comes on the screen? Good. Okay, now type in the following name. Ransom, as in kidnapping . . . what? Nothing, forget it. R-A-N-S-O-M. Comma. Shirlee. With two e's at the end, instead of an e-y. S-H-I-R-L-E-E . . . Okay, good. What comes on? . . . Okay, keep it there, Monica. I'm going to get a pencil and you tell me the birthdate and the address."

She began writing. I got up, read over her shoulder:

Ransom, Shirlee. DOB: 1/1/22
Rural Route 4, Willow Glen, Ca. 92399.

"Okay, thank you, Monica."

I said, "Ask her about a Jasper Ransom."

She looked up at me quizzically, said: "Monica, don't clear your screen yet. Type in ADD SRCH. Wait for the blinking prompt again . . . Got it? Okay, now Ransom, same name as before, comma Jasper . . . No. *J.* . . . Right. Jasper. Good . . . It is? Okay, give me the birthdate."

She wrote: *DOB 12/25/20. Same address.*

"Thank you again, Monica. Got a lot left to do? . . . Then take off early. I'll see you tomorrow." She hung up. "Two elderly Ransoms for the price of one, darling."

She looked at the paper again and pointed to the birthdates. "New Year's and Christmas. Cute. What's the chance of that? Who are these people?"

"I don't know," I said. "Willow Glen. Got a state map?"

"No need," she said. "I've been there. It's out in the boonies—San Bernardino County, near Yucaipa. When the kids were little I used to take them down there to pick apples."

"Apples?"

"Apples, darling. Little red round things? Keep the doctor away? Why the surprise?"

"I didn't know apples grew down there."

"They used to. Then one year we went down there and there was nothing left—all the U-pick places closed down, the trees dead and dying. We're talking boonies, Alex. Nothing's out there. Except Miss New Year's and Mr. Christmas."

28

The San Bernardino Freeway propelled me, like a pea through a shooter, past an exurban blur of industrial parks, ticky tack housing developments and auto lots wider than some small towns. Just beyond Pomona and the County Fairgrounds, the scenery shifted to ranches, egg farms, warehouses, and freight yards. Running parallel to the south side of the freeway were railroad tracks. Cotton Bowl and Southern Pacific boxcars sat stagnant on the rails. The rear third of the train was meshed compartments crammed with gleaming little Japanese sedans. A brief burst of architectural fervor past Claremont and then everything got quiet.

I drove through empty, sun-scorched hills, past smaller farms and ranches, sloping fields of alfalfa, horses grazing sluggishly in the heat. The Yucaipa exit narrowed to a single lane that ran alongside a tractor graveyard. I slowed and cruised past a string of aluminum-sided trailers billed as "The Big Mall," an untended taco shack, and a boarded-up shop advertising "Very Rare Antiques."

Willow Glen shared billing on a road sign with a Bible college twenty miles south and a state agricultural depot. The directional arrow aimed me over a covered bridge and onto a razor-straight road that cut through more farmland—citrus and avocado plantings, ramshackle stables, and untended fields. Broad slabs of blank brown space were broken by trailer parks, tin-roofed juke joints, and cinder-block churches, and surrounded by the granite drapery of the San Bernardino Mountains.

The mountains faded from rawhide to lavender-gray in the distance, the upper peaks merging with a pearly mist of sky. Heat percolated up from the lowlands, softening the contours of the pines that clung to the mountainsides, creating fringed silhouettes that recalled ink bleeding into blotting paper.

Willow Glen Road materialized as the left arm of a boulevard stop in the middle of nowhere, a sharp hook past a splintered sign advertising fresh produce and a "Jumbo Turkey Ranch," long vacated. The blacktop twisted and climbed toward the mountains, then up into them. The air got cooler, cleaner.

Ten miles in, a few apple orchards appeared: freshly tilled small plots backed by frame houses and surrounded by barbed wire and windbreak willows, the trees cut low with wide crotches, for handpicking. Cherry-sized orbs peeked out from under sage canopies of leaf. Harvest looked to be a good two months away. Homemade signs on stakes driven into the road shoulder welcomed the U-pick crowd but there didn't seem enough fruit to provide more than a day's desultory picking. As the road climbed higher, neglected orchards began to dominate the landscape—larger, dusty stretches filled with dead trees, some felled, others whittled to limbless, gray-white spikes.

The asphalt ended at twin telephone-pole-sized posts banded with Chamber of Commerce and service club badges. A chain dangling from between the posts supported a sign that read WILLOW GLEN VILLAGE. POP. 432.

I stopped, looked past the sign. The village seemed to be nothing more than a tiny rustic shopping mall shaded by willows and pines and fronted by an empty parking lot. The trees parted at the far end of the lot, and the road continued as compressed dirt. I drove in, parked, and stepped out into clean, dry heat.

The first thing that caught my eye was a large black-and-white llama nibbling hay in a small corral. Behind the corral was a narrow frame house painted barn-red and trimmed in white. The sign over the doorway read WILLOW GLEN FUN CENTER AND PETTING ZOO. I searched for human habitation, saw none. Waved at the llama and got a ruminant stare in return.

A handful of other buildings, all small, all wooden, shingle-roofed and unpainted and connected to one another by planked walkways. HUGH'S WOODCARVER'S PARADISE. THE ENCHANTED FOREST ANTIQUE SHOPPE. GRANNY'S TREASURE TROVE, GIFTS AND SOUVENIRS. Every one shuttered tight.

The ground was cushioned by pine needles and willow leaves. I walked through it, still searching for company, spotted a flash of white and a jet of smoke rising from behind the woodcarver's shop.

Low-hanging branches blocked the view. I walked past them, saw a series of weathered wood booths bolted together under a single, brand-new red roof. As I got closer, the air got sweet—the heavy sweetness of honey mixed with the tang of apples. The trees receded and I was standing in a bright clearing.

One of the booths was labeled APPLE PRESS & CIDERY, another CLOVER HONEY. But the sweet smoke was coming from next door, a green-shuttered section designated GOLDEN DELICIOUS CAFÉ. DEEP DISH PIE. COBBLER. The café's façade was whitewashed planks and stained-glass windows—windows decorated with black boughs, pink-white blossoms, green, red, and yellow apples. The door was open. I went in.

Inside everything was spotless and whitewashed—picnic tables and benches, a white ceiling fan recirculating hot, honeyed air, a Formica-topped counter and three white Naugahyde stools, hanging plants, an old brass cash register, and a mimeographed poster advertising a Yucaipa astrologer. A young woman sat behind the counter drinking coffee and reading a biology textbook. Behind her a pass-through window provided a view of a stainless-steel kitchen.

I sat down. She looked up. Nineteen or twenty, with a sharply upturned nose, clipped curly blond hair, and wide dark eyes. She wore a white shirt and black jeans, was slim but hippy. A green-apple badge on her shirt said WENDY.

She smiled. Maura Bannon's age. Less sophisticated, no doubt, but somehow older than the reporter.

"Hi. What can I get you?"

I pointed to her coffee cup. "How about some of that, for starts."

"Sure. Cream and sugar?"

"Black."

"Would you like a menu?"

"Thanks."

She handed me a plasticized rectangle. The selection surprised me. I'd expected burgers and fries, but a dozen entrees were listed, some of them complex, with a nod toward *nouvelle,* each tagged with letters indicating the proper wine: C for Chardonnay, JR for Johannisberg Riesling. On the back of the menu was a full wine list—good-quality French and California vintages as well as a locally produced apple wine described as "light and fruity, similar in nose and flavor to Sauvignon blanc."

She brought the coffee. "Something to eat?"

"How about an apple picker's lunch?"

"Sure." She turned her back on me, opened a refrigerator and various drawers and cabinets, tinkered for a while, put cutlery and a linen napkin on the counter, and served up a platter of perfectly sliced apples and thick wedges of cheese, garnished with mint.

"Here you go," she said, adding a whole-wheat roll and butter molded into flowers. "The goat cheese is really good, made by a family of Basques out near Loma Linda. Organically fed animals."

She waited.

Olivia's eggs still sat in my stomach. I took a small bite. "Terrific."

"Thanks. I'm studying food presentation in college, want to run my own place some day. I get to use working here as part of my independent studies."

I pointed at the textbook. "Summer school?"

She grimaced. "Finals. Tests aren't my specialty. More coffee?"

"Sure." I sipped. "Kind of quiet today."

"Every day. During picking season, September through January, we get a handful of tourists on weekends. But it's not like it used to be. People know about cherry picking in Beaumont but we haven't gotten much publicity. It didn't used to be that way—the village was built in 1867; people used to go home with bushel baskets of Spartans and Jonathans. But city people came and bought up some of the land. Didn't take care of it."

"I saw dead orchards on the way up."

"Isn't it sad? Apples need care—just like children. All those doctors and lawyers from L.A. and San Diego bought the orchards for taxes, then just let them die. We've been trying—my family and me—to get the place going again. The Orange County *Register* might run a piece on us—that would sure help. Meanwhile we're getting the jam and honey going, starting to do real good with mail order. Plus, I cook for the rangers and aggie commissioners passing through, get my independent study taken care of. You with the state?"

"No," I said. "What's with the llama?"

"Cedric? He's ours—my family's. That's our house behind his pen—our village house. Mom and my brothers are in there, right now, planning out the zoo. We're going to have a full-fledged petting zoo by next summer. Keep the little kids busy so the parents can shop. Cedric's a doll. Dad got him in trade—he's a doctor, has a chiropractic practice down in Yucaipa. That's where we live most of the time. There was this circus coming through—gypsies or something like that, in these painted wagons, with accordions and tape machines. They set up in one of the fields, passed the hat. One of the men sprained his back doing acrobatics. Dad fixed him up but the guy couldn't pay, so Dad took Cedric in trade. He loves animals. Then we got the idea for the petting zoo. My sister's studying animal husbandry at Cal Poly. She's going to run it."

"Sounds great. Does your family own the whole village?"

She laughed. "I *wish*. No, just the house and Cedric's pen and these back shops. The front shops are owned by other people but they're not around much. Granny—from the gift shop—died last summer and her family hasn't decided what they want to do. No one believes the Terrys are going to turn Willow Glen around, but we're sure going to try."

"The population sign said four thirty-two. Where's everyone else?"

"I think that number's high, but there are other families—a few growers; the rest work down in Yucaipa. Everyone's on the other side of the village. You have to drive through."

"Past the trees?"

Another laugh. "Yeah. It's hard to see, isn't it? Set up kind of to trap people." She looked at my plate. I gobbled in response, pushed it away half-finished. She was undeterred. "How about some deep-dish? I baked some just twenty minutes ago."

She looked so eager that I said, "Sure."

She set a big square of pastry before me, along with a spoon, and said, "It's so thick, this is better than a fork." Then she refilled my coffee cup and waited again.

I put a spoonful of pie in my mouth. If I'd been hungry, it would have been great: thin, sugary crust, crisp chunks of apple in light syrup, tinged with cinnamon and sherry, still warm. "This is terrific, Wendy. You have a bright future as a chef."

She beamed. "Well, thank you much, mister. If you want another piece, I'll give it to you on the house. Got so much, my hog brothers are only going to scarf it down without thanking me, anyway."

I patted my stomach. "Let's see how I do with this."

When I'd struggled through several more mouthfuls, she said, "If you're not the state, what brings you up here about?"

"Looking for someone."

"Who?"

"Shirlee and Jasper Ransom."

"What would you want with them?"

"They're related to a friend of mine."

"Related how?"

"I'm not sure. Maybe parents."

"Can't be a very close friend."

I put down my spoon. "It's complicated, Wendy. Do you know where I can find them?"

She hesitated. When her eyes met mine they were hard with suspicion.

"What's the matter?" I asked.

"Nothing. I just like folks to be truthful."

"What makes you think I haven't been?"

"Coming up here talking about Shirlee and Jasper maybe being someone's parents, driving all the way up here just to send regards."

"It's true."

"If you had any idea who—" She stopped herself, said, "I'm not going to be uncharitable. Let's just say I never knew them to have any relatives—not in the five years I've lived here. No visitors either."

She looked at her watch and tapped her fingers on the countertop. "You finished, mister? 'Cause I have to close up, do more studying."

I pushed my plate away. "Where's Rural Route Four?"

She shrugged, moved down the counter and picked up her book.

I stood up. "Check, please."

"Five dollars even."

I gave her a five. She took it by the corner, avoiding my touch.

"What is it, Wendy? Why're you upset?"

"I know what you are."

"What am I?"

"Bank man. Looking to foreclose on the rest of the village, just like you did with Hugh and Granny. Trying to sweet-talk all the other deed holders, buy up everything cheap so you can turn it into some *condo* project or something."

"You're a terrific cook, Wendy, but not too hot as a detective. I have nothing to do with any banks. I'm a psychologist from L.A. My name is Alex Delaware." I pulled ID out of my wallet: driver's license, psychology license, med school faculty card. "Here, see for yourself."

She pretended to be bored, but studied the papers. "Okay. So what? Even if you're who you say you are, what's your business here?"

"An old friend of mine, another psychologist named Sharon Ransom, died recently. She left no next of kin. There's some indication she's related to Shirlee and Jasper Ransom. I found their address, thought they might want to talk."

"How'd this Sharon die?"

"Suicide."

That drained the color from her face. "How old was she?"

"Thirty-four."

She looked away, busied herself with cutlery.

"Sharon Ransom," I said. "Heard of her?"

"Never. Never heard of Jasper and Shirlee having kids, period. You're mistaken, mister."

"Maybe," I said. "Thanks for lunch."

She called after me: "All of Willow Glen is Rural Route Four. Go past the schoolhouse about a mile. There's an old abandoned press. Turn right and keep going. But you're wasting your time."

I exited the village, endured fifty yards of potholes before the dirt smoothed and the RURAL ROUTE 4 sign appeared. I drove past more orchards and several homesteads graced by sprawling wood houses and fenced with low split rails, then a flag on a pole marking a two-story stone schoolhouse shaped like a milk carton and set in the middle of an oak-shaded, leaf-carpeted playground. The playground bled into forest, the forest into mountain. Name-tagged mailboxes lined the road: RILEY'S U-PICK AND PUMPKINS (CLOSED). LEIDECKER. BROWARD. SUTCLIFFE . . .

I drove past the abandoned apple press before realizing it, backed up, and pulled to the side of the road. From that distance it looked like scrap: corrugated steel sides ulcered with rust and caving inward, mere fringes of tar-paper roof remaining, exposing age-blackened rafters, neck-high weeds scrambling for the light. Surrounding the building was sunken land littered with spare parts, deadwood, and weeds that had reached the sun, been baked to summer straw.

Turn right and keep going. I saw no road, no entry, remembered Wendy's distrust and wondered if she'd led me wrong.

I kept the engine running and got out. Four o'clock, but sun was still pouring it on and within moments I was sweating. The road was silent. My nose picked up a skunk scent. I shaded my eyes with my hand, looked around, and finally saw a bald spot in the weeds—the barest outline of a pathway running alongside the press. A shiny depression in the straw where rubber tires had finally vanquished the tangle.

I thought of walking, didn't know how far in I had to go. Returning to the car, I backed up until I found a dip in the shoulder and nosed down into the sunken field.

The Seville didn't take well to rural travel; it skidded and slid on the slick straw. Finally I got some traction and was able to negotiate my way onto the path. I nudged the car forward, past the press, into an ocean of weeds. The depression turned into a dirt path and I picked up speed, crossed a broad field. At the far end was a copse of weeping willows. Between the lacy leaves of the trees, hints of metal—more corrugated buildings.

Shirlee and Jasper Ransom didn't seem like hospitable sorts.

Wendy had thought it unlikely they'd ever been parents, had stopped herself before explaining why.

Not wanting to be "uncharitable."

Or had she been afraid?

Perhaps Sharon had escaped them—escaped this place—for good reason, constructing fantasies of a pure and perfect childhood in order to block out a reality too terrible to confront.

I wondered what I was getting myself into. Let a Jasper/Shirlee fantasy of my own float by: mammoth rural mutants, toothless and walleyed in filthy overalls, surrounded by a pack of slavering, fanged mutts, and greeting my arrival with buckshot.

I stopped, listened for dogs. Silence. Telling myself to keep the old imagination in check, I gave the Seville gas.

When I reached the willows, there was no place for the car to enter. I turned off the ignition, stepped out, walked under the drooping boughs and through the copse. Heard the trickle of water. A voice humming tunelessly. Then came to the habitat of Jasper and Shirlee Ransom.

Two shacks on a small plot of dirt. A pair of tiny, primitive buildings sided with irregularly cut wood and roofed with tin. In place of windows, sheets of wax paper. Between the shacks was a wooden outhouse, complete with a crescent hole in the door. A rope clothesline was strung between the outhouse and one of the shacks. Faded garments were pinned to the hemp. Beyond the outhouse was a water tank on metal braces; next to it, a small electric generator.

Half the property was planted with apple trees—a dozen or so infant seedlings, staked and tagged. A woman stood watering them with a garden hose connected to the water tank. Water dribbled out from between her fingers, making it appear as if she were leaking, feeding the trees with her own body fluid. The water spattered on the ground, settled in muddy swirls, turned to dirt soup.

She hadn't heard me. Sixties, squat and very short—four foot eight or nine—gray hair cut in a pageboy, and flat, doughy features. She squinted, mouth open, accentuating an underslung jaw. A thatch of whiskers sprouted from her chin. She wore a one-piece smock of blue print material that resembled bed sheeting. The bottom hem was uneven. Her legs were pale and thick, pudding-soft and unshaven. She grasped the hose with both hands as if it were a live snake and concentrated on the water dribble.

I said, "Hello."

She turned, squinted several times, raising the hose in the process. The water squirted against the trunk of one of the saplings.

A smile. Guileless.

She waved her hand, tentatively, like a child meeting a stranger.

"Hello," I repeated.

"Hullo." Her enunciation was poor.

I came closer. "Mrs. Ransom?"

That perplexed her.

"Shirlee?"

Several rapid nods. "Tha's me. Shirlee." In her excitement, she dropped the hose and it began to twirl and spit. She tried to grab it, couldn't, caught a jet of water full in the face, cried out, and threw up her hands. I retrieved the muddy rubber coil, bent it and washed it off, and gave it back to her.

"Thanku." She rubbed her face on the shoulder of her smock, trying to dry it. I took out a clean handkerchief and dabbed at her face.

"Thanku. Sir."

"Shirlee, my name is Alex. I'm a friend of Sharon's."

I steeled myself for an outpouring of grief, got another smile. Brighter. "Pretty Sharon."

My heart ached. I forced the words out, nearly choked on the present tense. "Yes, she is pretty."

"*My* Sharon . . . letter . . . want to see it?"

"Yes, I do."

She looked down at the hose, appeared lost in thought. "Wait." Slowly, deliberately, she backed away from the saplings and made her way to the water tank. It took a long time for her to turn off the spigot, even longer to coil the tubing neatly on the ground. When she was through, she looked at me with pride.

"Great," I said. "Nice trees."

"Pretty. Apple. Mizz Leiderk gave them me and Jasper. Baby tree."

"Did you plant them, yourselves?"

Giggle. "No. Gabe-eel."

"Gabriel?"

Nod. "We take real good care."

"I'm sure you do, Shirlee."

"Yes."

"Can I see that letter from Sharon?"

"Yes."

I followed her flatfooted shuffle into one of the shacks. The walls were unpainted drywall streaked with waterstains; the floor, plywood; the ceiling, bare beams. A particle-board partition had been used to bisect the space. One half was a utility area—small refrigerator, electric hot plate, ancient washer with rollers. Boxes of soap powder and insecticide sat next to the fridge.

On the other side was a low-ceilinged room floored with a sheet of orange indoor-outdoor carpeting. A white-painted cast-iron bed draped with an army-surplus blanket nearly filled the space. The blanket was tucked tight, with military corners. Against one wall was an electric heater. The sun streamed in, golden and gentle, through wax-paper windows. A broom was propped in one corner. It had seen good use: The place was spotless.

The only other furniture was a small raw pine dresser. A box of crayons sat on top, along with several pencils worn down to nubs and pads of pulp paper neatly stacked and weighed down with a rock. The top sheet was a drawing. Apples. Primitive. Childish.

"Did you draw this, Shirlee?"

"Jasp. He a good drawer."

"Yes, he is. Where is he now?"

She left the cabin, pointed toward the outhouse. "Making."

"I see."

"Draw real good."

I nodded agreement. "The letter, Shirlee?"

"Oh." She smiled wider, cuffed the side of her head with one fist. "I forget."

We returned to the bedroom. She opened one of the dresser drawers. Inside were precisely ordered piles of garments—more of the same bleached-out stuff I'd seen on the clothesline. She slid one hand under the clothes, retrieved an envelope, and handed it to me.

Smudged with fingerprints, handled to tissue-fineness. The postmark, Long Island, New York, 1971. The address written in large block letters:

MR. AND MRS. JASPER RANSOM
RURAL ROUTE 4
WILLOW GLEN, CALIFORNIA

Inside was a single sheet of white stationery. The letterhead said:

FORSYTHE TEACHERS COLLEGE FOR WOMEN
WOODBURN MANOR
LONG ISLAND, N.Y. 11946

The same block lettering had been used for the text:

DEAR MOM AND DAD:

I'M HERE AT SCHOOL. THE PLANE RIDE WAS GOOD. EVERYONE IS BEING NICE TO ME. I LIKE IT, BUT I MISS YOU VERY MUCH.

PLEASE REMEMBER TO FIX THE WINDOWS BEFORE THE RAINS COME. THEY MAY COME EARLY, SO PLEASE BE CARE-FUL. REMEMBER HOW WET YOU GOT LAST YEAR. IF YOU NEED HELP MRS. LEIDECKER WILL HELP. SHE SAID SHE WILL CHECK TO SEE IF YOU ARE O.K.

DAD, THANKS FOR THE BEAUTIFUL DRAWINGS. I LOOKED AT THEM WHEN I WAS ON THE PLANE. OTHER PEOPLE SAW THEM AND SAID THEY WERE BEAUTIFUL. GOOD ENOUGH TO EAT. KEEP DRAWING AND SEND ME MORE. MRS. LEIDECKER WILL HELP YOU SEND THEM TO ME.

I DO MISS YOU. IT WAS HARD TO LEAVE. BUT I DO WANT TO BE A TEACHER AND I KNOW YOU WANT THAT TOO. THIS IS A GOOD SCHOOL. WHEN I AM A TEACHER I WILL COME BACK AND TEACH IN WILLOW GLEN. I PROMISE TO WRITE. TAKE CARE OF YOURSELVES.

LOVE,
SHARON
(YOUR ONLY LITTLE GIRL)

I slipped the letter back into the envelope. Shirlee Ransom was looking at me, smiling. It took several seconds before I could speak.

"It's a nice letter, Shirlee. A beautiful letter."

"Yes."

I handed it back to her. "Do you have more?"

She shook her head. "We had. Lots. Big rains came in, and whoosh." She waved her arms. "Everything wash away," she said.

"Dollies. Toys. Papers." She pointed to the wax-paper windows. "Rain comes in."

"Why don't you put in glass windows?"

She laughed. "Mizz Leiderk says glass, Shirlee. Glass is good. Strong. Try. Jasp say no, no. Jasp likes the air."

"Mrs. Leidecker sounds like a good friend."

"Yes."

"Was . . . is she Sharon's friend too?"

"Teacher." She tapped her forehead. "Real smart."

"Sharon wanted to be a teacher too," I said. "She went to school in New York to become a teacher."

Nod. "Four-set college."

"Forsythe College?"

Nod. "Far away."

"After she became a teacher, did she come back here to Willow Glen?"

"No. Too smart. Calfurna."

"California?"

"Yes. Far away."

"Did she write you from California?"

Troubled look. I regretted the question.

"Yes."

"When's the last time you heard from her?"

She bit her finger, twisted her mouth. "Crismus."

"Last Christmas?"

"Yes." Without conviction.

She'd talked about a sixteen-year-old letter as if it had arrived today. Thought California was some distant place. I wondered if she could read, asked her:

"Christmas a long time ago?"

"Yes."

Something else atop the dresser caught my eye: a corner of blue leatherette under the apple drawings. I pulled it out. A savings passbook from a bank in Yucaipa. She didn't seem to mind my intrusion. Feeling like a burglar anyway, I opened the book.

Several years' worth of transactions in an unwavering pattern: $500 cash deposits on the first of each month. Occasional withdrawals. A carry-over balance of $78,000 and some change. The account was in trusteeship for Jasper Ransom and Shirlee Ransom, co-tenants. The trustee, Helen A. Leidecker.

"Money," said Shirlee. Proud smile.

I put the book back where I'd found it.

"Shirlee, where was Sharon born?"

Look of bafflement.

"Did you give birth to her? Did she come out of your tummy?"

Giggles.

I heard footsteps and turned.

A man came in. He saw me, hitched up his pants, raised his eyebrows, and shuffled over to his wife's side.

He wasn't much bigger than she—barely over five feet—and about her age. Balding, with virtually no chin and very large, very soft-looking blue eyes. A fleshy nose tunneled between the eyes, shadowing a protruding upper lip. His mouth hung slightly open. He had only a few, yellowed teeth. An Andy Gump face, coated with fine white hair that resembled soap film. His shoulders so narrow that his short arms seemed to grow out of his neck. His hands dangled at his sides and ended in pudgy hands with splayed fingers. He wore a white T-shirt several sizes too large for him, gray work pants tied with a string around the waist, and high-top sneakers. The pants were pressed. His fly was open.

"Ooh, Jasp," said Shirlee, hiding her mouth with her hand and pointing.

He looked puzzled. She giggled and pulled up his zipper, patted him playfully on the cheek. He blushed, looked down.

"Hi," I said, holding out my hand. "My name is Alex."

He ignored me. Seemed preoccupied with his sneakers.

"Mr. Ransom . . . Jasper—"

Shirlee broke in. "Don' hear. Nuthin'. Don' talk."

I managed to catch his eye and mouthed the word *hello*.

Blank stare.

I offered my hand again.

He threw rabbity glances around the room.

I turned to Shirlee. "Could you tell him I'm a friend of Sharon's?"

She scratched her chin, contemplated, then screamed at him:

"He know Sharon! Sha-ron! Sha-ron!"

The little man's eyes grew wide, darted away from mine.

"Please tell him I like his drawings, Shirlee."

"Drawings!" shouted Shirlee. She did a crude pantomime of a moving pencil. *"He like draw-wings! Draw-wings!"*

Jasper screwed up his face.

"Draw-wings! Silly Jasp!" More pencil movements. She took him by the hand and pointed to the stack of papers on the dresser, then rotated him and pointed to me.

"Drawings!"

I smiled, said, "They're beautiful."

"Uhh." The sound was low-pitched, guttural, straining. I remembered where I'd heard something like it. Resthaven.

"Draw-wings!" Shirlee was still shouting.

"It's all right," I said. "Thank you, Shirlee."

But by now she was performing from her own script. *"Drawings! Go! Go!"* She gave his flat buttocks a shove. He trotted out of the shack.

"Jasp' gofer drawing," said Shirlee.

"Great. Shirlee, we were talking about where Sharon was born. I asked you if she came out of your tummy."

"Silly!" She looked down and stretched the fabric of her dress tight over her abdomen. Stroked the soft protrusion. "No baby."

"Then how did she get to be your little girl?"

The doughy face lit up, eyes brightening with guile.

"A present."

"Sharon was a present?"

"Yes."

"From who?"

She shook her head.

"Who gave her to you as a present?"

The headshake grew stronger.

"Why can't you tell me?"

"Can't!"

"Why not, Shirlee?"

"Can't! Secret!"

"Who told you to keep it secret?"

"Can't! Secret. *Seek-rut!"*

She was frothing at the mouth, looked ready to cry.

"Okay," I said. "It's good to keep a secret if that's what you promised."

"Secret."

"I understand, Shirlee."

She sniffled, smiled, said, "Uh-oh, water time," and walked out.

I followed her to the yard. Jasper had just come out of the other shack and was walking toward us clutching several sheets of paper. He saw me and waved them in the air. I walked over and he shoved them at me. More apples.

"Great, Jasper. Beautiful."

Shirlee said, "Water time," and glanced at the hose.

Jasper had left the door of the other shack open and I walked in. A single unpartitioned space. Red carpeting. A bed sat in the center, canopied and covered with lace-edged quilting. The fabric was speckled with green-black mold and rotted through. I touched a piece of lace. It turned to dust between my fingers. The headboard and canopy frame were muddy with oxidation and gave off a bitter odor. Above the bed, hanging from a nail driven crookedly into the drywall, was a framed Beatles poster—a blowup of the "Rubber Soul" album. The glass was streaked and cracked and flyspecked. Against the opposite wall was a chest of drawers covered with more decayed lace, perfume bottles, and glass figurines. I tried to pick up a bottle but it stuck to the lace. A trail of ants streamed over the chest top. Several dead silverfish lay strewn among the bottles.

The drawers were warped and hard to open. The top one was empty, except for more bugs. Same with all the others.

A sound came from the doorway. Shirlee and Jasper were standing there, holding each other, like scared children weathering a storm.

"Her room," I said. "Just the way she left it."

Shirlee nodded. Jasper looked at her, imitated her.

I tried to picture Sharon living with them. Being raised by them. *Martinis in the sun-room . . .*

I smiled to cover my sadness. They smiled back, also covering—a servile anxiety. Waiting for my next command. There was so much I wanted to ask them, but I knew I'd gotten as many answers as I ever would. I saw the fear in their eyes, searched for the right words.

Before I found them the doorway filled with flesh.

He wasn't much more than a kid—seventeen or eighteen, still peach-fuzzed and baby-faced. But enormous. Six-five, two ninety, perhaps thirty of it baby fat, with pink skin and a short neck broader than his moon face. His hair was cut in a blond crewcut and he was trying, without much success, to grow a mustache. His mouth was tiny and petulant, his eyes half-obscured by rosy cheeks as large and round as softballs. He wore faded jeans and an extra-extra-large black cowboy shirt with white piping and pearl buttons. The sleeves were rolled as far as they could go—midway up pink forearms as thick as my thighs. He stood behind the Ransoms, sweating, giving off heat and a locker-room odor.

"Who're you?" His voice was nasal, hadn't totally crossed over to manliness.

"My name's Alex Delaware. I'm a friend of Sharon Ransom."

"She doesn't live here anymore."

"I know that. I drove up from—"

"He bothering you?" he demanded of Shirlee.

She winced. "Hullo, Gabe-eel."

The kid softened his tone, repeated his question as if used to doing so.

Shirlee said, "He like Jasp drawings."

"Gabriel," I said, "I'm not out to cause any—"

"I don't care what you're out to do. These people are . . . special. They need to be treated special."

He lowered an enormous paw onto each of the Ransoms' shoulders.

I said, "Your mother's Mrs. Leidecker?"

"What of it?"

"I'd like to speak with her."

He bunched his shoulders and his eyes became slits. Except for his size it would have seemed comical—a little boy playing at machismo. "What's my mom got to do with it?"

"She was Sharon's teacher. I was Sharon's friend. There are things I'd like to talk to her about. Things that shouldn't be discussed in present company. I'm sure you know what I mean."

The look on his face said he knew exactly what I meant.

He moved back from the doorway a bit and said, "Mom doesn't need any upsetting either."

"I've no intention of upsetting her. Just talking."

He thought for a while, said, "Okay, mister, I'll take you to her. But I'll be there all the time, so don't be getting any ideas."

He moved completely out of the doorway. The sunlight returned.

"Come on, you guys," he told Jasper and Shirlee. "You should get back to those trees, make sure each of them gets a good soak."

They looked up at him. Jasper handed him a drawing.

He said, "Great, Jasp. I'll add it to my collection." Overenunciating. Then the man-child bent low and patted the head of the childish man. Shirlee grabbed his hand and he kissed her lightly on the forehead.

"You take care of yourselves, you hear? Keep watering those trees and soon we'll have something to pick together, okay? And don't talk to strangers."

Shirlee nodded gravely, then clapped her hands and giggled. Jasper smiled and gave him another drawing.

"Thanks again. Keep up the good work, Rembrandt." To me: "Come on."

We started to leave. Jasper ran after us, grunting sounds. We stopped. He gave me a drawing, turned away, embarrassed.

I raised his weak chin with my hand, mouthed "Thank you,"

overenunciating just as the boy had. Jasper's grin said he understood. I held out my hand. This time he gave it a weak shake and held on.

"Come on, mister," said Gabriel. "Leave them be."

I patted the little man's hand and pried it loose, followed Gabriel toward the willows, jogging to keep pace. Before stepping under the weeping green branches, I looked back and saw the two of them, hand in hand, standing in the middle of their dirt lot. Staring after us as if we were explorers—conquistadors setting out for some brave new world that they could never hope to see.

He'd parked a big restored Triumph motorcycle in back of the Seville.

Two helmets, one candy-apple red, the other starred and striped, dangled from the handlebars. He put on the red one, climbed on, and kick-started the bike.

I said, "Who told you I was here? Wendy?"

He ran his hand over his bristle-top and tried to stare me down.

"We take care of each other, mister."

He gave the bike gas, set off a dust storm in the dry weeds, then did a wheelie and peeled out. I jumped into the Seville, trailed him as quickly as I could, lost sight of him past the abandoned press, but found him a second later, headed back toward the village. I put on speed, caught up. We passed the mailbox that bore his family name, kept going until the schoolhouse, where he decelerated further and signaled right. He shot up the driveway, circled the playground, came to a halt at the schoolhouse steps.

He climbed the stairs, taking three at a time. I followed, noticed a wooden sign near the entrance.

WILLOW GLEN SCHOOL
ESTABLISHED 1938
ONCE PART OF THE BLALOCK RANCH

The letters were rustic and burned into the wood. Same style on the sign marking La Mar Road, a private road in Holmby Hills. As I stopped to take that in, Gabriel made it to the top of the stairs, threw open the door, and let it swing shut behind him. I ran up, caught it, and walked into a big, airy schoolroom that smelled of fingerpaint and pencil shavings. On the brightly painted walls were health and safety posters, crayon drawings. No apples. Blackboards hung on three walls, below Palmer penmanship guides. An American flag dangled over a large, round clock that put the time at 4:40. Facing each blackboard were about ten wooden school desks—the old-fashioned type, with narrow tops and inkwells.

A partners' desk faced all three seating groups. A fair-haired woman holding a pencil sat behind it. Gabriel stood over her, whispering. When he saw me, he straightened and cleared his throat. The woman put the pencil down and looked up.

She appeared to be in her early forties, with short wavy hair and broad, square shoulders. She wore a short-sleeved white blouse. Her arms were tan, fleshy, ending in dainty, long-nailed hands.

Gabriel whispered something to her.

I said, "Hello," and came closer.

She stood. Six feet or close to it, and older than a first impression suggested—late forties or early fifties. The white blouse was tucked into a knee-length brown linen skirt. She had heavy breasts, a thin, almost pinched waist that accentuated the breadth of her shoulders. Beneath the tan was a bed of ruddiness—a suggestion of the same coral tone that blanketed her son like some perpetual sunburn. She had a long, pleasant face enhanced by carefully applied makeup, full lips, and large, luminous, amber eyes. Her nose was prominent, her chin cleft and firmly set. An open face, strong and weathered.

"Hello," she said, without warmth. "What can I do for you, sir?"

"I wanted to talk about Sharon Ransom. I'm Alex Delaware."

Hearing my name changed her. She said, "Oh," in a weaker voice.

"Mom," said Gabriel, taking her arm.

"It's all right, honey. Go back to the house and let me talk to this man."

"No way, Mom. We don't know him."

"It's all right, Gabe."

"Mo-om."

"Gabriel, if I tell you it's all right, then it's all right. Now kindly get back to the house and attend to your chores. The old Spartans back of the pumpkin patch need pruning. There's still plenty of corn to husk, and the pumpkin vines need tying."

He grunted, gave me the evil eye.

"Go, Gabey," she said.

He removed his hand from her arm, shot me another glare, then pulled out his key ring and stomped out, muttering.

"Thank you, honey," she called out just before the door closed.

When he was gone, she said, "We lost Mr. Leidecker last spring. Since then, Gabe's been trying to replace his dad and I'm afraid he's grown overly protective."

"A good son," I said.

"A wonderful one. But he's still just a child. The first time people meet him, they're overwhelmed by his size. They don't realize that he's only sixteen. I didn't hear his bike start. Did you?"

"No."

She walked to a window and yelled down: "I said *back home,* Gabriel Leidecker. Get those vines propped up by the time I get back or it's curtains for you, kid."

Protest noises floated up from below. She stood in the window, hands on hips. "Such a baby," she said with affection. "Probably my fault—I was much harder on his brothers."

"How many children do you have?"

"Five. Five boys. All married and gone except for Gabey. Subconsciously I probably want to keep him immature."

She shouted, "Scoot!" and waved out the window. The rumble of the Triumph filtered up to us.

When the silence returned, she shook my hand and said, "I'm Helen Leidecker. Forgive me for not greeting you properly. Gabe didn't tell me who you were or what you were about. Just that some city stranger was snooping around the Ransoms' place and wanting to talk to me." She pointed to the school desks. "If you don't mind one of those, please sit down."

"Brings back memories," I said, squeezing behind a front-row seat.

"Oh, really? Did you attend a school like this?"

"We had more than one room, but the setting was similar."

"Where was that, Dr. Delaware?"

Dr. Delaware. I hadn't given her my title. "Missouri."

"A midwesterner," she said. "I'm originally from New York. If someone had told me I'd end up in a sleepy little hamlet like Willow Glen, I'd have thought it hilarious."

"Where in New York?"

"Long Island. The Hamptons—not the wealthy part. My people serviced the idle rich."

She went back behind her desk and sat.

"If you're thirsty," she said, "there's a cooler full of drinks around back, but I'm afraid all we've got is milk, chocolate milk, or orange drink." She smiled, got younger again. "I've repeated that so many times it's etched indelibly into my brain."

"No thanks," I said. "I had a big lunch."

"Wendy's a wonderful cook, isn't she?"

"Wonderful early warning system too."

"As I said, Dr. Delaware, this is a sleepy little hamlet. Everyone knows everything about everybody."

"Does that include knowledge of Shirlee and Jasper Ransom?"

"Especially them. They need special kindness."

"Especially now," I said.

Her face collapsed, as if suddenly filleted. "Oh, gosh," she said, and opened a desk drawer. Taking out an embroidered handkerchief, she dabbed at her eyes. When she turned them on me again, grief had made them even larger.

"They don't read the papers," she said, "can barely read a primer. How am I going to tell them?"

I had no answer for that. I was weary of searching for answers. "Do they have other family?"

She shook her head. "She was all they had. And me. I've become their mother. I know I'm going to have to deal with it."

She pressed the handkerchief to her face like a poultice.

"Please excuse me," she said. "I'm as shaky as the day I read about it—*that* was a horror. I just can't believe it. She was so beautiful, so alive."

"Yes, she was."

"For all intents and purposes I was the one who raised her. And now she's gone, blotted out. As if she never existed in the first place. Such a damned, ugly waste. Thinking about it makes me *angry* at her. Which is unfair. It was *her* life. She never asked for what I gave her, never . . . Oh, I don't know!"

She averted her face. Her makeup had started to run. She reminded me of a parade float the morning after.

I said, "It *was* her life. But she left a lot of people grieving."

"This is more than grief," she said. "I've just been through that. This is worse. I thought I knew her like a daughter, but all these years she must have been carrying around so much pain. I had no idea—she never expressed it."

"No one knew," I said. "She never really showed herself."

She threw up her hands and let them drop like dead weights. "What could have been so terrible that she lost all hope?"

"I don't know. That's why I'm up here, Mrs. Leidecker."

"Helen."

"Alex."

"Alex," she said. "Alex Delaware. How strange to meet you after all these years. In a way I feel I know you. She told me all about you—how much she loved you. She considered you the one true love of her life, even though she knew it could never work out because of your sister. Despite that, she admired you so deeply for the way you devoted yourself to Joan."

She must have read the shock on my face as pain and gave me a look rich with sympathy.

"Joan," I said.

"The poor thing. How's she doing?"

"About the same."

She nodded sadly. "Sharon knew her condition would never really improve. But even though your commitment to Joan meant you could never commit fully to anyone else, she admired you for it. If anything, I'd say it intensified her love for you. She talked about you as if you were a saint. She felt that kind of family loyalty was so rare nowadays."

"I'm hardly a saint," I said.

"But you are a good man. And that old cliché remains valid as ever: They're hard to find." A faraway look came onto her face. "Mr. Leidecker was one. Taciturn, a stubborn Dutchman, but a heart of gold. Gabe has some of that goodness—he's a kind boy. I only hope losing his dad so young doesn't harden him."

She stood up, walked over to one of the blackboards, and made a few cursory swipes with a rag. The effort seemed to exhaust her. She returned to her seat, straightened papers, and said, "It's been a year for losses. Poor Shirlee and Jasper. I so dread telling them. It's my own doing. I changed their lives; now the change has wrought tragedy."

"There's no reason to blame you—"

"Please," she said gently. "I know it's not rational, but I can't help the way I feel. If I hadn't gotten involved in their lives, things would have been different."

"But not necessarily better."

"Who knows," she said. Her eyes had filled with tears. "Who knows."

She looked at the clock on the wall. "I've been cooped up in here all afternoon grading papers. I could really use a stretch."

"Me too."

As we descended the schoolhouse steps I pointed to the wooden sign.

"The Blalock Ranch. Weren't they into shipping, or something?"

"Steel and railroads. It was never really a ranch. Back in the twenties, they were competing with Southern Pacific for the rail lines connecting California with the rest of the country. They surveyed San Bernardino and Riverside for an inland route and bought up a good chunk of both counties—entire villages at a time. They paid top dollar to get Willow Glen land away from the apple farmers who'd homesteaded it since the Civil War. The result was a huge spread that they called a ranch. But they never grew or raised anything on it, just fenced it in and posted guards. And the railroad was never built—the Depression. After World War Two, they started selling some of the smaller parcels back to private people. But several of the big tracts were snapped up by another corporation."

"Which one?"

She patted her hair. "Some aviation concern—the one run by that mad billionaire, Belding." She smiled. "And that, Dr. Delaware, is your California history lesson for the day."

We entered the playground, strolled past swings and slides, headed toward the forest that carpeted the foot of the mountains.

"Does Magna still own land here?" I asked.

"Plenty of it. But *they* won't sell. People have tried. For all intents and purposes that keeps Willow Glen a backwater speck. Most of the old families have given up, sold out to rich doctors and lawyers who use the orchards for tax write-offs and run them down— capped irrigation lines, no pruning or fertilizing. Most of them don't even bother to come up and harvest. In some places the earth's turned hard and dry as cement. The few growers who've stayed have become suspicious and mistrustful—they're convinced it's all part of a conspiracy to run things down so the city folk can buy what's left on the cheap and put up condominiums or something."

"That's what Wendy thought."

"Her folks are newcomers, really pretty naïve. But you have to admire them for trying."

"Who owns the land Jasper and Shirlee live on?"

"That's Magna land."

"Is that common knowledge?"

"Mr. Leidecker told me, and he was hardly a gossip."

"How'd they end up there?"

"No one knows. According to Mr. Leidecker—I wasn't living here then—they showed up at the general store to buy groceries back in 1956—back when there was a general store. When people tried to talk to them, Jasper waved his hands and grunted and she giggled. It was obvious they were retarded—children who'll never grow up. The prevailing theory is that they escaped from some institution, maybe wandered away from a bus and ended up here by accident. People help them when it's needed, but in general no one pays them much mind. They're harmless."

"Someone pays them mind," I said. "Five hundred dollars a month."

She gave a hand-in-the-cookie-jar look. "I beg your pardon."

"I saw their bankbook. Sitting on top of the dresser."

"On the dresser? What am I going to do with those two? I've told them so many times to keep that book hidden, tried to get them to let me keep it at my place. But they think it's some kind of symbol of freedom, won't part with it. They can get really stubborn when they want to. Jasper, especially. Did you see those wax-paper windows on their shacks? After all these years, he still refuses to have glass installed. Poor Shirlee freezes in the winter. Gabe and I have to bring down piles of blankets, and by the end of the season they're mildewed beyond repair. The cold doesn't seem to bother Jasper. Poor thing needs to be told to come in from the rain."

She shook her head. "On top of the dresser. Not that anyone from around here would hurt them, but that's a lot of money to advertise. Especially for two defenseless innocents."

"Who sends it?" I asked.

"I've never been able to find out. It arrives, like clockwork, on the first of every month, posted from the central depot in Los Angeles. Plain white envelope, a typed address, no return. Shirlee has no clear concept of time, so she can't say how long she's been receiving it, only that it's been a long time. There was a man—Ernest Halverson—used to deliver the mail until he retired in '64. He thought he remembered envelopes arriving as early as 1956 or '7, but he'd had a couple of strokes by the time I talked to him and his memory wasn't perfect. All the other old-timers are long gone."

"Was it always five hundred?"

"No. Used to be three, then four. It went up to five after Sharon left for college."

"Thoughtful benefactor," I said. "But how could they be expected to handle that kind of money?"

"They couldn't. They were living like animals until we began taking care of them. Wandering into town every couple of weeks with two or three twenty-dollar bills, trying to buy groceries—they had no idea how to make change or how much things were worth. People are honest here; they never took advantage."

"Wasn't there curiosity about where they were getting the money?"

"I'm sure there was, but Willow Glen folk don't pry. And no one realized how much money they were hoarding. Not until Sharon discovered it—thousands of dollars wadded up under the mattress, or just loose in a drawer. Jasper had used several of the bills for art projects—drawing mustaches on the faces, folding them into paper airplanes."

"How old was Sharon when she made the discovery?"

"Almost seven. It was 1960. I remember the year because we had unusually hard winter rains. Those shacks were originally built for storage, with only a thin cement pad underneath, and I knew they'd be hit hard, so we went over—Mr. Leidecker and myself. Sure enough, it was dreadful. Their plot was half-flooded, boggy, the dirt running off like melted chocolate. Water had perforated the wax paper and was pouring in. Shirlee and Jasper were standing knee-deep in mud, scared and totally helpless. I didn't see Sharon, went looking for her, and found her in her shack, standing on top of her bed wrapped in a blanket, shivering and shouting something about green soup. I had no idea what she was talking about. I took her in my arms to warm her, but she kept shouting about soup.

"When we got outside, Mr. Leidecker was pointing, all wide-eyed, at bits of green paper stuck in the mud and washing away in the flood. Money, lots of it. At first I thought it was play money—I'd given Sharon some board games—but it wasn't. It was real. Between Mr. Leidecker and myself, we managed to salvage most of it—we hung the wet bills over our hearth to dry them, put them in a cigar box and kept them safe. First thing after the rains stopped, I drove Shirlee and Jasper down to Yucaipa and set up the bank account. I sign for everything, take a little out for expenses, make sure they save the rest. I've managed to teach them a little elementary math, how to budget, how to make change. Once they finally learn something, they can usually retain it. But they'll never really understand what they've got—quite a tidy little nest egg. Along with Medi-Cal and Social Security, the two of them should be comfortable for the rest of their days."

"How old are they?"

"I have no idea, because they don't. They have no papers, didn't even know their birthdays. The government had never heard of them, either. When we applied for Social Security and Medi-Cal, we estimated their ages, gave them birthdates."

Miss New Year's and Mr. Christmas.

"You applied when Sharon left for college."

"Yes. I wanted to cover all bases."

"How did you come up with Sharon's birthdate?"

"She and I decided on one, when she was ten." She smiled. "July Fourth. Her declaration of independence. I put 1953. I got a really good fix on her age from the doctor I took her to—bone-age X-rays, teeth, height and weight. She was somewhere between four and five."

She and I had celebrated a different birthday. May 15. May 15, 1975. A rare splurge for dinner and dancing and lovemaking. Another fiction. I wondered what *that* date symbolized.

"Any possibility," I asked, "that she was their biological child?"

"Unlikely. The doctor examined all of them and said Shirlee was almost certainly sterile. So where did she come from, right? For a while I lived with the nightmare that she was someone's kidnapped baby. I went down to San Bernadino and checked six years' worth of papers from all around the country, found a couple of cases that sounded possible, but when I followed them up, I learned that both of those children had been murdered. So her origins remain clouded. When you ask Shirlee about it, she just giggles and says Sharon was given to them."

"She told me it was a secret."

"That's just a game with her—playing secret. They're really just like children."

"What's the prevailing theory about how they got her?"

"There really isn't one. Mind you, the doctor wasn't absolutely certain Shirlee couldn't conceive—'highly unlikely' was the way he put it. So I suppose anything's possible. Though the notion of two poor souls like that producing something so exquisite is . . ." She trailed off. "No, Alex, I have no idea."

"Sharon must have been curious about her roots."

"You'd expect her to be, wouldn't you? But she never really went through any identity search. Not even during adolescence. She knew she was different from Shirlee and Jasper but she loved them, accepted things the way they were. The only conflict I ever saw was the summer before she left for college. That was really hard for her—she was excited and frightened and tremendously guilty about abandoning them. She knew she was taking a giant step, and things would never be the same."

She stopped, bent, picked up an oak leaf and twirled it between her fingers. The sky between the trees was darkening. Unintimidated by city lights, the stars were burning pinholes through the blackness.

"When's the last time Sharon visited here?" I asked.

"A long time ago," she said, making it sound like a confession. "Once she broke away, she found it very painful to return. That may sound callous, but her situation was unique."

We walked on. The schoolroom windows shone through the dark: butter-colored rectangles. We hadn't gone far, had been walking in circles.

"Her last visit," she said, "was in 1974. She'd just graduated from college, had been accepted to graduate school, and was moving down to L.A. I threw a little party for her at my house. Mr. Leidecker and the boys wore starched white shirts and matching ties, and I bought new outfits for Shirlee and Jasper. Sharon arrived looking lovely, a real picture. She brought gifts for all of us, a handmade wooden checkers set for Shirlee and a tin of fancy colored pencils from England for Jasper. She also gave them a graduation picture—full cap and gown with an honors tassel."

"I didn't see that back at the shack."

"No, somehow they managed to lose it. Just like the money. They never knew what they had, still don't. You can understand why Sharon would have no place here. It's a miracle she survived before I found her."

"Shirlee did show me a letter. How often did she write?"

"Not regularly—what was the point? They're only marginally literate. But she called me regularly, to see how they were doing. She really cared about them."

She threw away the leaf. "It was so hard for her—please understand that. She really struggled with breaking away; the guilt was nearly overwhelming. I told her she was doing the right thing. What was the alternative? Being stuck forever as a caretaker?" She stopped. "Oh. I'm so sorry. That was thoughtless."

For a moment I was puzzled by her embarrassment.

"Joan," I said.

"I think your devotion is wonderful."

I shrugged. Dr. Noble. "I'm comfortable with my choice."

"Yes. Sharon said you were. And that's my point. She had to make *her* own choices. She couldn't be bound by some strange twist of fate."

"When did she tell you about Joan?"

"About six months after the graduation party—her first year of grad school. She called to ask about Shirlee and Jasper, but she sounded troubled. I could tell something else was on her mind. I asked if she wanted to get together and to my surprise she said yes. We met for lunch in Redlands. She looked like a real professional woman, perfectly groomed, mature. But sad—a blue angel. I asked her why. She said she'd met the man of her dreams, spent a lot of time describing your virtues. I said, sounds like he's perfect—why the long face? Then she told me about Joan, how it would never work out because of her."

"Did she tell you what caused Joan's problems?"

"The drowning? Oh, yes. How terrible, and you a little boy, watching."

She touched my arm in a gesture of comfort. "She understood, Alex. She wasn't bitter or angry."

"Is that all that was troubling her?"

"That's all she talked about."

"When did you see her next?"

She bit her lip. "Never. That was the last time. She did continue to call. But less and less frequently. Half a year later, the calls stopped. But we got cards on Christmas, Fruit-of-the-Month packages." She managed a weak smile. "Everything but the apples."

Several yards later she said, "I understood. Though I'd helped her shed her old life, I was still part of it. She needed to make a complete break. Years later, when she got her Ph.D., she sent me an invitation to her commencement. She'd made it to the top, finally felt secure enough to reconnect."

"Did you go?"

"No. It arrived late—the day after the ceremony. Mail mix-up, happens all the time on a rural route."

No mail mix-up had prevented the monthly cash payments to the Ransoms. I said nothing.

"All those years," she said, "I felt I understood her. Now I realize I was deluding myself. I barely knew her."

We walked toward yellow windows. I said, "How did you and Sharon actually meet?"

"My old do-gooder busybody personality asserting itself. It was shortly after my marriage, right after Mr. Leidecker brought me back here, in 1957."

She shook her head, said, "Thirty years," then nothing else.

I said, "Moving from the big city to Willow Glen must have been pretty jarring for you."

"Oh, it was. After college I got a position teaching at a private school on the Upper East Side of Manhattan—children of the rich.

Nights, I volunteered at the USO—that's where I met Mr. Leidecker. He was in the army, taking courses at City College courtesy of Uncle Sam. He came into the hall one night, looking absolutely forlorn. We struck up a conversation. He was very handsome, very sweet. So different from the fast, shallow men I'd been encountering in the city. When he talked about Willow Glen, he made it sound like paradise. He loved the land—his roots here run deep. His family came out from Pennsylvania for the Gold Rush. Got as far as Willow Glen and settled for Golden Delicious—he always used to say that. Two months later, I was married, a schoolmarm in a one-room school."

We reached the stone building. She looked up at the sky. "My husband was a taciturn man, but he knew how to tell a tale. He played the guitar beautifully and sang like a dream. We made a good life together."

"Sounds wonderful," I said.

"Oh, it was. I came to love this place. The people here are solid and decent; the children are almost touchingly innocent—even more so before we got cable TV. But one always makes trade-offs. Once upon a time, I fancied myself an intellectual—not that I was, but I did love to attend poetry readings in Greenwich Village, visit art galleries, listen to the band-shell concerts in Central Park. I loved the whole city scene. New York was a lovely place, back then. Cleaner, safer. Ideas seemed to burst right out of the sidewalks."

We were at the bottom of the schoolroom stairs. The light from above spilled over her face, lit flames in her eyes. Her hip brushed against mine. She moved away quickly and fluffed her hair.

"Willow Glen is a cultural desert," she said, climbing. "I belong to four book clubs, subscribe to twenty monthly periodicals, but believe me, it's no substitute. In the beginning I made Mr. Leidecker drive me to L.A. for the Philharmonic, San Diego for the Shakespeare Festival at the Old Globe. He did it without complaining, good soul that he was. But I knew he detested it—he never stayed awake through a single show—and eventually I stopped putting him through it. The only play I've seen in years is the one I write myself—the Christmas pageant that the children put on. 'God Rest Ye Merry Gentlemen' accompanied by my off-key piano thumping."

She laughed. "At least the children enjoy it—they're not very sophisticated around here. At home the emphasis is on making a living. Sharon was different. She had a rapacious mind, just loved to learn."

"Amazing," I said, "considering *her* home life."

"Yes, truly amazing. Especially when you consider the state she was in when I first laid eyes on her. The way she blossomed was a miracle. I feel privileged to have been part of it. No matter how things turned out."

She choked back tears, pushed the door, and walked quickly to her desk. I watched as she tidied up.

"How," I repeated, "did the two of you actually meet?"

"Right after I got here, I kept hearing my pupils talk about a family of 'retards'—*their* term, not mine—living out behind the old abandoned cider press. Two grown-ups and a little girl who ran around naked and chattered like a monkey. At first I thought it was just schoolyard fantasy, the kind of thing children love to make up. But when I mentioned it to Mr. Leidecker, he said, 'Oh, sure. That's Jasper and Shirlee Ransom. They're feebleminded but harmless.' Just shrugged it off, the old village idiot thing. 'What about the child?' I asked. 'Is she feebleminded too? Why hasn't she been enrolled in school? Has she been inoculated? Has anyone bothered to give her a decent checkup or seen to it that she gets proper nutrition?' That made him stop and think and he got a bothered look on his face. 'You know, Helen,' he said, 'I never much thought about that.' He was ashamed—that's the kind of man he was.

"The very next afternoon after school, I drove down the road, found the press, and went looking for them. It was just as the children had described: Tobacco Road. Those pathetic shacks—and they were a lot worse before we fixed them up. No indoor plumbing, electricity, or gas heat, water from an old hand pump with God knows what kind of organisms in it. Before we supplied the trees, just a dry dirt patch. Shirlee and Jasper just standing there, smiling at me, following me around but not putting up a lick of protest when I went into their shack. Inside, I got my first surprise. I'd expected chaos, but everything was scrubbed down with lye soap, extremely well-kept—all the clothes folded neatly, beds you could bounce a dime on. And the two of them are very diligent about their hygiene, though they do neglect their teeth."

"Well-trained," I said.

"Yes. As if someone had drilled the basics into them—which supports the institution theory. Unfortunately, that training didn't extend to child care. Sharon was filthy, that gorgeous black hair so dusty it looked tan, all matted and tangled with burrs. The first time I laid eyes on her she was up in one of the willow trees, crouched on a limb, naked as a jay, with something shiny in her hands. Staring down with those huge blue eyes. Looking, indeed, like a little monkey. I asked Shirlee to have her come down. Shirlee called up to her—"

"Called her by her name?"

"Yes. Sharon. That we didn't have to improvise. Shirlee kept calling, begging her to come down, but Sharon ignored her. It was clear there was no parental authority, they couldn't control her. Finally, after I pretended to ignore her, she scampered down, kept her distance and stared at me. But not afraid—on the contrary, she seemed actually happy to see a new face. Then she did something that really took me by surprise. The shiny thing she'd been holding was an open jar of mayonnaise. She stuck one hand into it, scooped out a big glob, and began eating it. Flies smelled it and began crawling all over her. I took the jar away. She squawked, but not too loudly—she craved discipline. I put my arm around her. She seemed to like that. She smelled foul, looked like one of those feral children you hear about. But despite that, she was absolutely gorgeous—that face, those eyes.

"I sat her down on a stump, held up the mayo jar and said, 'This is eaten with tuna or ham. Not by itself.' Shirlee was listening. She started to giggle. Sharon took her cue, laughed, and ran her greasy hands through her hair. Then she said, 'I like it by itself.' Clear as a bell. It shocked me. I'd assumed she was retarded, too, had little or no speech. I took a close look at her and saw something—a quickness in her eyes, the way she responded to my movements. Definitely something upstairs. She was also very well coordinated: When I commented on what an excellent climber she was, she showed off for me, shinnied up the tree, did cartwheels and handstands. Shirlee and Jasper watched and clapped their hands. To them she was a toy.

"I asked them if I could take her with me for a few hours. They agreed without hesitation, even though they'd never met me. No parent-child bond, though they were clearly delighted with her, kissed and hugged her a lot before we left."

"How did Sharon react to being taken away?"

"She wasn't happy, but she didn't fight it. She especially didn't like it when I tried to cover her—with a blanket. Funny thing is, once she got used to clothes, she never liked to take them off—as if being naked reminded her of the way she'd been."

I said, "I'm sure it did," and thought of backseat love.

"She actually became quite a fashion plate—used to pore over my magazines and cut out the outfits she liked. She never liked pants, only dresses."

Fifties dresses.

I said, "What was it like the first time you brought her home?"

"She allowed me to take her by the hand, and climbed up into the car as if she'd ridden in one before. During the ride I tried to talk to her, but she just sat there, staring out the window. When we reached my house, she got out, squatted, and defecated on the driveway. When I gasped, she seemed genuinely surprised, as if doing that sort of thing was perfectly normal. It was obvious there'd been absolutely no limit-setting of any sort. I took her inside, sat her on the commode, washed her up, combed out the tangles—at that point she began screaming bloody murder. Then I dressed her in one of Mr. Leidecker's old shirts, sat her down, and fed her a proper dinner. She ate like a lumberjack. Got off the chair and started to squat again. I hauled her into the bathroom, made her mind. That was the beginning. She knew I cared."

"But she did talk fluently?"

"It was strange, uneven. Sometimes whole phrases would pour out, then she'd be at a loss to describe something simple. She had giant holes in her knowledge of the world. When she got frustrated she'd start to grunt and point like Jasper. But not in any sort of sign language—I was trained in American Sign, and neither she nor Jasper knew it, though I've taught him a little bit since. He has his own primitive language—when he bothers to communicate at all. That's the environment she was living in before I found her."

"From that to Ph.D.," I said.

"I told you it was a miracle. She learned astonishingly quickly. Four months of steady drilling to get her talking properly, another three to teach her to read. She was ready for it, an empty glass waiting to be filled. The more time I spent with her, the clearer it became that not only wasn't she retarded, she was gifted. Highly gifted."

And previously educated. By someone who'd taught her about cars, whole phrases . . . then punched holes in her knowledge of the world.

Helen had stopped talking, was holding her hand to her mouth, breathing deeply. "All for nothing."

She looked at the clock on the wall. "I'm sorry, I have to go now. I hitched a ride with Gabe. He bought me a helmet with his own money—how could I refuse? Poor thing's probably beside himself, suspecting God knows what."

"I'd be happy to give you a lift."

She hesitated, then said, "All right. Give me a couple of minutes to close up."

30

Her house was large and peak-roofed and floodlit, trimmed generously with white gingerbread, and set back from the road behind half an acre of thriving orchard. Gabe's bike was parked near the front porch, next to an old Chevy truck and a Honda Accord. She led me around to the side door and we entered through the kitchen. Gabe sat at the table, his back to us, husking corn and listening to loud rap music on a ghetto blaster not much smaller than the Honda. Ears of corn were piled chin-high. He worked slowly but steadily, bobbing in time to the music.

She kissed the top of his head. He gave her a sympathy-begging look of misery. When he saw me, the misery turned to anger.

She turned down the volume on the blaster.

He said, "What's with *him?*"

"Don't be rude, Gabriel! Daddy taught you better than that."

The mention of his father made him look like a small, lost child. He pouted, picked up an ear of corn, tore off the husk, and idly shredded the silk.

His mother said, "Dr. Delaware is a guest. You will stay for dinner, Doctor?"

I had no need of food but was hungry for facts. "Be pleased to," I said. "Thank you very much."

Gabe mumbled something hostile. The music was still loud enough to block out his words, but not his meaning.

"Clean up and set the table, Gabriel. Perhaps nutrition will restore your manners."

"I ate, Mom."

"What did you have?"

"Chicken pie, the rest of the potatoes, the snap beans, the pumpkin bread."

"All the pumpkin bread?"

Kid's grin. "Yup."

"And for dessert?"

"The ice cream."

"Leave any for sweet-toothed Mom?"

The grin faded. "Sorry."

"That's okay, sweetie," she said, tousling his hair. "I need to cut down—you did me a favor."

He spread his hands over the pile of corn and gave her an imploring look. "Look how much I got done. Can I quit for tonight?"

She crossed her arms, tried to look stern. "All right. You'll pick up with the rest tomorrow. What about homework?"

"Did it."

"All of it?"

"Yes, ma'am."

"Fine. You're free on bail."

He stood, gave me a look that said, Don't let me get you alone, and made a show of cracking his knuckles.

"I've told you not to do that, Gabriel. You'll ruin your hands."

"Sorry."

She kissed him again. "Now, off with you." He made it to the doorway, said, "Uh, Mom?"

"What is it?"

"Can I go into town?"

"That depends on what you're going to do there."

"Russell and Brad called. There's a movie at the Sixplex in Redlands."

"Which one?"

"Top Gun."

"Who's driving?"

"Brad."

"All right, just as long as it's not Russell in that souped-up Jeep of his—one near-miss is enough. Do I make myself clear, young man?"

"Yes, ma'am."

"All right. Don't betray my trust, Gabe. And be home by eleven."

"Thanks." He lumbered out, so happy to be free that he forgot to glare at me.

*   *   *

The dining room was big and dark, and the smell of lavender permeated the papered walls. The furniture was old, carved black walnut. Heavy drapes masked the windows, and faded family portraits in antique frames hung in the empty spaces—a pictorial history of the Leidecker clan at various stages of development. Helen had once been beautiful, her looks enhanced by a generous smile that might never be resuscitated. Her four older sons were shaggy-haired beanpoles who resembled her. Their father was a yellow-bearded, barrel-chested precursor to Gabe—who'd started life as a bald, pink, squinting sphere of suet. Sharon was in none of the pictures.

I helped set the table with china and silver and linen napkins, noticed a guitar case on the floor, next to the china cabinet.

"Mr. Leidecker's," she said. "No matter how many times I told him to put it away, it always ended up there. He played so well, I really didn't mind. Now I just leave it there. Sometimes I feel it's the music I miss the most."

She looked so low that I said, "I play."

"Do you? Then by all means."

I opened the case. Inside was an old Gibson L-5, vintage thirties, nestled in blue plush. Mint condition, the inlays undamaged, the wood freshly polished, the gold plating on the tailpiece and tuners gleaming as if new. It gave off that wet-cat odor that old instruments acquire. I lifted it, strummed the open strings, tuned.

She'd gone back into the kitchen and called out: "Come in here so I can listen."

I brought the guitar in, sat down at the table, and fingered a few jazz chords while she fixed chicken, mashed potatoes, corn, beans, and fresh lemonade. The guitar had a warm, rich tone and I played "La Mer," using Django's liquid gypsy arrangement.

"Very pretty," she said, but I could tell that jazz—even warm jazz—wasn't her thing. I switched to finger-picking, played something melodic and countrified in C-major, and her face got young.

She brought the food to the table—huge quantities of it. I put the guitar away. She seated me at the head, positioned herself to my right, and smiled nervously.

I was taking a dead man's place, felt something was expected of me, some protocol that I could never hope to master. That and the ceremonious way she filled my plate put me in a melancholy mood.

She toyed with her food and watched me while I forced myself to eat. I got down as much as I could, paid compliments in between bites, and waited until she'd cleared the dishes and brought apple pie before saying:

"The graduation picture that the Ransoms lost. Did Sharon give one to you?"

"Oh, that," she said. Her shoulders drooped and her eyes moistened. I felt as if I'd thrown a drowning survivor back into icy waters. Before I could say anything, she sprang up, disappeared down the hall.

She returned with an eight-by-ten photo in a maroon velvet stand-up frame, handed it to me as if passing the sacrament, and stood over me as I studied it.

Sharon, beaming, in crimson cap and gown with a gold tassel and shoulder braid, her black hair longer, flowing over her shoulders, her face radiant, without blemish. The epitome of all-American college womanhood, staring off into the distance with youthful optimism.

Envisioning a rosy future? Or just some campus photographer's idea of what proud parents liked for their mantels?

In the bottom left-hand corner of the photo was gold-leaf lettering.

EPHEGIANS, CLASS OF '74
FORSYTHE TEACHERS COLLEGE FOR WOMEN
LONG ISLAND, N.Y.

"Your alma mater?" I said.

"Yes." She sat down, held the picture to her bosom. "She always wanted to be a teacher. I knew Forsythe was the right place for her. Rigorous and protective enough to cushion her from the shock of going out into the world—the seventies were a rough time and she'd led a sheltered life. She loved it there, got straight A's, graduated *summa cum laude*."

Better than Leland Belding . . . "She was very bright," I said.

"She was a brilliant girl, Alex. Not that some things weren't a struggle in the very beginning—toilet training, for one, and all the social things. But I just dug my heels in and stuck with it—good practice for when I had to train my boys. But anything intellectual she absorbed like a sponge."

"How did your boys get along with her?"

"No sibling rivalry, if that's what you mean. She was tender with them, loving, like some terrific older sister. And she wasn't threatening because she went home every night—in the beginning *that* was hard for me. I wanted so much to adopt her, make her all mine and let her lead a normal life. But in their own way Shirlee and Jasper did love her, and she loved them too. It would have been wrong to destroy that, wrong to rob those two of the only precious thing they owned. Somehow they'd been given a jewel. My job was to polish her, keep her safe. I taught her about being a lady, brought her pretty things—a pretty canopied bed, but kept it there, with them."

"She never spent the night with you?"

She shook her head. "I sent her home. It was best."

Years later, with me, she'd sent herself home. *I have trouble sleeping anywhere but my own bed.* Early patterns ... early trauma ...

"She was happy just the way things were, Alex. She *thrived.* That's why I never called in the authorities. Some social worker from the city would have come down, taken one look at Shirlee and Jasper and stuck them in an institution for the rest of their lives, with Sharon farmed out to a foster home. Paperwork and bureaucracy— she'd have slipped between the cracks. My way was best."

"Summa cum laude," I said, tapping the photo. "Certainly seems so."

"She was a pleasure to teach. I tutored her intensively until she was seven, then enrolled her in my school. She'd done so well she was actually ahead of her classmates, ready for third-grade work. But her social skills were still weak—she was shy around children her own age, accustomed to playing with Eric and Michael, who were still babies."

"How did the other children relate to her?"

"At first as an oddity. There were lots of cruel comments, but I put an end to them right away. She never did get really sociable, wasn't what you'd call popular, but she did learn to mix when it was necessary. As they got older the boys started to notice her looks. But she wasn't into that kind of thing, was mostly concerned with getting good grades. She wanted to be a teacher, to make something of herself. And she was always at the head of the class—that wasn't just my bias, because when she went down to Yucaipa for junior high and high school, she got consistent straight A's, including honors courses, and her scores on the S.A.T. were among the highest in the school. She could have gotten in anywhere, didn't need me for acceptance to Forsythe. As it was, they gave her a full scholarship plus stipend."

"When did she change her mind about becoming a teacher?"

"Beginning of her senior year. She'd majored in psychology. Given her background, you could see why she'd be interested in human nature—no offense. But she never said anything about actu- ally *becoming* a psychologist until she went to a Careers Day at Long

Island University—representatives of various professions sitting at tables, handing out literature and counseling students. She met a psychologist there, a professor who really impressed her. And apparently she impressed him as well. He told her she'd make an excellent psychologist, was quite adamant about it to the point of offering to sponsor her. He was moving to Los Angeles, guaranteed her acceptance to graduate school there if she wanted it. It was a real boost for her—to see herself as a doctor."

"What was this professor's name?"

"She never told it to me."

"You never asked her?"

"She was always a private person, told me what she wanted me to know. I came to learn that the worst way to get anything out of her was to ask. How about some pie?"

"I'd love to, but I'm really full."

"Well, I'm going to have some. I crave something sweet. I just really crave that, right now."

I learned nothing more through a half hour of photo albums and family anecdotes. Some of the snapshots *featured* Sharon—lithe, smiling, beautiful as a child, enchanting as a teenager, mothering the boys. When I commented on them, Helen said nothing.

By nine o'clock an awkwardness had settled between us: Like two kids who'd gone further than they should have on the first date, we were pulling back. When I thanked her for her time, she was eager to see me leave. I left Willow Glen at five after, and was back on Route 10 forty-five minutes later.

My freeway companions were semis hauling produce, flatbeds loaded with specimen trees and hay. I started to feel logy and tried listening to music. That made me even drowsier and I pulled off near Fontana, into the lot of a combo self-serve Shell station and twenty-four-hour truck stop.

Inside were scuffed gray counters, red vinyl booths mended with duct tape, rotating racks of freeway toys, and hard, heavy silence. A couple of broad-backed teamsters and one sunken-eyed drifter sat at the counter. Ignoring over-the-shoulder glances, I took a corner booth that provided the illusion of privacy. A thin waitress with a port-wine stain on her left cheek filled my cup with industrial-strength liquid caffeine, and I filled my mind with a tempest of questions.

Sharon, Queen of Deception. She'd risen, literally, from the muck, made "something of herself" in fulfillment of Helen Leidecker's Pygmalion dream.

That dream had been tinged by selfishness—Helen's desire to relive her urban intellectual fantasies through Sharon. But no less sincere for that. And she'd wrought a remarkable transformation: a wild child tamed. Chiseled and buffed into a paragon of scholarship and good breeding. Top of the class. *Summa cum laude.*

But Helen had never been given all the pieces to the puzzle, had no idea what had taken place during the first four years of Sharon's life. The formative years, when the mortar of identity is blended, the foundation of character set and hardened.

I thought once again of that night I'd found her with the silent partner photo. Naked. Regressed to the days before Helen had found her.

A two-year-old boy's tantrum kept coming to mind.

Early trauma. Blocking out the horror.

What horror for Sharon?

Who'd raised her for the first three years of her life, bridging the gap between Linda Lanier and Helen Leidecker?

Not the Ransoms—they were too dull to have taught her about cars. About language.

I remembered the two of them, gazing after Gabe and me as we left their dirt patch. Their sole souvenir of parenthood, a letter.

Your only little girl.

She'd used the same phrase to refer to another set of parents. Noël Coward bon vivants who'd never existed—not in Manhattan, Palm Beach, Long Island, or L.A.

Martinis in the sun-room.

Wax-paper windows.

Separating the two, a galactic abyss—the impossible leap between wishful thinking and dismal reality.

She'd tried to bridge that gap with lies and half-truths. Fabricating an identity out of the fragments of other people's lives.

Losing herself in the process?

Her pain and shame must have been terrible. For the first time since her death, I let myself feel really sorry for her.

Fragments.

A Park Avenue snippet from well-born Kruse.

A car crash orphan story lifted from Leland Belding's bio.

A ladylike demeanor and love for erudition from Helen Leidecker.

No doubt she'd sat at Helen's feet, absorbing stories about the way the "idle rich" comported themselves out in the Hamptons. Had enhanced her knowledge, as a Forsythe student, strolling past the gated entrances of sprawling beach estates. Collecting mental images like bits of broken seashell—images that enabled her to paint me a too-vivid picture of chauffeurs and clam spouts, two little girls in a pool house.

Shirlee. *Joan.*

Sharon Jean.

She'd rotated the story of the drowned twin one way for Helen, another for me, lying—to those she ostensibly loved—with the ease of brushing her hair.

Pseudo-twinship. Identity problems. Two little girls eating ice cream. Mirror-image twins.

Pseudo multiple personality.

Elmo Castelmaine was certain "Shirlee" had been born crippled, which meant she couldn't be one of the children I'd seen in the sawtooth-edged photo. But he was relying on information Sharon had provided.

Or lying himself. Not that there was any reason to doubt him, but I'd grown allergic to trust.

And what was to say the crippled woman was really a twin? A relation of any kind? She and Sharon had shared general physical traits—hair color, eye color—that I'd accepted as proof of sisterhood. Accepted what Sharon had told me about Shirlee because at the time there'd been no reason not to.

Shirlee. If that was even her name.

Shirlee, with two e's. Sharon had made a point of the two e's. Named after her adoptive mother.

More symbolism.

Joan.

Another mind-game.

All those years, Helen had said, *I felt I understood her. Now I realize I was deluding myself. I barely knew her.*

Welcome to the club, Teach.

I knew that the way Sharon had lived and died had been pro-grammed by something that had taken place before Helen had discovered her gorging on mayonnaise.

The early years . . .

I drank coffee, explored blind alleys. My thoughts shifted to Darren Burkhalter, his father's head landing on the backseat, like some bloody beachball. . . .

The early years.

Unfinished business.

Mal had chalked up another victory: he'd get a new Mercedes, and Darren would grow up a rich kid. But all the money in the world couldn't expunge that image from a two-year-old mind.

I thought about all the misborn, afflicted children I'd treated. Tiny bodies hurled into life's storm with all the self-determination of dandelion husks. Something told to me by a patient came to mind, the bitter farewell comment of a once self-confident man, who'd just buried his only child:

If God exists, Doc, he fucking well has a nasty sense of humor.

Had some sick joke dominated Sharon's formative years? If so, who was the comedian?

A small-town girl named Linda Lanier was one half of the biologic equation; who'd supplied the other twenty-three chromosomes?

Some Hollywood hanger-on or one-night-stand mattress jockey? An obstetrician with an after-hours sideline scraping away life? A billionaire?

I sat in that café and thought about it for a long time. And kept coming back to Leland Belding. Sharon had grown up on Magna land, lived in a Magna house. Her mother had made love to Belding— *office boys* knew that.

Martinis in *his* sun-room?

But if Belding had sired her, why had he abandoned her? Palmed her off on the Ransoms in exchange for squatting rights and paper money in an unmarked envelope.

Twenty years later, the house, the car.

Reunion?

Had he finally acknowledged her? Created an heir? But he was supposed to have died six years before that.

What of his other heir—the other little ice cream eater?

Double-abandonment? Two dirt patches?

I considered the little I knew about Belding: obsessed with machines, precision. A hermit. Cold.

Cold enough to set up the mother of his children?

Hypothetical. Ugly. I dropped my spoon. The clatter broke through the silence of the truck stop.

"You okay?" said the waitress, standing over me, coffeepot in hand.

I looked up. "Yeah, sure, I'm fine."

Her expression said she'd heard that one before. "More?" She hefted the pot.

"No, thanks." I pushed money at her, stood, and left the truck stop. Had no trouble staying awake all the way to L.A.

31

I got home just after midnight, adrenaline-jolted and drunk on riddles. Milo rarely went to bed before one. I called his house. Rick picked up the phone, projecting that odd, groggy vigilance that E.R. docs acquire after years on the front lines.

"Dr. Silverman."

"Rick, it's Alex."

"Alex. Oh. What time is it?"

"Twelve-ten. Sorry for waking you."

"S'okay, no sweat." Yawn. "Alex? What time is it, anyway?"

"Twelve-ten, Rick."

Exhalation. "Oh. Yeah. I can see that. Confirmed by the luminescent dial." Another yawn. "Just got in an hour ago, Alex. Double shift. Couple hours of down time before the next one kicks in. Must have dozed off."

"Seems a reasonable response to fatigue, Rick. Go back to sleep."

"No. Gotta shower, get some food down. Milo's not here. Stuck on night watch."

"Night watch? He hasn't done that for a while."

"Didn't *have* to for a while. Seniority. Yesterday. Trapp changed the rules. Pig."

"That's the pits."

"Not to worry, Alex, the big guy'll get even. He's been pacing a lot, got that look in his eye—half pit bull, half pit bull."

"I know the one. Okay, I'll try him at the station. Just in case, please leave him a message to call me."

"Will do."

"Goodnight, Rick."

"Good morning, Alex."

I phoned West L.A. Detectives. The cop who answered sounded groggier than Rick. He told me Detective Sturgis was out, had no idea when he was returning.

I got into bed and finally dozed off. I awoke at seven wondering what progress Trapp had made with the Kruse killings. When I went out on the terrace to get the papers, Milo was out there, slumped in a chaise longue, reading the sports section.

I said, "How 'bout them Dodgers, big fella." The voice was someone else's, hoarse and thick.

He lowered the paper, looked at me, then out over the glen. "What army camped in your mouth?"

I shrugged.

He inhaled deeply, still taking in the view. "Ah, the good life. I fed your fish—could swear that big black-and-gold one's growing teeth."

"I've been training him on shark chum. How's life on the night watch?"

"Peachy." He stood and stretched. "Who told you?"

"Rick. I called you last night, woke him up. Sounds like Trapp's back on the warpath."

He grunted. We went into the house. He fixed himself a bowl of Cheerios and milk, stood at the counter and spooned the cereal down nonstop before pausing to catch his breath.

"Hand me a napkin. Yeah, it's a regular funfest working the twilight zone. Paperwork on the cases that the guys from P.M. conveniently neglect to finish processing, lots of DUI's and overdoses. Toward the end of shift, most of the calls are bullshit, everyone talking and moving *real* slow—bad guys and good guys. Like the whole damned city's on Quaaludes. I caught two DB's, both of which turned out to be accidentals. But at least I get to check out some heterosexual corpses." He smiled. "We all rot the same."

He went to the refrigerator, took out a container of orange juice, poured a glass for me and kept the carton for himself.

I said, "To what do I owe the pleasure?"

"Show-and-tell time. I was driving back home, listening to the scanner, when something interesting popped up on Beverly Hills' frequency—burglary call on North Crescent Drive."

He recited the address.

"The Fontaines' house," I said.

"Green Mansions, itself. I detoured to get a look-see. Guess who the detective turned out to be? Our old buddy Dickie Cash—guess he hasn't sold his screenplay yet. I spun him some yarn about it maybe being related to a hot-prowl homicide out in Brentwood, and got the basic details: Break-in occurred sometime during the early morning hours. Sophisticated job—there was a high-tech security system but the right wires were cut and the alarm company never picked up a tweet. Only reason anyone caught on was that a neighbor spotted an open door out to the rear alley early this morning—our little friend playing Chames Bond, no doubt. Cash let me inside the house. Real good taste, those two—master bedroom has a mural of big, pink, drooling lips. The inventory of missing items is fairly typical for that neighborhood—some porcelain and silver, couple of wide-screen TVs, stereo equipment. But plenty of really expensive stuff left behind: three more TVs, jewelry, furs, better silver, all easy to fence. Not much of a haul after all that wire-cutting. Dickie was intrigued but not inclined to do much about it in view of absentee victims, the fact that they weren't courteous enough to leave a forwarding with his department."

"What about the basement museum?"

He ran his hand over his face. "Dickie doesn't *know* about any museum, and guilty as it made me feel, I didn't educate him. He did show me the elevator but there was no key or the access code to operate it—not listed with the alarm company either. But if they ever do get down there, ten to one the place will look like Pompeii after the big lava party."

"Tying up loose ends," I said.

He nodded. "Question is, who?"

"Any idea where the Fontaines are?"

"Bahamas. Bijan's dad was less than helpful. Beverly Hills Cab only had a record of taking them to the airport. But I did manage to trace the car storage company and, through them, the travel agency. First-class passage, L.A. to Miami, ditto to Nassau. They kept moving after that but the agent couldn't or wouldn't say where. There was no way for me to push the issue. My guess is one of the smaller remote islands—bad phone lines, rum drinks named after birds and monkeys, banks that make the Swiss look nosy. Kind of environment where someone with cash could stay cozy for a long time."

He finished the juice, then the cereal, raised the bowl to his lips and drank the milk.

"Where've you been, anyway?" he said. "And what were you calling me about last night?"

I told him what I'd learned in Willow Glen.

"Weird," he said, "very weird. But I don't hear any crime—unless she *was* kidnapped as a kid. Am I missing something?"

I shook my head. "I want to run some ideas by you."

He filled the bowl again. "Run."

"Let's say Sharon and her twin were the result of an affair between Leland Belding and Linda Lanier—a party-girl thing that went further than usual. According to Crotty he singled her out; she used to go to his office. Linda kept the pregnancy secret because she was worried Belding would force her to terminate."

"How could she know that?"

"Maybe she knew he didn't like children, or maybe she was making an educated guess—Belding was a cold man, shunned relationships. The last thing he would have wanted was an heir he hadn't planned. Make sense so far?"

"Go on."

"Crotty saw Lanier and Donald Neurath together—playing coochy-coo. What if Neurath was her doctor as well as her lover—they met on a professional level and it went further."

"Theme of the loop."

"The loop was a cartoon of their relationship, compressed for posterity."

He sat back, put his spoon down. "She starts as a party girl with Belding, takes it further. Starts as a patient with Neurath, takes it further."

"She was beautiful. But more than that. An expert seductress—she had to have had something special for Belding to pick her out from all the other party girls. As her gynecologist, Neurath would be among the first to know she was pregnant—maybe *the* first. If he'd gotten deeply emotionally involved with her, finding out she was carrying another man's child could have made him angry, jealous. What if he offered to abort it and she refused? He then threatened to tell Belding. Linda's back was up against the wall. She told her brother, and his extortionist's mind came up with a plot: seduce Neurath on film. Get leverage. Cable worked at the studio, had access to equipment. It wouldn't have been hard for him to set it up."

Milo chewed on that for a long time, then said, "And Cable, being a sleazeball, figures out how to make some extra cash on the deal—sells a copy of the loop to some collector."

I nodded. "Gordon Fontaine or someone else who eventually sells it to him. Years later, Paul Kruse comes across it, sees the resemblance to Sharon and gets curious. But that's jumping the gun. Let's stick with Linda for a moment. When her pregnancy shows, she leaves town, gives birth—to twins—sometime between spring and summer of '53. Now she figures it's safe to tell Belding: Aborting a fetus is one thing; rejecting two adorable girl babies is another. Maybe brother Cable builds up her confidence—visions of dollar signs would be dancing in front of *his* eyes. Linda pays Belding a visit, shows him the girls, states her demand: Make an honest woman out of me or shell out enough money so the kids, Uncle Cable, and I can live happily ever after."

Milo gave a sour look. "Sounds just like the kind of stupid scam stone losers always try to pull. The dumb story you piece together after they've ended up on a slab."

"It *was* stupid. The Johnsons were penny-ante players. They gravely underestimated the threat they posed to Belding—and his lack of compassion. The twins would be his sole heirs. His entire fortune was at stake—monstrous loss of control for a man used to being master of his own destiny. This is a man who didn't believe in sharing the wealth, never took his business public. He wouldn't have tolerated a single careless afternoon coming back to haunt him. As Linda talked to him, the wheels started turning. But he didn't show it—put on a happy face, played the proud papa. Expressed his good will by putting all of them up in that penthouse on Fountain. Bought them a car, furs, jewels, instant entree to the Good Life. And all he asked in return was that they keep the babies a secret until the moment was right to go public—buying himself a little time. The Johnsons complied, a pair of hicks in hog heaven. Up until the day they died. And the twins remained a secret."

"Cold," said Milo.

"But it makes sense, doesn't it? Hummel and DeGranzfeld were Belding's boys. Narcotics detectives, in a perfect position to set up a phony dope bust. Bankrolled by Belding, they could get their hands on plenty of heroin. They kept the uniforms outside, went into that apartment alone to set up the shoot-out, arrange the crime scene. But getting rid of Linda and Cable solved only part of Belding's problem. He was still stuck with two little babies he didn't want. Under the *best* of circumstances, raising twins is a challenge. For someone like Belding the prospect would have been overwhelming—a lot scarier than designing girdles or buying up companies. So he resorted to habit—*bought* his way out of it. And his deal with the Ransoms was a lot cheaper than any he would have had to cut with Linda and Cable. The same arrangement with Sharon's twin and some other couple."

Some other dirt lot. No Helen Leidecker. The other girl ending up crippled, or . . .

"Set up his own kids' mother to be ripped off, then sold them. Ultra-cold."

"He was a cold man, Milo, a misanthrope who preferred machines to people. He never married, never developed normal attachments, ended up a hermit."

"According to the hoax book."

"According to everyone. Seaman Cross just embellished reality. And you know babies get abandoned all the time. With a lot less reason. Casa de los Niños was full of them."

"Why the Ransoms?" he said "What connection would a billionaire have with people like that?"

"Maybe none. When I say Belding did these things, I don't mean literally. He probably never got his hands dirty, had some intermediary, like Billy Vidal, handle it—that was *his* specialty: procuring people for Belding's needs. Where the intermediary found them, who knows? But their being retarded would be a plus, not a minus. They'd be passive, obedient, not likely to get greedy or ask questions. They think concretely, are stubborn—good at keeping secrets. Or forgetting. I had an exhibition of that just yesterday. On top of that, they were *anonymous*—neither of them even knew their birthdays; no government agency had any record of them. Not until 1971, when Sharon went away to college and Helen Leidecker decided they needed extra protection and took it upon herself to file for Medi-Cal and Social Security. If she hadn't, I'd never have found them."

Milo said, "If Ransom hadn't named the crippled woman after Shirlee."

"Yes. And I don't profess to understand that—she was full of weird symbols. But be that as it may, giving a child to Shirlee and Jasper was equivalent to erasing that child's identity. Perhaps Belding never even expected her to survive. But Helen Leidecker discovered her, tutored her, sent her out into the world."

"Out to Kruse."

"Kruse went to that Careers Day at L.I.U. under the guise of altruism. But he was a predator—a lecher and a power junkie, always on the prowl for new disciples. Maybe he was attracted by Sharon's looks or maybe he'd seen Linda Lanier's loop and was struck by the resemblance. In either case, he turned on the charisma, got her talking about herself, saw how evasive she was about her background, and grew even more intrigued. The two of them were a perfect match for mind control: she, molded by Helen, no real roots. He, lusting to play Svengali."

"Jim Jones and the Kool-Aid gang." Milo's big face had darkened with anger.

"On a one-to-one level," I said. He got up and brought back a beer.

As he drank I said, "He took her under his wing, Milo. Convinced her she'd make a great psychologist—her grades made that realistic—brought her out to California with him, set her up in grad school, set himself up as her adviser. He supervised her cases, which always involves some therapy. He turned it into intensive therapy. For Kruse that meant bizarre communications, hypnotic manipulation. Like many people with confused identities, she was an excellent hypnotic subject. His power role in their relationship increased her susceptibility. He age-regressed her, exposed early childhood memories that intrigued him further. Some sort of early trauma that she was unaware of on a conscious level—maybe even something about Belding. Kruse started snooping."

"And making movies."

I nodded. "An updated version of her mother's loop—part of the 'therapy.' Kruse probably presented it to her in terms of reattaching her to her roots—to mother love. His game was controlling her—building up one part of her, tearing down another. Using hypnosis, he could suggest amnesia, keep her consciously unaware. End up knowing more about her than she knew herself. He fed her bits of her own subconscious in calculated nibbles, kept her dependent, insecure. Psychological warfare. No matter what you saw in Vietnam, he was an expert. Then, when the time was right, he turned her loose on Belding."

"Big bread, big-time control."

"And I think I know exactly when it happened, Milo. The summer of '75. She disappeared with no explanation, for two months. The next time I saw her, she had a sports car, a house, a damned comfortable life-style for a grad student without a job. My first thought was that Kruse was keeping her. She knew that, even made a joke about it, told me the inheritance story—which we now know was bullshit. But maybe, in a sense, there was some truth to it. She'd put in a claim on her birthright. But it played havoc with her mind, accentuated her identity problems. The time I found her staring at the twin picture, she was in some kind of trance, almost catatonic. When she realized I was standing there, she went crazy. I was sure we were through. Then she called me up, asked me to come over and came on to me like a nymphomaniac. Years later she was doing the same thing with her patients—patients Kruse set her up with. She never got her license, remained his assistant, worked out of offices he paid the rent on."

I felt my own rage grow. "Kruse was in a position to help her, but all the bastard did was play with her head. Instead of treating her, he had her write up her own case as a phony case history and use it for her dissertation. Probably his idea of a joke—thumbing his nose at the rules."

"One problem," said Milo. "By '75, Belding was long dead."

"Maybe not."

"Cross admitted he lied."

"Milo, I don't know what's true and what's not. But even if Belding was dead, Magna lived on. Lots of money and power to leech off. Let's say Kruse leaned on the corporation. On Billy Vidal."

"Why'd they let him get away with it for twelve years? Why'd they let him live?"

"I've been turning that over in my mind and I still can't come up with an answer. The only thing I can come up with was that Kruse also had something on Vidal's sister, something they couldn't risk coming out. She endowed his professorship, set him up as department head. I've been told it was gratitude—he treated a child of hers, but in her husband's obituary there was no mention of children. Maybe she remarried and had some—I was going to check on that before I found out about Willow Glen."

"Maybe," said Milo, "the Blalock thing is just a cover—Vidal using his sister as a screen, with the payoff really coming from Magna."

"Maybe, but that still doesn't explain why they let him get away with it for so long."

He got up, paced, drank beer, had another.

"So," I said, "what do you think?"

"What I think is you've got something there. What I also think is we may never get to the bottom of it. People thirty years in the grave. And it all depends on Belding being the daddy. How the hell you going to verify that?"

"I don't know."

He paced some more, said, "Let's get back to the here and now for a sec. Why did Ransom kill herself?"

"Maybe it was grief over Kruse's death. Or maybe it wasn't suicide. I know there's no proof—I'm just hypothesizing."

"What about the Kruse killings? Like we said before, Rasmussen's not exactly your corporate hit man."

"The only reason we latched on to Rasmussen was that he talked about doing terrible things around the time the Kruses were murdered."

"Not just that," he said. "Asshole had a history of violence, killed his own father. I *liked* all that psych stuff you dished out—killing Daddy all over again."

"To paraphrase an expert, that ain't evidence, pal. Given Rasmussen's history, *terrible things* could mean anything."

"Fucking pretzel," he said. " 'Round and around."

"There's someone who could clear it up for us."

"Vidal?"

"Alive and well in El Segundo."

"Right," Milo said. "Let's just waltz into his office and announce to his secretary's assistant's gofer that we want an audience with the big boss—friendly little chat about child abandonment, blackmail, inheritance claims, multiple murder."

I threw up my hands, went to get a beer of my own.

"Don't get miffed," he called after me. "I'm not trying to piss on your parade, just striving to keep things logical."

"I know, I know. It's just damned frustrating."

"How she died, or the things she did when she was alive?"

"Both, Sergeant Freud."

He used his finger to draw a happy face in the frost of his glass. "Something else. The twin photo—how old were the girls in it?"

"About three."

"So they couldn't have been separated from birth, Alex. Meaning either both were cared for by someone else, or both were given to the Ransoms. So what the hell happened to the sister?"

"Helen Leidecker never mentioned a second girl living in Willow Glen."

"Did you ask her?"

"No."

"Didn't bring up the picture?"

"No. She seemed . . ."

"Honest?"

"No. It just didn't come up."

He said nothing.

"Okay," I said, "flunk me in Freshman Interrogation."

"Easy," he said. "Just trying to get a clear picture."

"If you get one, share it with me. Goddammit, Milo, maybe the damned picture wasn't even Sharon and her sister. I don't know what the hell is real anymore."

He let me stew, then said, "Suggesting you let go of it all would be stupid, I suppose."

I didn't answer.

"Before you indulge yourself in self-contempt, Alex, why not just give the Leidecker woman a call? Ask her about the picture, and if you get a weird reaction, that'll be the tip-off that she hasn't been Honest Annie. Which could mean more cover-up—as in the twin was hurt under suspicious circumstances and she's trying to protect someone."

"Who? The Ransoms? I don't see them as abusers."

"Not abusers—neglecters. You yourself said they weren't parent material, could barely cope with one kid. Two would have been impossible. What if they turned their back at the wrong moment and one twin had an accident?"

"As in drowning?"

"As in."

My head was spinning. I'd crammed all night, was still floundering. . . .

Milo leaned over and patted my shoulder. "Don't fret. Even if we can't take it to court, we can always sell it to the movies. Show Dickie Cash the way it's done."

"Call my agent," I said.

"Have your people call my people and let's take a power bran muffin."

I forced a smile. "Have you checked Port Wallace birth records yet?"

"Not yet. If you're right about Lanier going home to have her baby, hometown would be the perfect place—assuming she never read Thomas Wolfe. How about you give a call down there and see what you come up with? Start with the Chamber of Commerce and find out the names of any hospitals doing business back in '53. If you're lucky and they hold on to records, a little lying will pry it out of them—say you're some kind of bureaucrat. They'll do anything to get rid of you. If nothing pans out, check out the county registrar."

"Call Helen; call Port Wallace. Any more assignments, sir?"

"Hey, you want to play sleuth, develop a taste for the tedious stuff."

"The safe stuff?"

He scowled. "Damn *right,* Alex. Think back to what the Kruses and the Escobar girl looked like. And how fast the Fontaines lit out for Coconut Country. If you're right about a tenth of this, we're dealing with people with very long arms."

He made a circle with thumb and forefinger, released the finger as if flicking away a speck of dust. "Poof. Life is fragile—something *I* got from Freshman Philosophy. Stay inside; keep your doors locked. Don't take candy from strangers."

He rinsed out his bowl, put it in the drainer. Saluted and began to leave.

"Where are *you* off to?"

"Got something I have to follow up on."

"The something that kept you from calling Port Wallace? Stalking the wild Trapp?"

He glowered at me.

I said, "Rick assured me you're going to get him."

"Rick should stick to cutting up people for fun and profit. Yeah, I'm gunning for the scrote, found a soft spot. On top of his other virtues, he has a penchant for females of the underage persuasion."

"How underage?"

"Teenage jailbait. When he was back in Hollywood Division he was heavily into the Police Scouts—earned himself a departmental commendation for public service beyond the call of blah blah. Part of that service was providing personal guidance to some of the more comely young lady scouts."

"How'd you find this out?"

"Classic source: disgruntled former employee. Female officer, Hispanic, couple of years behind me in the academy. She used to work the Hollywood Evidence Room, took leave to have a baby. After she returned, Trapp made her life so miserable, she opted for stress disability and quit. Few years ago I ran into her downtown, day of her final hearing. Racking my brains for a hook into Trapp made me remember. She really hated him. I looked her up and paid her a visit. She's married to an accountant, got a fat little kid, nice split level in Simi Valley. But even after all these years, talking about Trapp made her eyes bulge. He used to grope her, make racist comments— how Mexican girls lost their virginity before their baby teeth, what brown-nose really means—all of it delivered in a Tio Taco accent."

"Why didn't she report it when it was happening?"

"Why didn't all those kids at Casa de los Niños tell anyone what was happening to *them*? Fear. Intimidation. Back then the city didn't believe in sexual harassment. Filing a complaint would have meant exposing her entire sexual history to Internal Affairs and the press, and she'd been known to party. These days her consciousness is raised. She realizes how badly she got screwed and is sitting on a lot of rage. But she hasn't talked about it to anyone—certainly not hubby. After she spilled her guts, she made me swear I wouldn't drag her into anything, so I've got knowledge that I can't use. But if I can find corroboration, the bastard's good as gone."

He walked to the door. "And that, my friend, is where I'm choosing to focus my extracurricular attention."

"Good luck."

"Yeah. I'll work it from my end; maybe it'll all connect and we'll meet in Gloccamorra. Meanwhile, watch your rear."

"You too, Sturgis. Yours ain't scorchproof."

I got Helen Leidecker's number from San Bernardino information. No answer. Frustrated but relieved—I hadn't relished testing her integrity—I found a U.S. atlas and located Port Wallace, Texas in the southernmost part of the state, just west of Laredo. A faint black speck on the Texas side of the Rio Grande.

I called the operator for the South Texas area code, dialed 512 information, and asked for the Port Wallace Chamber of Commerce.

"One second, sir," came the drawled reply, followed by clicks and several computer squeaks. "No such listing, sir."

"Are there any government offices listed in Port Wallace?"

"I'll check, sir." Click. "A United States Post Office, sir."

"I'll take that."

"Hold for that number, sir."

I called the post office. No answer there either. Checked my watch. Eight A.M. here, two hours later there. Maybe they believed in the leisurely life.

I called again. Nothing. So much for my assignments. But there was still plenty to do.

The research library had a single listing for Neurath, Donald. A 1951 book on fertility published by a university press and housed, across campus, in the biomedical library. The date and subject matter fit, but it was hard to reconcile an abortionist with the author of something that scholarly. Nevertheless, I made the trek to BioMed, consulted the Index Medicus, and found two other articles on fertility, authored in 1951 and 1952 by a Donald Neurath with a Los Angeles address. The L.A. County Medical Association Directory features photos of members. I found the one from 1950 and flipped to the N's.

His face jumped out at me, slicked hair, pencil-line mustache, and lemon-sucking expression, as if life had treated him poorly. Or maybe it was living too close to the edge.

His office was on Wilshire, just where Crotty had put it. A member of AMA, education at a first-rate medical school, excellent internship and residency, an academic appointment at the school that loosely employed me.

The two faces of Dr. N.

Another split identity.

I hurried to the BioMed stacks, found his book and the two articles. The former was an edited compendium of current fertility research. Eight chapters by other doctors, the last one by Neurath.

His research involved the treatment of infertility with injections of sex hormones to stimulate ovulation—revolutionary stuff during a period in which human fertility remained a medical mystery. Neurath emphasized this, listed previous treatments as slapshot and generally unsuccessful: endometrial biopsies, surgical enlargement of the pelvic veins, implantation of radioactive metal in the uterus, even long-term psychoanalysis combined with tranquilizers to overcome "ovulation-blocking anxiety stemming from hostile mother-daughter identification."

Though researchers had begun to make a connection between sex hormones and ovulation as early as the 1930's, experimentation had been limited to animals.

Neurath had taken it a step further, injecting half a dozen barren women with hormones obtained from the ovaries and pituitaries of female cadavers. Combining the injections with a regimen of temperature-taking and blood tests in order to get a precise fix on the time of ovulation. After several months of repeated treatments, three of the women became pregnant. Two suffered miscarriages, but one carried a healthy baby to term.

While stressing that his findings were preliminary and needed to be replicated by controlled studies, Neurath suggested that hormonal manipulation promised hope for childless couples and should be attempted on a large scale.

The 1951 article was a shorter version of the book chapter. The one from '52 was a letter to the editor, responding to the '51 article, by a group of doctors who complained that Neurath's treating of humans was premature, based on flimsy data, and his findings were tainted by poor research design. Medical science, the letter emphasized, knew little about the effects of gonadotropic hormones on general health. In addition to not helping his patients, Neurath might very well be endangering them.

He countered with a four-paragraph retort that boiled down to: the ends justified the means. But he hadn't published further.

Fertility and abortion.

Neurath giveth; Neurath taketh away.

Power on an intoxicating level. Power lust loomed as the motivating force behind so many of the lives that had brushed up against Sharon's.

I wanted very much to speak to Dr. Donald Neurath. Looked him up in the current County Directory and found nothing. I kept backtracking. His last entry was 1953.

Very busy year.

I searched the *Journal of the American Medical Association* for obituaries. Neurath's was in the June 1, 1954 issue. He'd died in August of the previous year, age forty-five, of unspecified causes, while vacationing in Mexico.

Same month, same year as Linda Lanier and brother Cable.

The effects of gonadotropic hormones . . .

Ahead of his time.

Pieces began to fall into place. A new slant on an old problem— improbable, but it explained so many other things. I thought of something else, another part of the puzzle crying out for solution. Left BioMed and headed for the north side of campus. Running, feeling light-footed, for the first time in a long time.

The Special Collections Room was in the basement of the research library, down a long quiet hall that discouraged casual drop-ins. Smallish, cool, humidity-controlled, furnished with dark oak reading tables that matched the raised panels on the walls. I showed my faculty card and my requisition slip to the librarian. He went searching and came back shortly with everything I wanted, handed me two pencils and a pad of lined paper, then went back to studying his chemistry book.

There were two other people hunkered down for serious study: a woman in a batik dress examining an old map with a magnifying glass, and a fat man in a blue blazer, gray slacks, and ascot, alternating trifocaled attention between a folio of Audubon prints and a lap-top computer.

By comparison, my own reading material was unimpressive. A pile of small books bound in blue cloth. Selections from the L.A. Social Register. Thin paper and small print. Neatly ordered listings of country clubs, charity galas, genealogical societies, but mainly a roster of The Right People: addresses, phone numbers, ancestral minutiae.

Self-congratulation for those whose fascination with the us-them game hadn't ended in high school.

I found what I wanted quickly enough, copied down names, connected the dots until the truth, or something damned close to it, began to take shape.

Closer and closer. But still theoretical.

I left the room, found a phone. Still no answer at Helen Leidecker's. But a sleepy male voice answered in Port Wallace, Texas.

"Brotherton's."

"Is this the post office?"

"Post office, tackle and bait, pickled eggs, cold beer. Name your game, we're game."

"This is Mr. Baxter, State of California Bureau of Records, Los Angeles Branch."

"L.A.? How's the quake situation?"

"Shaky."

Hacking laugh. "What can I do for y'all, California?"

"We've received an application from a certain party for a certain state job—a position that requires a full background check, including proof of citizenship and birth records. The party in question has lost her birth certificate, claims she was born in Port Wallace."

"Background check, huh? Sounds pretty . . . covert."

"I'm sorry, Mr. Brotherton—"

"Deeb. Lyle Deeb. Brotherton's dead." Chuckle. "Unloaded this dump on me in lieu of a poker debt, three months before he passed on. Got the last laugh."

"I'm not at liberty to say more about the details of the position, Mr. Deeb."

"No prob, Cal, love to help a fellow civil-servicer, 'ceptin' I cain't, 'cause we got no birth certificates in Port Wallace—not much of anything other than shrimp boats, black flies, and wetbacks and the Immigration playing grab-ass all up and down the river. Records are up in San Antonio—you'd best check there."

"What about hospitals?"

"Just one, Cal. This ain't Houston. Dinky place run by Baptist naturopaths—not sure if they're even legit. They service mostly the Mexicans."

"Were they servicing back in '53?"

"Yep."

"Then I'll try there first. Do you have the number?"

"Sure." He gave it to me, said, "Your party in question's born down here, huh? That's a real small club. What's the name of this party?"

"The family name is Johnson; mother's first name, Eulalee. She might also have gone under Linda Lanier."

He laughed. "Eula Johnson? Birth in 1953? Ain't that a hoot, you folks getting all covert and everything? Meanwhile it's public knowledge. Hell, California, you don't need no official records for that one—that one's famous."

"Why's that?"

He laughed again and told me, then said, "Only question is, *which* party you talking about?"

"I don't know," I said, and hung up. But I knew where to find out.

32

The same vine-crusted fieldstone walls and mentholated air, the same
long, shady stretch past the wooden slab sign. This time I was
driving—L.A. legitimate. But the silence and the solitude and the
knowledge of what I was about to do made me feel like a trespasser.

I pulled up in front of the gates and used the phone on the stand
to call the house. No answer. I tried again. A male mid-Atlantic voice
answered: "Blalock residence."

"Mrs. Blalock, please."

"Who shall I say is calling, sir?"

"Dr. Alex Delaware."

Pause. "Is she expecting you, Dr. Delaware?"

"No, but she'll want to see me, Ramey."

"I'm sorry, sir, she isn't—"

"Tell her it concerns the exploits of the Marchesa di Orano."

Silence.

"Would you like me to spell that, Ramey?"

No answer.

"Are you still with me, Ramey?"

"Yes, sir."

"Of course, I could talk to the press instead. They always love a
human interest story. Especially one with heavy irony."

"That won't be necessary, sir. One moment, sir."

Moments later the gates slid open. I got back in the car and
drove up the fish-scale drive.

The verdigris roofs of the mansion were gold at the peaks where
the sunlight made contact. Emptied of tents, the grounds looked even

more vast. The fountains threw off opalescent spray that thinned and dissipated while still arcing. The pools below were shimmering ellipses of liquid mercury.

I parked in front of the limestone steps and climbed to an immense landing guarded by statuary lions, recumbent but snarling. One of the double entry doors was open. Ramey stood holding it, all pink face, black serge, and white linen.

"This way, sir." No emotion, no sign of recognition. I walked past him and in.

Larry had said the entry hall was big enough to skate in. It could have accommodated a hockey stadium: three stories of white marble, rich with moldings, flutings, and emblems, backed by a double-carved white marble staircase that would have put Tara to shame. A concert-hall-sized chandelier hung from the gold-leaf coffered ceiling. The floors were more white marble inlaid with diamonds of black granite and polished to glass. Gilt-framed portraits of dyspeptic-looking Colonial types hung between columns of precisely pleated ruby velvet drapes tied back with beefy gold cord.

Ramey veered right with the smoothness of a limousine on legs, and led me down a long, dim portrait gallery, then opened another set of double doors and showed me into a hot, bright sun-room—a Tiffany skylight forming the roof, one wall of beveled mirror, three of glass that looked out onto infinite lawns and impossibly gnarled trees. The flooring was malachite and granite in a pattern that would have given pause to Escher. Healthy-looking palms and bromeliads sat in Chinese porcelain pots. The furniture was sage and maroon wicker with dark-green cushions, and glass-topped tables.

Hope Blalock sat on a wicker divan. Within her reach was a bar on wheels holding an assortment of decanters and a crystal pitcher frosted opaque.

She didn't look nearly as robust as her plants, wore a black silk dress and black shoes, no makeup or jewelry. She'd drawn her hair back in a chestnut bun that gleamed like polished hardwood, and she stroked it absently as she sat at the very edge of the divan—barely lowering rump to fabric, as if daring gravity.

She ignored my arrival, continued staring out through one of the glass walls. Ankles crossed, one hand in her lap, the other gripping a cocktail glass half-filled with something clear in which an olive floated.

"Madam," said the butler.

"Thank you, Ramey." Her voice was throaty, tinged with brass. She waved the butler away, waved *me* toward a chair.

I sat opposite her. She met my gaze. Her complexion was the

color of overcooked spaghetti, overlaid with a fine mesh of wrinkles. Her aqua-blue eyes could have been beautiful but for sparse lashes and deep, gray sockets that made them stand out like gems in dirty silver. Frown lines tugged at her mouth. A halo of post-menopausal down encircled her unpowdered face.

I gazed at her glass. "Martini?"

"Would you care for a splash, Doctor?"

"Thank you."

The wrong answer. She frowned, touched one finger to the pitcher and dotted the frost. "These are vodka martinis," she said.

"That will be fine."

The drink was strong and very dry and made the roof of my mouth ache. She waited until I'd swallowed before taking a sip, but took a long one.

I said, "Nice sun-room. Have them in all your homes?"

"Just what kind of doctor are you?"

"Psychologist."

I might have said witch doctor. "But of course. And just what is it you want?"

"I want you to confirm some theories I have about your family history."

The skin around her lips turned white. "My family history? What concern is that of yours?"

"I just got back from Willow Glen."

She put her glass down. Her unsteadiness made it rattle against the tabletop.

"Willow Glen," she said. "I believe we used to own land there, but not any longer. I fail to see—"

"While I was there I ran into Shirlee and Jasper Ransom."

Her eyes widened, squeezed shut, and reopened. She gave a hard, forced blink, as if she hoped she could make me disappear. "I'm sure I don't know what you're talking about."

"Then why did you agree to see me?"

"The lesser of two evils. You mention my daughter, make vulgar threats about going to the press. People of our station are constantly subjected to harassment. It behooves us to know what kind of baseless rumors are being circulated."

"Baseless?" I said.

"And vulgar."

I sat back, crossed my legs, and sipped. "It must have been hard for you," I said. "Covering for her all these years. Palm Beach. Rome. Here."

Her lips formed an O. She started to say something, shook her head, favored me with another hand wave, and gave a look that said I was something the maid had neglected to sweep up. "Psychologists. Keepers of secrets." Brassy laugh. "How much do you want? *Doctor.*"

"I'm not interested in your money."

A louder laugh. "Oh, *everyone's* interested in my money. I'm like some bag of blood crusted with leeches. The only question is how *much* blood each of them gets."

"Hard to think of Shirlee and Jasper as leeches," I said. "Though I suppose, over time, you've been able to turn things around and see yourself as the victim."

I got up, inspected one of the bromeliads. Gray-green striped leaves. Pink flowers. I touched a petal. Silk. I realized all the plants were.

"Actually," I said, "the two of them have done quite well for themselves. Much better than you ever expected. How long did you figure they'd last, living out there in the dirt?"

She didn't reply.

I said, "Cash in an envelope for people who didn't know how to make change. A dirt lot, two shacks, and let's-hope-for-the-best? Very generous. As was the other gift you gave them. Though at the time, I imagine, you didn't view it as a gift. More of a throwaway. Like old clothes to your favorite charity."

She shot to her feet, shook a fist that trembled so violently she had to restrain it with her other hand. "Who the hell *are* you! And *what* do you want!"

"I'm an old friend of Sharon Ransom's. Also known as Jewel Rae Johnson. Sharon Jean Blalock. Take your pick."

She sank back down. "Oh, God."

"A close friend," I said. "Close enough to care about her, to want to understand how and why."

She hung her head. "This can't be happening. Not again."

"It isn't. I'm not Kruse. I'm not interested in exploiting your problems, Mrs. Blalock. All I want is the truth. From the beginning."

A shake of the gleaming head. "No. I . . . It's impossible— wrong of you to do this."

I got up, took hold of the pitcher and filled her glass.

"I'll start," I said. "You fill in the blanks."

"Please," she said, looking up, suddenly no more than a pale old woman. "It's over. Done with. You obviously know enough to understand how I've suffered."

"You haven't a patent on suffering. Even Kruse suffered—"

"Oh, spare me! Some people reap what they sow!"

A spasm of hatred passed across her face, then settled on it, changing it, damaging it, like some palsy of the spirit.

"What about Lourdes Escobar, Mrs. Blalock? What did she sow?"

"I'm not familiar with that name."

"I wouldn't expect you to be. She was the Kruses' maid. Twenty-two years old. She just happened to be in the wrong place at the wrong time and ended up looking like dog food."

"That's disgusting! I had nothing to do with anyone's death."

"You set wheels in motion. Trying to solve your little problem. Now, it's finally solved. Thirty years too late."

"Stop!" She was gasping, hands pressed to her chest.

I looked the other way, fingered a silk palm frond. She breathed theatrically for a while, saw it wasn't working, and settled down to a silent smolder.

"You have no right," she said. "I'm not strong."

"The truth," I said.

"The truth! The truth—and *then* what?"

"And then nothing. Then I'm gone."

"Oh, yes," she said. "Oh, yes, of course, just like your ... trainer. With your pockets empty. And fairy tales come true."

I came closer, stared down at her. "No one trained me," I said. "Not Kruse or anyone else. And let me tell you a fairy tale.

"Once upon a time there was a young woman, beautiful and rich—a veritable princess. And like a princess in a fairy tale she had everything except the thing she wanted the most."

Another hard, forced blink. When her eyes opened, something behind them had died. She needed both hands to bring her glass to her lips, put it down empty. Another refill. Down the hatch.

I said, "The princess prayed and prayed, but nothing helped. Finally, one day, her prayers were answered. Just like magic. But things didn't turn out the way she thought they would. She couldn't handle her good fortune. Had to make *arrangements*."

She said, "He told you everything, the monster ... He promised me ... Damn him to hell!"

I shook my head. "No one told me anything. The information was there for the looking. Your husband's obituary in 1953 listed no children. Neither do any of your Blue Book entries—until the following year. Then two new entries: Sharon Jean. Sherry Marie."

Hands back on chest. "Oh my God."

I said, "It must have frustrated a man like him, having no heirs."

"*Him!* A *man's* man, but his seed was all water!" She took a long swallow of martini. "Not that it stopped him from blaming me."

"Why didn't the two of you adopt?"

"Henry wouldn't hear of it! 'A Blalock by blood, m'girl!' Nothing else would do!"

"His death created an opportunity," I said. "Brother Billy saw that and seized the moment. When he showed up a few months after the funeral and told you what he had for you, you thought your prayers had been answered. The timing was perfect. Let everyone think old Henry had finally come through—in spades. Bequeathed you not one but *two* beautiful little baby girls."

"They *were* beautiful," she said. "So tiny, but already beautiful. My own little girls."

"You renamed them."

"Beautiful new names," she said. "For a new life."

"Where did your brother tell you he got them?"

"He didn't. Just that their mother had fallen on hard times and couldn't care for them anymore."

Hard times. The hardest. "Weren't you curious?"

"Absolutely not. Billy said the less I knew—the less any of us knew—the better. That way, when they got older and started to ask questions, I'd be able to honestly say I didn't know. I'm sure you disapprove, Doctor. You psychologists preach the gospel of open communication—everyone bleeding all over everyone else. I don't see that society is any better for your vile meddling."

She emptied her glass again. I was ready with the pitcher.

When she'd finished most of the refill, I said, "When did things start to go bad?"

"Bad?"

"Between the girls."

She closed her eyes, put her head back against the cushion. "In the beginning, things were lovely—*exactly* like a dream come true. They were *bookends,* so perfect. Perfect blue eyes, black hair, pink cheeks—a pair of little bisque dolls. I had my seamstress fashion them dozens of matching outfits: teensy gowns and bonnets, chemises and booties—their feet were so tiny, the booties were no larger than a thimble. I took a shopping excursion to Europe, brought back the loveliest things for the nursery: an entire collection of *real* bisque dolls, hand-printed wall coverings, a pair of exquisite Louis Quatorze cradles. Their bedroom always smelled sweet, with fresh-cut flowers and sachets that I prepared myself."

She lowered her arms, allowing the glass to tilt. A rivulet of liquid ran down the side and speckled the stone floor. She didn't move.

I broke into her reverie. "When did the troubles start, Mrs. Blalock?"

"Don't pick at me, young man."

"How old were they when the conflict became apparent?"

"Early . . . I don't recall exactly."

I stared, waited.

"Oh!" She shook a fist at me. "It was so long ago! How on earth can I be expected to remember? Seven, eight months old—I don't know! They'd just started crawling and getting into everything—how old are babies when they do that?"

"Seven, eight months sounds right. Tell me about it."

"What's there to tell? They were identical but were so different, conflict was inevitable."

"Different in what way?"

"Sherry was active, dominant, strong—in body and spirit. She knew what she wanted and went right for it, wouldn't take no for an answer." She gave a smile. Satisfied. Strange.

"What was Sharon like?"

"A wilted flower—ephemeral, distant. She sat and played with one thing over and over and over. Never demanded a thing. One never knew what was on her mind. The two of them established their roles and played them to the hilt—leader and follower, just like a little stage play. If there was a bit of candy or a toy that they both wanted, Sherry would just move right in, bowl Sharon over, and take it away. In the very beginning Sharon put up some resistance, but she never won, and soon she learned that, one way or the other, Sherry was going to triumph."

That strange smile again. Applauding that triumph.

The smile I'd seen so many times on the faces of ineffectual parents saddled with extremely disturbed, aggressive youngsters.

He's so aggressive, such a tiger. Smile.

She beat up the little girl next door, really demolished her, the poor thing. Smile.

He's a real ass-kicker, my boy. Gonna get into serious trouble one day. Smile.

The do-as-I-feel, not-as-I-say smile. Legitimizing bullying. Granting permission to knock down, gouge, scrape, pummel, and, above all, *win.*

The kind of off-kilter response guaranteed to get a therapist hmm-ing and noting "inappropriate affect" in the chart. And knowing treatment wouldn't be easy.

"Poor Sharon really did get knocked around," Mrs. Blalock said.

"What did you do about it?"

"What *could* I do? I tried reasoning with them—told Sharon she needed to face up to Sherry, be more self-confident. I informed Sherry in no uncertain terms that this was no way for a young lady to behave. But the moment I was gone, they'd revert to type. I do believe it was a little game between them. Collaboration."

She was right about that, but she'd gotten the players wrong.

She said, "I'm long past blaming myself. Their characters were predetermined, programmed from the very start. In the end Nature triumphs. That's why your field will never amount to much."

"Was there anything positive about their relationship?"

"Oh, I suppose they loved each other. When they weren't fighting, there were the usual hugs and kisses. And they had their own little nonsense language that no one else understood. And despite the rivalry, they were inseparable—Sherry leading, Sharon tagging behind, taking her licks. But always, the fighting. Competition for everything."

Strange phenomenon, mirror-image monozygotes ... given an identical genetic structure there should be no differences at all. ...

"Sherry always won," she was saying. Smile. "By the age of two she'd become a real little martinet, a little stage director, telling Sharon where to stand, what to say, when to say it. If Sharon dared not to listen, Sherry lashed out, slapping and kicking and biting. I tried to separate them, forbade them to play with one another, even got them separate nannies."

"How'd they react to being separated?"

"Sherry threw tantrums, broke things. Sharon just huddled in the corner, as if in a trance. Eventually, they always managed to sneak back and reconnect. Because they needed each other. Weren't complete without each other."

"Silent partners," I said.

No reaction.

"I was always the outsider," she said. "It wasn't a good situation, not for any of us. They drove me to distraction. Getting away with hurting her sister wasn't good for Sherry—it hurt her too. Perhaps even more than it hurt Sharon—bones may mend, but once injured, the mind never seems to set properly."

"Were Sharon's bones ever actually broken?"

"Of course not!" she said, as if addressing an idiot. "I was speaking figuratively."

"How serious were her injuries?"

"It wasn't child abuse, if that's what you're getting at. Nothing we had to call a doctor for—clumps of hair pulled out, bites, scratches. By the time she was two, Sherry knew how to raise a nasty bruise, but nothing serious."

"Until the drowning."

The glass in her hand began to shake. I filled it, waited until she'd drained it, kept the pitcher at hand. "How old were they when it happened?"

"A little over three. Our first summer away together."

"Where?"

"My place in Southampton."

"The Shoals." Item one on a list I'd just read in a social register: Skylark in Holmby Hills. Le Dauphin in Palm Beach. An unnamed flat in Rome. Her real children.

"Another sun-room," I said. "A latticed pool house."

My knowing shook her further. She swallowed hard. "You seem to know everything. I really don't see the need—"

"Far from everything." Refill. I smiled. She looked at me with gratitude. Boozer's version of the Stockholm syndrome. "Bottoms up."

She drank, shuddered, drank some more, said, "Here's to glorious, glorious truth."

"The drowning," I said. "How did it happen?"

"It was the last day of holiday. Early autumn. I was up in my sun-room—I love sun-rooms—merging with Nature. I've had sun-rooms in all of my homes. The one at The Shoals was the finest, more of a pavilion, actually, an Old English look, comfy and warm. I was sitting there, looking out at the Atlantic—it's a more intimate ocean, the Atlantic, don't you think?"

"Definitely."

"Compared to the Pacific, which is so . . . undemanding. At least that's what I've always believed."

She held her glass up, squinted, sloshed vodka.

I said, "Where were the girls?"

She tightened her grip on the glass, raised her voice: "Ah, *where* were the girls! Playing, what else do little girls do! Playing down on the beach! With a nanny—a slab-faced English pudding! I paid her passage from Liverpool, gave her my best old gowns, lovely quarters. She came with recommendations, the slut. Flirting with Ramey, with the hired help—with anything in pants. That day, she was batting her lashes at the groundsman and took her eyes off the girls. They snuck into the pool house—the *latticed* pool house— which was supposed to be locked and wasn't. Heads rolled that day. They rolled."

She emptied her glass, belched softly, and looked mortified.

I pretended not to notice, said, "Then what happened?"

"Then—*finally*—the *pudding* realized they were gone. Went looking for them, heard laughter from the pool house. When she got there, Sherry was standing by the side of the pool, slapping her knees. Laughing. The idiot asked where Sharon was. Sherry pointed to the pool. The stupid pudding looked over and saw one arm sticking out of the water. She jumped in, managed to pull Sharon out. The pool was filthy—ready to be drained until spring. Both of them got slimy—it served the slut right."

"And Sherry kept laughing," I said.

She let go of the glass. It rolled down her lap, hit the stone floor, and shattered. The shards formed a wet gemlike mosaic that transfixed her.

"Yes, laughing," she said. "Such merriment. Through it all."

"How seriously was Sharon injured?"

"Not seriously at all. Just her pride. She'd swallowed some water, the dumb cluck fiddled with her, and she vomited all of it up. I arrived just in time to see that—all that brown water shooting out of her. Revolting."

"When did you realize it hadn't been an accident?"

"Sherry marched up to us, thumping her little chest, saying 'I push her.' Just like that: 'I push her,' as if she was proud of it. I thought she was joking away her fear, told Ramey to take her away, give her some warm milk and soft biscuits. But she struggled, began screaming: 'I push her! I push her!'—claiming credit! Then she broke away from him, ran over to where Sharon was lying, and tried to kick her—to roll her over, back into the pool."

Shake of head.

Smile.

"Later, when Sharon was feeling better, she confirmed it. 'Sherry push me.' And there was a bruise on her back. Tiny little knuckle marks."

She stared at the liquid on the floor with longing. I dribbled some martini into another glass and handed it to her. Eyeing the miserly portion, she frowned but drank, then licked the rim with the look of a child flouting table manners.

"She wanted to do it again, right in front of me. Wanted me to *see* it. That's when I knew it was . . . serious. They couldn't . . . had to be . . . separated. Couldn't be together, ever again."

"Enter brother Billy."

"Billy always took good care of me."

"Why the Ransoms?"

"They worked for us—for Billy."

"Where?"

"In Palm Beach. Making beds. Cleaning."

"Where did they come from—originally?"

"A place. Near the Everglades. One of our acquaintances—a very fine doctor—took in the feeble-minded, taught them honest labor, how to be good citizens. Trained properly, you know, they make the best workers."

Everything scrubbed down with lye soap . . . all the clothes folded neatly, beds you could bounce a dime on . . . as if someone had trained them in the basics a long time ago.

Living near the swamps. All that mud. They'd have felt right at home on their dirt patch. Green soup . . .

"The doctor and Henry were golf chums," she was saying. "Henry always made a point of hiring Freddy's—the doctor's—imbeciles, for grounds work, fruit-picking, repetitive things. He believed it was our civic responsibility to help."

"And you were helping them further when you gave them Sharon."

She missed the sarcasm, seized on the rationalization. "Yes! I knew they couldn't have children. Shirlee'd been . . . fixed. Freddy had all of them fixed, for their own good. Billy said we'd be giving her—them—the greatest gift anyone could give while solving our problem at the same time."

"Everyone comes out a winner."

"Yes. Exactly."

"*Why* did it have to be done?" I said. "Why not keep Sharon at home and send Sherry away for some kind of treatment?"

Her reply sounded rehearsed. "Sherry needed me more. She was really the needy one—and time's borne me out on that."

Two progeny in the Blue Book, 1954 through 1957. After that, only one.

My guesses turned to fact, the pieces finally fitting. But it sickened me, like a bad-news diagnosis. I loosened my tie, clenched my jaw.

"What did you tell your friends?"

No answer.

"That she'd died?"

"Pneumonia."

"Was there a funeral?"

She shook her head. "We let it be known we wanted things private. Our wishes were respected. In lieu of flowers, donations to Planned Parenthood—thousands of dollars were donated."

"More winners," I said. I felt like throttling a little insight into her. Instead, I slipped on the therapist's mask, pretended she was a patient. Told myself to be understanding, nonjudgmental . . .

But even as I smiled, the horror stayed with me. The bottom line, just another sickening, sordid child-abuse case, psychopathology fueling cruelty: a weak, dependent woman, despising her weakness, projecting that hatred onto the child she saw as weak. Seeing another child's viciousness as strength. Envying it, *feeding* it:

One way or the other, Sherry was going to triumph.

She was tilting her head back, trying to suck nourishment from an empty glass. I was cold with rage, felt a chill in my bones.

Even through the haze of intoxication she picked up on it. Her smile vanished. I lifted the pitcher. She held up one arm, ready to ward off a blow.

I shook my head, apportioned more martini. "What did you hope to accomplish?"

"Peace," she said, barely audible. "Stability. For everyone."

"Did you get it?"

No answer.

"No surprise," I said. "The girls loved each other, needed each other. They shared a private world they'd created. By separating them, you destroyed that world. Sherry would have had to get worse. Much worse."

She looked down, said, "She put it out of her mind."

"How did you go about doing it?"

"What do you mean?"

"The mechanics of the transfer. How exactly did you do it?"

"Sharon knew Shirlee and Jasper—they'd played with her, been kind to her. She liked them. She was happy going off with them."

"Going off where?"

"On a shopping trip."

"That never ended."

The arm rose in defense, again. "She was happy! Better off, not being pummeled!"

"What about Sherry? What explanation did she get?"

"I . . . I told her that Sharon had . . ." She submerged the rest of her sentence in vodka.

I said, "You told her Sharon had died?"

"That she'd been in an *accident* and wouldn't be coming back."

"What kind of accident?"

"Just an accident."

"At Sherry's age, she would have assumed the drowning did it— that she'd killed her sister."

"No, impossible—ridiculous. She'd seen Sharon survive—this was days after!"

"At that age none of that would have made a difference."

"Oh, no, you can't accuse me of . . . No! I didn't—wouldn't ever have done anything so cruel to Sherry!"

"She kept asking for Sharon, didn't she?"

"For a while. Then she stopped. Put it out of her mind."

"Did she stop having nightmares too?"

Her expression told me all my years of schooling hadn't been wasted. "No, those . . . If you know everything, why are you putting me through this?"

"Here's something else I know: After Sharon was gone, Sherry was terrified—separation anxiety's the primal fear at three. And her fear kept climbing. She started to lash out, get more violent. Began taking it out on you."

Another good guess. "Yes!" she said, eager to be the victim. "She threw the most horrid tantrums I'd ever seen. More than tantrums—fits, animal fits. Wouldn't let me hold her, kicked me, bit me, spit at me, destroyed things—one day she walked into my bedroom and deliberately broke my favorite Tang vase. Right in front of me. When I scolded her, she snatched up a manicure scissors and went for my arm. I needed stitches!"

"What did you do about this new problem?"

"I started to think more seriously about her origins, her . . . biology. I asked Billy. He told me her lineage wasn't . . . choice. But I refused to be discouraged by that, made improving her my main project. I thought a change of scenery might help. I closed up this house, took her back with me to Palm Beach. My place there is . . . tranquil. Rare palms, lovely big bay windows—one of Addison Mizner's best. I thought the ambience—the rhythm of the waves—would calm her."

"A couple of thousand miles between her and Willow Glen," I said.

"No! That had nothing to do with it. Sharon was out of her life."

"Was she?"

She stared at me. Began to cry, but without tears, as if she were a dry well, had nothing to draw upon.

"I did my best," she finally said in a strangled voice. "Sent her to the best nursery school—the *very* best. I'd attended it myself. She had dance lessons, equestrian training, charm school, boat rides, junior cotillion. To no avail. She wasn't good around other children; people started to talk. I decided she needed more of my individual attention, *devoted* myself to her. We went to Europe."

A few thousand more miles. "To your place in Rome."

"My atelier," she said. "Henry gave it to me when I was studying art. On the way there, we took the grand tour—London, Paris, Monte Carlo, Gstaad, Vienna. I bought her a darling set of miniature luggage to match mine, had a whole new wardrobe made up for her—even a little fur coat with matching hat. She loved dressing up. She could be so sweet and charming when she wanted. Beautiful and poised, just like royalty. I wanted her exposed to the finer things in life."

"To compensate for her *origins.*"

"Yes! I refused to see her as incorrigible. I loved her!"

"How did the trip go?"

She didn't answer.

"Throughout all of this, did you ever consider reuniting her with Sharon?"

"It . . . came to mind. But I didn't know how. I didn't think it was best. . . . Don't look at me like that! I was doing what I thought was best!"

"Did you ever think of Sharon—of how she was doing?"

"Billy gave me reports. She was fine, doing just fine. They were sweet people."

"They *are*. And they did a damned good job of raising her, considering what they had to work with. But did you really expect them to make it?"

"Yes, I did! Of course I did. What do you take me for! She was *thriving*! It was the best thing for her."

Mayonnaise from a jar. Wax-paper windows. I said, "Until last week."

"I . . . I don't know about that."

"No, I'm sure you wouldn't. Let's get back to Sherry. Given her social problems, how did she do in school?"

"She went through ten schools in three years. After that we used tutors."

"When did you first take her to Kruse?"

She looked down at her empty glass. I rationed another inch. She polished it off. I said, "How old was she when he started treating her?"

"Ten."

"Why didn't you seek help before then?"

"I thought I could work things out myself."

"What made you change your mind?"

"She . . . hurt another child, at a birthday party."

"Hurt how?"

"Why must you know this? Oh, all right, what's the difference? I'm already stripped raw! They were playing pin the tail on the donkey. She missed the donkey and got angry—she despised losing. Tore off her blindfold and stuck the pin into a little boy's rear—the birthday boy. The child was a brat; the parents were *nouveau riche* social climbers, utterly without sense. They made a mountain out of a molehill, threatened to call the police unless I took her to someone."

"Why'd you choose Kruse?"

"I knew him socially. My people had known his people for generations. He had a lovely home not far from mine with a beautiful office suite on the ground floor. Complete with a private entrance. I thought he'd be discreet."

She laughed. A drunken, strident laugh. "I don't seem to be much for . . . prescience, do I?"

"Tell me about the treatment."

"Four sessions a week. One hundred twenty-five dollars a session. Payment for ten sessions in advance."

"What diagnosis did he give you?"

"He never gave me one."

"What about treatment goals? Methods?"

"No, nothing like that. All he said was that she had serious problems—character problems—and needed intensive therapy. When I tried to ask questions he made it very clear that everything that went on between them was *confidential.* I was forbidden to be involved at all. I didn't like that, but he was the doctor. I assumed he knew what he was doing. I stayed *completely* out of it, had Ramey drive her to her appointments."

"Did Kruse help her?"

"In the beginning. She'd come home from seeing him and be calm—almost too calm."

"What do you mean?"

"Sleepy. Drowsy. I know now that he was hypnotizing her. But whatever benefits that brought didn't last. Within an hour or two she was the same old Sherry."

"Meaning what?"

"Defiance, foul language. That terrible temper—still breaking things. Except when she wanted something—then she could be the most charming little doll in the world. Sweet as sugar, a real actress. She knew how to twist people to her needs. *He* taught her how to do it even better. All the time I thought he was helping her, he was teaching her how to manipulate."

"Did you ever tell him about Sharon?"

"He wouldn't let me tell him anything."

"If he had, would you have told him?"

"No. That was . . . in the past."

"But eventually you did tell him."

"Not until later."

"How much later?"

"Years. She was a teenager—fourteen or fifteen. He called me late at night, caught me off-guard. He liked to do that. All of a sudden he'd completely changed his tune. All of a sudden it was *imperative* I be involved. Come in to be *evaluated.* Five years of going nowhere and now he wanted me on the couch! I wanted no part of such a thing—by then I'd realized that it was useless, her personality wasn't going to change. She was the prisoner of her . . . genes. But he wouldn't take no for an answer, kept calling me, badgering me. Dropping in to chat when I was entertaining guests. Pulling me aside at parties and telling me that she and I were a . . . what was the word he used? . . . a *dyad.* A *destructive dyad.* Two people on a psychological seesaw, trying to knock each other off. Her behavior affected mine; mine, hers. In order for her to stop doing all those terrible things, we needed to *equalize* our communications, find emotional *homeostasis* or some rubbish like that. I felt he simply wanted to control me, and I wasn't about to give in. But he was like a . . . a drill. Kept at it, simply wouldn't give up. Still, I was able to resist." Prideful smile. "Then things got much worse and I caved in."

"Worse in what way?"

"She started doing . . . teenage things."

"Running away?"

"Disappearing. For days at a time—completely without warning.

I'd send Ramey out for her but he rarely found her. Then, out of nowhere, she'd come crawling back, usually in the middle of the night, all disheveled, filthy, crying, promising never to do it again. But she always did."

"Did she talk about where she'd been?"

"Oh, the next morning she'd be boasting, telling me horrid tales in order to make me suffer—crossing the bridge and heading over to the colored part of town, things like that. I never knew how much to believe—didn't want to believe any of it. Later, when she was old enough to drive, she'd take off in one of my cars and vanish. Weeks later, the credit card bills and traffic tickets would start trickling in and I'd find out she'd been traipsing all over—Georgia, Louisiana, dull little towns I'd never heard of. What she did there God only knows. One time she went to Mardi Gras and came home painted green. I finally took away her driving privileges when she ruined my favorite car—a lovely old Bentley painted lilac, with etched windows. Henry's gift to me on our tenth. She drove it into the ocean, just left it there and walked away. But she always managed to find a set of keys, be off again."

One way or the other, Sherry would triumph.

No smile, now.

I remembered what Del had told me about the needle marks, said, "When did she get into drugs?"

"When she was thirteen, Paul had tranquilizers prescribed for her."

"He wasn't an M.D., wasn't allowed to prescribe."

She shrugged. "He got her those drugs. Prescription tranquilizers."

"What about street drugs?"

"I don't know. I suppose so. Why not? Nothing could stop her from doing what she wanted."

"During this period, how often was Kruse seeing her?"

"When she chose to go. He billed me even if she didn't show up."

"What was the official schedule?"

"No change—four sessions a week."

"Did you ever question him? Ask why years of treatment hadn't improved her?"

"He . . . he was hard to approach. When I finally raised the issue, he got very angry, said she was irreparably disturbed, would never be normal, would need treatment all her life just to *maintain.* And that it was my fault—I'd waited too long to bring her in, couldn't expect to wheel a jalopy into a garage and have a Rolls-

Royce emerge. Then he'd start in again, pressuring me to come in for evaluation. She was getting worse and worse. He broke me down—I agreed to talk to him."

"What about?"

"The usual rubbish. He wanted to know about my childhood, did I dream at night, why I'd married Henry. How things made me *feel*. He always talked in a low monotonous voice, had shiny things in his office—little toys that moved back and forth. I knew what he was doing—trying to hypnotize me. Everyone in Palm Beach knew he did that kind of thing. He did it at parties, at the Planned Parenthood ball—made people quack like ducks for amusement. I resolved not to give in. It was difficult—his voice was like warm milk. But I fought it, told him I didn't see what any of that had to do with Sherry. He kept pushing. Finally I blurted out that he was wasting his time, she wasn't even mine, was the product of some slut's bad genes. That made him stop droning and he looked at me strangely."

She sighed, closed her eyes. "My heart sank. Trying to resist him, I'd said too much, given him just what he needed to bleed me dry."

"You'd never told him she was adopted?"

"I never told *anyone*—from the day I . . . got her."

"How did he react to finding out?"

"Broke his pipe in half. Slammed his hand on the desk. Took me by the shoulders and shook me. Told me I'd wasted his time all these years and severely damaged Sherry. Said I didn't care about her, was a terrible mother, a selfish person—my communications were *perverse*. My secretiveness was what had made her what she was! He kept going on like that, attacking me! I was in tears, tried to leave the office but he stood in the doorway and blocked me, kept hurling abuse. I threatened to scream. He smiled and said go ahead, by tomorrow all of Palm Beach would know. Sherry would know. The moment I stepped out the door, he'd call her, tell her how I'd lied to her. That broke me. I knew it would be the final straw between us. I begged him not to tell, begged him to have pity. He smiled, went back behind his desk and lit another pipe. Just sat there puffing and looking at me as if I were trash. I was whimpering like a baby. Finally, he said he'd reconsider on condition that I be honest from now on—completely *open*. I . . . I told him everything."

"What exactly did you tell him?"

"That the father was unknown, the mother a tart who'd fancied herself an actress. That she'd died soon after the baby was born."

"You still didn't tell him about Sharon."

"No, no."

"You weren't worried Sherry would tell him?"

"How could she tell him something she didn't know? It was out of her head—I'm sure of that because she never mentioned it, and when she was angry she threw everything else in my face."

"What if she chanced to open up an old Blue Book?"

She shook her head. "She didn't like books, didn't read—never learned to read well. Some sort of blockage the tutors couldn't break through."

"But Kruse found out anyway. How?"

"I have no idea."

But I did: a college Careers Day, spotting his former patient. Discovering it wasn't his former patient at all, but a carbon copy, mirror-imaged . . .

She was saying, "He bled me for years, the monster. I hope he's writhing in eternal hellfire."

"Why didn't brother Billy fix that for you?"

"I . . . I don't know. I told Billy. He always told me to have patience."

She turned away from me. I doled out more martini but she didn't drink it, just held her glass and straightened her posture. Her eyes closed and her breathing got shallow. A boozehound's tolerance, but it wouldn't be long before she passed out. I was phrasing my next question for maximum impact when the door swung open.

Two men stepped into the sun-room. The first was Cyril Trapp in white polo shirt, pressed designer jeans, Topsiders, and black Members Only jacket. California Casual betrayed by the tension in his white-blotched face and the blue steel revolver in his right hand.

The second man kept his hands in his pockets as he examined the room with the practiced eye of a pit boss. Older, mid-sixties, tall and wide—big bones padded with hard fat. He wore a doeskin-colored western suit, brown silk shirt, string tie gathered by a large smoky-topaz clasp, peanut-butter-colored lizard boots, and a straw cowboy hat. His skin tone matched the boots. Forty pounds heavier than Trapp, but the same hatchet jaw and thin lips. His eyes settled on me. His stare was that of a naturalist studying some rare but hideous specimen.

"Mr. Hummel," I said. "How are things in Vegas?"

He didn't answer, just moved his lips the way denture wearers do.

"Shut up," said Trapp, pointing the gun at my face. "Put your hands behind your head and don't move."

"Friends of yours?" I said to Hope Blalock. She shook her head. Her eyes were electric with fear.

"We're here to help you, ma'am," said Hummel. His voice was badlands *basso profundo*, coarsened by smoke and drink, and desert air.

Ramey came in, all spotless black serge and starched white. "It's all right, madam," he said. "Everything's in order." He looked at me with tight fury and I knew who'd called in the goon squad.

Trapp stepped forward, waved the revolver. "Get those hands behind you."

I didn't move fast enough to suit him, and the weapon was pressed hard under my nose.

Hope Blalock gasped. Ramey went to her side.

Trapp put a little more weight behind the gun. Looking at all that metal crossed my eyes. I tightened reflexively. Trapp leaned harder.

Royal Hummel said, "Easy." He came around behind me. I heard a ratchet slip, felt cold metal around my wrists.

"Not too tight, son?"

"Perfect. *Uncle* Roy."

"Shut the fuck up," said Trapp.

Hope Blalock winced.

Hummel said, "Easy, C.T.," and patted the back of my neck. His touch bothered me more than the gun. "Close your eyes, son," he said, and I obeyed. The pressure of the revolver was replaced by something tight and elastic around my head. Banding my eyes so tight I couldn't open them. Strong hands gripped me under my arms. I was lifted so that only my shoe tips touched the floor, propelled forward like a kite in a headwind.

It was a very big house. They dragged me for a long time before I heard a door open, felt hot air on my face.

Trapp started laughing.

"What?" said his uncle, stretching the word to two syllables.

"How we got this joker. Fucking butler did it."

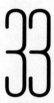

They searched me, confiscated my watch, keys, and wallet, and put me in a vehicle that smelled brand-new.

"Settle down, son," said Hummel, easing me into the backseat and removing the cuffs. He slammed the door. I heard him go around to the front; then the engine started—muted, as if my ears were stuffed.

I peeled back an inch of blindfold and inspected the interior: blackened windows that let in only hints of light. A black glass partition sealing off the rear compartment. A cell lined in gray vinyl—rock-hard bench seats, nylon carpeting, cloth roof. No dome light. No ornamentation at all, not a clue to make or model. The plain-wrap styling of a midsize economy American sedan—a bottom-of-the-line Dodge, Ford, or Olds, but with a twist: no door handles. No ashtrays or seat belts. No metal at all.

I ran my hands over the doors, trying to find some hidden latch. Nothing. A hard rap on the partition brought no response. San Quentin on wheels.

We began to move. I peeled off the blindfold. Heavy-duty black elastic, no label. It already stank of the fear in my sweat. I heard the spatter of gravel, muted like the ignition. Soundproofing.

I pressed my face to the window, saw only my reflection in the darkened glass. I didn't like the way I looked.

We picked up speed. I sensed it the way you sense acceleration in an elevator—a pit-of-the-stomach lurch. Cut off from the world, I had only my fear to listen to; I might have been in a crypt.

A sudden turn made me slide across the seat. When the car

straightened, I kicked the door, then karate-kicked it hard. No give. I pounded the windows until my hands hurt, attacked the partition. Not even a hint of vibration.

I knew then that I'd be there as long as they wanted me to. My chest went tight. Any road noise the soundproofing let in was blotted out by the pounding of my heart.

They'd robbed me sensorily; the key was to regain my bearings. I searched for mental signposts; the only thing left was time. But no watch.

I began counting. One thousand one. One thousand two. Settled back for the ride.

After about forty-five minutes the car came to a stop. The left rear door opened. Hummel bent low and peered in. He wore mirrored sunglasses and held a long-nosed chrome-plated Colt .45 parallel to his leg.

Behind him was cement flooring. Sepia-tinged darkness. I smelled auto fumes.

He raised his other hand to his crotch and unbound his shorts. "Transfer time, son. Gonna have to cuff you again. Bend forward."

No mention of the fact that I'd removed the blindfold. I stuffed it behind the seat and did what he asked, the good little prisoner. Hoping compliance would buy me the privilege of vision. But the moment my hands were bound, on went the elastic.

I said, "Where are we going?" Stupid question. Helplessness does that to you.

"For a ride. C'mon, C.T., let's hustle."

A door slammed. Trapp's voice said, "Let's move this turkey." Amused. A moment later I smelled Aramis, heard the buzz of his whisper in my ear. "Fucking butler did it. Isn't that a hoot, faggo?"

"Tsk, tsk," I said. "Bad language for a born-again."

Sudden bee-bite pain behind my ear: a finger flick. "Shut the fu—"

"C.T.," said Hummel.

"All right."

Double arm-grip. Footsteps echoing. The auto fumes stronger.

An underground parking lot.

Twenty-two paces. Stop. Wait. Mechanical hum. Gears grinding, something sliding, ending with a clang.

Elevator door.

A push forward. Slide shut. Click. Rapid climb. Another push. Out in the heat, the stench of gasoline so powerful I could taste it.

More cement. A loud whoosh, growing louder. Very loud. Gasoline . . . No, something stronger. An airport smell. Jet fuel. *Whoosh whoosh.* Gusts of cool air slicing through the heat.

Propellors. A slow chug picking up speed. Helicopter rotor.

They dragged me forward. I thought of Seaman Cross, driven blindfolded to a landing strip less than an hour from L.A. Flown to Leland Belding's dome. Somewhere out in the desert.

The rotor noise grew deafening, scrambling my thoughts. Gusts of turbulence slapped my face, plastered my clothes to my body.

"There's a step here," Hummel shouted, putting pressure under my elbow, pushing me, lifting me. "Step up, son. There you go—good."

Climbing. One step, two step. Mother, may I . . . Half a dozen, still more.

"Keep going," said Hummel. "Now stop. Put your foot forward. There we go. Good boy." Hand on my head, pushing down. "Duck, son."

He placed me in a bucket seat and belted me in. A door slammed. My ears clogged. The noise level dropped a notch but remained loud. I heard radio stutter, a new voice from the front: male, military-flat, saying something to Hummel. Hummel answered back. Planning. Their words drowned out by the rotor.

A moment later, we lifted off with a surge that bounced and buffeted me like a pachinko ball. The copter swayed, rose again, gained stability.

Suspended in midair.

I thought again of Seaman Cross's nose dive from celebrity to death. Missing notes in a public storage vault. Books recalled. Locked up, raped. Head in the oven time.

If you're right about a tenth of this, we're dealing with people with very long arms. . . .

The copter kept climbing. I fought the shakes, worked hard at pretending this was an E ride at Disneyland.

Up, up and away.

We'd been traveling for more than two hours by my slow count when more radio noises burped from the front of the cabin and I felt the copter take a drop in altitude.

More radio stutter. One decipherable word: "Roger."

We dipped for landing. I remembered reading somewhere that copters cruised between 90 and 125 knots. If my counting was near-accurate, that meant a 200- to 250-mile trip. I mentally traced a circle with L.A. at its center. Fresno to Mexico longitudinally. From the Colorado desert to somewhere over the Pacific on the east-west axis.

No shortage of desert in three directions.

Another sharp drop. Moments later we hit solid ground.

"Smooth," said Hummel. In seconds I felt his breath, hot and spearminted, on my face, heard him grunt as he loosened the belt.

"Enjoy the ride, son?"

"Not bad," I said, borrowing someone else's voice—some Milquetoast's quavering tenor. "But the movie stank."

He chuckled, took hold of my arm, guided me out of the copter and down.

I stumbled a couple of times. Hummel kept me upright and moving, not breaking half a step.

The old heave-ho march—he'd probably used it on a thousand Vegas drunks.

We walked for a slow-count of four hundred. The air was very hot, very dry. Silent.

"Stay here," he said, and I heard the horsey clump of his departing boot-steps, then nothing.

I stood there, unguarded, for a three-hundred count. Three hundred more.

Ten minutes. Left to my own devices.

Another five minutes and I started to wonder if he was coming back. Three more and I hoped he was.

His walking away meant escape would be folly. I tried to picture where I was—at the edge of a precipice? Playing target at the end of a shooting range?

Or simply dropped in the middle of nowhere, gift-wrapped brunch for the scorpions and the buzzards.

Donald Neurath's obituary came to mind . . . unspecified causes while vacationing in Mexico.

Maybe Hummel was bluffing. I considered moving. Uncertainty locked my joints. I was a man with one foot on a land mine, immobility my life sentence.

I stood there, counting, sweating, trying to maintain. Enduring the molasses drip of time slowed by fear. Finally I forced myself to take a single step forward—a baby step. Mother, may I? Please?

Solid ground. No fireworks.

Another step. I swung one foot out in a slow arc, testing—no tripwires—was inching forward when an electric whine sounded from somewhere behind me.

Stop and go. Whine stop whine.

A golf cart or something like it. Coming closer. Footsteps.

"Cute little dance, son," said Hummel. "We could use the rain."

He put me in the cart. It had shallow seats and no roof. We rode under a blazing sun for about fifteen minutes before he stopped, eased me out, and led me through revolving doors into a building air-conditioned to frigidity. We passed through three more doors, each one opening after a series of clicks, then made a quick right-hand turn, went thirty more paces, and entered a room that smelled of disinfectant.

"Stay loose and no one'll hurt you," he said.

Multiple footsteps shuffled forward. Off came the handcuffs. Several sets of hands pinioned my arms and legs, braced my head, tilted it back. Fingers filled my mouth, pried under my tongue. I gagged.

My clothes were stripped off. The hands ran a marathon over my body, ruffled my hair, probed my armpits, my orifices—deftly, quickly, without a hint of prurient interest. Then I was dressed again, buttoned and zipped, all of it over in a couple of minutes.

I was walked through two more clicking doors and deposited in a big, deep chair—leather, tannically fragrant.

The door closed.

By the time I yanked off the blindfold, they were gone.

The room was big, dark, done in Neo-Home-on-the-Range: plank walls, Navajo rugs over distressed pine floors, wagon-wheel chandelier brass-chained from a beamed cathedral ceiling, a set of armchairs fashioned of cowhide stretched on a stag antler frame, wall-size oil paintings of tired-looking cowboys, and bucking-bronco bronzes.

In the center of the room was a big claw-footed, leather-topped desk. Behind it a wall display of flintlocks and engraved antique rifles ran from floor to ceiling.

Behind the desk sat Billy Vidal, bright-eyed and brush-cut, square-jawed and perfectly seamed. His strong-tea tan was set off nicely by an ivory-colored turtleneck under a white cashmere V-neck. No cowboy gear for the chairman of Magna; he was Palm Beach polished, golf-course fit. His hands lay flat on the desktop, manicured, baby smooth.

"Dr. Delaware, thank you for coming."

His voice didn't fit with the rest of him—a hoarse, wispy croak, cracking between words.

I said nothing.

He looked straight at me with pale eyes, held the stare for a while, then said, "That was an icebreaker that fell flat." His last words petered out to a lip-sync. He cleared his throat, produced more laryngitic whisper. "Sorry for any inconvenience you've been caused. There didn't seem to be any other way."

"Any other way for what?"

"To arrange a chat between us."

"All you had to do was ask."

He shook his head. "The problem was timing. Until recently I wasn't sure it was wise for us to meet. I've been debating that issue since you started asking questions."

He coughed, tapped his Adam's apple. "But today, when you visited my sister, you made the decision for me. Things had to be done quickly and carefully. So once again, I'll apologize for the *way* you were brought here, and hope we can put that to rest and move on."

I could still feel the chafe of the cuffs around my wrists, thought of the copter ride, mainlining fear while waiting for Hummel and his golf cart, fingers up my ass.

Cute little dance, son. I knew my rage would weaken me if I let it take over.

"Move on to what?" I said, smiling.

"Our discussion."

"Of what?"

"Please, doctor," he rasped, "don't waste precious time being coy."

"Short on time, are you?"

"Very much so."

Another staring match. His gaze never wavered but his eyes lost focus and I sensed he was somewhere else.

"Thirty years ago," he said, "I had the opportunity to witness an atomic test conducted jointly by the Magna Corporation and the U.S. Army. A festive event, by invitation only, out in the Nevada desert. We spent the night in Las Vegas, had a wonderful party, and drove out before sunrise. The bomb went off just as the skies lightened—a supercharged sunrise. But something went wrong: a sudden shift in the winds and all of us were exposed to radioactive dust. The army said there was little risk of contamination—no one thought much about it until fifteen years ago, when the cancers began appearing. Three quarters of those present that morning are dead. Several others are terminally ill. It's only a matter of time for me."

I studied his well-fed face, all that glowing bronze dermis, said, "You look healthier than I do."

"Do I *sound* healthy?"

I didn't answer.

"Actually," he said, "I *am* healthy. For the time being. Low cholesterol, excellent lipids, a heart as strong as a blast furnace. A few lumps in my esophagus removed surgically last year, no evidence of spread." He pulled down the collar of the turtleneck, exposed a hot-pink, puckered scar.

"Delicate skin, I develop keloid scars—do you suppose I should bother with plastic surgery?"

"That's up to you."

"I've considered it, but it seems such a foolish conceit. The cancer's bound to return. Ironically, the treatment includes radiation. Not that treatment has made much of a difference for any of the others."

He folded his collar back in place. Tapped his Adam's apple.

"What about Belding?" I said. "Was he exposed?"

He smiled, shook his head. "Leland was protected. As always."

Still smiling, he opened a desk drawer, took out a small plastic squeeze bottle and shot some kind of atomized spray down his throat. He deep-swallowed a couple of times, put the bottle back, reclined in his chair, and smiled wider.

I said, "What is it you want to discuss?"

"Matters that seem to interest you. I'm willing to satisfy your curiosity on condition that you stop turning over rocks. I know your intentions are honorable but you don't realize how destructive you could be."

"I don't see how I could add to the destruction that's already taken place."

"Dr. Delaware, I want to leave this earth knowing everything's been done to cushion certain individuals."

"Such as your sister? Isn't cushioning her what caused all of it, Mr. Vidal?"

"No, that's incorrect—but then, you've seen only part of the picture."

"And you're going to show me all of it?"

"Yes." Cough. "But you must give your word that you'll stop probing, let things finally rest."

"Why pretend that I have a choice?" I said. "If I don't give you what you want, you can always squash me. The way you squashed Seaman Cross, Eulalee and Cable Johnson, Donald Neurath, the Kruses."

He was amused. "You believe *I've* destroyed all those people?"

"You, Magna, what's the difference?"

"Ah. Corporate America as Satan Incarnate."

"Just this particular corporation."

His laugh was feeble and breathy. "Doctor, even if I did have an interest in ... *squashing* you, I wouldn't. You've acquired a certain ... aura of grace."

"Oh?"

"Oh, yes. Someone cared deeply about you. Someone lovely and kind—dear to both of us."

Not dear enough to stop him from erasing her identity.

I said, "I saw that someone talking to you at the party. She wanted something from you. What?"

The pale eyes closed. He pressed his fingers to his temples.

I said, "From Holmby Hills to Willow Glen. Five hundred dollars a month, in an unmarked envelope. Doesn't sound as if she was *that* dear to you."

He opened his eyes. "Five hundred? Is that what Helen told you?" He produced another wheezy laugh, wheeled his chair back, put his feet on the desk. He wore black silk corduroy slacks, tan lambskin kilties with argyle socks. The soles of the shoes were polished, unmarked, as if they'd never touched the ground.

"All right," he said. "Enough shilly-shallying. Tell me what it is you think you know—I'll correct your misconceptions."

"Meaning you find out how much trouble I could cause you, then act accordingly."

"I understand how you could see it that way, Doctor. But what I'm really after is preventive education—giving you the whole picture, so that you no longer have any *need* to cause trouble."

Silence.

He said, "If my offer doesn't appeal to you, I'll have you flown back home immediately."

"What are my chances of arriving there alive?"

"One hundred percent. Barring acts of God."

"Or God pretending to be the Magna Corporation."

He laughed. "I'll try to remember that one. What is it then, Doctor? The choice is yours."

I was at his mercy. Going along meant learning more. And buying time. I said, "Go ahead, educate me, Mr. Vidal."

"Excellent. Let's do it like gentlemen, over supper." He pushed something on the desk front. The gun display wall half-rotated, revealing a closet-sized passageway with a screen door that he opened to fresh air.

We stepped onto a long, covered patio, supported by gray-brown turned-wood columns and paved with rust-colored Mexican tile. Thick-trunked bougainvillea rooted in clay pots wound their way around the columns and up to the roof, where they spread. Straw baskets of donkey-tail and jade plant hung from the rafters. A large round table was covered with sky-blue damask and set for two: earthenware dishes, hammered-silver flatware, crystal goblets, a centerpiece of dried herbs and flowers. He'd been sure of my "choice."

A Mexican waiter appeared from nowhere and held out my chair. I walked past him, crossed the patio, and stepped out into the open air. The sun's position said dusk was approaching, but the heat was midday strong.

I stepped back far enough from the building to take it in entirely: long, low, single-storied, textured mock-adobe walls, windows trimmed with the same gray-brown wood used for the columns. Flagstone walkways cut a swath through an acre or two of lawn bordered by yellow gazania. Beyond the grass was dry dust and an empty horse corral. Past the corral, more dust, miles of it, the biscuit-colored monotony broken only by clumps of aloe and Joshua tree, and paint-by-number splotches of ashen shadow.

And backing all of it, the source of the shadows: granite mountains. Majestic, black-tipped, knife-edged against a sapphire sky. Picture-postcard mountains, so perfect they could have been a photographer's backdrop.

My eyes swept downward, to a particular spot on the lawn, seeking out a wooden garden bench. Nothing. But my memory placed one there anyway.

A posing spot.

Two little girls in cowgirl suits, eating ice cream.

I looked back at Vidal. He'd sat down, was unfurling his napkin, saying something to the waiter as his wine glass was filled.

The waiter laughed, filled my glass, and left.

The former Billy the Pimp held his hand out to my chair.

I took another look at the mountains, saw only stone and sand now. The play of light and shadow on inanimate surface.

All the memories wiped out.

Vidal beckoned.

I walked back to the patio.

34

He ate fiercely, obsessively, an impeccably mannered cobra. Striking at his food, cutting it into tiny pieces and tenderizing it to purée before ingesting. Guacamole ostentatiously mixed tableside by the waiter, using a rough stone mortar and pestle. A salad of wild greens and marinated onions. Homemade corn tortillas, newly churned butter, barbecued swordfish steaks, six kinds of salsa, pork loin roast in some kind of sweet, piquant sauce. A Chardonnay and a Pinot Noir he took pains to inform me were estate-bottled at a Sonoma winery run by Magna exclusively for its own consumption.

A couple of times I saw him wince after swallowing, wondered how much of his pleasure was gustatory, how much appreciation that his mouth still worked.

He'd accepted a second portion of pork before he noticed my untouched food.

"Not to your liking, Doctor?"

"I'd rather be educated than eat."

Smile. Dice. Purée. The human Veg-O-Matic.

"Where are we?" I asked. "Mexico?"

"Mexico," he said, "is a state of mind. Someone witty once said that, though for the life of me I can't remember who—probably Dorothy Parker. She said all the witty things, didn't she?"

Cut, chew. Swallow.

I said, "Why did Sharon kill herself?"

He lowered his fork. "That's an end point, Doctor. Let's proceed chronologically."

"Proceed away."

He drank wine, winced, coughed, kept eating, sipped some more. I looked out at the desert as it darkened to madder-brown. Not a sound, not a bird in the sky. Maybe the animals knew something.

Finally he pushed his plate away and tapped his fork on the table. The Mexican waiter appeared, along with two heavy black-haired women in long brown dresses. Vidal said something in rapid Spanish. The table was cleared and each of us was served a pewter bowl of green ice cream.

I took a taste. Cloyingly sweet.

"Cactus," said Vidal. "Very soothing."

He took a long time with the dessert. The waiter brought coffee flavored with anise. Vidal thanked him, dismissed him, and dabbed his lips.

"Chronological order," I said. "How about starting with Eulalee and Cable Johnson."

He nodded. "What do you know about them?"

"She was one of Belding's party girls; he was a petty crook. A pair of small-town hustlers trying to make it in Hollywood. Not exactly major league dope dealers."

He said, "Linda—I always knew her as Linda—was an exquisite creature. A diamond in the rough, but physically magnetic—that intangible something that can't be bought at any price. Back in those days we were surrounded by beauties, but she stood out because she was different from the rest—less cynical, a certain pliability."

"Passivity?"

"I suppose someone in your line of work would look at it as a flaw. I saw it as an easygoing nature, felt she was the right woman to help Leland."

"Help him with what?"

"Become a man. Leland didn't understand women. He froze up when he was around them, couldn't . . . perform. He was far too intelligent to miss the irony—all that money and power, the country's most eligible bachelor and still a virgin at forty. He wasn't a physical person, but every kettle has its boiling point and the frustration was getting in the way of his work. I knew he'd never solve the problem by himself. It fell upon my shoulders to find a . . . guide for him. I explained the situation to Linda. She was amenable, so I arranged for the two of them to be together. She was more, Dr. Delaware, than a *party girl.*"

I said, "Sexual favors for a fee. Sounds like something else."

He refused to be offended. "Everything has its price, Doctor.

She was simply doing, thirty years ago, what a sexual surrogate would do today."

I said, "You didn't just pick her for her personality."

"She was beautiful," he said. "Likely to stimulate."

"That's not what I meant."

"Oh?" He sipped his coffee, said, "Tepid," and rapped his spoon on the table three times. The waiter appeared out of the darkness with a fresh pot. I wondered what else was concealed out there.

He drank the steaming liquid, looked as if someone had poured acid down his throat. It took several moments before he tried to speak, and when he did I had to lean forward to hear: "Why don't you tell me what you're driving at."

"Her sterility," I said. "You picked her because you thought she was unable to bear children."

"You're a very bright young fellow," he said, then raised his cup to his lips again and hid behind a cloud of steam. "Leland was a very squeamish man—that was part of his problem. Not having to worry about taking precautions *was* a point in her favor. But a minor factor, a bit of messiness that could have been dealt with."

"I was thinking of something a bit messier," I said. "An heir born out of wedlock."

He drank more coffee.

I said, "Why'd you think she couldn't conceive?"

"We did background checks on all the girls, had them undergo complete physical exams. Our research revealed that Linda had gotten pregnant several times during her youth but had miscarried almost immediately after conception. Our doctors said it was some sort of hormonal imbalance. They pronounced her incapable of bearing children."

Animal husbandry in reverse. I said, "How'd she do with old Leland?"

"She was marvelous. After a few sessions he was a new man."

"What were his feelings toward her?"

He put down his cup. "Leland Belding didn't feel, Doctor. He was as close to mechanical as a human being could be."

Ellston Crotty's words came back to me: *Like some frigging camera on legs. I remember thinking what a cold bastard he was.*

"Even so," I said, "patients and surrogates usually develop some sort of emotional bond. Are you saying none developed between them?"

"That's exactly what I'm saying. It was like tutoring—learning

French. Leland received her in his office; when they were through he showered, dressed, and resumed his business and she went about hers. I knew him better than anyone and that wasn't much—I never felt I had access to his thoughts. But my guess is he saw her as another of his machines—one of the more efficient ones. Which isn't to say he disparaged her. Machines were what he admired most."

"What about her feelings toward him?"

A moment's pause. A fleeting look of pain. "No doubt she was impressed with his money and power. Women are drawn to power—they'll forgive anything in a man but helplessness. And she also saw his helpless side. So I'd imagine she viewed him with a mixture of awe and pity, the way a doctor might regard a patient with a rare disease."

He'd framed his words theoretically. But the pained look kept pushing through the charm-façade.

I knew then that Linda Lanier had become more to him than a harem girl on assignment. Knew I couldn't touch that.

"Theirs was purely a business arrangement," he said.

"Cozy, until brother Cable stepped in."

The façade slipped another rung. "Cable Johnson was despicable. When he and Linda were adolescents he sold her to the local boys for money—she was fourteen or fifteen. That's how she got pregnant all those times. He was pure filth."

One procurer damning another.

I said, "Why didn't you consider him a risk factor when you set Linda up as a surrogate?"

"Oh, I did, but I thought the risk had been dealt with. At the time I hired Linda, Johnson was locked up at the county jail for theft—facing a stay at the penitentiary as a repeat offender. He was dead-broke, unable to come up with ten dollars' bond on a hundred-dollar bail. I obtained his freedom, got him a job at Magnafilm at an inflated salary. The idiot didn't even have to show up for work—the check was mailed to his rooming house. All that was required on his part was staying away from her. A very generous arrangement, wouldn't you say?"

"Not compared to a piece of the Belding fortune."

"The fool," he said. "There wasn't an iota of a chance of his getting a penny, but he was a compulsive criminal, couldn't stop conniving."

"Enter Donald Neurath, M.D. Fertility expert and meal ticket."

"My, my," said Vidal. "You're a thorough researcher yourself."

"Was Neurath in on the extortion scheme?"

"He claimed not, said they presented themselves as a married couple—poor, childless Mr. and Mrs. Johnson. He insisted he hadn't been fooled, had sensed something wrong about them and refused to take her on as a patient. But Johnson convinced him, somehow."

"You know how," I said. "A trade. The porn loop in exchange for hormonal treatment for Linda."

"More filth," he said.

I said, "Still, Neurath knew too much. You had to finish him off somewhere out in Mexico—not far from here, I'd bet."

"Doctor, Doctor, you give me too much credit. I've never *finished off* anyone. Donald Neurath drove down here voluntarily, to offer information. He owed money to loan sharks, was hoping for payment. I refused. On the way back, his car broke down—or so I've been told. He died of exposure—the desert does its damage quickly. As a medical man, he should have been more prepared."

I said, "Is that how you connected him to Cable's scheme?"

"No. Linda came to me saying she could no longer work with Leland. Bearing a to-whom-it-may-concern note written on Neurath's stationery. In it he claimed she'd contracted some sort of vaginal infection. At first, I didn't suspect anything. Everything looked bona fide. I gave her ten thousand dollars' severance pay, and wished her well. Later, of course, I put it all together."

"How did Belding react to her leaving?"

"He didn't. By that time he was feeling his oats, testing out his newfound confidence on other women. As many as he could get his hands on. Eventually, he began to flaunt it."

Belding's transformation from recluse to playboy. The timing fit.

"What happened next?"

"Nearly a year later, Cable Johnson called me. Informed me I'd better meet with him if I knew what was good for Leland. We met at some tawdry downtown hotel, Johnson drunk and gloating like a top dog, strutting around, very proud of himself. He told me Linda had given birth to Leland's babies. He'd taken her to Texas to do it; now they were back and 'the squeeze was on.'"

Vidal raised his coffee cup, thought better of it, and put it down. "Oh, he thought he was a smart one. Had it all figured out. Cuffing my shoulder as if we were old friends, offering me cheap gin from a filthy bottle. Singing rude limericks and saying that now the Johnsons and the Beldings were going to be *kinfolk*. Then he told me to wait, left the room, and came back a few minutes later with Linda and his *little gifts*."

"Three gifts," I said.

He nodded.

Triplets. All that hormonal tinkering doing strange things to the egg, increasing the chance of multiple birth. Common medical knowledge today, but Neurath had been ahead of his time.

"Port Wallace's sole claim to fame," I said. "Jewel Rae, Jana Sue. And poor Joan Dixie, born blind, deaf, paralyzed."

"The pathetic little thing," he said. "Some sort of brain damage—the place he dragged Linda to was primitive. Joan almost died at birth." He shook his head, closed his eyes. "She was so tiny—not much bigger than a fist. It was a miracle she survived. Linda carried her around in a basket, kept cooing at her, massaging her limbs. Pretending her twitches were voluntary movement. Pretending she was normal."

"Something like that would be tough for a squeamish man to take."

"*All three* of them disgusted him. He'd always despised children; the idea of triplets made him ill. He was the ultimate engineer—accustomed to machine specifications, precision. Had absolutely no tolerance for anything that deviated from his expectations. Of course, Joan's deformities were an additional insult—the implication that he'd taken part in creating something defective. I knew him, knew how he'd react. I wanted to keep all of it from him, work things out in my own way. But Cable wanted it all, right now. *Kinfolk.* Linda had held on to a key to Leland's office. She went there one night when he was working late, brought the babies."

He shook his head. "The poor, stupid girl, believing the sight of them would ignite his paternal pride. He listened to her, told her what she wanted to hear. The moment she was gone he phoned me and ordered me over for a 'problem solving session.' Not that he wanted my input—he'd come to a decision: All of them would have to be eliminated. Permanently. I was to be the angel of death."

"The babies were supposed to be killed?"

He nodded.

"All the villainy foisted on a dead man," I said. "Some good storm trooper carried out the order."

He drank, hacked, pulled a squeeze bottle out of his pocket and sprayed his throat.

"I saved those babies," he said. "Only I could have done it; only I had enough of Leland's trust to disagree with him and get away with it. I told him infanticide was absolutely out of the question. If it ever came out he'd be ruined—Magna would be ruined."

"A pragmatic approach."

"The only one he understood. I pointed out that the babies could be given up for adoption in such a way that any link to him would be permanently obscured. That he could draft a new will specifically excluding any blood relatives, known or unknown, from inheriting a dime. At first he didn't want to hear it, kept insisting the only way out was the 'unambiguous option.' I told him I'd carried out his assignments without questioning, but I'd quit before carrying out this one. And if those babies died, I couldn't guarantee my silence. Was he prepared to eliminate me, as well?

"That angered—and shocked—him. From childhood no one had ever told him no. But he respected me for standing up to him, eventually agreed to my plan."

"Nifty plan," I said. "Including a consolation prize for your sister."

"It was just after Henry's death. She'd sunk into a deep depression—widowhood, childlessness. Had been in seclusion since the funeral. I thought having the girls would do wonders for her. And she's not an imaginative woman. Would never ask where they came from, never want to know."

"Was Joan included in the deal?"

"No. *That* Hope couldn't have handled. The corporation purchased a sanitarium in Connecticut, and Joan was placed there. She got excellent care. In the process, we learned about health care management, ended up buying up several other hospitals."

"New names, new lives," I said. "Except for the Johnsons. Was it you or Belding who thought of the dope dealer angle?"

"That . . . it wasn't supposed to happen the way it did."

"I'm sure Linda and Cable would be comforted to know that."

He tried to speak. Nothing came out. Atomized his throat, waited, and produced soft tones dry as a death rattle.

"It was never intended that Linda would . . . be part of it. She wasn't supposed to be there, was supposed to be out shopping. She posed no threat. With her brother out of the way, she could have been dealt with. I would have dealt with her. But her car didn't work; she was phoning for a taxi when things started to happen. Cable grabbed her, the filth, used her as a *shield*. She was shot by accident."

"No way," I said. "She wouldn't have let her children be taken from her without a fuss. She had to die. You either knew that from the beginning or chose not to see it when you set up the bust. That glitzy suite on Fountain—all the jewels, furs, cars—were to lull her and Cable into thinking Belding was agreeing to their terms. But both of them were dead the moment she stepped into his office with those babies."

"You're wrong, Dr. Delaware. I had everything arranged."

"Let's give you the benefit, then, and say someone rearranged your arrangement."

He gripped the edge of the table. The look in his eyes overpowered the tan, the clothes, all that cultivated charm.

"No," he croaked. "It was a mistake. Her idiot scum brother killed her—using her the way he'd always done."

"Maybe he did. But Hummel and DeGranzfeld would have killed her anyway on Belding's orders. He was pleased with the job they'd done, rewarded them with Vegas jobs."

He said nothing for a long time. Something—could it be real?—seemed to be eating at him, devouring him from within. He looked through me. Back into another time.

"Nonsense," he said.

"Are you the father?" I asked.

Another long silence. "I don't know." Then: "Leland and I have the same blood type: O positive. Along with thirty-nine percent of the population."

"Nowadays there are precise tests."

"What would be the point?" His voice rose, cracked and died. "I saved them. Placed them in a good home. It was enough."

"Not for Sharon. She ended up naked, eating mayonnaise from a jar. Another plan gone wrong?"

He closed his eyes, grimaced, getting older by the second. "It was for the good of both of them."

"So I've been told."

"Sherry was a frightening child. I'd seen the signs of violence in her from the time she could walk. It worried me. I wondered about a bad seed—the Johnsons came from a long line of miscreants. Eventually it became clear that Hope couldn't handle both of them. Sharon was being persecuted—battered. It was escalating steadily. Something had to be done. When Sherry tried to drown her, I knew the time had come. But Leland couldn't find out about it. He'd forgotten completely about them, hadn't mentioned a word since the transfer. I knew he'd regard any change in plans as evidence that my way of dealing with the situation wasn't working. Would insist on doing it his way."

"What did you tell him?"

"That Sharon had accidentally drowned. *That* set well with him."

His lips began to tremble. He placed a manicured hand over his mouth to conceal the loss of control.

"Why banish Sharon?" I said. "Why not Sherry?"

"Because Sherry was the one who bore *watching*—she was unstable, a loaded gun. Having her out there unsupervised was too risky—for both of them."

"That's not the only reason," I said.

"No. Hope wanted it that way. She felt closer to Sherry, felt Sherry needed her more."

"Punish the victim," I said. "From a mansion to a dirt patch. Two retarded people as caretakers."

"They were *good* people," he said. He began coughing and, unable to stop, shook his head from side to side, gasping for breath. His eyes filled with water and he had to hold on to the table for support.

Finally he was able to speak, but so softly I had to lean forward to hear: "Good people. They'd worked for me. I knew they could be trusted. The arrangement was supposed to be temporary—a way to buy time for Sharon until I came up with something else."

"A way to wipe out her identity," I said.

"For *her* sake!" His whisper was harsh, insistent. "I'd never have done anything to harm her."

Hand to mouth, again. Uncontrollable coughing. He placed a silk handkerchief to his lips, spit something into it.

"Excuse me," he said. Then: "She had her mother's face."

"So did Sherry."

"No, no. Sherry had the features. But not the face."

We said nothing for a long time. Then, suddenly, as if forcing his way out of a sentimental stupor, he sat up, snapped his fingers. The waiter brought him a glass of ice water and was gone. He drank, cleared his throat, touched his Adam's apple, swallowed hard. Forcing a smile, but looking drained, defeated. A man who'd sailed through life in first class, only to find out the cruise had gone nowhere.

I'd arrived at this place hating him, prepared to stoke my hate. But I felt like putting my arm around him.

Then I thought of dead bodies, a pile of them, and said, "Your temporary plan stretched to permanence."

He nodded. "I kept searching for another way, some other arrangement. Meanwhile, Shirlee and Jasper were doing a yeoman job—amazingly so. Then Helen discovered Sharon, made her a protégée, began molding her in a fine way. I decided nothing could be better than that. I contacted Helen; we reached an agreement."

"Helen was paid?"

"Not with money—she and her husband were too proud for that. But there were other things I could do for them. Scholarships for her children, aborting a plan to sell off corporate acreage in Willow Glen for development. For over thirty years, Magna's guaranteed to purchase any agricultural surpluses and compensate for any losses below a specified level. Not just for Helen—for the entire town."

"Paying them not to grow apples," I said.

"An American tradition," he said. "You should taste Wendy's honey and cider. Our employees love them."

I remembered Helen's complaint:

They won't sell. . . . For all intents and purposes that keeps Willow Glen a backwater speck.

Keeping Shirlee and Jasper and their charge away from prying eyes . . .

"How much does Helen know?" I asked.

"Her knowledge is very limited. For her sake."

"What will become of the Ransoms?"

"Nothing will change," he said. "They'll continue to live wonderfully basic lives. Did you see any signs of suffering on their faces, Doctor? They don't want for anything, would be considered well-off by most people's standards. Helen looks out for them. Before she came along, I did."

He allowed himself a smile. Smug.

"All right," I said, "you're Mother Teresa. So how come people keep dying?"

"Some people," he said, "deserve to die."

"Sounds like a quotation from Chairman Belding."

No answer.

I said, "What about Sharon? Did she deserve to die for trying to learn who she was?"

He stood, stared down at me. All self-doubt gone, once again The Man In Charge.

"Words can communicate only so much," he said. "Come with me."

We headed out toward the desert. He aimed a penlight at the ground, highlighting pitted soil, mammalian clumps of scrub, saguaro cactus stretching skyward.

About a half-mile in, the beam settled on a small, streamlined

Fiberglas vehicle—the golf-cart I'd visualized during my ride with
Hummel. Dark paint, a roll bar, knobby, off-road tires. A forward-
slanting *M* on the door.

He got behind the wheel and motioned me in. No blindfold for
this ride. I was either trusted or doomed. He flipped several switches.
Headlights. The whine of the electric engine. Another flip and the
hum rose in frequency. We moved forward with surprising speed,
twice as fast as the bumper-car pace Hummel had taken—the sadist.
Faster than I'd thought possible from an electric machine. But then,
this was high-tech territory. The Patent Ranch.

We rode for more than an hour without exchanging a word,
sailing across stretches of chalky wasteland. The air was still hot and
grew fragrant, a mild herbaceous scent.

Vidal coughed a lot as the vehicle churned up clouds of fine clay
dust, but he continued to steer with ease. The granite mountains
were faint pencil marks on black construction paper.

He flipped another switch and made the moon appear, gigantic,
milky-white, and earthbound.

Not the moon at all, but a giant golf ball, illuminated from
within.

A geodesic dome, perhaps thirty feet in diameter.

Vidal pulled up to it and parked. The surface of the dome was
white plastic hexagonal panels framed in tubular white metal. I
looked for the booth Seaman Cross had described, the one he'd sat in
while communicating with Belding. But the only access to the building was a white door.

"The Basket-Case Billionaire," I said.

"A stupid little book," said Vidal. "Leland got it into his head
that he needed to be chronicled."

"Why'd he pick Cross?"

We got out of the cart. "I haven't the slightest idea—I told you
he never let me inside his head. I was out of the country when he
cooked up the deal. Later he changed his mind and demanded Cross
fold up his tent in return for a cash payment. Cross took the money,
but went ahead with the book. Leland was very displeased."

"Another search-and-destroy mission."

"Everything was handled legally—through the courts."

"Burglarizing his storage locker wasn't exactly working within
the system. Did you use the same guys for the Fontaine break-in?"

His expression said that wasn't worth responding to. We started
walking.

I said, "What about Cross's suicide?"

"Cross was weak-willed, couldn't cope."

"You're saying it was a genuine suicide?"

"Absolutely."

"If he hadn't done himself in, would you have let him live?"

He smiled and shook his head. "As I told you before, Doctor, I don't *squash* people. Besides, Cross was no threat. No one believed him."

The door was white and seamless. He placed his hand on the knob, looked at me, and let the message sink in:

Cross had poisoned the well when it came to Leland Belding stories.

No one would believe me. This day had never occurred.

I looked up at the dome. Starlight made it shimmer, like a giant jellyfish. The plastic panels gave off a new-car smell. Vidal twisted the knob.

I stepped in. The door closed behind me. A moment later, I heard the buggy depart.

I looked around, expecting screens, consoles, keyboards, a Flash Gordon tangle of electronic pasta.

But it was just a big room, interior walls sheathed in white plastic. The rest could have come out of any suburban tract home. Ice-blue carpet. Oak furniture. Console TV. Stereo components topping a record cabinet. Prefab bookcase and matching magazine basket. An efficiency kitchen off to one side. Potted plants. Framed samplers.

Apple drawings.

And three beds arranged parallel to one another, as in a bunk room. Or ward: the first two were hospital setups with push-button position controls and chromium swivel tables.

The nearest one was empty save for something on the pillow. I took a closer look. It was a toy airplane—a bomber, painted dark, with a forward-slanting *M* on the door.

In the second, a crippled woman lay under a cheerful quilt. Immobile, gape-mouthed, some gray streaking her black hair, but otherwise unchanged in the six years since I'd last seen her. As if disability had so dominated her body it rendered her ageless. She took a deep sucking breath and air came out in a squeak.

A waft of perfume filtered through the new-car ambience. Soap and water, fresh grass.

Sharon sat on the edge of the third bed, hands folded in her lap. A smile, tissue-thin, graced her lips.

She wore a long white dress that buttoned down the front. Her hair was combed out, parted in the middle. No makeup, no jewelry. Her eyes purplish in the light of the dome.

She fidgeted under my stare. Long fingers. Arms smooth as butter. Breasts straining against the dress. Silk. Expensive, but it resembled a nurse's uniform.

"Hello, Alex."

Shirlee Ransom's swivel table held tissues, a hot water bottle, a mucus aspirator, a water pitcher, and an empty drinking glass. I picked up the glass, rolled it between my palms, and put it down.

"Come," she said.

I sat down next to her, said, "Risen like Lazarus."

"Never gone," she said.

"Someone else is."

She nodded.

I said, "The red dress? Strawberry daiquiris?"

"*Her.*"

"Sleeping with your patients?"

She shifted so that our flanks touched. "*Her.* She wanted to hurt me, didn't care she was hurting others in the process. I didn't know a thing until the cancellations started pouring in. I couldn't understand it. Everything had been going so well—mostly short-term cases, but everyone liked me. I phoned them. Most of them refused to talk to me. A couple of wives got on, full of rage, threatening. It was like a bad dream. Then Sherry told me what she'd done. Laughing. She'd been staying with me, had taken my office key and made a copy. Used it to get into my files, picked out the ones who sounded *cute,* offered them free follow-up visits and ... *did* them, then *dumped* them. That's the way she put it. When I was calm enough, I asked her *why.* She said she'd be damned if she'd let me play doctor and lord it over her."

She placed her hand on my thigh. Her palm was wet. "I knew she resented me, Alex, but I never imagined she'd carry it that far. When we first got together, she acted as if she loved me."

"When was that?"

"My second year of grad school. Autumn."

Surprised, I said, "Not the summer?"

"No. Autumn. October."

"What was the family business that prevented you from going to San Francisco?"

"Therapy."

"Conducting or receiving?"

"My therapy."

"With Kruse."

Nod. "It was a crucial time. I couldn't leave. We were dealing with issues ... It really was family business."

"Where were you staying?"

"His house."

I'd gone there, looking for her, watching Kruse's face split in two. . . .

Have a nice day . . .

"It was pretty intense," she said. "He wanted to monitor all the variables."

"You had no trouble sleeping there?"

"I . . . No, he helped me. Relaxed me."

"Hypnosis."

"Yes. He was preparing me—for meeting her. He thought it would be a healing process. For both of us. But he underestimated how much hatred remained."

She stayed calm but the pressure of her hand increased. "She was pretending, Alex. It was easy for her—she'd studied acting."

Some gravitate to the stage and screen. . . . "Interesting career choice," I said.

"It wasn't a career, just a fling. Just like everything else. First she used it to get close to me, then again to target what she knew was dearest to me: you; then, years later, my work. She knew how much my work meant to me."

"Why didn't you get licensed?"

She tugged her earlobe. "Too many ... distractions. I wasn't ready."

"Paul's opinion?"

"And mine."

She pressed against me. Her touch felt burdensome.

"You're the only man I've ever loved, Alex."

"What about Jasper? And Paul."

The mention of Kruse's name made her flinch. "I mean romantic love. *Physical* love. You're the only one who's ever been *inside* of me."

I said nothing.

"Alex, it's true. I know you suspected things, but Paul and I were never like that. I was his patient—sleeping with a patient's like incest. Even after therapy stops."

Something in her voice made me back off. "Okay. But let's not forget Mickey Starbuck."

"Who?"

"Your co-star. *Checkup*."

"Was that his name? Mickey? All I knew about him was that he was an actor whom Paul had treated for cocaine addiction. Back in Florida. I've never been to Florida."

"Her?"

She nodded.

I said, "Who cast her?"

"I know what it looks like, but Paul thought it might be curative."

"Radical therapy. Working it through."

"You'd have to see it in context, Alex. He'd worked with her for years without much success. He had to try something."

I looked away, took in my surroundings. Hooked rug on the blue carpet. The samplers spouting truisms. No goddam place like home.

Spaceship homey. As if extraterrestrials had swooped down on a specimen-hunt, plundered Middle America of its clichés.

When I turned back, she was smiling. A shiny smile. Too shiny. Like glaze before crackling.

"Alex, I understand how strange all this must sound to you. It's hard to sum up so many years in just a few minutes."

I smiled back, let my confusion show. "It's overwhelming—the dynamics—how it all fits together."

"I'll do my best to clear it up for you."

"I'd appreciate that."

"Where would you like me to start?"

"Right at the beginning seems as good a place as any."

She put her head on my shoulder. "That's the problem. There really is no beginning," she said, in the same disembodied voice she'd used years ago, to talk about the death of her "parents." "My primal years are a blur. I've been *told* about them, but it's like hearing a story about someone else. That's what therapy was about, that summer. Paul was trying to unblock me."

"Age regression?"

"Age regression, free association, Gestalt exercises—all the standard techniques. Things I've used myself with patients. But nothing worked. I couldn't remember a thing. I mean, intellectually I *understood* the defensive process, knew I was repressing, but that didn't help me in *here*." She placed my hand on her belly.

"How far back could you recall?" I asked.

"Happy times. Shirlee and Jasper. And Helen. Uncle Billy told me you met her yesterday. Isn't she an exceptional person?"

"Yes, she is." *Yesterday.* It seemed like centuries. "Does she know you're alive?"

She winced as if bitten. Hard tug on the lobe. "Uncle Billy said he'd take care of it."

"I'm sure he will. What were you and he talking about at the party?"

"*Her.* She was forcing herself on me again—dropping in at all hours, waking me up, screaming and cursing, or crawling into bed with me and mauling me, trying to suck my breasts. Once I caught her with scissors, trying to snip off my hair. Other times, she'd arrive stoned or drunk on her daiquiris, get sick all over the place, lose bladder control on the carpet. I kept changing the locks; she always found a way to get in. She ate pills like candy."

Old scars between the toes. "Was she shooting dope?"

"She used to, years ago. I don't know, maybe she started again—cocaine, speedballs. Over the years, she must have overdosed at least a dozen times. I had one of Uncle Billy's doctors on call twenty-four hours a day, just for pumping her stomach. By the day of the party she'd really deteriorated and was trying to take me down with her. Kept saying we were going to be *eternal* roomies. I was scared, just couldn't handle it anymore. So I asked Uncle Billy to handle it. Even after all she'd put me through, it was rough, knowing she'd be put away. So seeing you there at the party really lifted my spirits. A week before, I'd been at Paul's house and Suzanne was doing the calligraphy for the invitations. I saw your name on the list, felt such a surge of feeling for you."

She took my hand and ran it down toward her mons. I felt heat, heaviness, the soft mesh of pubic hair through silk.

"I hoped you'd attend," she said. "Checked a couple of times to see if you'd RSVP'd, but you hadn't. So when our eyes met I couldn't believe it. Destiny. I knew I had to try to make contact." She kissed my cheek. "And now you're here. Hello, stranger."

"Hello." I sat there and allowed her to kiss me some more, run her fingers through my hair, touch me. Endured it and kissed back and knew how hookers feel. Sweat broke out on my forehead. I wiped it on my sleeve.

She said, "Would you like water?" Got up and poured me some from Shirlee's pitcher.

I used the time to clear my head. When she came back I said, "Was Paul treating you for anything other than unblocking the past?"

"Actually it didn't start out as real therapy—just clinical supervision, the usual stuff about how my feelings and communications style affected my work. But as we got into it, he could see that I had . . . identity problems, a poor sense of self, low self-esteem. I felt incomplete. And guilty."

"Guilty about what?"

"Everything. Leaving Shirlee and Jasper—they're *darling*. I really cared for them, but I never felt I *belonged* to them. And Helen. Even though she'd basically raised me, she wasn't my mother—there was always a wall between us. It was confusing."

I nodded.

"That first year of grad school," she said, "there was a lot of pressure, being expected to actually help *other* people. It terrified me—that's why I broke down in practicum. I guess, down deep, I agreed with what the others were saying, felt like an impostor."

"Everyone feels that way at first."

She smiled. "Always the therapist. That's what you were that night. My rock. When I saw your name on the party list I guess I thought history might repeat itself."

I said, "Before you met Sherry—before you knew about her—did you ever fantasize about having a twin?"

"Yes, all the time, when I was a child. But I never gave much credence to that. I was the type of kid who fantasized about *everything*."

"Was there one twin image that kept recurring?"

Nod. "A girl my age who looked exactly like me, but was confident, popular, assertive. I named her Big Sharon, even though she was exactly my size, because her personality *loomed.* Paul said I saw myself as puny. Insignificant. Big Sharon stayed behind the scenes but she could always be counted on to help when things got rough. Years later, when I took my first psych course, I learned that kind of thing was normal—kids do it all the time. But I was doing it even into adolescence, even in *college.* I was embarrassed about it, afraid I'd talk in my sleep and my roommates would think I was weird. So I made a conscious effort to get rid of Big Sharon and finally grow up. Eventually, I managed to suppress her out of existence. But she came out under hypnosis, when Paul was probing. I began talking about her. Then *to* her. Paul said she was my partner. My silent partner, hanging around in the background. He said everyone has one—that's really what Freud was getting at with ego, id, superego. That it was okay to have her—she was nothing more than another part of me. That was a very affirmative message."

"And in autumn he decided to introduce you to your real silent partners."

She tightened. The glazed smile took hold of her face again.

"Yes. By then the time was right."

"How did he arrange it?"

"He called me into his office, said he had something to tell me. That I'd better sit down—it might be traumatic. But it would definitely be significant, a growth experience. Then he hypnotized me, gave me suggestions for deep muscle relaxation, transcendent serenity. When I was really mellow, he told me I was one of the luckiest people in the world because I had a real silent partner—two partners, actually. That I was one of three. *Triplets.*"

She turned, faced me, took both my hands in hers. "Alex, all those feelings of not being complete—the attempt to fill the hole with Big Sharon—had been my subconscious mind not allowing me to forget, despite the repression. The fact that I'd been able to talk to Big Sharon in therapy was a sign to him that I'd reached a higher level, was ready to get in touch with my identity as one third of a whole."

"How'd finding out make you feel?"

"At first it was wonderful. A wave of happiness washed over me—I was *drunk* with joy. Then, suddenly, everything got cold and dark and the walls started closing in."

She wrapped her arms around me, held me tight.

"It was unreal, Alex—unbelievably horrible. As if someone was stepping on my chest, crushing me. I was sure I was about to die. I tried to scream, but no sound came out. Tried to stand up and fell, began *crawling* toward the door. Paul picked me up, held me, kept talking in my ear, telling me everything was all right, to breathe slowly and deeply, get my breathing rhythmic, it was just an anxiety attack. Finally I managed to do it but I didn't feel normal. All my senses were *stuffed*. I was ready to *burst*. Then something came out, from deep inside of me—a terrible scream, louder than I'd ever screamed before. Someone else's scream—it didn't sound like me. I tried to step away from it, sit in the therapist's chair and watch someone else scream. But it *was* me and I couldn't stop. Paul clamped his hand over my mouth. When that didn't work, he slapped my face. Hard. It hurt but it felt good, if you can understand that. To be cared for."

"I understand," I said.

She said, "Thank you," and kissed me again.

"Then what?"

"Then he held me till I was calm. Stretched me out on the floor and let me lie there and put me deeper in hypnosis. Then he told me to open my eyes, reached into his shirt pocket—I can still see it: he was wearing a red silk shirt—and handed me a snapshot. Two little girls. Me and another me. He said to look on the back, he'd written something there. I did: *S and S, Silent Partners.* He said that was my catechism, my healing mantra. And the photo was my icon—he'd gotten it for me to keep. When in doubt or troubled, I should use it, fall into it. Then he told me to fall into it then and there and began telling me about the other girl. That her name was Sherry. She'd been his patient for years, long before he met me. The first time he saw me, he thought it was her. Meeting both of us was a miracle— miraculous karma—and his goal in life since then had been reuniting us into a functioning unit. A family."

"How long had he kept her existence from you?"

"Just a short time. He couldn't tell me about her until she agreed. She was his patient—everything was confidential."

"But to get her to agree, he must have told *her* about *you.*"

She frowned, as if working on a difficult puzzle. "That was different. Ours was a supervision therapy—he viewed me as a fellow professional, thought I could handle it. It had to start somewhere, Alex. Breaking the circle."

I said, "Of course. How did she react to learning about you?"

"At first she refused to believe him, even after he showed her a copy of the photo. Claimed it was trick photography, took a long time to accept the fact that I existed. Paul told me she'd been raised without love, had trouble bonding. Looking back, I realize he was warning me, right from the beginning. But I was in no state to consider negative input. All I knew was that my life had changed—magically. *Triplets,* the empty vessel *filled.*"

"Two out of three," I said.

"Yes, a moment later I realized that and asked about my other partner. He said we'd gone far enough, ended the session. Then he served me herb tea and a light dinner, had Suzanne give me a massage, drove me home and told me to try on my new identity."

"Home," I said. "Who gave you the house?"

"Paul did. He told me it was a rental property of his that no one was using and he wanted me to live in it—I needed a new place for my new life. This one was perfect for me, harmonious, in synchrony with my vibrations."

"Same with the car?"

"My little Alfa—wasn't that a cute car? It finally gave out last year. Paul said he'd bought it for Suzanne but she couldn't learn to drive a stick shift. He said after everything I'd been through, I deserved a little fun in my life so he was giving it to me. It wasn't till later, of course, that I learned he'd been serving as a conduit—but he did put everything together, so in a sense, everything did come from him."

"I can see that," I said. "What happened once you got home?"

"I was exhausted. The sessions had taken a lot out of me. I got into bed and slept like a baby. But that night I woke up in a cold sweat, panicky, having another anxiety attack. I wanted to call Paul, was too shaky to dial the phone. Finally I managed to breathe myself calm, but by then my mood had changed—I was really depressed, didn't want to speak with anyone. It was like falling head-first into a bottomless well—falling endlessly. I got under the covers, trying to escape. For three days I didn't dress or eat or get out of bed. Just sat staring at that snapshot. The third day was when you found me. When I saw you I went crazy. I'm sorry, Alex. I lost control."

She touched my cheek.

"Don't worry," I said. "Long forgotten. What happened after I left?"

"I stayed that way for a while. Some time later—I'm really not sure how long it was—Paul came by to see how I was doing. He cleaned me up, dressed me, and took me back to his place. For a week I did nothing but relax, stayed up in my . . . in a room there.

Then we had another session, even deeper hypnosis, and he told me about the separation."

"What did he tell you?"

"That we'd been put up for adoption at birth and wrenched apart at three because Sherry kept trying to hurt me. He said it wasn't the right way to handle it, but that our adoptive mother had problems of her own, couldn't handle both of us. She liked Sherry more, so I was given away."

She'd taken pains to speak in an offhand voice, but something raw and frigid had come into her eyes.

"What is it?" I said.

"Nothing. Just the irony. She lived like a princess all her life, but her soul was impoverished. I ended up being the lucky one."

"Did you ever meet Mrs. Blalock?"

"No. Not even at the party. Why should I? She was a name to me—not even a face. Someone else's mother."

I gazed at the plastic walls of the dome and said nothing. Let my eyes rest on the husk in the next bed.

"When did Paul tell you about partner number two?"

"Third session, but there wasn't much to tell. All he knew was that she'd been born disabled, was institutionalized somewhere."

"Someone filled you in. Uncle Billy?"

"Yes."

"The handsome paternal lawyer?"

"After all these years, you remember? Amazing." Trying to sound pleased, but edgy. "As a matter of fact, Uncle Billy always wanted to be a lawyer. He even applied to law school, but he got caught up with other things and never went."

"When did he come into the picture?"

"The second time Paul sent me home. Maybe a week after we . . . parted. I was doing much better, putting things in perspective. The doorbell rang. An older man with a beautiful smile was standing there. With candy and flowers and a bottle of wine. He said he was the brother of the woman who'd given me away—he apologized for that, said I shouldn't hate her, though he understood if I did. That she was an inadequate person but he'd always looked after me. Both as an uncle and an emissary of my father."

She looked over at the empty bed. "Then he told me who my father was."

I said, "How'd it feel learning you were Leland Belding's heir?"

"Not as strange as you'd think. Of course I'd heard of him,

knew he was a genius and rich, and it *was* strange finding out we were related. But he was dead, gone, no chance for any connection. I was more concerned with living ties."

She hadn't answered the question. I let it pass. "How did Uncle Billy chance to find you?"

"Paul had traced my roots and found *him*. He said he'd wanted to meet me for years, had been unsure of what to say or do and stayed away out of fear of doing the wrong thing. Now that the cat was out of the bag, he wanted me to hear everything from the source.

"I told him I knew about Sherry and we talked a little about her—I could tell he wasn't fond of her, but he didn't push it and I didn't challenge him. I wanted to know about my other sister, about my roots. We sat there and drank wine and he told me everything— how the three of us were the love children of Mr. Belding and an actress whom he'd loved very much but couldn't marry for social reasons. Her name was Linda. She died of childbirth complications. He showed me a picture. She was very beautiful."

"An actress," I said. When she didn't react, I said, "You look like her."

"That's quite a compliment," she said. "We were also miracle children—premature, tiny at birth, and not expected to live. Linda became sick, with septicemia, but she never stopped thinking about us, praying for us. She named us just minutes before she died. Jana, Joan, and Jewel Rae—that's me. And though we all made it, Joan had multiple deformities. Despite being rich and powerful, Mr. Belding was in no position to raise her—or any of us. He was painfully shy—actually phobic about people, especially children. From what Uncle Billy described, a bit agoraphobic as well. So Uncle Billy had us adopted by his sister. He'd thought she'd turn out to be a better mother than she did. All these years both he and Mr. Belding felt tremendously guilty about letting us go.

"I told him Paul was going to arrange a meeting with Sherry and he said he knew. Then I asked if he could arrange one with Joan."

"So he and Paul were working together."

"They were cooperating. He was evasive about Joan, but I kept pressing him and finally he told me she was somewhere in Connecticut. I said I wanted to see her. He said there was no point—she was severely disabled, had no conscious mind to speak of. I said not only did I want to see her, I wanted to be with her, to take care of her. He said that was impossible—she required full-time care and that I should concentrate on my education. I said she was a part of me. I'd never be able to concentrate on anything else again unless I could have her with me. He thought about that, asked if I could take some time off from school, and I said sure. We drove straight to a private airport, hopped on a corporate jet to New York, then took a limousine to Connecticut. I know he thought the way she looked would change my mind. But it only made me more resolute. I lay down in bed next to her, hugged her, kissed her. Felt her vibrations. When he saw that, he agreed to move her out here. The corporation bought Resthaven and set up a private wing for her. I got to interview attendants, hand-picked Elmo. She became part of my life. I came to really love her. Loved the other patients, too—I've always felt at home with the defective. If I had it all to do over again, I would have spent my life working with them."

At home. The only real home she'd known had been shared with two retarded people. A textbook insight, but she wasn't getting it.

I said, "And you changed her name."

"Yes. A new name symbolizes a new life. Both Jana and I had been given S names; I thought Joan should have one too. To fit in."

She got up, sat by her sister's side, and touched the sunken cheeks.

"She goes on forever," she said. "She's been a constant in my life. A real comfort."

"Unlike your other partner."

That cold look again. "Yes, unlike her." Then a smile. "Well, Alex, I'm pooped. We've covered a lot of ground."

"There are a few other things, if you don't mind?"

Pause. For the first time since I'd known her, she looked drawn. "No, of course not. What else would you like to know?"

There was plenty, but I was looking at her smile: stuck to her without being part of her—like a clown's makeup. Too wide, too bright. A prodrome—early warning of something. I ordered my thoughts, said, "The story you told me about being orphaned—the accident in Majorca. Where did that come from?"

"A fantasy," she said. "Wishful thinking, I guess."

"Wishing for what?"

"Romance."

"But the way you tell it, the true story of your parents is pretty romantic. Why embellish?"

She lost color. "I . . . I don't know what to tell you, Alex. When you asked me about the house, that story came out—just poured out of me. Does it matter after all these years?"

"You really have no idea where it came from?"

"What do you mean?"

"It's identical to the way Leland Belding's parents died."

She turned ghostly. "No, that couldn't ..." Then, again, the glazed smile. "How strange. Yes, I can see why that would intrigue you."

She thought, tugged her ear. "Maybe Jung was right. The collective unconscious—genetic material transmitting images as well as physical traits. Memories. Perhaps when you asked me, my unconscious kicked in. I was remembering him. Eulogizing him."

"Maybe," I said, "but something else comes to mind."

"What's that?"

"It was something Paul told you under hypnosis, then suggested you forget. Something that surfaced anyway."

"No. I ... there were no suggestions for amnesia."

"Would you remember if there were?"

She stood, clenched her hands, held them stiff at her sides.

"No, Alex. He wouldn't have done that." Pause. "And what if he did? It would only have been to protect me."

"I'm sure you're right," I said. "Pardon the armchair analysis. Occupational hazard."

She looked down at me. I took her hand and she relaxed.

"After all," I said, "he did tell you about the drowning—which was pretty emotionally loaded stuff."

"The drowning," she said. "Yes. He did tell me that. I remember it clearly."

"And you told me. And Helen." Twisting and turning the truth like wood in a lathe.

"Yes, of course I did. You were the people I felt close to. I wanted both of you to know."

She pulled away, sat down on the opposite end of the bed. Bewildered.

I said, "It must have been a terrible experience, being forced under water, someone trying to kill you. Especially at that age. The primal age."

She turned her back to me. I listened to the arrhythmic hiss and squeak of Shirlee's breathing.

"Alex?"

"Yes?"

"Do you think lies are ... a combination of elements?" Her voice was empty, dead, like that of a torture victim. "Fiction combined with repressed truth? That when we lie, what we're really doing is taking truth and changing its temporal context—bringing it forward from the past to the present?"

I said, "It's an interesting theory." Then, "If you feel up to it, I'd like to hear about how you and Sherry finally met."

"A couple of days after Uncle Billy visited me, Paul came by and told me she was ready."

"Back to his house."

"Yes. He put me up in my room and told me to meditate, be sure to get a good night's sleep. The next morning he brought me down to the living room. Everything was set up with big soft pillows and dim lighting. He told me to wait, and left. A moment later he reappeared. With her.

"When I saw her a jolt of electricity shot up my spine. I couldn't move. She must have been going through the same thing, because both of us just stared at each other for a long time. She looked *exactly* like me except she'd dyed her hair platinum-blond and was wearing sexy clothes. We started to smile—at precisely the same moment. Then we started giggling, then laughing out loud, threw out our arms and ran toward each other—it was like running into a mirror. A few minutes later and we were talking away as if we'd been best friends all our lives.

"She was funny and sweet—nothing at all like Paul had described. Not selfish or spoiled the way Uncle Billy had implied. It was obvious she wasn't highly educated, which surprised me because I knew she'd grown up rich. But she was bright. And well-bred—her posture, the way she crossed her legs. She told me she was studying to be an actress, had already starred in one film. I asked her the title but she just laughed and changed the subject. She wanted to know all about grad school, all about psych, said she was so proud that I was going to get a Ph.D. We really hit it off, discovering that we liked the same foods, used the same toothpaste and mouthwash and deodorant. Noticing little mannerisms we had in common."

"Like this?" I tugged on my earlobe.

"No." She laughed. "I'm afraid that's all me."

"Did she talk about her home life?"

"Not much that first time—we really didn't want to talk about anything but *us*. And she hadn't been told about Joan yet—Paul said she wasn't ready for that. So we concentrated on just the two of us. We stayed in that room all day. The first time I had a hint of anything negative was when we got on the topic of men. She told me she'd *done* lots of men, so many she'd lost count. She was sounding me out—wanted to see if I approved or disapproved. I wasn't judgmental, but told her I was a one-man woman. She refused to believe that at first, then said she hoped he was one hell of a man. That's when I told her all about you. For a moment a scary look came into her eyes—predatory. Hungry. As if she *hated* me for loving. But then it disappeared so quickly that I thought I'd imagined it. If I'd known better, I would have protected you, believe me, Alex. Protected us."

"When did it start going bad?"

Her eyes moistened. "Soon after, though I didn't realize it at the time. We were supposed to go shopping together, but she didn't show. When I got back to Paul's house, he told me she'd packed her bags and left town without telling anyone. That it was her pattern—she had no impulse control. Not to worry, it wasn't my fault. She finally came back, two weeks later, in terrible shape—bruised, groggy, unable to remember anything that had happened other than that she'd ended up in a bar in Reno. From that point on, that's what it was like—drop in, drop out. Fugue states, drug abuse."

"Jana. Your dissertation."

That jolted her.

I said, "I read it. I was interested—in you. Whose idea was it?"

"It started out as a joke. I'd just been through a rough month with her—a couple of overdoses, lots of verbal abuse. And I was under pressure, needed to come up with a dissertation topic or apply for an extension from the department—my second one. I was unloading on Paul about how much she frustrated me, how hard she was making it for me. That it would have been easier to be her therapist than her sister. He laughed at that, said being her therapist was no picnic either. We talked about the loss of control that comes from dealing with people like that. Then he said, why didn't I put myself in the therapist role—as a means of establishing some sense of control in the relationship—and write it all down."

"Working it through."

"Paul said she owed it to me."

"Sounds like Paul was angry at her too."

"He was frustrated—all those years, and she kept getting worse. Deteriorating. Toward the end she was downright paranoid, near psychotic."

"Paranoid about what?"

"Everything. The last time she came back—the time she wrecked my practice—she was convinced I was out to get her, that I was revealing her personal secrets to my patients, humiliating her. It came from her own pain, but she was projecting it onto me—blaming me, the way she'd done years before."

"Tell me about that."

"It was a long time ago, Alex."

"I'd still like to hear about it."

She thought for a while, shrugged and smiled. "If it's that important to you."

I smiled back.

She said, "It happened after she got married—to Italian nobility, a marchese named Benito di Orano whom her mother introduced her to. Ten years younger than her, suave, handsome, heir to some sort of shoe company—another impulsive thing—they'd only known each other a week, flew to Liechtenstein and had a civil ceremony. He bought her a Lamborghini, moved her into his villa overlooking the Spanish Steps. Paul and I hoped she'd finally settle down. But Benito turned out to be a sadist and a druggie. He beat her, doped her up, took her to the family palazzo in Venice, crammed her with dope, and gave her to his friends—as a party favor. When she woke up, he told her he'd had the marriage annulled because she was trash, then kicked her out. Literally.

"She crawled back to the States like a worm, burst into my office in the middle of a session, screaming and bawling and begging me to help her. I called Paul. Both of us tried to calm her down, persuade her to admit herself. But she wouldn't cooperate and she wasn't a clear and present danger, so there was nothing we could do, legally. She stomped out, cursing both of us. A few days later she was the old Sherry again—foul-mouthed, popping pills, back on the road, constantly on the move. From time to time I heard from her—middle of the night phone calls, postcards that tried to be friendly. Once or twice I even drove out to the airport to see her between planes. We'd chat, have drinks, pretend everything between us was okay. But her rage hadn't dissipated. The next time she came back to L.A. to stay, she got close to me again, then started in with her *follow-up visits*. God, I loved my work, Alex. Still miss it."

"What brought things to a head?"

"The party. She loved parties as much as I hated them. But Paul wanted *me* at this one—ordered *her* to stay away. She argued, threw a fit. He told her that both of us couldn't go and I'd be the one. This was for psychologists. Professionals only. A special occasion for him and he wouldn't see it ruined by her acting-out. That set her off—she attacked him, tried to stab him with a pair of scissors. The first time she'd ever gotten physical with him. He overpowered her, gave her a large dose of barbiturates, and locked her in her room. Saturday night, right after the party, he let her out. Told me she looked calm, was actually pleasant—remorseful. Forgive and forget."

"How did you handle the party?" I asked. "Meeting Mrs. Blalock's friends."

"For them I was Sherry—smiling and looking sexy. It wasn't that hard—there wasn't much substance to her. For all the psych people I was me. The two groups didn't mingle at all, and mostly I stayed with Uncle Billy."

Magpies and swans . . .

"Forgive and forget," I said. "But she'd done neither."

She stared at me. "Must we go further, Alex? It's so ugly. She's gone now, out of my life—out of our lives. And I have a chance for a new start."

She raised my hand to her lips. Licked the knuckles.

"Hard to begin without ending," I said. "Closure. For both of us."

She sighed. "For you," she said. "Only for you. Because you mean so much to me."

"Thanks. I know it's hard, but I really think it's best."

She squeezed my hand. "I got your message on Sunday. I was disappointed, but I could tell from your voice that it wasn't farewell. You were nervous, had left the lines open."

I didn't argue.

"So I was thinking about whether to call you, or wait until you called me to set up another date. I decided to wait, let you move at your own pace. You'd been on my mind all day and when the knock on my door sounded, I thought it *was* you. But it was her. All covered with blood. And laughing. I asked her what had happened— had she been in an accident? Was she okay? And then she told me. Laughing. What she'd done—the horror of it and she was laughing!"

Sharon burst into tears, began shaking violently, doubled over and held her head.

"She didn't do it by herself," I said. "Who helped her?"

She shook some more.

"Was it D.J. Rasmussen?"

She looked up, tear-streaked, mouth open. "You knew D.J.?"

"I met him."

"Met him? Where?"

"At your house. Both of us thought you were dead. We came there to pay our last respects."

She tore at her face. "Oh, God, poor, poor D.J. Until she told me what she'd . . . what they'd done, I'd never known he was one of her . . . conquests."

"He was the only one she held on to," I said. "The most vulnerable. The most violent."

She groaned and straightened, pulled herself to her feet and began circling the room, slowly, like a sleepwalker, then faster and faster, tugging her earlobe so hard I thought she'd tear it off.

"Yes, it was D.J. She laughed when she told me that, laughed about how she'd gotten him to do it—using dope, booze. Her body. Mostly her body. I'll never forget the way she put it: 'I did *him,* so he'd do *them.*' Laughing, always laughing, about all the *blood,* how Paul and Suzanne had begged. And poor Lourdes, so sweet, leaving, on her way out, when they caught her coming down the stairs. Sunday was her day off—she'd stayed late to help tidy the house. Laughing, about how *she'd* tied them, watched as D.J. *did* them— with a baseball bat and a gun. Him thinking all the time that it was *me* he was doing it for—*me* who'd used him."

She ran over and sank to her knees. "That's what amused her the most, Alex! That he'd never known the truth—all the time he thought he was doing it for *me!*"

She took hold of my shirt, pulled me to her, to her breasts. "She said that made *me* a murderer too. That when you really got down to it, we were one and the same!"

I helped her up, then lowered her back to the bed. She lay down, curled fetally, eyes wide open, arms wrapped around her trunk like a straitjacket.

I patted her, stroked her, said, "She wasn't you. You weren't her."

She uncurled her arms and put them around me. Drew me down, bathed my face with kisses. "Thank you, Alex. Thank you for saying that."

Slowly, gently, I drew myself away, still patting. Saying, "Go on. Get it out." The therapist's prompt . . .

She said, "Then her laughter got crazy—weird, hysterical. All of a sudden she stopped laughing completely, looked at me, then down at herself, all the blood, and started to tear off her clothes. Coming down hard. Realizing what she'd done: By destroying Paul, she'd destroyed herself. He was everything to her, the closest she'd ever come to a father. She needed him, depended on him, and now he was gone and it was her fault. She fell apart, right before my eyes. Decompensating. Sobbing—not play-acting now, real tears—just wailing like a helpless baby. Begging me to bring him back, saying I was smart, I was a doctor, I could do it.

"I could have calmed her down. The way I'd done so many

times before. Instead, I told her Paul was never coming back, that it was her fault, she'd have to pay, no one would be able to protect her from this one, not even Uncle Billy. She looked at me in a way I'd never seen before—scared to death. Like a condemned woman. Started in again, begging me to bring Paul back. I repeated that he was dead. Said the word over and over. Dead. Dead. Dead. She tried to come to me for comfort. I pushed her away, slapped her hard, once, twice. She backed away from me, stumbled, fell, reached into her purse and took out her daiquiri flask. Drank it, slobbering and crying, letting it dribble down her chin. Then out came her pills. She took handfuls of them, began gobbling them down. Stopping every few seconds to stare at me—daring me to stop her, the way I'd done so many times before. But I didn't. She lurched into my bedroom, still carrying her purse—stark naked, but with the purse, she looked so . . . pathetic.

"I followed her in. She took something else out of the purse. A gun. A little gold-plated pistol I'd never seen before. *My new toy,* she said. *Like it? Got it on Rodeo fucking Drive. Broke it in today.* Then she pointed it at me, tightened her finger on the trigger. I was sure I was going to die, but I didn't beg, just remained calm, looked her straight in the eye, and said, 'Go ahead, spill some more innocent blood. Get filthier, you worthless piece of scum.'"

"Then the strangest look came onto her face. She said, 'I'm sorry, partner,' put the gun to her temple, and pulled the trigger."

Silence.

"I just sat there looking at her for a while. Watching her bleed, her soul pass out of her. Wondering where it was headed. Then I called Uncle Billy. He took care of the rest."

My chest hurt. I realized I'd been holding my breath and let it out.

She lay there, gradually loosening, getting dreamy-eyed. "And that's all there is, my darling. An ending. And a beginning. For us."

She sat up, smoothed her hair, loosened the top button of her dress, and leaned forward. "I'm cleansed now. Free. Ready for you, Alex—ready to give you everything, to give myself in a way I've never given to anyone. I've waited so long for this moment, Alex. Never thought it would come." She reached for me.

Now it was my turn to get up and pace.

"This is a lot to handle," I said.

"I know it is, darling, but we've got time. All the time in the world. I'm finally free."

"Free," I said. "And rich. I never thought of myself as a kept man."

"Oh, but you wouldn't be. I'm really not an heiress. Mr. Belding's will says the money stays in the corporation."

"Still," I said, "with Uncle Billy administering everything—the way he feels about you, life's bound to be pretty luxurious."

"No, it doesn't have to be. I don't need that. Money was never important to me—not for its own sake, or for the things it could buy. That was *her* thing. When she found out who she was, she freaked out, started screaming at Uncle Billy, accused him of ripping her off and threatened to take him to court. Such greed—she already had more than she needed. She even tried to get me to go along with her, but I refused. That really made her vicious."

"How far did she go with the threat?"

"Not far. Uncle Billy managed to calm her down."

"How?"

"I have no idea. But let's not talk about her anymore. Or money, or anything negative. I'm here, with you. In this wonderful place, where no one can find us or soil us. You and me and Shirlee. We'll make a family, be together forever."

She came toward me, lips parted for a kiss.

I held her at arm's length.

"It's not that simple, Sharon."

Her eyes went big. "I . . . I don't understand."

"There are problems. Things that don't make sense."

"Alex." Tears. "Please don't play games with me, not after what I've been through."

She tried pushing against me. I held her fast.

"Oh, Alex, please don't do this to me. I want to touch you, want you to hold me!"

"Sherry killing Kruse," I said. "It wasn't about the party—that may have been the final straw, but she'd been planning it, paying off D.J. Rasmussen for at least two weeks before then. Thousands of dollars. Priming him for the big job."

She gasped, reversed her movements, trying to free herself from my grasp. Still I held fast.

"No," she said. "No, I don't believe that! As bad as she was, that's not true!"

"It's true, all right. And you know it better than anyone."

"What do you mean?" And all at once her face—that flawless face—was ugly.

Ugly with rage. *Empathic failure* . . .

"What I mean is that you set it up. Planted the seeds. Sent her a six-year-old dissertation and confirmed her worst anxieties."

Her eyes went wild. "Go to hell."

She twisted, tried to free herself.

"You know it's true, Sharon."

"Of course it isn't true. She didn't read. She was a stupid, stupid girl, didn't *like* books! And you're stupid for even saying something like that!"

"This is one book she would have struggled through. Because you'd been priming her for it—using the same techniques Kruse used on you. Verbal manipulations, hypnotic suggestions. Things you suggested to her while she was under, then ordered her to forget—about Kruse and you, his liking you better. She was borderline from the beginning, but you pushed her over the border. The sad thing is, you'd gotten over there yourself, first."

She snarled, turned her fingers into claws and tried to sink her nails into my hands. We wrestled, panting. I managed to get both of her wrists in one hand, used the other to hold her fast.

"Let go of me, you bastard! Ow, you're hurting me! Fuck you, let go!"

"How long did it take, Sharon? To break her, turn her on Paul?"

"I didn't! You're crazy! Why would I?"

"To clean things up. Get free. Get rid of someone you finally realized had been manipulating you instead of helping you. What made *you* break? Finding the two of them? Up in her room, doing what they'd probably been doing for years? Or maybe she'd told you about it when you hypnotized her. Incest. The worst kind. Daddy fucking her. He was your daddy too. And, by doing it, fucking you over."

"No! No, no, no, no! You slime-bastard, you lying fucking bastard! No! Shut up! Get out, you fuck, you piece of shit!"

The filth poured out of her, the way I'd heard it pour out of her sister. The look on her face, that of the girl in the flame dress, loathing me. Murderous.

I said, "Two birds with one stone, Sharon. Turn Sherry on Kruse, then wait for her to come for you. You'd been planning it for months—at least half a year. That's when you told Elmo to get another job. You knew Resthaven was closing down, because Resthaven was something Uncle Billy had set up for Shirlee and you were taking Shirlee out of there. To your new home. You and me and Shirlee makes three. A new partnership."

"No, no! That's fucking crazy—you're out of your mind! She had D.J.—dangerous, violent, you said so yourself. Two against one! I'd have been crazy to put myself in that kind of danger!"

She fought one hand loose, finally got a nail in and ripped downward. I felt pain, wetness, shoved her away from me, hard. She flew backwards, the backs of her legs hit the bed, and she sprawled. Panting. Sobbing. Mouthing silent obscenities.

I said, "D.J. was no threat to you. Because all along, he thought it was you he'd been making it with, you who'd paid him to kill Kruse. Sherry couldn't risk blowing that, telling him he'd been deceived and having him turn on her. She had to take care of you by herself. Thought she'd be able to surprise you. But you had the advantage. She stepped right into your trap and you were ready. With your gold-plated twenty-two."

She kicked her feet in the air, waved her arms. Tantrum. Early trauma. Bad genes . . .

"Fucking . . . bastard . . . fuckdick slimebastard . . ."

"First you shot her," I said. "Then you poured dope and booze down her throat. A good forensic analysis would be able to show she'd swallowed all of it after she died, but there'll never be a forensic analysis, because Uncle Billy took care of it. Along with everything else."

"Lies, all lies, you fuck!"

"I don't think so, Sharon. And now you've got everything. Enjoy it."

I backed away from her.

"You can't prove a fucking thing," she said.

"I know," I said. And made it to the door.

A gurgling, roaring sound—the only thing I could think of was a cesspool overflowing—came from deep inside her. She picked up the water glass she'd gotten for me, drew her arm back, and threw it at me.

If it had hit, it would have done damage. I ducked. It bounced off the plastic wall, landed on the carpet with an ineffectual thud.

"Your right hand," I said. "At least I'm finally sure which side of the mirror I've been looking at."

She whipped her eyes down to her hand, stared at it as if it had betrayed her.

I left. Had to walk for a long time in the darkness before I stopped hearing her screams.

36

I heard the buggy before I saw it, a night-moth hum, coming from somewhere to my left. Then headlights swept the desert like some prison searchlight, washing over me, halting its arc, preserving me like a specimen in amber.

Within moments it was at my side.

"Step in, Doctor." Vidal's rasp. Only he, in the driver's seat.

As I took my seat he ran his penlight over the blood on my hand. The desert air had dried it to maroon grit.

"Superficial," I said.

"We'll take care of that when we get back."

Unconcerned.

"You heard everything," I said.

"Constant monitoring is necessary," he said. "She needs care, watching. You saw that for yourself."

"You're a big fan of show-and-tell," I said. "Taking Sharon to see Joan, hoping that would dissuade her. Putting Sharon on display for me, in hopes of shutting my mouth."

He began driving.

"What makes you think," I said, "that you'll be any more successful?"

"One can only try," he said.

We crossed the desert. More stars had come out, flooding the earth with icy light. Glazing it.

I said, "When did Belding die?"

"Years ago."

"How many years ago?"

"Before the girls were reunited. Is the exact date important?"

"It was to Seaman Cross."

"This isn't about Cross, is it?"

"What was the diagnosis?" I asked.

"Alzheimer's disease. Before the doctors gave us that, we just called it senility. A gradual, nasty fade."

"Must have been a strain on the corporation."

"Yes," he said, "but on the other hand, we had time to prepare. There were early signs—forgetfulness, wandering attention—but he'd always been an eccentric. His quirks concealed it for a while. Contacting Cross was the first thing that made me take notice—it was totally out of character. Leland had always been obsessed with his privacy, detested journalists of any sort. A change in habits indicated something seriously wrong."

"Like the playboy phase that preceded his breakdown."

"More serious. This was permanent. Organic. I realize now he must have felt his mind slipping away and wanted to be immortalized."

I said, "The things that Cross described—the long hair and nails, the altar, defecating openly. They were true, then. Symptoms."

"The book was a fraud," he said. "Fictional trash."

We drove on.

I said, "Convenient of Belding to die when he did. It spared him—and you—confronting Sharon and Sherry."

"Ever so rarely Nature acts in benevolent ways."

"If She hadn't, I'm sure you would have figured something out. Now he can remain a benevolent figure for her. She'll never know he wanted to kill her."

"Do you think that knowledge would be good for her— therapeutic?"

I didn't answer.

"My role in life," he said, "is to solve problems, not create them. In that sense, I'm a healer. Just like yourself."

The analogy offended me less than I'd have imagined. I said, "Taking care of others really has been your thing, hasn't it? Belding— everything from his sex life to his public image, and when that got hard to handle, when he started going for the night life, you were there to assume executive responsibility. Your sister, Sherry, Sharon, Willow Glen, the corporation—doesn't it weigh on you once in a while?"

I thought I saw him smile in the darkness, was certain he touched his throat and grimaced, as if it were too hard to talk.

Several miles later he said, "Have you reached a decision, Doctor?"

"About what?"

"About probing further."

"My questions have been answered, if that's what you mean."

"What I mean is, will you continue to stir things up and ruin what's left of a very ill young woman's life?"

"Not much of a life," I said.

"Better than any alternative. She'll be well taken care of," he said. "Protected. And the world will be protected from her."

"What about after you're gone?"

"There are men," he said. "Competent men. A line of command. Everything's been worked out."

"Line of command," I said. "Belding was a cowboy, never had one. But once he was dead, it was a different story. With no one to churn out patents, you had to hire creativity, reorganize the corporate structure. That made Magna more vulnerable to outside attack—you had to solidify your power base. Having all three of Belding's daughters under your thumb was one big step in that direction. How'd you get Sherry to back off from her legal threats?"

"Quite simple," he said. "I took her on a tour of corporate headquarters—our research and development center, the highest of high-technology enterprises. Told her I'd be happy to step down and have her run everything—she could be the new chairperson of Magna, bear the responsibility for fifty-two thousand employees, thousands of projects. The very thought terrified her—she wasn't an intellectual girl, couldn't balance a checkbook. She ran out of the building. I caught up with her and suggested an alternative."

"Money."

"More than she'd be able to spend in several lifetimes."

"Now she's gone," I said. "No more need to make payments."

"Doctor, you have an extremely naïve view of life. Money is the means, not the end. And the corporation would have survived—*will* survive, with or without me, or anyone else. When things attain a certain size, they become permanent. One can dredge a lake, not an ocean."

"What *is* the end?"

"Rhythm. Balance. Keeping everything *going*—a certain *ecology*, if you will."

A few minutes later: "You still haven't answered my question, Doctor."

"I won't stir anything up. What would be the point?"

"Good. What about your detective friend?"

"He's a realist."

"Good for him."

"Are you going to kill me anyway? Have Royal Hummel do his thing?"

He laughed. "Of course not. How amusing that you still see me as Attila the Hun. No, Doctor, you're in no danger. What would be the *point?*"

"For one, I know your family secrets."

"Seaman Cross redux? Another *book?*"

More laughter. It turned into coughing. Several miles later the ranch came into view, perfect and unreal as a movie set.

He said, "Speaking of Royal Hummel, there's something I want you to know. He'll no longer be functioning in a security capacity. Your comments on Linda's death gave me quite a bit of pause— amazing what a fresh perspective will do. Royal and Victor were professionals. Accidents needn't happen with professionals. At best, they were sloppy. At worst . . . You brought me insight late in life, Doctor. For that I owe you a large debt."

"I was *theorizing,* Vidal. I don't want anyone's blood on my conscience, not even Hummel's."

"Oh, for God's sake, will you please stop being melodramatic, young man! No one's *blood* is at stake. Royal simply has a new job. Cleaning our chicken coops. Several tons of guano need to be shoveled each day. He's getting on in years, his blood pressure's too high, but he'll manage."

"What if he refuses?"

"Oh, he won't."

He aimed the vehicle at the empty corral.

"You gave the silent-partner photo to Kruse," I said. "The girls were photographed over there."

"Fascinating the things one dredges up in old attics."

"Why?" I said. "Why'd you let Kruse go on for so long?"

"At one point, until recently, I believed he was helping Sharon— helping both of them. He was a charismatic man, very articulate."

"But he was bleeding your sister before he met Sharon. Twenty years of blackmail—of mind games."

He put the buggy in idle and looked at me. All the charm had dropped away, and I saw the same cold rawness in his eyes that I'd just witnessed in Sharon's. Genes . . . The collective unconscious . . .

"Be that as it may, Doctor. Be that as it may."

He drove quickly, stopped the buggy and parked.

We got out and walked toward the patio. Two men in dark

clothing and ski masks stood waiting. One held a dark piece of elastic.

"Please don't be frightened," said Vidal. "That will come off as soon as it's safe for both of us. You'll be delivered safe and sound. Try to enjoy the ride."

"Why don't I feel reassured?"

More laughter, dry and forced. "Doctor, it's been stimulating. Who knows, we may meet again one day—another party."

"I don't think so. I hate parties."

"To tell the truth," he said, "I've tired of them myself." He turned serious. "But given even a slim chance that we do come face to face, I'd appreciate it if you don't acknowledge me. Invoke professional confidentiality and pretend we've never met."

"No problem there."

"Thank you, Doctor. You've comported yourself as a gentleman. Is there anything else?"

"Lourdes Escobar, the maid. A true innocent victim."

"Compensation's been made in that regard."

"Dammit, Vidal, money can't fix everything!"

"It can't fix *anything*," he said. "If it makes you feel any better, during the time she lived in the States, half of her family was wiped out by the guerrillas. Same death, no compensation. Those who survived were tortured, their homes burned to the ground. They've been granted immigration papers, brought over here, set up with businesses, given land. Compared to life itself, admittedly feeble, but the best I can offer. Any additional suggestions?"

"Justice would be nice."

"Any suggestions about improving the justice that's been meted out?"

I had nothing to say.

"Well, then," he said, "is there anything I can do for *you*?"

"As a matter of fact, there is a small favor. An arrangement."

When I told him what it was, and exactly how I wanted it done, he laughed so hard it plunged him into a coughing attack that bent him double. He took out a handkerchief and wiped his mouth, spat, laughed some more. When he pulled the handkerchief away, the silk was stained with something dark.

He tried to talk. Nothing came out. The men in black looked at each other.

He finally found his voice again. "Excellent, Doctor," he said. "Great minds moving in the same direction. Now, let's attend to that hand."

37

I was dropped off on the University campus. Pulling the blindfold off, I made my way home on foot. Once inside my house I found I couldn't tolerate being there, threw some things into a bag, and called the exchange to say I'd be going away for a couple of days, to hold my calls.

"Any forwarding number, Doctor?"

No active patients or pending emergencies. I said, "No, I'll check in."

"A real vacation, huh?"

"Something like that. Goodnight."

"Don't you want to pick up the messages that are already on your board?"

"Not really."

"Oka-ay, but there's this one guy who's been driving me crazy. Called three times and got rude when I wouldn't give him your home number."

"What's his name?"

"Sanford Moretti. Sounds like a lawyer—says he wants you to work on a case for him or something like that. Kept trying to tell me you'd really want to hear from him."

My reply made her laugh. "*Doctor* Delaware! I didn't know you used that kind of language."

I got in the car and drove away, found myself heading west, and ended up on Ocean Avenue, off Pico. Not far from the Santa Monica Pier, which had closed up for the night and darkened to a knurled clump of rooftops over a thatch of bowed pilings. Not far from the (vulgar) Pacific, but no OC VU on this block. The sea breeze had taken leave; the ocean smelled like garbage. The street hosted beer-and-shot bars with Polynesian names and "day-week-month" motels given a wide berth by the auto club.

I checked into a place called Blue Dreams—twelve brown, salt-smudged doors arranged around a parking lot badly in need of resurfacing, the neon tubes in the VACANCY sign cracked and drained of gas. A pasty-faced biker-hopeful with a dangling crucifix earring manned the front desk—doing me the favor of taking my money while making love to a slab of fried catfish and staring at a California Raisins commercial. Candy and condom machines stood side by side in the shoulder-cramping lobby, along with a pocket-comb dispenser, and the California Penal Code's reflections on theft and defrauding an innkeeper.

I took a room on the south side, paying for a week in advance. Nine by nine, insecticide stink—no gnats here—a single narrow, filmed window exposing a slice of brick wall turned mauve by reflected streetlight, mismatched wood-grain furniture, skinny bed under a spread laundered to dishwater-colored fuzz, pay TV bolted to the floor. A quarter in the pay slot yielded an hour of fizzy sound and jaundiced skin tones. There were three quarters in my pocket. I tossed two out the window.

I lay on the bed, let the TV run down, and listened to noise. Bass thumps from the jukebox of the bar next door, so loud it seemed as if someone was being hurled against the wall in two-four time; angry laughter and truncated street-talk in English, Spanish, and a thousand undecipherable tongues, canned laughter from the TV in the adjacent room, toilet flushes, faucet hisses, movement cracks, door slams, car horns, a scatter of sharp reports that could have been gunshots or backfires or the sound of two hands applauding. And backing it all, the Doppler drone of the freeway.

An Overland symphony. Within moments I was robbed of twelve years.

The room was a sweatbox. I stayed inside for three days, subsisting on pizza and cola from a place that promised to deliver hot and cold and lied about both. For the most part I did what I'd been avoiding for so long. Had pushed away by chasing the inadequacies of others, throwing down cloaks over mudholes. Introspection. Such a prissy word for scooper-dips deep into the wellspring of the soul. The scooper honed sharp and jagged.

For three days I went through all of it: rage, tears, tension so visceral my teeth chattered and my muscles threatened to go into tetany. A loneliness that I would have gladly anesthetized with pain.

By the fourth day I felt sapped and placid, was proud I didn't mistake that for cure. That afternoon, I left the motel to keep my appointment: a sprint down the block to the sidewalk paper rack. The remaining quarter down the hatch and the evening edition was mine, gripped tightly under my arm, like pornography.

Bottom left of page one, complete with picture.

L.A.P.D. CAPTAIN CHARGED WITH SEXUAL MISCONDUCT RESIGNS

Maura Bannon
Staff Writer

A Los Angeles police captain, accused of having sexual relations with several underage female Police Scouts while on duty, resigned today after a police disciplinary board recommended dismissal.

The three-member Board of Rights panel ordered Cyril Leon Trapp, 45, terminated immediately from duty and recommended retroactive loss of all L.A.P.D. pensions, benefits and privileges. In accordance with what both Trapp's attorney and a police spokesman described as a negotiated settlement, Trapp agreed to register as a sex offender, forfeit appeal of the board's decision, sign an affidavit agreeing never again to work in law enforcement, and pay "substantial financial restitution, including full fees for medical and psychiatric treatment" to his victims, suspected of numbering over a dozen. In exchange, no criminal charges are being filed, an alternative which theoretically could have included indictments for statutory rape, narcotics abuse, sexual abuse of a minor and multiple misdemeanors.

The offenses, to which Trapp pleaded no contest, took place over a five-year period during which he served as a sergeant in the department's Hollywood Division, and may have continued while he was a lieutenant at the Ramparts Division and at the West Los Angeles Division, where he was promoted to captain, last year, following the sudden heart attack death of the previous captain, Robert L. Rogers.

While at Hollywood, Trapp's name also surfaced in connection with the burglary scandal in which police officers broke rear windows of stores and warehouses on their patrols, tripping burglar alarms, then notified the police dispatcher that they were handling the call. The officers then proceeded to loot the premises, using police cruisers to cart away stolen goods, then filed false burglary reports. No charges were filed against Trapp, who was characterized by prosecutors, at that time, as a "cooperative witness."

With regard to the current case, Trapp was accused of luring female scouts into his office under the guise of offering "career guidance," plying them with beer, wine, "premixed, canned cocktails," and marijuana before making sexual advances. Allegations of fondling were made in thirteen cases, with actual intercourse believed to have taken place with at least seven girls, ages 15 to 17. Though the Board of Rights refused to specify what led to the investigation of Trapp, a police source reports that one of the victims experienced emotional problems due to the molestation, was taken for counseling, and revealed to her therapist what had happened. The therapist then informed the Department of Social Services, who contacted the L.A.P.D.

Corroboration of the charges was received from several other victims. However, none of the girls was willing to testify in court, leading the District Attorney's office to conclude that successful criminal prosecution of Trapp was "unlikely."

When it was suggested that the settlement constituted a slap on the wrist for an individual who could have been sentenced to a substantial jail term, the board chairman, Cmdr. Walter D. Smith, said, "The Department wants to make it very clear that it will not tolerate sexual misconduct of any sort on the part of any officer, no matter how high-ranking. However, we are also sensitive to the emotional needs of victims and couldn't force these girls into the psychological trauma of testifying. The board's action today guarantees that this officer will never again work in law enforcement and will lose every cent he has earned as a police officer. To me that sounds like a pretty good deal."

Trapp's attorney, Thatcher Friston, refused to divulge his client's future plans, other than to say that the disgraced officer is "expected to leave the state, maybe even the country, to work in agriculture. Mr. Trapp's always been interested in poultry farming. Now perhaps he'll have a chance to try it."

I read it once more, tore it out of the paper, and folded it into a paper airplane. When I finally landed the plane in the toilet, I left the motel.

I went home, felt like a new tenant, if not a new man. Was sitting down at my desk ready to plow through accumulated papers when a knock sounded at the front door.

I opened it. Milo came in, wearing his police ID tag on the lapel of a brown suit that reeked of squad-room smoke, glaring at me under black brows, his big face clouded.

"Where the hell have you been?"

"Out."

"Out where?"

"I don't want to get into it right now."

"Get into it anyway."

I didn't speak.

He said, "Jesus! You were supposed to be making a few calls—doing the safe stuff, remember? Instead you disappear. Haven't you learned a goddamned thing!"

"Sorry, Mom." Then, when I saw the look on his face: "I did do the safe stuff, Milo. *Then* I disappeared. I left a message with my service."

"Right. Very comforting." He pinched his nose. " 'Dr. Delaware will be out for a couple of *da-ays.*' " Unpinch: " 'Where to, honey?' " Pinch. " 'He didn't sa-ay.' "

I said, "I needed to get away. I'm fine. I was never in danger."

He swore, punched his palm, tried to use his height to advantage by looming over me. I went back into the library and he followed me there, digging deep in his coat pocket and pulling out a crumpled piece of newsprint.

As he started to unfold it, I said, "Saw it already."

"I'll bet you have." He leaned on the desk. "How, Alex? How the *fuck*?"

"Not now," I said.

"What, all of a sudden it's let's-play-hide-and-seek time?"

"I just don't want to get into it right now."

"Bye-bye, Cyril," he said, to the ceiling. "For the first time in my life, wishes come true—it's like I've got this goddamned genie. Problem is, I don't know what he looks like, who or what to rub."

"Can't you just accept good fortune? Kick back and enjoy?"

"I like making my own fortune."

"Make an exception."

"Could you?"

"I hope so."

"Come on, Alex, what the hell's going on? One minute we're talking theory; the next, Trapp's neck-deep in shit and the speedboats are revving."

"Trapp's a very small part of it," I said. "I just don't want to paint the whole picture right now."

He stared at me, went into the kitchen and came back with a carton of milk and a stale bagel. Tearing off a chunk of bagel and washing it down, he finally said, "Temporary reprieve, pal. But some day—soon—we're gonna have ourselves a little sit-down."

"There's nothing to sit down about, Milo. It's like an expert once told me, no evidence, nothing real."

He held the stare a while longer before his face softened.

"Okay," he said. "I get it. No neat wrap-up. Case of the law-enforcement blue balls: You were angling for a love affair with Little Miss Justice, found you couldn't go all the way. But hell, you handled that kind of thing in high school, should be able to handle it now that you're all grown up."

"I'll let you know when I'm all grown up."

"Screw you, Peter Pan." Then: "How're you doing, Alex? Seriously."

"Good."

"All things considered."

I nodded.

"You look," he said, "as if you've been considering lots of things."

"Just tuning up the system . . . Milo, I appreciate that you care, appreciate all the things you've done for me. Right now I could really use being alone."

"Yeah, right," he said.

"See you later."

He left without another word.

Robin came home the next day, wearing a dress I'd never seen before and the look of a first-grader about to recite in front of the class. I accepted her embrace, then asked her what had brought her back.

"You're not happy to see me," she said.

"I am. You took me by surprise." I carried her suitcase into the living room.

She said, "I was thinking of coming down anyway." Slipping her arm through mine. "I missed you, really wanted to talk to you last night and called. The operator at the service said you'd gone away without telling anyone where or for how long. She said you'd sounded different, tired and angry—'cussing like a trucker.' I was worried."

"Charity time," I said, stepping back.

She looked at me as if for the first time.

I said, "I'm sorry, but right at this moment, I'm not going to be the man you want."

"I've pushed it too far," she said.

"No. It's just that I've had to do a lot of thinking. Long overdue."

She blinked hard, her eyes got wet, and she turned away. "Shit."

I said, "Some of it has to do with you; a lot of it doesn't. I know you want to take care of me—know that's important to you. But right now I'm not ready for that, couldn't accept it in a way that would give you what you want."

She slumped, sat down on the couch.

I sat facing her, said, "That's not anger speaking. Maybe *some* of it is, but it's not that simple. There are some things I need to work out for myself. Time I have to take."

She blinked some more, put on a smile that looked so painful, she might have just carved it in her flesh. "Who am I to complain about that?"

"No," I said, "this isn't about revenge. There's nothing to take revenge for—in the end, you did me a favor."

"Glad to oblige," she said. The tears began to flow, but she staunched them. "No, I won't do that—you deserve better than that. Don't do the crime if you can't do the time, right?"

I extended my hand. She shook her head, bit her lip.

"There was another man," she said. "Nothing serious—old flame from college, coffee and pie. I nipped it in the bud. But it came so close. I still feel I've betrayed you."

I said, "I've betrayed you too."

She gave a low moan and closed her eyes. "Who?"

"Old flame from college."

"Is she . . . Are you still . . ."

"No, it's not like that, never was like that. She captured my head, not my cock. Now she's gone forever. But it changed me."

She walked to the end of the room, folded her arms over her breasts and said nothing for a while. Then: "Alex, what's going to become of us?"

"I don't know. A happy ending would be nice. But I have a ways to go before I'm going to be much use to you—to anyone."

"I like you just the way you are."

"Like you, too," I said, so automatically that it made both of us laugh.

She faced me. I extended my hand. She came back, looked up at me. We touched, merged, began undressing each other wordlessly, fell back on the couch and made love there. Made sex. Competent, seamless union born of practice and ritual, so seamless it verged on incestuous.

When it was over, she sat up and said, "It's not going to be that easy, is it?"

I shook my head. "What is that's worthwhile?"

She peeled away from me, got up, stood in front of the picture window. Backlit, naked, curls hanging down her back like a cluster of grapes.

"The shop's probably a godawful mess," she said. "Messages slipped under the door, all those backed-up orders."

"Go ahead," I said. "Do what you need to do."

She turned, ran back to me, lay on me, sobbed on my chest. We stayed together, cheek to cheek, before the restlessness set in, then went our separate ways.

Sharon. Kruse. The Ratman. Even Larry. Enough problems among us to fill a textbook.

Alone again, I thought of mine, all the unfinished business. I dealt with it by taking the easy way out: found a number in my Rolodex and dialed.

Fourth ring: "Hello?"

"Mrs. Burkhalter? Denise? This is Dr. Delaware."

"Oh. Hi."

"If this is a bad time—"

"No, no, it's . . . I'm . . . It's funny, I was just thinking of you. Darren's still, uh, crying a lot."

"Some of that can be expected."

"Actually," she said, "he's crying more. Lots. Since the last time he saw you. And not sleeping or eating right."

"Has anything changed since the last time I saw you?"

"Just the money—though I can't feel that yet. It's not real. I mean, Mr. Worthy says it could take months for it to come in. Meanwhile, we're still getting bank letters and my husband's insurance company is still dragging their damned . . . Why am I going on like this? That's not what you want to hear about."

"I want to hear anything you want to tell me about."

Pause. "I'm real sorry. About the way I ran my mouth at you."

"That's okay. You've been through plenty."

"Isn't that the truth. From day one—" Her voice broke. "I keep going on about other stuff, and it's my baby I'm all shook about—crying and yelling and hitting at me, not wanting to know me like he used to. Meanwhile, all the waiting. No one's around. I don't know what to do—I just don't understand why all this is happening."

Another pause, this one mine. Therapeutic.

She sniffled through it.

I said, "I'm sorry, Denise. I wish I could take away your pain."

"Take it and stuff it in a bag and drop it in the sewer," she said. "Take everyone's."

"Wouldn't that be something."

"Yeah." Small laugh. "What should I do, Doc? With Darren."

"Has he been playing—the way he played in my office?"

"That's the thing," she said. "He won't. I give him the cars and tell him what to do, but he just looks at them and starts screaming."

"If you'd like to bring him in, I'd be happy to see him," I said. "Or if the drive's too long, I can refer you to someone closer."

"No, no, that was all . . . It's not too far. What else do I have to do all day but drive, anyway?"

"Then by all means come," I said. "I can see you tomorrow, first thing."

"Yeah, that would be great."

We made an appointment.

She said, "You're a nice man. You really know how to help a person."

That shored me up enough to make my second call.

Five minutes to twelve. Lunch break.

"Dr. Small."

"Hi, Ada. It's Alex. Brown-bagging it?"

"Cottage cheese and fruit," she said. "Battle of the bulge. Listen, I'm glad you called. I tried to reach Carmen Seeber, but her line's been disconnected and there's no record of a new one."

"This isn't about her," I said. "It's about me."

Her therapeutic pause.

The damned things worked. I said, "A lot's been piling up. I thought if you thought it would be appropriate for me to come in . . ."

"I'm always happy to see you, Alex," she said. "Do *you* have any concerns about the appropriateness of it?"

"Not at all. No, that's not true. I guess I do. Things have changed between us. It's hard slipping out of the colleague role, admitting helplessness."

"You're far from helpless, Alex. Just insightful enough to know you're not invulnerable."

"Insightful." I laughed. "Far from it."

"You called, didn't you? Alex, I understand what you're saying— shifting roles must seem like a step backward. But I certainly don't see it that way."

"I appreciate your saying that."

"I'm saying it because it's true. However, if you have doubts, I can refer you to someone else."

"Start over? No, I wouldn't want that."

"Would you like some time to think it over?"

"No, no. I might as well dive in, before I figure out some way to build up my defenses again."

"All right, it's settled then. Let me check my book." The sound of flipping pages. "How about tomorrow at six? The office will be quiet—you won't run into anyone you've referred."

"Six would be great, Ada. See you then."

"I'm looking forward to it, Alex."

"Me too. 'Bye."

"Alex?"

"Yes?"

"It's a very good thing you're doing."